Praise for

A LADY'S FORMULA FOR LOVE

"A witty, dazzling debut with a science-minded heroine and her broody bodyguard. Fiercely feminist and intensely romantic, *A Lady's Formula for Love* is a fresh take on historical romance that's guaranteed to delight readers."

—Joanna Shupe, author of *The Devil of Downtown*

"A brilliant scientist and her brooding bodyguard discover that love can find you when you least expect it. *A Lady's Formula for Love* is full of wit, charm, and intrigue. You don't want to miss this exciting debut from Elizabeth Everett."

—Harper St. George, author of *The Heiress Gets a Duke*

"Smart, sassy, sexy, and sweet... it's *The Bodyguard* meets *Pride and Prejudice*. Mr. Darcy, with his brooding sexiness, doesn't have a damned thing on Arthur Kneland. This book is an all-around winner."

—Minerva Spencer, author of the Academy of Love series

"A secret society of rule-breaking women . . . irresistible! You're going to love Elizabeth Everett's adventurous debut."

—Theresa Romain, author of the Holiday Pleasures series

"A sparking debut full of humor, heart, and sizzling romance."

—Jeanine Englert, award-winning author of *Lovely Digits*

"A fabulous debut filled with danger, imperfect but fierce found family, and the love story of two stubborn protectors, *A Lady's Formula for Love* is everything a romance reader who likes to ponder as well as cheer could want." —Felicia Grossman, author of the Truitts series

A LADY'S FORMULA FOR LOVE

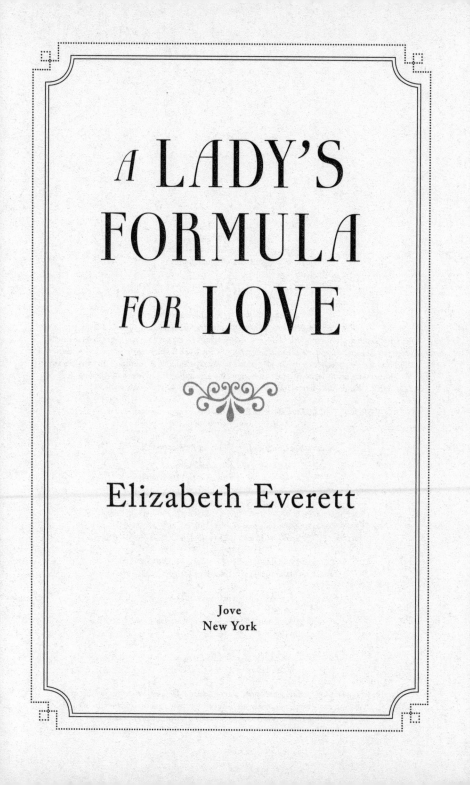

Elizabeth Everett

Jove
New York

A JOVE BOOK
Published by Berkley
An imprint of Penguin Random House LLC
penguinrandomhouse.com

Library of Congress Cataloging-in-Publication Data

Names: Everett, Elizabeth, author.
Title: A lady's formula for love / Elizabeth Everett.
Description: First edition. | New York: Jove, 2021. |
Series: [The secret scientists of London; vol 1]
Identifiers: LCCN 2020030432 (print) | LCCN 2020030433 (ebook) |
ISBN 9780593200629 (trade paperback) | ISBN 9780593200636 (ebook)
Classification: LCC PS3605.V435 L33 2021 (print) | LCC PS3605.V435 (ebook) |
DDC 813/.6—dc23
LC record available at https://lccn.loc.gov/2020030432
LC ebook record available at https://lccn.loc.gov/2020030433

First Edition: February 2021

Printed in the United States of America
1   3   5   7   9   10   8   6   4   2

Cover design by Rita Frangie
Book design by Alison Cnockaert

For my husband, a real-life romantic hero.

A LADY'S FORMULA FOR LOVE

1

London, 1842

ONLY AFTER THE second explosion did Violet start to worry.

Having retired for the night, rung for her maid, and poured herself a glass of brandy, Violet Hughes, or Lady Greycliff, decided to ignore the first blast. She tried to ignore the second one as well until she considered her housekeeper's reaction.

Violet paid Mrs. Sweet a small fortune to clean an astonishing variety of chemical compounds out of the walls, floors, and furniture of her home, Beacon House, and its adjoining property. She had neither the time nor the inclination to search the British Isles for another housekeeper who could remove scorch marks from damask.

The *third* explosion, however, sent Violet scurrying from her bedchamber and down the back staircase.

Linked to Beacon House, what once had been a series of outbuildings was now part of one structure with a front entrance the next street over. After sinking most of her funds into the construction of this addition, Violet had created London's first social club for ladies, Athena's Retreat. Even more dear to her heart was the club within the club. The public believed the Retreat to be a gathering place for ladies with a passing interest in the natural sciences. Behind closed doors, though, those same ladies were making discoveries advancing the fields of mathematics, biology, and chemistry, to name a few.

Loud, smoke-filled discoveries.

Before her, the thick oak door to the connecting hall stood open, revealing the club's first floor of hidden laboratories. An odor of sulfur and cheese hung in the air, along with an unsettling amount of green smoke.

"No cause for alarm," cried a hoarse voice, followed by a round of coughing. "Made a slight miscalculation. Nothing to worry over."

Violet cursed her luck as Mildred Thornton and her partner, Wilhelmina Smythe, emerged from a room where the smoke was thickest. The two ladies, affectionately known as Milly and Willy, had sworn they were no longer experimenting with unstable compound liquids.

"You told me you were investigating the properties of powders," Violet cried. "How did you manage to create an explosion from talc?"

"Whoops. Did we say *talc* powder? Apologies," rasped Milly. A fine veil of soot darkened her silver hair and settled like black beads in her eyebrows.

"All sorts of powders, dear," Willy chimed in. A foot taller than Milly and half as wide, she shook a cloud of ash from her skirts. "Talc powder, rice powder . . ." She lowered her voice and found something interesting to examine in the vicinity of her shoes. "Gunpowder . . ."

Violet helped Milly bat out a few smoldering embers on the mancheron trimming of her left sleeve. "Either way, what were you thinking?" she moaned.

"We were thinking how far ahead those insufferable Italians at the University of Turin are in the development of pyroglycerin," Milly said. "Although we cannot share our work with the world, a few men are privy to our research and take us seriously. England cannot afford to fall behind in this area."

Mrs. Sweet's voice could now be heard above the din, her lilting West Indian accent softening the severity of her shouted evacuation orders. Doors opened along the corridor as women emerged from their labs in various states of excitement. Many wore canvas aprons over their dresses, and some sported thick, padded gloves.

"Must we leave? My work is at a delicate stage," complained a fine-boned woman dressed in a modest, though expertly tailored, blue wool dress. "Who was it this time?"

"Letty," Violet greeted the petite mathematician. "Help me get everyone out of the laboratories and into the public rooms so we can decide what to do."

Miss Letitia Fenley, club secretary for Athena's Retreat, set about her duties at once, and Violet sent a prayer of thanks heavenward for her efficiency.

Twenty minutes later, Violet stood in the club's common area. Its decor echoed those in the men's clubs of St. James's Street. While oak wainscoting lined the lower half of the walls, the upper half had been painted a cheerful cranberry. At one end of the room, a fire blazed in a large hearth framed by a mantel of speckled marble.

"If I might have your attention," Violet called out.

Twenty or so women, ranging in age from eighteen to eighty-five, turned their faces to Violet. Despite the circumstances, her pride and joy in what they'd created here buoyed her spirits. These members of the true Athena's Retreat were sworn to secrecy—bound by a set of rules that encouraged the sharing of knowledge and the protection of one another.

Violet's bubble of happiness punctured at the sight of Mrs. Sweet, arms folded and lips pursed in a disapproving moue. Violet ventured a tentative wave in the housekeeper's direction.

Mrs. Sweet did not wave back.

Drat.

"We had a small accident this evening," Violet announced.

"You mean Milly and Willy were at it again." A dry, cultured voice cut through the amused murmuring.

"Ahem." Violet shot a warning glance at the commentator, Lady Phoebe Hunt. Violet had hoped to avoid a discussion of Milly and Willy's propensity for damage. "A benefit of Athena's Retreat connecting to my home, Beacon House, is the ability to pass off some of the phenomena that occur here as coming from my kitchen."

"Your cook is not going to like it," Letty noted.

"Thank you, Miss Fenley, for the reminder," Violet said. "As club president, I delegate it to you to figure out an alternate explanation for the noise and record the explanation in our club diary."

Letty blinked in consternation, but Violet had other concerns.

"We must cut our activities short tonight," she continued. "Otherwise, we risk exposing the truth of what happens behind the public rooms."

"Is the threat of explosion over?" Lady Phoebe leaned back and kicked one expensive boot onto a stool, flipping a hand in Milly's direction. "I don't want my work burned to a crisp because these two reckless—"

"Reckless? *Brilliant*, rather," Willy said. "Someday, our work will change the economy of the whole of Britain." The flapping of her cap, which hung from the side of her topknot like a singed flag, offset Willy's indignation as she waved her arms to make a point. "You, on the other hand, would rather feature in the gossip papers than finish your work. I haven't seen hide nor hair of any advances in the so-called process of electrolysis."

Violet interrupted this conversation before it turned into a protracted row. "Either way, can we call a halt to any experiments posing the threat of explosion? Please, remember we host our first public event in a month. Miss Fenley has advertised it as An Evening of Education and Elucidation."

"How appallingly alliterative," said Phoebe.

"It's An Evening of *Edification* and *Entertainment*," Letty reminded Violet.

"That's even worse," Milly whispered.

Violet took a moment to smooth her features into a ladylike blandness. "There is much to be gained by recruiting more members to our club, and everything to lose if we become a subject of ridicule. For tonight, a discreet exit would be best. Will you begin, Lady Phoebe?"

"Discreet may not be in the cards, my lady," Letty said. "It seems a handful of reporters have been waiting outside to speak with Lady Phoebe. Something about a wager with Lord Henderson?"

"He was tormenting Althea Dertlinger," Phoebe said with mock innocence. "All I did was wager I could fit my entire boot in his—"

"They were so noisy the neighbors alerted the watch," Letty said, addressing Violet. "When I asked Winthram to call us hackneys, he reported that a crowd had gathered at the entrance. Among them is your stepson, Lord Greycliff."

Double drat.

Dozens of women surrounded Violet as she ushered them to the cloakroom, where Winthram, the doorman, helped them with their coats and bonnets. Outside the club entrance, the throng of reporters waited for her and Phoebe to appear. Once the events of the night were finished, more bodies would envelop her as servants prepared her for bed.

Yet amid all these people, Violet Hughes had never felt so alone.

ARTHUR KNELAND WANTED to be alone.

In his line of work, a crowd was the ultimate enemy. The gaslight on this small street off Knightsbridge barely illuminated the wooden walkway below. Shadows large and squat wove between the writhing mass of figures around him.

Wafts of brimstone-scented air came from the town house as a procession of ladies exited the building.

"Not how you envisioned your first night of private employment, is it? You've gone from protecting heads of state to looking after my stepmother."

William Hughes, or Viscount Greycliff—Grey to his friends— stabbed the walkway with his gold-topped cane while he spoke. One might assume the cane an affectation. From experience, Arthur knew that Grey carried a dagger hidden in that cane and could use it.

They'd both worked for a small sub-rosa group run out of the prime minister's office tasked with carrying out sensitive operations. In situations where it would have been impolitic for the British government to officially be involved, Grey had played the part of an indolent nobleman while gathering information.

Arthur rarely worked with other agents. The exception, one god-awful night in Brussels with Grey—which had included the poisoning of an aide to the Grand Duke William, the rescue of two whores locked in the personal carriage of Prince Frederick, a gunfight, and a serious drinking session with the orchestra of the Théâtre Royal— had resulted in the closest Arthur ever came to friendship.

"Protecting a little widow is indeed a change of pace," Arthur said, thinking of those whores and the copious amount of terrible wine they could drink.

Silence met his observation. Grey was distracted by a petite blonde taking charge of the departing ladies.

"Funny how chaos seems to follow behind certain women," Grey muttered.

Chaos indeed. "I did mention how I'm anticipating a quieter life, didn't I?" Arthur said.

Grey pulled a face. "Tonight is an exception. Besides, it pays four times what you would have made as an employee of Her Majesty's government for a similar job. You're the last person I'd expect to finish out his years rusticating in the countryside, but if you want to buy that farm you've always talked about, you'll need a nice lump sum. Look, it isn't so bad as the year the PM sent you to America."

Arthur shuddered.

Americans. Loud, partial to superlatives, and friendly to an uncomfortable degree. Arthur had no use for such easy camaraderie. It didn't make sense to have friends in a profession where someone was always either being shot at or shooting someone else.

"You are the best bodyguard we have," Grey continued, "and I mean to wring the most out of you before you disappear into the wilds of the Highlands forever. I'll pay you enough to start your new life if you do this one small favor for me."

A new life. The words unnerved Arthur. "New" life meant better, didn't it? Yes, he'd always wanted to live out his days on a farm. He'd said the words so many times they'd disentangled themselves from reality.

Time to make them real.

Until then, Arthur considered the scene before them. "You're certain you want me to do this job? It's the first time I've been back in England in twenty years. People have a long memory for scandal. What happens if someone recognizes me? Seems like it might be more trouble than it's worth."

As he spoke, Arthur studied the crowd. Something was off.

"You worry too much. I'll be finished up north within a month, then you're free to go. Besides, the scandal is two decades old. Since then, you've guarded some of the most influential and powerful men in the world." Grey clapped a hand on Arthur's shoulder, his cool demeanor thawing. "Lady Greycliff is especially dear to me. I couldn't leave her with anyone else. I trust you."

Arthur slipped free of the casual touch, hoping he was worthy of

Grey's trust. At forty years old, he had dozens of assignments under his belt, and he'd failed only once.

One time too many.

The door to the town house opened, and the viscountess emerged, drawing the reporters' attention. He couldn't make out the details of her features from where he stood, yet he knew she was lovely the same way he knew the reporter closest to her had consumption, the disheveled and singed ladies who left in a hackney would return home to share the same bed, and the doorman seeing her out was not all he seemed.

"I am too old for this," he muttered, more to himself than to Grey. "After this commission, I am finished."

Arthur took a step forward as the lady made her way down the stairs, laughing at something one of the men in front of her had said. Beneath her voluminous shawl, she'd a well-rounded figure—sweetly curved hips and a generous bosom—and her curls were mussed as if she'd just risen from bed. The image took him aback.

"I promise, Arthur," Grey said, "this will be the easiest assignment you've ever taken. You won't even know you're working. In fact—"

Arthur never learned what Grey would have said. He was running straight toward the lady, who was now standing on the walkway beneath a first-floor window.

Barreling through the crowd of reporters, Arthur could finally see her face. Long, thick black lashes opened and closed, revealing dark brown eyes the color of coffee. Smaller than the men surrounding her, she had to tilt her perfect little chin up as she traded jokes. Her lips were the color of ripe plums and prompted a surprising stir of lust.

The world was full of women more beautiful than Violet Hughes. Arthur had met some of them, slept with some of them, and taken a massive head wound from one of them. None had called forth such an instantaneous, primal attraction.

At that moment, an explosion sent the second-floor windows shattering outward, and Arthur leaped the two-foot distance separating them. Estimating the amount of force necessary, he shielded her body without hurting her as they toppled to the ground.

What he hadn't counted on was the stupendously ugly armchair flying out the window, smashing to pieces inches from his face and sending splinters flying. Chaos broke out around them.

Rustication couldn't come soon enough.

2

AFTER VIOLET'S NIGHTLY ritual of brandy and a bath followed by a journey to her empty bed, she concluded her routine with one final step. She would imagine someone climbing into the bed from the opposite side, blowing out the candle, and taking her into their arms before falling asleep.

These nighttime visitors remained firmly in her head. Violet's late husband had insisted that a woman with a physical appetite was both unladylike and distasteful. Although she suspected this might not always be the case, she'd never searched out a real-life lover to prove him wrong. Her reputation was too important to the future of Athena's Retreat.

Worse, what if he was right?

In all those lonely nights, Violet had never conjured a pair of arms that surrounded her like this man's holding her now. The sensation of a warm, solid body against her stunned her more than the chaos and the scattered shards of glass and wood. The soles of shoes whipped past; all around, voices were raised in angry, frightened cries.

None of this touched her.

She was safe.

Not because the man holding her had rasped those words in her ear, although that was delightful, how his lips had brushed against the sensitive lobe. No. Something else told her everything would be well.

She had seen him before the explosion, standing next to Grey. In the commotion around her, the dark figure at Grey's side had remained preternaturally still until he burst into motion.

A typical reaction might have been to step back or shy away from a strange man hurling himself at you. Instead, as he came closer, Violet had the strangest urge to step *toward* him.

Nothing about his appearance signaled safety. He wore a dull brown frock coat, a few years out of date. He was tall, but not too tall. Broad, but no more than an average laborer. His top hat of felted wool was nondescript, as was his dark, curly hair and the whiskers halfway down the sides of his cheeks. Deep lines evidenced exposure to the elements over many years, and he'd broken his nose at some point.

In any other setting, he would have slipped her notice, as though he were a shadow or a slight blur at the edge of her vision.

Except she happened to look into his eyes.

Not even when she'd had no idea why he would have laid hands on her, in the seconds it took between the time he grabbed her until the explosion—not even then—was she frightened.

Cradling her head in one large hand to protect her skull from the fall, he held their bodies flush. When he'd pulled his mouth away from her ear and locked his gaze on hers, Violet had understood. Although they were an unremarkable shade of brown, his eyes were what told Violet she would be safe no matter what.

His glance swept her face, then traveled the length of her body before he turned his head to survey the crowd. The lack of expression and preternatural calm belied the intense vigilance in the depths of his gaze.

"Are you all right?" he asked.

Was she all right?

It had been so long since anyone had held her, let alone a man to whom she'd had an instant and powerful attraction. A million details filled her brain: the shape of his upper lip, the tiny drops of mist clinging to his lashes, the rapid pace of her heartbeat.

Her attention centered on the enveloping warmth of his body, her skin awakening beneath his hands. Could he feel her response? Would he be amused or appalled?

"Thank you for your bravery," Violet said, speaking into the man's cravat while he continued to shield her from the pandemonium.

"How lucky I am you landed in this spot," she continued. Glancing to where his hips pressed against hers, she blushed. "Not landed in *this* spot, as in where you currently rest. I mean to say, not . . . We're not resting, of course . . ."

He remained silent.

"Ahem," she said. "If you could please let me up, I will be better able to—"

"On the count of three, I will get you up," he said. "You stay in front of me as we head west. If anyone comes close, you are to drop to the ground and cover your head. One, two . . ."

On three, the man sprang to his feet and lifted Violet as though she weighed less than a feather. Astonishing. He was stronger than he appeared, beneath his coat. Examining the crowd, he gave her another set of orders.

"Stay close to the walls of the town houses. Crouch as low as you can without tripping over your skirts. Now, let's go."

He hadn't glanced at her again. Freed from his scrutiny, sanity returned, and Violet remained in place. Athena's Retreat was her responsibility. She could not leave before she had ensured that her club

members were unharmed and she fed the press a reasonable explanation.

"Did the explosion damage your hearing, my lady?" he asked, still
scanning the crowd.

"My hearing is undamaged, my head is whole, and my limbs are
intact thanks to you, sir. No injuries, just flustered, what with the explosions and the part where you were, er, resting."

Unless she had unknowingly suffered a head wound? What else
could explain her reaction? A nervous laugh escaped her, then died
beneath his flinty stare.

Violet swallowed. "While I am grateful, I must be certain no one
else is hurt. If you'll excuse me?"

"No."

Violet blinked. It *had* been a loud explosion. Was her rescuer the
one suffering from hearing loss?

She raised her voice to compensate for the damage to his ears. "I
am going this way," she enunciated, pointing toward the club.

An opaque gaze examined her, no hint of expression to give Violet
the slightest clue to what the man thought. For some reason, she
wanted him to think well of her.

"I can hear you perfectly well," he said without inflection. "You're
going nowhere but with me."

Violet let out a gasp as the man sidled one arm around her waist
and picked her up. No respectable man would haul a woman away like
this unless he had nefarious intentions.

She'd never been the object of nefarious intentions before. A ripple of excitement spread through her, followed by shame.

"I am not ungrateful. You are brave and"—Violet took a moment to
appreciate his form—"well-made and nice-smelling. I simply don't have
time to be rescued." Twisting in his arms, she caught sight of her stepson.

"Grey, can you explain to this gentleman I don't have time to be rescued?"

Grey pushed through the crowd to join them. "Let go, Arthur. You don't want anyone seeing you with her and drawing any conclusions."

The man, Arthur, set her down without warning, and she stumbled, whereby he reached out and steadied her. Grasping her elbow with the lightest of touches, he threw off enough heat to protect her from the cold.

"You didn't tell her I was coming," Arthur said to Grey.

Grey's mouth twisted to one side in a familiar expression. What was he up to?

"I was getting to that part before you took off running," Grey said. "How did you know, by the way?"

The large man at her side lifted his shoulders a scant inch. "It's my job to know. Let's go."

Violet braced herself, but Arthur politely gestured for her to precede him.

"Please, for once, let me be the one to make things right for you," Grey said with a brusque air, trusting that even if Violet had heard the emotion beneath the words, she would not mention it aloud.

When she did not immediately resist, he pressed his point. "If you come with us, I'll have my agents clean this up for you."

She considered for a moment, then shook her head. "This could not have happened at a worse time. I cannot leave until the members are safe and sound."

"I promise their safety will be assured," Grey said. "On top of that, I'll keep Mrs. Sweet from quitting."

"*That* would be helpful." Violet wrapped her shawl around her shoulders. "I would like an explanation, though. The next time something like this happens—"

"That is why I am here," Arthur said. "To make sure there is no next time."

YEARS AGO, ARTHUR had guarded a lepidopterist. Not because butterflies had anything to do with the fate of the British Empire. The scientist was the son of a Greek general and the target of assassins sent by the Ottoman sultan.

The way the lepidopterist would examine the minute markings on his specimens bore a chilling similarity to the way the two women seated across the room were staring at him right now, pinning him in place as he reached for a jam tart.

One woman was tall and dark, the other tiny and blond, and they shifted their piercing gazes between Arthur and Lady Greycliff.

"You will never even know he is here," Grey was saying. The younger man stood in the middle of the sitting room, having maneuvered his way around the piles of books, overstuffed ottomans, and tea tables with admirable grace, considering his large stature and the small amount of space.

Oblivious to her audience, Lady Greycliff paced in the opposite direction. When she moved, her enormous shawl billowed around her, sending papers flying and houseplants waving in her wake. Frenetic energy poured off her, setting a charge to the air around them. The way she held herself indicated that energy was a by-product of her *thinking*.

The types of folks who needed a bodyguard were often controversial or unsavory characters. Arthur had little experience in protecting the innocent. The lady appeared younger than her thirty years; those wide eyes that had fixed on him earlier had revealed an unnerving vulnerability. He was a tomcat being given a mouse to watch over.

"I can't ignore the presence of an assassin in my house," Lady Greycliff exclaimed.

Good Lord.

Now the ladies' stares morphed from intense curiosity to fierce disapproval.

"I'm not an assassin," Arthur told them.

"You look like an assassin," said the fierce little blonde, Miss Letitia Fenley.

"Well, I am not," Arthur assured her.

Earlier, Grey had privately recounted the rise of Miss Fenley's family, from humble butchers to owners of the largest shopping emporium in London.

"Letty Fenley doesn't have much use for the aristocracy, except when we contribute to her family's coffers," he'd said. "Every word out of a nobleman's mouth, she interprets as an order or an insult."

This might have explained her prickly demeanor toward Grey. From the way she studied the man when he wasn't looking, however, Arthur suspected a more personal reason for their antagonism.

"It isn't as though you would tell us if you were an assassin," said the tall, handsome woman next to Miss Fenley. Lady Phoebe Hunt, daughter of a marquess, was a sensation in London society circles. A woman who spoke up and spoke out, especially in opposition to whatever cause her father happened to champion. She'd high cheekbones and a full mouth, but her most dramatic feature was the spectacular amethyst hue of her eyes.

Arthur fought the urge to shift in his chair.

"If he were a halfway competent assassin, he'd take on that gaggle of reporters outside," Miss Fenley remarked. "If it weren't for them hounding Lady Greycliff, no one would have been any the wiser about tonight's explosions."

"He's not an assassin," Grey said. His jaw sawed back and forth in a rare sign of frustration. He'd been trying to get the women to leave for half an hour with no success. "He is a trained *counter*assassin. Mr. Kneland has protected important figures in Europe and the Americas over the last two decades. He kept Lord Dickerson alive despite three attempts on his life in the past year."

"Wait. Wasn't Dickerson shot?" asked Lady Phoebe. "Not a ringing endorsement if his clients are full of bullet holes."

"A bullet travels at roughly eight hundred and thirty feet per second," said Miss Fenley. "One must have extraordinary reflexes to stop it once it has discharged."

Lady Phoebe tipped her head. "He's not a young man. Slowing reflexes might be why he's retired."

"Did you get a discounted rate because he's old?" Miss Fenley asked Grey. "My father always says you get what you pay for. Couldn't you spring for a younger man?"

"I am sitting right here," Arthur observed. "I can hear you. And the bullet went through me into Dickerson."

The women blinked in surprise. They *had* forgotten him.

Arthur transferred his gaze to the ceiling and counted to twenty before he said something unforgivable.

"Hush, Letty," Lady Greycliff chastised. "Mr. Kneland rescued me quite efficiently earlier tonight." Her cheeks reddened, and he held back a smile, remembering her words to him.

Well-made and nice-smelling.

He'd received more practiced compliments, but none as genuine.

Miss Fenley's fists clenched her skirts. "Can we please come back to why he is here?"

She glared at Grey. "Club members have reported strange men loitering in the mews and the alley behind Athena's Retreat. Last week, the laboratory in which Lady Greycliff was working had its windows smashed in by bricks."

The daughter of a shopkeeper ought to be intimidated by a man as large and wellborn as Grey. Nonetheless, Miss Fenley was standing up to him on behalf of her friend, addressing him directly. "This started when Lady Greycliff agreed to help you with your government work, my lord."

Grey pinched the bridge of his nose. "That work was meant to be *secret.*"

Lady Greycliff winced. "I haven't told them what I'm working on—simply that it is vital. You see, I had a question about sulfuric acid and potassium hydroxide, so I consulted Phoebe."

Grey sighed. "Of course."

"Then there was the particularly complex equation when I took into account Dalton's law, and who better than Letty . . ." The lady broke off her explanation as a question occurred to her. "I've helped you with your government work before, and no one has found out. Why would this time be different?"

Arthur had had the same question. He studied the lady's friends with suspicion.

"I'm not sure." Grey glanced at Arthur, then away. "But I don't believe the explosion originating from the second floor was an accident."

"Whatever is happening must stop," said Lady Phoebe. "Athena's Retreat is hosting its first evening event for the public at the end of the month. We can't have assassins running loose when we are trying to convince the ton of our respectability."

Grey turned to Arthur, palms stretched in supplication. "Can you reassure them? I must leave tonight."

An orphaned farm boy from the Highlands, raised by an indifferent relative until sent to work, Arthur had never been allowed to forget his station in life. Still, after two decades living cheek by jowl with the wellborn of Europe, he knew better than most that titles were empty honorifics. Lacking a pedigree, he'd learned to use silent intimidation and a well-muscled body to get the attention of powerful men and women who would never otherwise have heeded him.

Arthur took his time standing now, sending a message. Without saying a word, he informed these women that he could be a threat.

Lady Greycliff's life was in danger. He needed everyone here to accept his command. Moving to the window, he twitched shut the curtain.

"Omnium Democratia is an illegal workers' organization formed in the Northeast and the Midlands, and now proselytizing in London. Originally, they were part of the Chartist movement, advocating for a reformation of Parliament and suffrage for all men."

"Of course it would be suffrage for all *men*," Miss Fenley muttered.

Arthur checked the latches on the windows and frowned. "Omnium Democratia grew impatient. They're far more radical now and not opposed to using violence to advance their aims."

"That rabble is all talk and no action, from what I hear," Lady Phoebe opined.

"They've graduated to action," Arthur said. "Their last rally turned violent. When the constables arrived, they encountered a new kind of weapon."

"A weapon? The broadsheets mentioned smoke and confusion." Miss Fenley regarded Lady Greycliff with concern. "You are developing a theory of pressurized gas. How does this relate to rioting?"

Lady Greycliff's face lit with interest and she explained. "They've fashioned small canisters containing two separate chambers, each holding a mixture of unknown origin. If shaken hard enough, the wall between the chambers collapses and the chemicals combine, creating a harmful gas."

"Depending on the amount inhaled," Arthur said, "the effects range from disorientation and nausea to severe damage to the eyes and lungs. Two constables went in hospital after the attack with damaged lungs and partial blindness. Last night, one of them died."

Lady Phoebe covered her mouth in sympathy.

"Why didn't the rioters get sick as well?" Letty asked.

"At the top is a siphon," Grey explained, "like the one created by Antoine Perpigna for carbonated water. The rioters aimed the siphons directly at the constabulary."

"I've figured out the composition of their poison," said Lady Greycliff. "Right now, the constables can use masks for protection, but the gas lingers. Any unlucky bystander could be affected. I have been developing a compound that neutralizes the gas in the air, but even with your help, it has been slow going."

"The Omnis are waging a futile campaign." Miss Fenley shook her head in resignation. "Violence won't force the peerage to find their conscience. An attack on their wealth would have more of an impact."

Grey peered down his nose at Miss Fenley. "Until you manage to unseat us amoral peers and upend centuries of political tradition, I'd like to prevent anyone else from suffering."

Turning his back on her scowl, he addressed Lady Greycliff. "There are thirty or so members of Athena's Retreat. All of them have family, friends, and even servants who might know of the club's existence. Any of them might be behind the explosion."

As her friends argued the impossibility of such a scenario, Lady Greycliff examined the glowing embers of the dying fire. An angry red scrape stood out against the ivory skin of her cheek. Arthur doubted she'd had time to clean it between fetching tea for the watch and soothing the frightened bystanders. She'd seen everyone off with words of comfort and promises that all would be as new by the end of the week.

If Arthur felt sorry for her, he'd break his cardinal rule: Never feel *anything* for his assignments.

That was all this beautiful woman should be to him.

An assignment.

"While Lady Greycliff develops an antidote," Arthur said, "I will protect both her and the formula. I shall pose as the club's majordomo, hired for extra security in light of the events of this evening."

He turned his focus to the women seated before him.

In his training many years ago, he'd learned that any object could be a weapon.

A chair leg could double as a club or a sword. A hat could suffocate someone. A hairpin could deliver a lethal dose of poison to someone's heart.

These three ladies could be turned to his advantage in this mission. The key was to think of them as objects, like anyone else who came into his life.

Merely a means to an end.

3

VIOLET SAID GOODBYE to Grey one last time, closed the door, and slumped against the wall. A pair of sinumbra lamps stood on either side of a large mirror in the foyer, their glass shades casting an eerie orange light across the black-and-white tiled floor.

When Violet's husband was very ill, she would wander the house at night in between bouts of nursing him, hammering out the details of complex formulas in her head as death hovered in the background. Here in Beacon House, the night was never silent, and she was intimately familiar with the origin of every click and squeak.

Therefore, she addressed her remarks to the large shadow in a corner without having to see him.

"You are awfully quiet for such a large man. How do you do it?"

Arthur emerged from a shallow indentation beneath the staircase. Flickering light brushed the hollows of his sun-browned cheeks.

"I have had twenty years of practice," he answered. "It pays to be quiet when one is a counterassassin. Even when hired at a discount."

Violet chuckled. "I don't expect you bargained for the three of us when Grey approached you," she said. "He calls us 'the coven,' you know. Did they scare you?"

"Yes," he said dryly.

Violet laughed in appreciation, happy a real person resided within the stoic figure. "Grey described the nature of your service before he left. He said the Queen offered you a medal ceremony after you saved Lord Dickerson, yet you refused."

Appearing unimpressed by the Queen's gesture, he moved away from the wall. Although his gaze remained fixed on her, Violet wouldn't have been surprised if he had memorized the exact position of the cut-glass bowl on the entry table and how many sconces were attached to the wall behind him.

They regarded each other in the dim hallway without awkwardness, an odd familiarity between them after the strange events of the night. She'd learned the shape of him before she'd even learned his name.

"Although he failed to warn me of your friends," Arthur said, "Grey did say you have a habit of collecting ladies under your wing."

"Letty and Phoebe are founding members of Athena's Retreat, not wounded birds. Although he complains when they are around, he misses them when they are not." She leaned toward Arthur with a conspiratorial air. "He'll never admit to it, however."

"You care for Grey."

"Yes," she said.

Ah. With his tone, Arthur had asked a question without asking the question—an estimable talent.

"Grey's father, Daniel, swept me off my feet the first month of my debut season." A familiar ache began in the pit of her stomach as she explained. "He was the epitome of sophistication and romance. He made every other man seem slow and callow in comparison, despite his age."

The low light kept Arthur's reaction to this confession a mystery— if he had one.

"Grey mentioned his father was charismatic," he said.

Violet tilted her head as she considered the word. "He projected such certainty—as if he had the answer to everything. As a young woman whose brain was filled with nothing but questions, I found this quality incredibly compelling."

So compelling she'd ignored the concerns of her family and the tiny warnings in her own head and rushed into marriage. Daniel had been just as hasty. Worried about Grey's health, he had believed a young wife would guarantee a chance at another child. He'd been enamored as well of the chance to mold a young woman with the promise of brilliance.

What they found most attractive about each other, however, quickly drove them apart. Daniel's certainty made him judgmental and controlling. Violet's brilliance did not spill over into the areas of politics and social maneuvering, where Daniel's interests lay.

"Folks with small minds enjoy pointing out that Grey is a few years older than me," she acknowledged.

Grey's childhood struggle with the falling sickness had isolated him as a child, although his seizures were rare by the time they met. In the early years of her marriage to his father, she'd researched cures and dispelled old-fashioned notions of cold baths and bloodletting as relief. They'd formed a friendship that grew closer as his father's flaws revealed themselves, but he'd left for the army soon after and rarely returned home, even after Daniel grew ill.

When the flood of midnight memories threatened to drown her, Violet cleared her throat and forced brightness into her tone, returning to Arthur's question. "Although he is not my natural son, Grey is my *family*."

Arthur cocked his head, hearing what she was not saying. This conversation beneath the conversation worked both ways.

He stood so still. His peace amid the chaos was what first drew her attention. As though an invisible circle of calm surrounded him. She wanted to cup her hand and dip it into that pool of calm, pour it over her or drink deep, whatever method necessary to find her own peace.

"Do you truly believe I am under threat?" This man was not one to waste his time. She asked anyway, hoping for a different answer. "Couldn't the second-floor explosion have been a coincidence?"

"Grey has a nose for danger. He wouldn't have asked me to stay in London and pay me what he's paying me if he didn't think your talents have made you a target."

Violet sighed. "I'm not as gifted as he thinks."

Her new protector moved closer, until her skirts brushed his shoes. Heat raced up her neck when she remembered his hand clasping the back of her head, his hips resting against hers, and the certainty of safety in his arms.

Her gloves had been dirtied and torn when she fell to the ground earlier. She'd left them off, and he caught her bare hand in his. In his large hands, her hand seemed alien—delicate and feminine rather than chapped and ungainly.

There were tiny scars across the backs of her hands and the tips of her fingers.

"Here is evidence you've performed a great many experiments." The matter-of-factness of his voice contrasted with the deliberate stroke of his thumb over the mound of her palm.

How long had it been since a man had touched Violet intimately? Excitement woke the nerves beneath her skin.

"Is Grey wrong? Are you the most accident-prone chemist in Europe, rather than the most brilliant?"

"He is . . ." Violet had to clear her throat for words to emerge. "He is overestimating my abilities."

Once again, she pictured the ferocity of Arthur's gaze on her face as the world had exploded around them.

"More important than my safety is the well-being of the women in the club next door. They already risk so much to come here night after night and do their work. Grey understands my devotion to the club, and I am grateful he sent you to us. Until he returns, please consider Beacon House your home."

Surprised at his cynical expression, she squeezed his hand. "You might find us unconventional. I like to think we are nevertheless a happy household. You must call me Violet."

His jaw tensed for one moment before his expression froze into a mask of indifference. "I am your bodyguard. Not your friend. Not a guest. Grey is paying me money to stay here and keep you safe."

A chill prickled the exposed skin of her neck at his words.

Arthur dropped her hand. "My task is to keep you alive and unhurt, nothing more nor less."

No frost chilled his voice, and no disdain crossed his face. Nothing in his tone or manner gave any hint to the feelings within, but in a blink, he stood two feet away, hands behind his back.

The loss of his touch left her light-headed. "I did not mean to offend," she said. "I meant to make you welcome in my home while you carry out your duties."

"Don't." The word dropped between them like a rock tossed into the water and cleared away the sensual haze as effectively as an icy splash. "Let me do my job. Anything more than that, and you become a distraction. Distraction leads to failure. In my line of work, if I've failed, it means you are dead."

A PLATE OF kippers on the table in front of him beheld Arthur with more sympathy than the ladies of Athena's Retreat had last night. Lucky for him, they hadn't witnessed his manner toward Lady Greycliff afterward.

What had Miss Fenley said? A bullet travels eight hundred and thirty feet per second. In the time it takes to look away, an assassin could complete their mission.

He'd seen it happen. Twenty years ago, Arthur had lost sight of his mission, and a man had died.

Pushing Violet away made sense. Must have been a trick of the light that made her smile appear to quaver, and her lively eyes turn wary and sad—nothing to do with him.

Now, his first morning on the job, he held a staring contest with his breakfast at a long oak table in the kitchen of Beacon House, an array of covered dishes set down the center. Around the table sat household staff in small clusters, talking and joking as they broke their fast, the smells of tea, eggs, porridge with nutmeg and cinnamon, salted mackerel, and rolls filling the air.

Mrs. Sweet walked among them, urging some to refill their plates, conferring with others about the chores ahead. The housekeeper exuded an aura of competence and dynamism, her dark brown skin glowing in the morning light coming through the sparkling kitchen windows. Turning her wide amber-colored eyes toward Arthur, she made her way to his side.

The staff, who had been peeking at him with curiosity since he'd planted himself among them, now turned his way.

"You will be happy to learn that Lady Greycliff has added to the staff at the club next door," Mrs. Sweet announced. "Mr. Kneland will be serving as the Retreat's majordomo."

Violet had revealed to the housekeeper Arthur's real purpose here. She spoke of her staff with as much warmth and affection as some might speak of their family and insisted that keeping secrets from Mrs. Sweet was impossible. To the rest of the domestics, he was simply a new hire.

"Thank you, Mrs. Sweet," he said. "It is obvious to me that you run this house with maximum efficiency and to great success. I see my role as taking the burdens off your shoulders, ensuring the security of Athena's Retreat, and trying to keep the business of the club separate from what goes on in Beacon House."

The staff approved. A few sighs of relief mingled in with their respectful nods.

Arthur wished the coven could take their lessons from the members of Lady Greycliff's household. As Mrs. Sweet introduced each of them to Arthur, they pledged their enthusiastic participation in any changes he might soon make. By the end of the afternoon, Arthur had a thorough overview of daily life in Beacon House. The servants were happy, well paid, and devoted to Lady Greycliff.

This was a problem.

What he needed were a few broken windows that awaited repairs, unpaid coalmen, and anonymous late-night visitors who gained access from secret entrances.

"If they don't pay the coalman, he has a grudge, alongside access to a house. It is the first place someone wanting to make mischief would enter and, therefore, the first place they would be caught," Arthur explained later in Mrs. Sweet's sitting room.

When he first called on her, he'd had a nasty shock. Shelves full of glass jars filled with various internal organs suspended in colored liquids ran up one wall. Opposite those shelves hung a fully articulated human skeleton.

When his gaze fell on a sheaf of paper illustrated with intricate anatomical drawings, he finally twigged to Mrs. Sweet's identity.

"Is every woman in this house a scientist?" he'd asked. "Is little Alice an ornithologist? Cook, is she a mathematician?"

"Don't be silly. Alice's interests lie in celestial mechanics, not zoology. I am studying to be a physician," Mrs. Sweet answered. "That is,

I am conducting preliminary studies on my own until I find a medical college to accept me."

Arthur sighed and took a seat. Mrs. Sweet hoped some medical college would take her? He'd never heard of a female doctor, let alone a Black female doctor.

Hope was a rare and precious commodity, especially in London. Around every corner stood an edifice to abandoned prospects and loss of faith. He said nothing, therefore, about her aspirations. It would do no good; dreams were sticky things, not easily banished.

He changed the subject to household scheduling while she laid out a tea tray. A plate of unappetizing biscuits lay between them— Mrs. Sweet did not approve of cakes—but the grassy peach smell of Darjeeling was pleasant enough.

"Too much sugar leads to a bilious liver," she explained.

His mam's kitchen was never without the scent of shortbread in the air. The silvery chime of his sister's laugh sounded in his ears, and a stray memory of how few tarts arrived from the oven to the table caused his stomach to rumble at the same time his throat tightened with loss.

Memories of his wee sister had ambushed him since he'd returned to England. The smell of crushed gorse and treacle would stop him in his tracks, and more than once he'd turned at the sound of tiny feet running behind him.

Hers wasn't the only ghost to greet his homecoming, however.

"I suppose that makes sense." Mrs. Sweet's voice pulled him back to the present when she referred to his earlier observations regarding coalmen. "Our staff is devoted to Lady Greycliff. She is exceptionally kind to the staff and more than generous with workmen and shopkeepers," she said. "Doesn't that mean you have fewer people to worry about?"

"It makes my work *more* difficult," he explained. "Say the lady received nighttime visitors. The maids wouldn't tell me. They'd want to protect her reputation. That leaves me ignorant of whether someone from outside has easy access to her bedroom window. A vulnerable point that an assassin could exploit."

Mrs. Sweet clucked in disdain. "I can assure you, Mr. Kneland, there are no sorts of immoral goings-on in *this* house. Lady Greycliff has had no visitors upstairs since her husband died."

Arthur chose to ignore the treacherous rush of satisfaction at that statement and held up a hand to halt her scold. "I put forth a hypothetical scenario. I am certain Lady Greycliff is a model of respectability." And loneliness? She was thirty years of age. With her beauty and good humor, why wasn't she remarried? "I am simply pointing out that your happy household makes my task more difficult."

Difficult or not, Arthur would treat this assignment like any other.

No matter how appealing his charge.

"AND THIS ROOM here functions as the club stillroom. As you can see, our herbs are labeled clearly. Saffron, sage, and so forth. You won't see anything out of the ordinary, Arthur."

Her bodyguard grimaced at the sound of his given name, but Violet refused to treat the man who might have to step between her and sudden death as though he were of no account.

Earlier today, she'd stopped in the kitchen and almost missed him sitting in a corner, chatting quietly to two of the footmen. Wearing black trousers and a dull grey coat, he resembled any other household servant. Shoulders stooped, weary feet propped on the bottom rung of another chair, he blended in with his surrounds, transformed from the vigilant and capable man she met the other night.

Her late husband had complained that Violet had no interest in any man who could not match her intellect. He said her failure as a hostess was because she didn't appreciate the company of those who preferred dancing to distillation.

Untrue. She enjoyed speaking with anyone who had a passion for what they did, whether a master carpenter or a member of Parliament.

Arthur Kneland was good at what he did, and she found it fascinating. She found *him* fascinating—every single bit of him. Nothing piqued Violet's interest more than a mystery, and this man's enigmatic demeanor hinted at secrets long buried.

"So if anyone were to wander through the club, it would appear to be a mirror image of a men's club," he said.

"Exactly. We present a benign facade to London. Instead of a billiards room, we have a stillroom. Instead of a cardroom, we have a crafting room," she said. "Even without revealing the depth of our secret scientific endeavors, the general public has become fascinated with us, and the press has seized hold of the idea. This is why Letty and Phoebe conceived the idea of an evening's entertainment. Society can come and see for themselves we do nothing out of the ordinary. Hopefully, we'll be left alone after that."

Arthur agreed. "Yes," he said, "it would be for the best if society lost interest in this place."

His dismissal disappointed her. Then again, why would this man be sympathetic to their work? Violet smoothed her skirts to hide her dismay.

Baskets heaped with dried petals stood to one side and the powdery scent of lavender filled the space between them.

"The fewer people aware of the club, the safer you'll be," he continued.

Last night, Violet had deliberated long and hard about Arthur's abrupt distancing in the hallway—truthfully, she'd deliberated *about* the long and hard of him. It took her ages to fall asleep.

What he'd said gave her pause. In his line of work, diversion from duty could get someone killed.

Was it not the same for her, in less dramatic terms? Athena's Retreat served as a sanctuary for its members. If her focus wavered, what would become of them?

Violet resolved to ignore Arthur's appeal and turn her mind to proper, ladylike concerns. There were refreshments to order and activities to plan—no time for speculation about the man standing so close in the dark.

"There are any number of stories about your club in the broadsheets," he said.

"Ah, yes. We wish to corrupt women by encouraging radical ideas." Violet began ticking off the most popular rumors. "Learning outside the home arts is dangerous to our fragile minds, leading us to contemplate even more disturbing subjects, such as politics or, even worse, suffrage. Also, we are unattractive and unmarriageable and must seek out one another's company to commiserate."

There were other stories out there, far more risqué, and even cruel. Violet assumed he'd heard them as well, but he gave no sign. "Why do men find the idea of our club so objectionable?" she asked.

"Men get nervous when women enjoy themselves without their company. You might discover that we are of limited use." Arthur answered in a dry tone, arms crossed over his chest.

"Oh, men have their uses," she said without thinking.

The constant roving of his gaze stilled.

For the love of . . . Violet had to stop saying things like that. How was she to convince society that Athena's Retreat was respectable if she couldn't tame her tongue?

"I meant to say there is more than one use for a man."

Wait. That didn't sound right, either.

He took pity on her and changed the subject. "Do the rumors make you angry?" he asked.

Was that a note of sympathy in his voice?

Violet searched his face for a hint of why he might have asked her such an odd question. He gave her nothing but the slightest tilt of his head, as if asking why she wouldn't answer.

Difficult to read a man like Arthur Kneland in the dark.

Difficult to read him anytime.

"Ladies don't get angry," she explained, Daniel's voice echoing behind the words. "We might, on occasion, be out of sorts, but only behind closed doors."

Her attempt at lightheartedness sounded flat and tinny in the small space, and Arthur nodded as if he hadn't heard the lie.

"Shall we continue our tour?" she asked.

As she passed, he stilled her with the touch of his fingertips. It had the force of a grip, so attuned was she to his body.

"Yes?" she asked, amazed she could even push the words past her lips.

"You are correct," he said in a low voice.

"About what?"

Sidling closer, the slow glide of a wolf across the darkness of the forest floor, he bent his head to murmur in her ear. "Us men, we do have our uses."

Violet's rock-solid resolve to remain unaffected melted into a puddle as Arthur preceded her out the door.

4

WHAT IF WE had a replica of Mount Vesuvius instead of a
punch bowl," Violet said, "and the punch flows up from the
bottom via a hidden pump?"

A volley of nos came hurtling toward her from different corners of
the room with such emphasis that if words were stones, she'd have
been black-and-blue.

"We're trying to keep our experiments *secret*," Phoebe declared, "including any recent discoveries in mechanical engineering. No pumps."

"That makes sense," Violet said with forced cheer.

Six women sat in the club's small meeting room and bent their
heads together, continuing their discussion of decorations for the upcoming event, Milly and Willy among them. Violet perched on a chair
to one side of the circle, eager to be included. Entertaining might never
have been her forte, but the success of the evening mattered so much
to the women of the club that she wanted to contribute something.

"We've heard back from a number of ladies' journals," Letty announced. "Three of them have agreed to print articles on the many
charitable works our club members engage in, and—"

"We do charitable works?" Willy inquired of no one in particular.

"Putting up with your explosions is charitable on my part," Phoebe muttered.

"As I was saying"—Letty's voice rose—"our respectability cannot be in doubt if the public is to accept Athena's Retreat. Now, does anyone else have suggestions?"

A cheerful fire crackled in counterpoint to soft, cultured voices as members finalized details. Each of Violet's suggestions met with pained looks and murmured declinations. Even Milly's ludicrous desire to serve lemonade made from dried, powdered, and then reconstituted lemons received more consideration than Violet's ideas. She'd discovered the meeting by accident when she caught sight of Phoebe's cloak over Winthram's arm and went in search of her.

A more suspicious woman would think her friends were trying to exclude her.

Letty leaned over and patted Violet's knee, speaking in a quiet voice. "I'm certain we can put your proposals into use at another event. We've already decided on a presentation of household innovations, a quick lecture and, finally, a few sets of country dancing."

The plans made sense. Violet sat back in her chair without interrupting again. Examining a row of stitches coming undone on her glove, she ignored the sting of hurt at the wariness with which the ladies regarded her—as though she were a maddened horse that might bolt.

The door opened, and a new servant entered, making his way over to Arthur, who'd been observing the meeting for the past hour. Arms crossed, mouth stern, he resembled a menhir, one of the old standing stones in the north. Vigilant and unmoving.

The servant's name was Thomas. Although Violet liked him, it irked her that, without any discussion, Arthur had supplemented her staff with people of his choosing. The result was that she was never more than a few steps away from him or someone he had trained. Such scrutiny made her uncomfortable and added to the nervousness she suffered as the night of the event drew near.

"You cannot be parsimonious with candles," Phoebe chastised. "These are the upper tiers of society. The rooms will reek of tallow."

Letty crossed her arms and sniffed. "We are paying for candles out of club funds. The high cost of beeswax may not have occurred to you, Lady Phoebe. Every extra expense diverts money from purchasing instruments and materials for the members' work."

Over the past few months, Violet's friends had been clashing more often.

They'd always been an unlikely trio.

"Brains, brass, and beauty," Phoebe had quipped about the three of them during their first planning meeting.

They'd met a few years before Daniel died. At a particularly boring ball hosted by Phoebe's father, the Marquess of Larkbrough, Violet had snuck off to the library and, to her great delight, found a copy of Avogadro's seminal work on the relative masses of elementary molecules. She'd been lost in the familiar pages when the door to the library flew open.

Backlit from the hallway, a tall figure posed at the entrance, wearing a diamond-and-emerald-encrusted tiara, which shimmered outrageously. Much like its owner.

"Excuse me. You must find somewhere else to cower. I am in anticipation of a fumbling yet amusing attempt at seduction in the next five minutes, and my would-be lothario has no taste for public approbation."

"I beg your pardon," Violet apologized, impressed by the young woman's aplomb, not to mention her vocabulary. She marked the page with her thumb. "I will absent myself at once."

The stranger held up a hand clad in an elbow-length velvet glove.

"One moment." She strode to the center of the room and pointed at the book in Violet's hands. "Is that the work of Amedeo Avogadro? Where do you stand on his theory of equal volumes of gas containing equal volumes of elementary molecules?"

Violet's mouth dropped open in surprise at this exquisitely coiffed noblewoman's familiarity with the Piedmontese scientist and his controversial theory. Although many women of the aristocracy were well educated, it had become unfashionable to flaunt such knowledge.

"Is he the fellow who posited that the pressure of a gas of fixed mass and volume is proportional to the gas's temperature?" a third woman asked as she hurried into the library, squinting in the dim light, first at Violet, then at Phoebe. "Or was that Gay-Lussac?" She didn't wait for an answer. Resting her fists on her narrow hips, the tiny woman cocked her head, examining Violet with interest.

"You're Lady Greycliff," the woman said to her. "You have a reputation as an eccentric." Her gaze swung around to Phoebe. "And you have a reputation as well, Lady Phoebe. My brother, Sam, was supposed to be escorting me tonight. I'm desperate to leave, but he's gone and disappeared on me." The interloper inspected the noblewoman with suspicion. "You haven't seen him, have you?"

"But . . . but . . . ." Violet clasped the book to her chest, buoyed with excitement. "How do you know Avogadro?" she asked the tall beauty. "And what do you know of Gay-Lussac?" she asked the petite blonde.

Thus began the first of many nights spent arguing, laughing, and drinking purloined port while the rest of London danced around them.

Rare as it was for a woman as wellborn as Phoebe to be engaged in science, Letty's education was even more extraordinary, considering her humble background. Despite their differences in class and temperament, Letty and Phoebe worked hand in glove to bring their dream of a haven for like-minded women into fruition. These days, the club ran smoothly, but their disparities frequently came to the fore. Letty had less patience with Phoebe's deliberate provocations, and Phoebe itched beneath Letty's scolds.

Violet loved them both. She admired their courage and outspokenness but wished that sometimes, such as right now, they were more like her: able to quash her anger, clench her teeth, and paste over everything with a placid expression.

A marvelous idea popped into her head, and Violet leaned forward in excitement. "I've a letter from a friend in Guernsey. She has an acquaintance, Mr. Warren De la Rue, who has been experimenting with electricity and a way to use it indoors to provide lighting. What if we lit the dance floor . . . ?"

Her words trailed off at the sight of Letty trying to rearrange her features from horrified to interested, eyeballs bulging as if she'd swallowed a twist of peppercorns. All the women in the room wore the same expression, except for Phoebe.

"Darling," Phoebe drawled. "You are the most brilliant woman I know, aside from myself, but conducting electricity inside of a crowded ballroom? We don't want another Saga of the Sagging Spoons or the Attack of the Lurid Langoustines."

A few women laughed, and Letty scowled so fiercely in their direction they developed hiccups.

Violet summoned her composure. "I was eighteen when that happened."

"You were the most infamous hostess in London," Phoebe reminded her. "We want to lull this crowd into believing we are a group of boring bluestockings who are fascinated by the cleaning properties of lemon juice and the life cycle of asters."

One of the older members, Lady Potts, shifted in her chair and sent a withering glance in Phoebe's direction.

"If you wish to lull anyone into thinking you are harmless, Lady

Phoebe, stop challenging young men to duels during dinner parties," she admonished.

"Pfft." Phoebe waved away the warning. "Any man who tries to put their hands where they don't belong should know I will call them out."

Anxious to continue, Letty raised her voice over the laughter. "It would be too dangerous to have anyone question how we managed to install electrical lighting without burning down the club."

"Maisy White could have figured that out," said Milly wistfully. The room fell silent at the name, and Violet pressed a hand to her stomach. Even Phoebe's smirk fell away.

A deep voice cut across their chatter. "There will be no Evening of Edification—"

"Elucidation," piped Willy.

". . . if we don't repair the damages caused by the unfortunate explosion of the other night," Arthur said from behind Violet's chair. She hadn't even heard his approach. "Lady Greycliff, have you a moment to spare to advise me on how you would like the work to be carried out?"

Letty frowned. She'd complained more than once in the past week about Arthur's constant presence. Phoebe, keen to stir the pot, took the opposite position. "How titillating, Violet, if you showed Mr. Kneland the site of your almost-demise."

"Why bother Lady Greycliff with such an errand?" Letty objected. "She can send for Winthram."

No longer able to tolerate their squabbling, Violet stood. "Excellent idea, Mr. Kneland. I should take stock of what might be salvageable. We'll need to watch our shillings if Phoebe has her way."

Arthur said nothing as he followed her toward the unobtrusive doorway that closed off the hidden parts of the club from the public areas.

She heard him anyway.

"I understand why they declined my offers of help," she said as if to herself. "Most of my domestic experiments were dramatic failures. The story of the langoustines is infamous." Stopping at the door, she peered back over her shoulder at him.

He held her stare, the familiar intensity tempered with a softer emotion. Sympathy? He seemed too hard a man to condone such feelings.

Shrugging off the urge to defend herself, Violet walked up the stairs toward the smoke-stained room, stopping when she spied the door to a chemistry lab left ajar.

"That door is supposed to be cl—"

Before she could finish her sentence, he'd pulled her behind him. Pressed against his back, she couldn't see a thing over his broad shoulders so Violet leaned in and sniffed the delicious aroma of male and soap. When he stepped into the lab, she almost fell forward.

"Stay," he ordered. The command set off a tiny wave of excitement. A strange, tickling awareness in her body woke at the dark rumble of his voice.

After a moment, he appeared at the door and allowed her inside. Someone had been careless. A cupboard stood open, exposing chemicals to the light.

"These are volatile," she explained as she cleared up. "This laboratory and the storage cabinet upstairs are designed specially in case of fires." She pointed to buckets of sand in the corner of the room. "With certain chemicals, water will make a fire worse."

Arthur inspected the buckets while Violet gave a brief explanation of combustion, then he wandered over to the washbasin. Turning a spigot, he nodded in approval when water streamed into the basin, then through a strainer into another pipe. "I saw something similar in a home when I was in America," said Arthur. "There, the pipes were hidden."

"America." She clasped her hands to her chest. "Is it as exciting as I imagine?"

Arthur grimaced. "I'd prefer being hit over the head with a dozen flying armchairs than going back to America. The people are loud, everything is needlessly outsized, and you cannot find a decent biscuit."

He surveyed the room, taking in the details of the work space. "I've never seen anything like this place. From the facade of the public rooms to the details of the laboratories, your club is an incredible accomplishment."

The compliment's matter-of-fact delivery shook her. Arthur spoke so rarely each of his words carried the weight of truth, as though he could not spare the energy to tell a lie. Happy warmth shot to her toes.

"An odd endeavor for a widow," he continued. No censure laced his words. "Was this a legacy of Grey's father? If he'd lived, would you have built this together?"

Pleasure collapsed, and Violet coughed to cover the terse laugh, schooling her expression. Memories crawled under her skin, and she inhaled deeply. During her marriage, Violet had struggled to breathe, no matter how many windows she opened or how loosely she tied her corset strings.

"I thought so once. When Daniel courted me, he knew of my passion for chemistry and promised not to stand in the way of my discoveries. My parents were hesitant to approve, but I insisted. He was so steady and sensible, while I spent so much time in my head. I thought he could keep me from floating away. Only . . ." Violet broke off, pulling the soothing scent of chemicals and wood polish into her lungs.

She'd been so lonely at her comeout. None of the other girls were interested in chemistry or physics, and none of the callow young men could be bothered to speak on the topics that interested her. While her peers drank and flirted, Violet had stood to the side, pretending interest in gossip and fashion—until she met Daniel.

How to explain without placing blame?

"Neither of us understood how much my duties as a wife would crowd out my work as a scientist. Once we were married, I put my theories aside to restore order to a household too long without a mistress. Daniel's second wife was a leading light in society. I believe he imagined I would follow her. So did I. Unfortunately, my enthusiasm for applying science to domestic arts dashed both our hopes."

All the members of Athena's Retreat told similar stories, regardless of their class or wealth. Violet's only surprise was how many of them were brave enough, or desperate enough, to seek her help.

"I couldn't set up an experiment if I had to attend a ball. I don't have room in my brain for more than one project," she explained. "One ball became ten. Two charity memberships became twenty. Then there was the estate. After two years of marriage, my husband became ill and needed my care."

Apoplexy had drained Daniel of his powerful intellect, and the decline had been difficult to watch. It left him querulous and childlike, demanding her full attention and resenting her work. The relief she'd felt at leaving Daniel's company for the solace of her theories was outweighed by the guilt that plagued her after he died.

"I would stay awake once everyone else had fallen asleep and try to carve out an hour or two to work on my formulas."

The distance between what Violet and Daniel believed marriage meant had taken time to sink in. Once it had, Violet spent her energy on bridging the divide instead of changing her expectations—or endeavoring to change Daniel's.

If she'd tried harder, could she have had everything?

"Other women with far more talent and potential do the same thing every day," she said. "They take care of everyone around them first, setting their heart's desires aside to make someone else's dreams come to life. I created Athena's Retreat for them. A place of respite from the outside world for a few hours."

Arthur cocked a brow at her story. "But why the deception? The work you do here is far more impressive than anything I've read in the popular press. Why not bring it into the open?"

"Show our work to the world? We cannot even study alongside men at university. We cannot own property. We cannot vote. Do you think men will allow us to outshine them with our scientific discoveries? Or let us threaten their beliefs?" Her voice rose with every word, jarring and out of place. Violet clamped her mouth shut, letting go of a slow exhalation through her nose.

"If you weren't a lady, I might think that made you angry," Arthur said with gentle irony.

The club's event brought Violet's insecurities to the fore. Daniel's ghost had hovered too close for comfort these last few months.

"A woman's anger is warped, petty, and unattractive to anyone unfortunate enough to witness it." When Violet spoke Daniel's criticism aloud, it sounded less incisive and more small-minded than she'd remembered.

"A man is allowed anger because the larger emotions are in his nature," she continued. "His anger is righteous or pure. When a male god is in a rage, mountains appear. If a goddess is cross, she turns a man into a tulip or her rival into a cow."

"I've never considered a woman's stronger emotions in that light." Arthur paused. "Does that mean if I make you angry, you'll turn me into a bull?"

Was he teasing her? A bit giddy, she took a risk.

"It means if you make me angry, I will turn you into a steer." Violet had no idea what expression she wore, but whatever Arthur saw in her face was enough to make this unflappable man pale. In the next moment, when it appeared, his smile was devastating enough to set off an explosion.

THE MUTED *THUD* from somewhere outside was not an explosion, but Arthur's body reacted before his thoughts could catch up, and he raced down the hall. He staggered to a halt when a door flew open and a tiny figure stumbled into the hallway.

In his shock, a startled curse slipped out. The diminutive woman flinched.

"I beg your pardon, miss. Er, madam, er . . ." Arthur tried to ascertain her age and status, but that feat was beyond him.

"It's Pettigrew. Mrs. Caroline Pettigrew. And you don't have to beg my pardon. You said exactly what I was thinking," the woman replied in a trembling voice.

It took a moment for his heart to stop pounding and the fear to leave him. He examined the person before him until he calmed down.

Mrs. Pettigrew was small—smaller than Letty Fenley even. She wore a long canvas apron over her full skirts and sensible, thick-soled shoes peeked out from beneath her dress.

"Good heavens, Caroline!" Violet came running up behind Arthur, slightly out of breath. "Whatever hap—Oh. Oh dear."

Violet opened and closed her mouth, groping for words.

What was there to say?

Mrs. Pettigrew's entire self was spattered in pink. An alarming, violent shade of pink, which Arthur was confident had never occurred in nature.

"Lady Greycliff, I am sorry. I don't . . ." Mrs. Pettigrew's hands fluttered with distress.

While Violet murmured something calming, Arthur took the opportunity to move past the woman and peer into the room. On a large table stood a cupboardful of dishes, champagne glasses, punch bowls, serving platters, and tea services. The rest of the room was bare, walls covered in whitewash.

Except for the huge zigzag lines of pink paint.

There were pink streaks on the ceiling, the floor, the ivory curtains, and, most unfortunately, all over the pretty white china cups and dishes.

Violet and Mrs. Pettigrew joined him and surveyed the damage together.

Mrs. Pettigrew moaned. "I wanted to test the new aerosol delivery system."

"Aerosol delivery system? What is that?" Arthur asked.

"Caroline has been working on the concept of an aerosol pump similar to the propellant in the canisters the Omnis use. I've asked her to help me." Violet took in the vast swaths of paint. "Why . . . why pink?"

"Since you haven't finished your antidote and I needed to experiment with a liquid, I filled my canister with leftover paint from the upstairs cupboard. Miss Fenley mentioned the club's china services showed signs of wear and we hadn't the funds to buy new. I meant to spray the rim of that teacup there as an initial experiment." Mrs. Pettigrew pointed to a lone teacup set apart from the other dishes.

"I had just pressed the nozzle when an enormous spider—as big as my fist—jumped from a tower of teacups onto my shoulder. I tried to shoo it off. In my panic, I threw the canister at it. The nozzle stuck, then the canister fell to the floor and rolled all over." She gestured to the shambles of the room as an illustration of what had followed.

Arthur looked about the chamber. He saw no sign of such a beast. Big as her fist? Was she exaggerating, or lying for a more sinister purpose?

"This can't be all the dishes and cups belonging to the club," Violet said. Her face fell when Mrs. Pettigrew nodded. "Oh. Drat."

"You always tell us, 'To every dark cloud there is a silver lining,'" Mrs. Pettigrew said. "It must be here somewhere. Some silver amidst the pink." She hung her head, setting one pink-gloved hand to her pink-lipped mouth in shame.

Violet examined the rows of glasses and stacks of plates, now streaked and spattered with the paint.

"It was stupid of me to do this," Mrs. Pettigrew moaned. "I've ruined the Evening of Information and Invigoration."

Head snapping up, eyes ablaze, Violet took Mrs. Pettigrew's hands in hers. "Do you remember the vow we took as members? We promised never to call ourselves 'stupid.' You are the opposite of stupid. You are brilliant. Your invention works—it might not be designed to ward off an enormous spider, but it *works*."

At Violet's words, Mrs. Pettigrew transformed from despairing to elated. "It does work, doesn't it? The problem before was the pressure-to-solvent ratio."

The disaster surrounding them melted away as the women chattered like magpies, about sulfates and pressure and solvents and springs. They leaped to examine the path of the paint, and within seconds, Violet was also covered in the pink mixture.

"As you can see," Mrs. Pettigrew said, "the paint carried a good three feet from where it began, and out to a width of seven feet."

"Amazing," cheered Violet. "Caroline, you have outdone yourself."

Arthur interrupted the conversation with a more pressing question. "Who else have you told about this invention?"

Mrs. Pettigrew's movements stilled as she examined the splotches of paint on her apron. "I suppose . . . Well, no one other than Lady Greycliff."

Each word dropped like a brittle stick, and Mrs. Pettigrew shrank in on herself. Arthur squinted at the woman with mistrust. Why would she cower over such a simple question? A guilty conscience?

Could coincidence alone account for the fact that the Omnis had developed a canister that emitted gas from a nozzle as well? And what was this nonsense about a giant spider?

"You invented this on your own? Without speaking to anyone?" Arthur didn't bother to cover his disbelief.

Mrs. Pettigrew's hands twisted imaginary tools as her shoulders rose in discomfort. "I have what Mr. Pettigrew calls an 'unquiet mind.' I get an idea in my head, and the urge to create consumes me until I finish it, whether I know what the result will be or not." The woman gazed at Violet. "There is no one outside of the club with whom I can speak. Mr. Pettigrew worked hard to secure his clerkship. If the bank managers find out about my tinkering, they might assume he's reaching above his station. He's warned me not to make any wild claims, to keep to myself and not to draw any attention to my projects."

She sighed. "What will he say when I come home covered in pink? What will the upstairs neighbors say? I've dropped hints that I go out to help with charitable works. What possible explanation could there be for . . . Is it in my hair as well?" Mrs. Pettigrew touched her cap, pink lashes fluttering with distress.

Violet pinched the bridge of her nose, then shook her head and lifted her shoulders. "We will use china from Beacon House. Due to a few unfortunate incidents of my own, we don't have any matching sets large enough for the Evening of Edification. Let's hope no one will notice if we mix patterns. Everything will work out for the best."

In a telling gesture, Violet's head ducked as she spoke, as if expecting someone to contradict her as she took command, bracing herself for a blow.

Unfortunately, my enthusiasm for applying science to domestic arts dashed both our hopes.

We promised never to call ourselves 'stupid.'

Embarrassed by the disconcerting tightness in his chest, Arthur strode to the table of dishes and made a show of examining them. What did he care if their event was ruined? A ridiculous waste of time and added work on his part.

He opened his mouth to tell them so, then peered over at Violet. "It is a very bright color. However, I find it appealing."

She turned to regard him with surprise.

Did sympathy prod him to speak? No, it was common sense. If she was worried about the Evening of Eduwhowhatsit, she'd have less time to work on the antidote. The faster she worked, the quicker he could quit her household.

Addressing Mrs. Pettigrew, he gestured to a dish with pink stripes down the center. "What if you fixed the nozzle and sprayed the entire plate with the paint? Or created new patterns? The result might be . . . innovative."

Mrs. Pettigrew cocked her head. "I suppose if I narrowed the opening and adjusted the propellant, I could better control the flow of paint. It's worth a try. What do you think, Lady Greycliff?"

Although she was answering Mrs. Pettigrew, Violet stared at Arthur when she spoke. "It's a marvelous, thoughtful idea."

"Yes, well . . ." He mistrusted her expression. Was it gratitude? This had been a gesture of expediency, not friendship. "You are needed here. I will call for Winthram to go over the damages with me instead."

Despite his clipped tone, Violet continued to beam as he took his leave, a wide smile lighting her face. Arthur fought its appeal.

He'd seen plenty of smiles before, and Violet's was simply one of many.

As he left the room, the lie followed on his heels.

5

THE DOORMAN HAD better things to do than watch Arthur study the burnt remains of the second-floor room where the explosion had occurred. He didn't say so, of course. Too well trained to comment on the proceedings, Winthram communicated his dissatisfaction by shifting his weight from side to side and puffing through pursed lips. His thick brows were many shades darker than the auburn hair pomaded back from his forehead, drawing attention to his bright blue eyes. Because he had no sideburns nor a hint of a beard, the few freckles splattered across the thin bridge of his nose stood out, the splayed constellation giving his face a mischievous air, at odds with his ill-concealed antagonism.

Arthur ignored him for the moment. Sitting on his haunches, he tried studying the undulating patterns of soot across the walls, but his thoughts kept circling back to Violet. Unlike the evidence of the explosion before him, some damage leaves no outward trace.

A lady doesn't get angry.

What must it be like to swallow one's rage, year after year? Did it resemble the pain of living with unspoken grief and guilt?

Arthur took hold of himself. Best to abandon such questions. He had no business trying to peer behind the formidable wall of relentless good humor Violet had maintained over the years. If he were to turn his attention toward a mystery, it should be the question of who set off the bomb. Quashing a surge of sympathy, he ran a finger through the rubble.

"Any number of chemicals are stored in here. One or two might have fallen from a wobbly shelf," the doorman opined.

"You think this explosion was accidental?" Arthur asked, sniffing at a chunk of plaster.

The young man threw his shoulders back and boasted, "I know who comes in and out of the club each night, sir. No one in this club didn't belong. The ladies would never do anything to hurt Lady Greycliff."

Arthur rose and walked out of the laboratory into the hallway. "This part of the building shares a wall with Beacon House, does it not?"

Winthram tucked his chin in a surly nod.

Knocking on the wall opposite the lab, Arthur's knuckles came away smudged with blackened whitewash. "Which room lies on the other side of this wall?"

Comprehension dawned on Winthram's face. On the other side of the wall, not two feet from the explosion site, lay Violet's bedchamber.

Violet's bedchamber.

The images those two words conjured comprised a bomb of their own.

It would be far easier to keep his distance if the woman weren't so damn compelling. Arthur rubbed his face, summoning attention back from his nether regions and onto the problem at hand.

"But . . . but who would want to hurt Lady Greycliff?" The doorman shook his head. "Nay. It doesn't make sense."

The business of sorting out motives for inflicting cruelty and pain made Arthur tired. Years of seeing people as objects—as weapons—had drained him. Would any humanity remain by the time he found a home? Did he even remember how to talk to another soul on a subject other than their likelihood of being murdered? He couldn't recall the last time he'd tried to make a friend.

No matter. Time enough to contemplate his unsuitability for society after he finished this job.

"Who would want to hurt Lady Greycliff?" Walking toward the doorman, Arthur allowed a touch of menace to show on his face. "Someone with secrets in their past. Who in this club might have something to hide?"

At Arthur's approach, Winthram widened his legs and stuck out his jaw in a pugnacious flourish. Good show, but Arthur smelled fear.

"This has nowt to do wi' me," Winthram insisted in his high-pitched voice, tossing his head as that fear peeled away the sharp point of his consonants, revealing a touch of the north. A thatch of auburn hair slipped over one eye at the gesture, no doubt nudged by a duplicitous cowlick that wouldn't be tamed despite the copious application of pomade.

"But you've been to a meeting or two of the Chartists, haven't you? If I asked around, would anyone have seen you at an Omnium Democratia meeting?" Arthur asked the questions as he backed Winthram against the dirty wall.

A bead of sweat rolled down Winthram's temple, and his hands clenched shut. "That was ages ago. I went to see m' brother. I don't have anything to do with anyone from home anymore. I would never—"

"Far as I can figure, that bomb was timed to go off when Lady Greycliff was in her bath. By the grace of God, something went wrong. Otherwise, she would be in pieces right now," Arthur said. "Your brother is Adam Winters, is he not?"

While Grey gave his stepmother free rein of Beacon House and its environs, he still kept watch over her. Before leaving for the north, he'd put notes in his files about Winthram's connection to Adam Winters. Once an influential member of the Chartist movement, Winters had been under surveillance by the Crown for suspicious activities, including working with Omnium Democratia. Violet had insisted to Grey that Winthram could be relied upon. It was her belief that Winthram would never allow any harm to come to the ladies of Athena's Retreat.

Arthur had long ago learned never to trust based on someone else's opinion.

"Heard Adam fell out with Lovett and the rest of the Chartist moderates after the convention in '37," said Arthur. "Now he's printing leaflets and giving speeches on the tyranny of the ruling class."

The doorman closed his eyes in acknowledgment, setting a hand to his stomach as if recovering from a punch.

Arthur gave him no time to think and pressed on with his questions.

"Quite the rabble-rouser, Adam. While he hasn't admitted to membership in Omnium Democratia, he has taken up their causes at his meetings. When was the last time the two of you spoke?"

"The last time we spoke ..." Winthram's voice broke, and he swallowed twice. "The last time we spoke was two years ago."

Arthur read misery and defiance on the man's face. Was there malice as well?

Winthram continued, his words slurring as he held back tears. "He told me I was dead to him, and I haven't seen him since. I left the name Winters behind after that day."

Grey's files contained facts; motivations were Arthur's responsibility to uncover. He cocked his head in query. "And the name Henrietta as well?"

Color flooded Winthram's cheeks. Defiant despite his sorrow, he dashed away tears and pushed back his shoulders.

"Henry," Winthram said. He touched a palm to his chest, giving himself the name with a tender dignity. "My name is Henry. And I would never let anyone hurt Lady Greycliff."

They considered one another in the silence that followed.

Winthram broke the stalemate as a question occurred to him. "Why would you think it were—was the Omnis? Members come here to do their science. Most of their talk is about compounds and re-agents, not elections or riots."

"Lady Greycliff is in a position to uncover one of the Omnis' se-crets," Arthur replied. He backed away and examined the scattered debris by his feet. "Plenty of them behind the doors of this club, aren't there?"

"What do you mean?"

"You." Arthur gestured to the room behind him. "All these ladies come here to hide their brains and their talents from the world. Pre-tending to embroider roses or glue seashells to boxes, when all the while they are making discoveries no one could imagine."

Winthram snorted. "They aren't hiding. It's outside the secrets are kept. Why don't you poke your nose around out there?"

Arthur shook his head in disagreement. "Someone knows what happened here last night. It's best we work together. Don't you want to help me figure this out?"

"We want to keep Lady Greycliff safe, but no one here will trust you," said Winthram. "This is a place made *by* us and *for* us. If you come in here without understanding who we are or why we are here? Then there is no place for a man like you on this side of the wall."

VIOLET TOLD HERSELF not to take offense when Phoebe and the others dismissed her suggestions. The future of Athena's Retreat was more important than her ego. Even so, she had withdrawn to the place she felt safest. The faint scent of ethanol and graphite settled like a fog around her, and she tapped her toes in contentment.

With the aid of talented craftsmen, Violet had designed a private workroom on the third floor of Beacon House by combining three rooms into one, raising the ceiling and elongating the windows to let in copious natural light. The north side held bookshelves crammed with volumes of varying heights and thickness alongside dozens of jars filled with all manner of chemicals. Rows of drawers in long, low cabinets brimmed with dried powders and piles of useful materials, such as thick silk threads and boiled lemon drops. Next to the green-tiled hearth sat a comfy stuffed couch she used as a bed when she was too tired to go to her chambers.

"Heaven," she whispered.

Taking a seat at her worktable, she turned her head a fraction of an inch, letting her gaze slip over the top half of the page open in a note-book.

Even five years after Daniel's death, a pall of guilt often accompanied her research. She should give her work to Grey's office. They could find someone else to figure out the antidote, although at a slower pace. The club members needed her sole attention.

"Half an hour. If I don't figure something out, I'll send it away," Violet whispered to herself.

A tingling spread from her toes to her fingertips as she sank into the work. A few hours later, she examined a complex equation in pursuit of a solution. If the reaction was endothermic, where delta symbolized the heat of the reaction, then . . .

"No. Don't scurry away from me. I have to follow your trail," she crooned to the mixture of symbols and integers thumbing their nose at her.

This was where she belonged. Not stuffed into a gown and propped up before the intrusive stares of disapproving matrons. In her head, it made no difference if she was fat or thin, plain or pretty, no matter if her parties were a success or if she could maintain small talk for an hour. When she worked, she forgot how lonely her nights and how long her days stretched out before her. She hummed a low song of satisfaction and scribbled out an error.

A single heavy knock sounded on the door, which opened before she could tell whoever it was to go away.

"Lady Greycliff?"

Violet's head snapped up, theories cracking apart beneath the sound of Arthur's voice.

In the doorway, he stood staring at her as though she were naked. Violet peeked to ascertain that she was not, thank goodness, naked. One never knew.

She blinked.

Why whenever Arthur walked into the room did her thoughts run into a million different *naughty* directions? Whatever insight she had gained with the formula now slithered away from her.

She put a hand to her forehead, trying in vain to press the solutions back into her slothlike brain.

"Why are you staring at me like that?" Violet asked, heat creeping over her cheeks.

"How long have you been in here?"

"Not long enough. I have almost figured out this last set of formulas, and I need a few more minutes of quiet. Lovely to see you." Violet waved her hand in the direction of the doorway, hoping he would take the hint.

Instead, Arthur moved toward her in that manner he possessed— stealthy yet purposeful. Despite her frustration, a thrill of lust woke her senses at the sight.

She must remember her resolve. A proper lady did not allow for thrills.

Having reached the opposite side of the table from her, Arthur narrowed his eyes. "When was the last time you changed your clothes?"

"What an odd question." Violet looked down. "If you must know, this dress is not even a year old. No . . . two, three . . . perhaps more." She shook her head to clear her thoughts, and swayed, dizzy at the sudden movement.

"When was the last time you ate or drank anything?" Arthur asked.

Thick purple curtains hung over the windows, blocking out extraneous light and hiding the time of day. Sweet-smelling beeswax candles tilted into a tarnished candelabra lit her work space. Judging by the candle stubs, she hadn't left her work since . . . yesterday? That couldn't be right.

"I had luncheon at some point today. I think. I do remember dinner. Is it still Thursday?" Violet said.

Arthur's brows raised, then lowered, in concern.

Gracious, how long *had* she been working?

"Why don't you leave off and have a dish of tea?" Arthur asked.

"A dish of tea? How am I to think of tea when I've made a connection between this work and my original research into Avogadro's law?" Violet began to explain how equal volumes of gases at the same temperature and pressure could contain equal numbers of molecules, but her throat hurt.

"Now that you mention it"—she tried to force her legs to unbend, groaning at the stiffness in her joints—"I am parch—Oh, oh no."

Violet fell to the floor in a clumsy heap, pins and needles burning her limbs. "That's odd. My legs have stopped working."

Arthur was there before she'd finished her sentence, scooping her up in his arms. "Johnson," he called out to a passing footman as he carried her from the workroom. His low voice made pleasant vibrations against Violet's side. "If you could ask Mrs. Sweet to send a tea tray for Lady Greycliff."

"Put me down. My legs fell asleep is all."

Already, sensation had returned to her toes, but he insisted on carrying her.

Oh well. If a brooding, desirable man must sweep her into an embrace, she may as well enjoy it.

Violet sniffed at his waistcoat. The man smelled like winter and soap. How ridiculously attractive.

"You're quite strong," she told him.

"Hmm."

Inured to flattery, was he?

"Most other men would be breaking a sweat right now, carrying a woman of my size up and down the stairs," she observed.

His thick black brows met as he frowned. "What do you mean? You are . . ." His glance dropped to her bosom, tracing the curves from her chest to her waist to her hips.

He cleared his throat and shifted her in his arms. When he spoke again, his voice was low. "You are not too heavy."

"You are going above and beyond your duties," she told him.

Was it her imagination, or did he pull her even closer? "It is no hardship," he said.

"Nevertheless. Thank you." There might have been an electric current attached to those last two words, the way Arthur regarded her. Hadn't anyone thanked him before?

"How could you forget to eat?" he asked.

Violet rested her head against his chest when he turned a corner then kept it there, lulled by the warmth of his body and the sensation of security.

"I've tried to explain what happens when I fall into my work. I've never found the right words. It's as if I lose the tether between my brain and my body."

Better she would lose the tether between her brain and her tongue. Her words sounded unnatural, and a lady shouldn't be speaking about her body, especially not to a . . . What was Arthur? Not a servant, and he'd made clear he wasn't a friend.

Something else? Something more?

He shouldered open the door to her private rooms and stepped around a pile of books. This first chamber she used to entertain close friends. Through a connecting door lay her bedroom.

The request popped out of her mouth.

"Can you bring me to my bed, Arthur?" The dryness in her throat turned her question into a whispered plea.

Time froze.

For her, at least. In a metaphorical sense, that is, because time is always in motion. But goodness—those eyes. They saw right through her layers of fabric: the dress, the corset, and the chemise beneath. The look Arthur gave her was hungry and fierce, and it did something peculiar and amazing to her insides.

Good thing he still held her, for her body went soft and pliant as if she were a flower opening for the sun. She ran the tip of her tongue over the bowed edge of her top lip. In response, he tightened his grip. Violet's heart lurched.

Was he going to do it?

Languidly, he lowered her legs, supporting her back with one strong arm. Her muscles quivered with tension as she held on to his shoulders and let herself sway against him. His brown eyes grew darker, and he searched her upturned face. A lick of lightning crested beneath her skin.

He was going to kiss her.

She was going to kiss him back.

This oversized lust she'd been stricken with since she first saw him would be sated—unless her heart hammered itself right out of her chest.

He made loose bracelets with his long fingers, stroking upward to her elbows, sending shivers of anticipation in his wake. Violet pressed her breasts against him, wishing away the layers of canvas and wool.

Then, with devastating abruptness, he set his hands on her shoulders and stepped away.

"I see you are well enough to stand on your own," he said. "Johnson is taking too long. I'll go fetch your tea myself."

Oh.

How could she have been so stupid?

Humiliation chilled the space between them. Violet turned her head in embarrassment at the tightness in her throat and a horrible scratchiness behind her eyes. Daniel had warned her time and again that her desire for physical contact was unattractive. Violet's reaction to Arthur's touch must have scared him away.

She forced a laugh past the lump in her throat. "It isn't your job to bring me tea. I'm feeling better anyway. I lost sight of the time." Glancing at the clock on her mantel, Violet gasped, shock overtaking the hurt.

"There is a meeting of the club chemists in less than an hour," she cried. "Much as Letty tries to keep them in line, Lady Peckinpaugh is forever one-upping Miss Makepeace with her formulas, and the two of them have burned more than a few holes in the carpet when comparing solvents. I must go."

Refusing to retreat, Arthur folded his arms in that way he had of turning from flesh to stone. "You will remain here until you've had tea. The meeting of club chemists was Thursday at four."

"Yes, I know. Today at . . . Was?"

"Today is Friday," he said.

Violet put a hand to her forehead in surprise, only to find Arthur bending over her, concern tightening his jaw.

"Have you a fever?" he said. "Are you ill?"

"Please let it be fever and not the harbinger of things to come," she cried. "If my brain becomes any more sluggish, I will end up wearing hats on my feet and shoes around my neck. Friday, you say? Who went and misplaced Thursday on me?"

A spontaneous grin cracked the granite of his face. Violet staggered back, dumbfounded. She'd caught a glimpse of him smiling before, but this—this smile—it transformed him into a warm-blooded man, not just a presence.

She pointed at him in accusation. "You are smiling."

As fast as it had appeared, the smile vanished, and his face settled back into its natural state of hardened detachment. Too late.

"Too late," she warned him. "I saw it. I made you smile."

Embarrassed, he found something on the floor to examine. The vulnerability of the gesture touched her. As he inspected his shoes, the tiniest crease appeared at the corner of his mouth for an instant, then disappeared again.

Twice! She'd done it twice.

"It isn't as though you called water from a stone," he groused.

"I find it on par with similar miracles," she said.

When he looked up, the grin was gone, and his thick brows were drawn in worry. "Fevers can be dangerous. You must be careful."

"Of course." Violet placed her hand on his arm, the wool of his jacket brushing against her palm. "Thank you for taking care of me."

A frisson of the earlier tension climbed her spine when he covered her bare hand with his.

"It is no hardship," he answered, staring at their joined hands.

His answering pressure was slight, and if she hadn't been waiting for it, she might have missed its significance. Her first tentative step toward him was rewarded when he looked up from her hands without hiding the hunger in his gaze.

This would happen. Arthur would take her in his arms, bring her to the bed next door, and—

"Hullo, old bird."

Violet jumped in fright at the sound of her door slamming back against the wall. Her visions of kisses melted away at the sight of a giant blond man standing in her doorway.

Crossing the room, he clasped her hand in both of his. "Got carried away with your work again? Did you forget I was coming today?"

Drat.

"And who is this?" Arthur asked with a disinterested air. A wall of ice had formed around her bodyguard, dousing whatever embers of lust they'd kindled.

Double drat.

"George Willis, Earl Grantham, I'd like you to meet Mr. Arthur Kneland," Violet managed to stammer even as her face went up in flames.

Grantham glanced at Arthur as though she'd pointed out a new piece of furniture, then flashed a set of strong white teeth at her. "I came as quick as I could to your summons for rescue. Here to spend my every waking moment seeing to your pleasure. I'm all yours, Vi."

Triple drat to the power of five.

6

⁂

EARL GRANTHAM SAT on a cushion of blue brocade. None too subtly, he flexed his muscles as he stretched his arm across the back of a sofa in Violet's formal parlor, examining Arthur with a curious gaze.

Having read the gossip sheets Cook let lie around the kitchen, Arthur had fleshed out the sparse entry on the earl that Grey had left behind in the dossiers.

Once a soldier in the 24th Foot, Grantham had taken a title upon the death of a distant relative without heirs. The gossip sheets made much of his friendship with Prince Albert and his popularity with the ladies of the ton. Grey had also mentioned that Grantham had grown up in a house on Violet's family's estate.

"Grey wrote to me that he'd engaged a man to watch Vi while he went north," Grantham said. "Suppose you work for that lot in the PM's office. Off protecting despots and butchers."

"Despots who ally themselves with the Crown," Arthur said, careful to keep a level tone. "Butchers who kill to our kingdom's benefit."

As if he hadn't heard Arthur's answer, the big man yawned and stretched his massive arms above his head. "Kneland. Scottish?"

Arthur nodded.

"Seems I remember that name in connection to something . . ."

"Common enough name," Arthur said, a slither of anxiety sliding through his belly.

"Lady Greycliff called me back to London to squire her around while she drums up support for an event at the Retreat." The earl paused. "On the small side for a counterassassin, aren't you?"

Whereas a man Grantham's size would make a satisfying *thunk* upon hitting the ground.

Before Arthur could test out this theory, Violet came rushing into the room. She'd changed out of the dress she'd worn earlier. Her cheeks were flushed, and she looked pretty.

No, not simply pretty.

Desirable.

For a moment, their eyes locked and her flush deepened. She'd wanted to kiss him earlier, leaning forward, eyelids fluttering closed and lips parted. He'd almost let her, too. He'd imagined how it would taste, that mouth. Soft and sweet, warm and inviting. Everything he'd denied himself since his first assignment.

The sheer delight in her face when she spoke of her work, an untrammeled spark in her despite her insecurity, fascinated him. Retirement would mean a retreat from a life lived in the company of strangers, punctured by bursts of terrible violence. In Violet's presence, for the first time in years, he hadn't been an observer. They had a . . . connection.

Dangerous. Allowing yourself to care was like living on quicksand. At any moment, the people you cared for would be swallowed forever. This woman turned him back into the fool boy he'd been almost twenty years ago. Chills pricked Arthur's gut.

It needed to stop.

That fool boy had thought himself a hero, and the man he was supposed to protect had wound up dead.

Arthur could not bear to fail again.

"So, you *did* forget I was coming," Grantham chided Violet with a teasing pout.

"No," Violet said. She was a terrible liar.

The earl chuckled. "You are a terrible liar."

She mock-scowled. "I am a brilliant liar. Who convinced you to lick the pump handle on Boxing Day for good luck?"

"I was seven," Grantham growled. "Too young to know when a lady spoke with a serpent's tongue. Anyway, that was the last time I fell for one of your stories. I saw through you the next summer when you tried to convince me that bats see with their ears."

"They don't see with their ears. They navigate by sound. There is some interesting work done by an Italian—"

"Right. Good thing you begged me to come to your aid. How long did you go without eating this time? You look dreadful." Grantham's voice, a deep, rich baritone, had none of the ennui the fashionable set liked to adopt. Sounding genuine in his concern, the earl also asked whether she'd rested.

"On the list of phrases one should never use with a lady, 'You look dreadful' ranks fairly high." Her rejoinder came from the middle of the room, where she'd positioned herself between the two men.

Arthur should leave. Violet had much to discuss with this handsome earl who oozed charm from his every pore. Enough to kill one's appetite, that oozing.

Instead, he opened his gob and stepped into it. "Lady Greycliff is peaked, owing to her hard work on the assignment Grey left for her. Genius takes its toll."

Violet's jaw dropped, then snapped shut again. She covered her grin as though her pleasure might be unseemly. Her delight in even the smallest of compliments was as sweet and addictive as sugar.

Grantham stared at Arthur with mild surprise but addressed his words to Violet. "Genius, eh? Well, genius, I'm in town for a few weeks. Mama is . . ." He bit his lip.

Violet frowned in sympathy. "I am selfish to take you away from her and the estate," she said with concern. "You should go back."

Arthur agreed.

"No, my cousin Mrs. Applewhite and her daughter are staying to keep Mama company until Lizzie is finished with school. She comes out next spring."

"Don't tell me Elizabeth is almost old enough to be presented," Violet marveled. "Why, I can scarcely believe it. I remember waving goodbye to her when she left for the academy."

Grantham beamed. "She's a top student. Knows about those thing-amabobs you can only see with one of those whoseyercallits."

"You mean a cell. Yes, my aunt has written to me of Elizabeth's work. I am fascinated by her theories of cell division . . ."

As Violet chattered on about his sister, Grantham cleared his throat and stared pointedly, first at Arthur, then at the door.

Arthur, entertained by the veins popping from the big man's neck, pretended not to understand.

Giving up on his attempts at subtlety, Grantham interrupted Violet's reverie. "Time moves fast—for both of us. Makes me think I ought to come to the point sooner rather than later."

"Come to the point?" Violet asked.

The earl glanced over at Arthur once more. Arthur's feet remained glued to the floor.

Grantham frowned. "Grey's at an age where he'll want to settle down. What are you going to do—stay at Beacon House as a dowager?" The tone of voice was gentle, but the words were a reproach nonetheless.

"We've agreed I am going to buy it from him," she explained. "Once he returns from this last assignment."

"Giving him one more excuse to keep accepting missions he doesn't want and put off starting a family?" Grantham asked.

Perhaps Violet hadn't considered this outcome. She wrung her hands in consternation, her pretty mouth twisted around words she wouldn't say.

Arthur knew he should dispel the tension, but nothing came to him. Countless times, he'd stood to the side, watching people's lives play out as though he were a picture hanging on the wall, pretending invisibility while drama unfolded. For the first time in years, he cared about the outcome. How to intervene?

"Why not come home with me to Morningside for a fortnight," Grantham said, "instead of worrying about explosions and whatnot. A visit from you would do wonders for Mama's health." A serious note entered his voice. "I don't like the thought of you alone here without Grey."

Violet's eyebrows rose in consternation. "You are a dear to be worried, Grantham, but Mr. Kneland has me well in hand."

All three of them froze for a moment. Glancing over at Arthur, Violet colored a luscious shade of crimson. "Not well in *his* hand, of course. Not that he's had me. In his hands, you see. Except for that one time," she stammered.

Grantham's gaze transferred between Arthur and Violet, his brows lowering in suspicion.

"What I mean to say is that I was in his hands, but his hands were not . . . Never mind. Let's forget the subject of hands. Or any other body parts. His, at any rate. And mine. Or mine and his. Together."

Pretending to cough, Arthur covered his mouth to hide his amusement.

Violet crossed her arms. "Ahem. So, in conclusion, I am well, and no one had their hands on anyone else—it was the rest of our bodies that one time on the ground. You must be exhausted from your trip. Shall we catch up over tea? Say, tomorrow?"

"I beg your pardon?" asked Grantham.

Violet clapped her hands to her cheeks in shock. "I said . . . tea. Speaking of tea, I am famished. I'll go check on whether Cook has anything set aside for me."

"That part in the middle," Grantham said. "About the rest of your bodies?"

Violet inched her way toward the door. "Friday is generally stew. I'm mad for stew."

Grantham made to rise at the same time Arthur took a step toward her. They might have ended in an awkward tug-of-war if a scream hadn't torn through the tension.

The earl was damned fast for such a big bastard. He and Arthur hit the doorway at the same time. For a few seconds, both were wedged into the exit. Grantham was taller by an inch or so, but Arthur took pleasure in the certainty that he could break the man's ribs in two seconds flat, had he a mind to.

Feck. What was he thinking? This wasn't the time or the place to engage in a pissing contest, nor was Violet a prize to be fought over. Arthur jerked backward and let Grantham fall forward and knock himself into the opposite wall.

When another scream rent the air, Arthur pushed everything else out of his head.

On the second-floor landing Alice stood, pointing to Violet's laboratory.

"There is someone in Lady Greycliff's workrooms," she cried.

Even before she'd finished her sentence, Arthur leaped past her.

Slamming open the door, he surveyed the room. Almost lost beneath the whomp of heavy footsteps coming up behind him was the quiet squeak of a rusty hinge. Vaulting past the well-used armchair by the fire, Arthur made toward a door at the back of the room, standing partway open.

It had been closed when he'd come into the room earlier.

The door led to a small closet. Within stood a low cabinet holding a porcelain bowl and a beak-shaped contraption made of steel. On the opposite wall sat a single window higher than a man's head. A figure in black hung from the ledge of the narrow window, a sheaf of papers under one arm. Arthur sprang and grabbed the thief's leg.

The intruder dropped the papers, gripped the windowsill, and kicked at Arthur's face. Arthur hung on, despite the blows, and was trying to pull himself up the thief's legs when the closet filled with people.

"My goodness, Arthur, be careful," Violet called.

"What are you playing at?" bellowed Grantham.

As Arthur turned his head to respond, the thief dug a heel into his eye. Blinding pain shot through his face, and he fell, cracking the back of his head against the floor, doubling over when Grantham tripped and landed squarely on Arthur's chest.

"Move, Kneland," Grantham growled. "The man is getting away."

Move? Arthur would have had a few choice words to deliver if his lungs hadn't been flattened by the giant fool.

Grantham scrambled to his feet and used the cabinet as a springboard to jump after the thief. The figure in black was faster, though, slithering through the window before the earl could reach him.

Still winded, Arthur rolled to his side and heaved himself up. Racing down the servants' stairs, he shouted for the footmen to block the back gate.

Too late.

By the time Arthur burst through the kitchen door and into the mews, the thief was gone.

GRANTHAM KNELT ON one knee and examined the hard earth at the back of the house. Meanwhile, Arthur finished speaking with two footmen, his jaw clenched and his face white with tension as he issued a series of terse orders.

Dusk shaded the hollows of his eyes. Lifting his face to the sharp winds, he sniffed the air as if he could find the would-be thief by scent alone.

Grantham rose from his haunches and brushed off his trousers.

"Anything?" Arthur asked in an abrupt masculine way of speech they'd adopted since the thief got away.

Grantham shook his head. "Few chips of paint. Nothing that would help us."

"Well. That's that, I suppose," Violet said. "No self-respecting thief will try to break into Beacon House again."

"He shouldn't have been here in the first place," Grantham bit out in accusation.

Arthur tensed, and Violet intervened. "It was my fault. Mr. Kneland warned me to keep my workroom windows locked. I forgot."

She turned to Grantham. "Thank you for your help. Now, if you will both excuse me. I must go—"

"Not so quick," said Arthur.

"You cannot consider the matter closed," Grantham said.

"But I do," Violet insisted. "The two of you nearly caught him. Why would he come back? I will be more careful locking the windows."

Feeling vulnerable, despite the presence of two large men at her side, she peered around the kitchen garden. Violet could attribute the explosion to an experiment gone wrong and the bricks to silly boys. The appearance of a thief in her private rooms, however, meant no longer hiding from the truth. Someone wanted her to stop.

"Your composure is a credit to you, my lady," said Arthur. "You've been very brave."

Oh. Very brave? Violet preened a little.

He then spoke to Grantham. "Lady Greycliff is safe as long as she follows my direction."

"Safe? With her windows wide-open?" Grantham asked. The men had forgotten her and now faced off against one another.

If Miss Meredith Pickering were here, she would be taking copious notes. Miss Pickering's area of expertise was the mating behaviors of large predators. From what Violet gathered, it consisted of similar shows of aggression.

"Miss Pickering would be in raptures right now if she saw their antics." Phoebe's whispered observation gave Violet an unpleasant jolt.

"Indeed. I didn't hear you coming." She turned to greet her friend. "Hello, dear."

Phoebe resembled a winter queen, in her gorgeous blue ankle-length, ermine-trimmed paletot. By contrast, Violet had raced out of the house wearing nothing but a shapeless old gown, her worn petticoats making themselves known when a gust of frigid wind found its way under her skirts.

"Do you remember the lecture she gave last month?" Phoebe continued. "After a confrontation, the male predators mark their territory with musk."

"Ugh." Violet shuddered. "Not to worry. This isn't mating behavior, because they don't . . ." Her words trailed off at the cynical amusement on Phoebe's face.

"Grantham seems ready to tear out Mr. Kneland's throat," Phoebe said. "What happened here? I was passing by and saw the commotion."

"A thief got into my workroom and tried to steal my research," Violet explained. "Grantham wants me to leave Beacon House for the time being."

Phoebe's amused expression melted into concern. "A woman should never back down because a man told her so. However, broken windows, a bomb, and now an attempted theft? Darling, consider doing as he says."

She watched as Grantham ran his fingers through his hair, heedless of how tousled it looked. "He means well. Of that, there was never any doubt in my mind."

Like a cat toying with a mouse is how Phoebe behaved with most men of her acquaintance, and for many years, a man's unsuitability was her catnip. She danced circles around her hapless suitors, pawns in a war they had no idea Phoebe was waging with her father.

For a time, she'd fallen in with a more measured crowd, Grantham among them, who took an interest in philanthropy, the arts, and politics, to a genteel degree. She'd surprised even Letty with a newfound understanding of workers' conditions. Violet had encouraged Phoebe's friendship with Grantham, and for a while there had been talk of an engagement. Despite Grantham's sometimes arrogant exterior, he'd a fine mind, a subtle sense of humor, and a generous heart. All qualities beneficial to Phoebe, who struggled to find peace.

Phoebe had ended the courtship the instant she sensed everyone's approval. "It wasn't Grantham's fault. With him, I turned into the person society wanted me to be," she'd told Violet. "The more I conform, the less I am myself. Besides, Papa did not turn purple and forbid me to see him again."

Phoebe's wicked grin had twisted, pulling her alabaster skin taut with misery. "Nothing kills the romance like a father's endorsement."

With the severing of the courtship, Phoebe had slid back into old habits, and the scandal sheets were again full of unflattering analogies to predators and hapless prey.

Upon spying Phoebe outside Beacon House, Grantham paled. Good manners prevailed, however, and he joined them to make his bow.

"This was bold, even for the Omnis," he said.

"Unsurprising for a group that calls for a secret ballot, the abolishment of the monarchy, and an end to the House of Lords," Violet observed.

"Yes," Phoebe said, reverting to her familiar sarcastic drawl. "As if the lower classes were intelligent enough to be trusted with the vote. Bold indeed." She tapped a finger to her chin. "Abolishing lords isn't a bad idea, however. Nothing but a holding room for overfed, inbred, and useless old men."

Grantham tugged at his cravat, eyeing the gate and its promise of escape. "I don't suppose you consider me an exception to that description, Lady Phoebe?"

Phoebe's laugh, as dry as paper, rubbed against Violet's raw nerves. "I meant my father," she said. "A man not born to a title like yourself might not agree. Those of us raised by such men know better."

Grantham stiffened, and Phoebe laughed again.

Their bickering added to a dull throbbing that hammered at Violet's temples. To her embarrassment, she swayed, in the beginnings of a faint. She did not want Grantham here, assuming the role of an older brother. She did not want to listen to Phoebe's sly digs.

Were there other women who suffocated in plain sight? Others who shoved their objections into small, dark places in their guts, choking on their dissatisfaction and dismay?

The puddled shadows at her feet doubled in size as Arthur came to stand beside her. Tension ebbed from her cramped muscles as his calm enveloped her in gentle waves.

Violet leaned into the offer of comfort, fleeting as it might be.

How could it be she stood in the company of so many and still felt so alone?

7

COME," ARTHUR ORDERED in a low rumble, slipping his arm around her waist, and they left behind Phoebe's acid taunts and Grantham's sputtered replies. He escorted Violet into the kitchen, where Mrs. Sweet greeted them. Three lines of worry marred the smooth skin of her forehead. "I trust you will put an end to this goings-on, Mr. Kneland?" She turned to Violet. "Not to worry, my lady. Cook is making a healing broth of my own recipe. Kelp, bitter greens, and fish stock. It feeds the blood and wakes the brain."

Violet sent a silent plea Arthur's way, widening her eyes and shaking her head in the negative. Mrs. Sweet had a preternatural talent for diagnosis, but her cures often tasted of disappointment and unwashed stockings.

"I shall see to it Lady Greycliff eats plenty of that broth, Mrs. Sweet. However, she is overset now." Arthur gave Violet a nudge. She nodded slyly, then fanned her face, trying to appear distressed.

It didn't take too much effort. How mortifying to be seen swooning. Arthur must think her a proper ninny.

"I'll have her rest in my office." He led Violet to a narrow corridor at the opposite end of the kitchen from Mrs. Sweet's rooms.

The butler's office was a large, well-appointed space. The walls were the color of weak tea, and someone had hung a cheap print of Glencoe above the fireplace. A sturdy desk sat pushed against one wall, and two overstuffed armchairs sagged in a corner.

Violet refused Arthur's offer of a seat, and he knelt to pile coals in the fireplace.

"Grey didn't tell me you were thinking of marrying. My felicitations," he said without inflection.

"I am not getting married," Violet insisted. "Grantham did not come home to court me."

"No?" he asked, sounding indifferent. "He spoke as though marriage had been discussed."

Her toe made a tiny arc across the uneven wooden floorboards. "I've known him since childhood. It would be . . . easy," she confessed. "I can help him adjust to the responsibilities of the earldom. He's popular and could build the reputation of Athena's Retreat." She paused. "I should like to have a family."

Arthur said nothing while she tasted the flinty truth of that sentence. It sounded normal. Not at all pathetic that a thirty-year-old woman with a title and all her teeth hadn't already accomplished such a thing.

As though he was holding the conversation with them, Arthur addressed the pile of coals. "Makes sense. No bothering with courtship or romance or any such nonsense."

"Exactly," she said. "From a scientific view, there's no evidence that an emotional state defined as 'love' contributes to healthy children or a successful marriage."

Strange how something so rational could sound unappealing.

Grantham wouldn't care what she wore or if she managed to put on a dinner party. He wouldn't care much about anything she did so long as she managed the estate and looked after his mother.

A terrifying idea occurred to her.

"Are you . . ." Violet had to force the question from her lips. "Are *you* married?"

He stared as though she'd asked, "Are you American?" A combination of shock and disdain.

"I am not. Although . . ." His thick black brows drew together. "I am planning to buy a farm once I am finished here. I suppose I'll need a wife. Or a housekeeper. Since I'm in London, I could put an advert in the papers," he said, speaking about the prospect of finding a helpmate in the same manner one considered finding livestock or furniture.

"Of course you'll need a wife," she said. "How else are you to have children?"

"Children?" he said. "Never."

Was that fear in his voice?

"Do you not enjoy children?" she asked.

He stabbed at the coals with his poker. "Don't come across enough to like or not like them. Moving to the countryside. Remote. Not many doctors outside of cities and towns. Anything could happen."

His words were weighted like stones. Gathering clouds suffocated the faint light in the rooms, and Violet had difficulty reading the lines of his face. She debated whether to ask who he'd lost. Upon reflection, she kept the question to herself. Walls were designed to hold things up as well as to keep things from spilling out. Like her own, his barriers were well constructed.

When a footman rapped at Arthur's door, Violet almost jumped out of her shoes, and the moment was lost. Goodness, she'd done more than her share of jumping today.

"We talked to the staff next door," the footman said. "No one saw a thing."

"Thank you." Arthur waited until the door shut to return to his fire-making duties.

Violet sighed. "I owe you an apology."

His head jerked up, and he stared at her. Although practiced at masking his expressions, he couldn't fully hide his reaction.

Was he surprised? Wary?

"Apology for what?" he asked. He fixed his attention back on the fire, his motions slow and deliberate as he waited for her explanation.

Moving closer to the fireplace, she examined a handful of small soapstone figures on the mantel. Something told her these next words would be significant.

"I told myself the explosion was an accident. After your warnings, it was ill-done of me to leave the windows open. I must also apologize for seeming to come undone. A lady never loses her composure." After all, fear was as unattractive as anger.

"It is frightening to be the victim of theft," he said.

"Nevertheless." Violet rubbed her hands together, chilled at the prospect of what might have happened had she been alone in her workroom when the thief entered.

"Cold?" he asked.

When she nodded, he stood and pulled a tattered quilt from the back of the chair opposite her.

"I won't let anything happen to you."

An hour ago, she would have believed him. Now everything had changed, and her home was no longer safe. The deep crimson circle at his temple, where the thief had kicked him, had darkened to blue. What if something happened to him? To the ladies?

"Violet?" he asked.

The use of her given name startled her. He snapped open the quilt and held her glance.

"I *will* keep you safe."

Even if she'd imagined the subtle inflection, she hadn't missed the way he'd paced the garden earlier, like a tiger denied its prey.

"I know you will," she assured him.

Grateful, she bent forward and let him settle the blanket across her shoulders. Leaning back again, Violet found herself encircled in his arms as he pulled the quilt around her.

A faded scar bisected the end of his left eyebrow. Her glance darted to his lips, then back to his eyes. Tiny lines of gold streaked through the irises of dark chocolate. She hadn't noticed them the first night, when he held her in his arms and told her she would be safe.

"You have to do as I say from now on," he said.

Hypnotized by the gilded highlights in his irises, she answered him without deliberation.

"I'll do anything you ask."

He didn't smile at her impulsive declaration. Instead, he pulled her closer, tightening his grasp, so the quilt trapped her arms at her side, leaving her at his mercy.

"Anything?" he asked.

Outside the circle cast by his attention, another world existed. The kitchen boy called out to one of the footmen as they clattered up the back stairway. Cook and the maids exchanged desultory gossip as they laid the table for the servants' supper. Outside Beacon House came the rumble of traffic, but traffic didn't shake the floor.

His scrutiny bound her closer than the soft quilt he'd wrapped her in. Her body trembled, tiny quakes from the tips of her toes to her parted lips.

She'd wanted him to kiss her earlier. Now, she *needed* him to kiss her. To hold her before this need shook her apart and into pieces.

With the lightest brush of satin against her skin, he touched his lips to hers, leaving a trail of fire like the tail of a shooting star.

Too short. Not enough. Close to perfect.

She'd let her eyelids flutter shut at the sensation. Now she opened them and met his stare with her own.

"I'm sorry, I didn't hear that," she said. "Could you repeat it?"

A puff of laughter answered her before his lips settled back onto her own in the gentlest of touches. Once, twice, grazing her in sweet reassurance.

Before he pulled away, she stood on her toes and pressed her mouth against his, her tongue darting out to tease his intransigent lips, tasting a suggestion of apricots. Dropping back to her heels, Violet was dizzy with hope and light-headed with fear.

Had she gone too far?

Tenderness fled his face, replaced with an avid hunger. Hot and greedy, his tongue swept her mouth, tangling with hers as he held her immobile beneath his kisses. Again and again, he imprinted his taste on her, and she opened herself to him.

He kissed her with urgency, as though she might flee his touch. Instead, she burrowed even closer to him, straining against the confines of the blanket. She nipped at his bottom lip, and he made a noise, low in his throat, that reverberated through to her core. She longed to drag him to the floor with her and let him cover her body. Instead, he pulled away.

They stared at each other in silence until the sound of popping coal jerked their gazes apart. Her lips were tender and throbbing, and wonder ran through her veins.

"Remember your promise," he rasped. "I will hold you to it."

Sweet mother-of-pearl, the man could kiss. Violet sniffed the heady scent of soap and linen and virile male.

"Yes, of course. Hold me to it. Hold me firmly to it," she said, her words awkward and thick. Lust had left her muddleheaded.

One corner of his mouth turned down, a wry nod to her inelegant assurance, but he gave no other sign that what had passed between them had had any effect.

How could that be? If he hadn't kept hold of the quilt, she'd be pooled in a spineless heap at his feet.

Arthur let the quilt edges fall at her sides and nonchalantly knelt before the fireplace to add more coal. As if she needed a fire after that display. More like an ice bath! Two seconds of kissing Arthur had aroused her more than anything she'd done in her entire marriage.

At that moment, Violet vowed to seize the day. Or rather, seize the man. She would prove Daniel wrong and find a way to make herself desirable.

No more imaginary lovers to keep her company at night.

She wanted the real thing.

MRS. SWEET WAS not to be denied. She interrupted the two of them, taking Violet's pulse and red cheeks as proof that the lady needing physicking.

Arthur stayed in the corner and watched as the staff hovered over Violet with affection and concern. A crew of outcasts and misfits. Not dissimilar from the women on the other side of the wall in Athena's Retreat.

Violet proved to be dangerously kind. She left herself vulnerable to betrayal with no apparent fear of consequences. Stupid or saintly? Whichever she was, this made his job more difficult.

Add to that his own unfathomable behavior. What on earth was he doing, kissing her? Had a twenty-year exile not been enough to cure him of any desire to become involved in the lives of his assignments?

Her fear had unraveled him. At that moment, he couldn't think of any other way to give her comfort.

Ignoring that he'd had the option of reassuring her with a pat on the shoulder, Arthur focused on the occupants of the kitchen. How had the thief known where she kept her papers? Experience had taught him over and over that no one could be trusted, no matter how kind or concerned they seemed.

"Will you catch them?"

Winthram leaned against the wall and echoed Arthur's pose, arms at his side, ready to draw a knife.

"It would be a sight easier if everyone here followed my directions," Arthur answered.

Winthram rolled his lower lip under as Cook poured Violet another cup of tea and Mrs. Sweet pressed one of her nasty biscuits on her.

"She's too trusting, my lady," the doorman said. "Won't set watch at the door between the public rooms and the back part where they do their work."

Arthur waited while the young man deliberated whether to continue. Eventually, Winthram faced him, concern tightening the corners of his eyes. "I'm not complaining. They don't want anyone spying on their comings and goings. One lady, Mrs. White, her husband twigged to what she did here. Jealous type. Beat her something fierce, then locked her up at home 'for her own good.' My Lady Greycliff was sick for days over it."

Nothing about this had appeared in Grey's dossiers. A deep and terrible rage ignited in Arthur's belly. By God, how he loathed men like White. Arthur had dismissed some of Violet's concerns for the club members as silly. He should have known better.

"Why didn't you tell me this before?" Arthur demanded. "I'll need his direction right away."

Winthram held a hand up. "Wasn't White. He died from apoplexy a few months later, and Lady Phoebe took Mrs. White away someplace north."

The implications of the story settled into Arthur's brain, and his estimation of Lady Phoebe rose.

Winthram nodded toward Violet with his chin. "We tried to tell him she weren't here the night he dragged her home, but her name was printed in the book they signed into. From then on, we weren't allowed to keep track of who goes in or out."

Violet finished her tea, and Mrs. Sweet hurried her off to her rooms. The rest of the servants cleared away the dishes, the soft murmurs of conversation weaving a blanket of normalcy.

"Where'd you say you were from?" inquired a high voice at Arthur's elbow.

Arthur glanced at the little maid, Alice, noting her ragged cuticles and the chewed end of one braid. The girl pushed her toe into the floor, hiding her hands behind her back when she caught the direction of his stare.

"Didn't," he said.

"Mrs. Sweet said you were from the Highlands. I am, too, from near Dingwall. Do you know it?" Wide grey eyes stared at him with avid curiosity.

A girl from a big family might be tempted to send more than her paltry wages home. Wouldn't take much to bribe a maid to delay warning of a thief in her lady's rooms. Could be nerves, or could be guilt that pinched her thin, pale face.

"No."

The girl might well be innocent, but he wasn't here to make idle chatter with the staff. How *did* one make idle chatter? He'd a fair idea it involved discussing weather. What was there to discuss about weather? Hot, cold, wet, and dry.

"We're talking serious business here, Alice," Winthram chided. "Go dust."

Alice scrunched her nose in distaste. "Hate dusting. Worse than calculus."

She didn't argue, however, and took herself off. Winthram clucked his tongue against his teeth. "Complains about everything, that child."

Arthur made a noncommittal noise, hiding his amusement that a man of eighteen or so would consider a girl a few years younger to be a child.

"What I said before," Winthram said, "that none of us will help you . . ." He frowned. "I changed my mind. We have to protect her."

"Lady Greycliff?" Arthur clarified.

"All of them. We have to protect all of them, because no one else will."

8

"Yᴇᴛ ᴀɴᴏᴛʜᴇʀ ᴍᴀɴ pretending to be someone he's not," Mrs. Sweet complained. "When will this end, Mr. Kneland?"

Arthur stifled a sigh as he argued with the housekeeper two days after the thwarted burglary. He'd never worked a job where folks had so many questions. In other households, he'd growled an order or two and the servants jumped to obey.

Not here.

Someone at Beacon House was keeping secrets. How else had the thief known when Violet had left her workroom and it was safe to steal the papers? If Winthram was to be believed—and Arthur still had his doubts—only club members had been in the Retreat the night of the explosion. Which of them might have set it off?

"Thomas is trained in domestic operations, Mrs. Sweet. You have a head footman and added security for Lady Greycliff, all in one. If you let him schedule the day staff here and at the club, it is one less chore for you. This is temporary."

Thomas had already been an agent for five years when Arthur joined the prime minister's covert group. The older man took young

Arthur under his wing at first, imbuing his lessons with steady logic and dry humor. Thomas's relaxed demeanor and infectious laugh had ingratiated him into households where the group needed an inside man. He and Arthur had worked together sporadically in the years since Arthur left England, Thomas preferring his overseas assignments in warmer climes. Lucky for Arthur, Grey had managed to poach Thomas from another mission and reassign him to Beacon House.

Mrs. Sweet, however, proved impervious to both Thomas's charms and Arthur's assurances. "I don't need a head footman. I need two more parlor maids. I am run off my feet with work for this evening event. How are we to feed these extra mouths?"

Thomas tried to mollify her. "The boys and I are happy to eat at a chophouse, ma'am."

"A chophouse?" Mrs. Sweet set her hands on her hips. "Those kitchens are filthy. You won't get your proper fill of greens, either."

Before Thomas could make the mortal mistake of suggesting they could do with fewer greens and more beefsteak, an interruption occurred in the form of a sturdily built older woman balancing a fearsome tower of hennaed hair.

Marching into the kitchen, Lady Potts called for the servants' attention.

"The connecting doors between Beacon House and the club were left open," the woman complained. "And in the hubbub of this Evening of Epochs and Edification business, I forgot to latch shut the doors on a few of my cages. A handful of my friends have decided to peek in on you all. But it—"

The oath that escaped Mrs. Sweet's lips in response made Arthur's ears turn pink. Cook uttered an exclamation slightly less salty than Mrs. Sweet's and grabbed a broom, poking the bristles into every corner, as the footmen who had been lounging at the table went racing up the servants' staircase and Alice clambered on a wobbly stool, skirts pulled above her ankles.

Undeterred by the pandemonium, the lady raised her voice over the *thud* of the kitchen boy fainting dead away. " 'Tis feeding time, and we must gather them up. Be careful not to step on them. Tarantulas are delicate little creatures."

Thomas's ebony skin lightened to a sickly grey, and he shot Arthur a dark look.

Damn.

While Lady Potts commandeered the staff to retrieve her five or six—possibly seven—runaway experiments, Arthur decided that now was an excellent opportunity to check the security on another floor.

He most definitely was *not* taking advantage of the confusion to escape Thomas's ire.

Unfortunately, Thomas had expert tracking skills, and he followed hard on Arthur's heels, cornering him at the far end of the second-floor corridor.

"You said this was a simple job, Kneland," Thomas complained, peering along the baseboards. "Said I could do it with both hands tied behind m' back. Don't seem simple from here."

"Take it up with Grey," Arthur replied. "He told me I'd be looking after an absentminded little widow. Easiest job in the world, he said. Anyway, what's there to complain about? Grey's paying three times what we'd get for a job. And there are greens, don't forget."

"For the love of all that is holy! There are three of them in here!" shouted a footman from the front parlor at the other end of the hall. A colossal crash followed in the distance, and a maid screamed.

Thomas stared at Arthur and raised one bushy white eyebrow.

Arthur stared back.

Thomas tapped a toe.

Arthur surrendered, issuing a wan smile. "I forgot you didn't care for spiders."

"Really? You forgot Cairo?"

Forgetting Cairo would be ideal, but some things could not be unseen. Still, one must carry on.

Thomas pinned him with a disbelieving stare. "What about the baboon spiders on that job in Malindi? Now, you and Grey have dragged me to the one house in England where tarantulas are running loose."

"Sorry," Arthur said.

Thomas blinked, then narrowed his gaze. "Sorry, eh? What are you doing here, Kneland? Thought you were headed straight for the Highlands. Why didn't you tell Grey to find someone else?"

The dregs of a dream curdled in Arthur's stomach. The landlord who owned Arthur's childhood home had enclosed the land. Like most small landholdings in rural Scotland, it had been consolidated into one vast private property. The farmhouse was gone, and sheep grazed where he once played. A lengthy search for someplace else to rest his head awaited him once he finished here.

"Takes time and money to find a farm up north these days. Grey promised me the funds," Arthur explained. "Haven't you considered getting out of the game?"

"Aye, but you won't find me withering away in the countryside. I'm thinking of leaving the service and going to work for the Company out in Jalalabad." Genuine pleasure lit Thomas's face. Baboon spiders aside, he grew restless living in one place for too long.

At that moment, a cry for help came from the library, and Arthur sighed. He ought to apologize to Mrs. Pettigrew for his initial disbelief. Spiders as big as a fist, indeed.

"I'll take care of that. You take Winthram off for a pint until it's safe to come back. I don't trust him. It's too much of a coincidence that his brother is with the Omnis."

"He seems to like you well enough," Thomas said. "Follows you around and listens to your every word."

"I hadn't noticed," Arthur lied.

"He reminds me of a green boy I met, oh, twenty years ago." Thomas winked. "Took a while, but the boy grew into a good man."

Arthur grunted. "Save your twinkling eyes and pretty stories for Mrs. Sweet." He turned and walked down the hall, shoulders hunched, as another crash came from upstairs.

"No one said anything about spiders," Thomas called after him. "If I'd known about the spiders . . ."

Arthur waved his hand in acknowledgment before entering the library.

It took a moment for his vision to adjust to the dimness. He knew Violet was in here by her scent alone. A combination of dried flowers and wet slate had haunted him into the wee hours after their kiss.

There had been no logical explanation for that kiss, and the urge to pull her close and set his mark on her—as though a kiss could be a token of protection.

What a foolish notion. A kiss couldn't stop a bullet or lower a fever.

He might have been lust-addled enough to do more than kiss her if her heavy-lidded eyes hadn't peered at him with an unrecognizable emotion.

Unrecognizable it would remain.

An intense physical attraction could be understood and indulged. Once. Anything more meant crossing a line that involved feelings. Feelings led to complications.

Complicating a mission meant increasing the odds of a mission's failure.

"Oh, Arthur," Violet called. "I'm glad to see you."

From a precarious perch on a wall of shelves so high her cap brushed the ceiling, Violet stood, legs akimbo, one foot on a ladder, the other on a shelf. "I tried to reach a particular volume when the ladder slipped out from under me. It's stuck now on the carpet, and I can't get down."

This will be the easiest assignment you've ever taken. You won't even know you're working.

"What is the commotion out there?" Violet asked as he moved toward her.

"You shouldn't be alone in here," Arthur said. "Where is the footman I assigned to you?"

"I'm capable of picking a book off the shelf by myself." Violet waved her hand to brush away his concern, with a disconcerting wobble. "I—Oh! Get it off, get it off!" she shrieked, twisting and turning like a leaf in the wind.

Instinct took over. Arthur flung his arms out in time to catch her fall. A small, hairy body went flying overhead, bounced twice off the floorboards, and skittered out the door.

"My, you are efficient," Violet said with good cheer, remarkably unaffected by her near-fatal tumble. "How did I manage to survive before you came?"

Arthur's heart raced at the close call, a spike of anger overtaking his relief. "Do you understand how close you came to breaking your neck? What were you thinking, climbing so high without securing the ladder?"

Violet blinked at his tone. He set her on her feet, ashamed of his anger.

"I didn't mean to frighten you," she whispered.

"Frighten *me*?" That hadn't been fear racing in his veins. Had it? Arthur willed his heart to slow. "I am not frightened. I simply wish to do my job without distraction. Instead, you forget to eat, you leave your windows open, and today you are falling off shelves . . ."

Arthur faltered when her head dropped as if she were contemplating the carpet beneath her slippers. Truth be told, he *had* been terrified when she fell. What if he couldn't have been there in time?

What would happen if he failed her?

He cleared his throat and gentled his voice in apology. "At least refrain from tossing yourself off bookshelves before mealtime. If I must save your life every five minutes, I'm happier doing it on a full stomach."

When she smiled, a tiny dent appeared below her pillowy lower lip. "Do you forgive me?" she asked.

He'd never considered a dimple to be erotic. On her face, though, it turned into a marker of where to place the tip of his tongue.

Her bosom rose and fell from the excitement, and a deep crimson flush rode high on her rounded cheeks.

"There is nothing to forgive." He examined her red face. "Are you feeling well?"

Clearing her throat, she patted her cheeks. "All this excitement is going to my head," she said.

"A headache can presage a fever," he warned her.

"No, I meant literally. You see, my heart beat faster, which in turn pumped my blood through the circulatory system at an increased rate, leading to the color in my face." Her awkwardness disappeared, words spilling forth in her excitement. "William Harvey was the first scientist to study the physiology of blood circulation. There's much we don't understand. I've heard . . ."

Something happened when Violet explained a scientific theory.

She glowed.

Her stained, work-worn hands flew up with a sudden grace, illustrating a point as if pulling the knowledge from the air. What a beautiful sight, watching her revel in imparting secrets of how the world worked.

". . . and such reactions are intensified as the stimulation increases. Am I speaking too fast?" Violet asked. "I don't want to leave you behind."

There wasn't a trace of irony in her words.

I don't want to leave you behind.

My God, this woman made him feel seen in a way he hadn't been since childhood. A man used to living in the shadows, an afterthought until called forth by violence—her attention unmoored him.

"You haven't left me behind." The stark truth fell out of him. "I am right here with you."

Violet beamed.

As it had before, restless energy crackled between them, charged with their unspoken attraction. Violet's lush mouth parted, and her tongue darted out to moisten her plump lower lip. Evidence of her circulation theory fluttered in the hollow of her throat as her pulse sped under his regard.

"I wish . . ." She broke off. "I mean to say . . ." All the confidence she'd radiated moments before vanished. Her movements slowed, and she held her left hand close to her side—little finger angled away from the center of her body. Poised to protect herself from injury.

A surge of protectiveness filled Arthur's chest when it struck him: This beautiful, vibrant woman had no faith in her own desirability, no idea of her allure. That foolish talk of how anger and passion made her unattractive had found its way into her head.

Kissing might be what she needed.

What if he . . . ?

Before Arthur could finish his thought, Earl Grantham barged into the library.

"There you are. Footmen are running around like lunatics, and you two are alone together in a dark room staring at each other like gudgeons. Again. Shouldn't you be over at the club, Vi, setting out chairs or blowing something up?"

Arthur hastened to the other side of the room, grateful for the interruption.

Yes, that was gratitude racing in his veins. Not an urge to throw Grantham out the window.

Oblivious to the tension, Grantham wandered over to a settee and took a seat. "You might consider apologizing for leaving me alone with Phoebe the other day. That woman is—"

"One of the sharpest minds I know," finished Violet.

"I was going to say *mean*," Grantham complained. "Phoebe Hunt is mean."

"She's wounded," Violet said. "You understand how those in pain can lash out."

Grantham's ears pinked. "I'm not the one who caused the pain. I offered to protect her, if you'll recall. If she'd married me, her father would have had no power over her."

Violet moved to the window, checking the fit of her cap in her reflection. "Phoebe fights her own battles, and a marriage shouldn't be a rescue attempt."

Grantham cleared his throat and changed the subject. "You've put off two parties this week already. You called me back to London for a reason."

He threw a packet of envelopes on the low table before him. "If you want the event to be well attended, you must make calls, drop into a musicale or two, and . . ." He broke off his grumpy tirade and essayed a chuckle when Violet scowled. "Do not make that face. A lady's reputation is everything. Come now, it will be like old times, the two of us plotting together. After all, for the club to be a success, *you* must succeed as well. Isn't that right, Kneland?"

VIOLET KEPT QUIET while Arthur and Grantham discussed the question of her security at several social events. What was she supposed to say? *Get out, Grantham. I am intent on seducing this man*? She had been on the brink of extending an invitation to Arthur to join her later tonight in her bedchamber.

She was 100 percent certain she would have gone through with it. Well . . . 73 percent certain. Now the momentum was lost. It would take ages for her to gather her courage again.

Arthur had turned her upside down and inside out with his kisses. There were times when Violet had convinced herself that Daniel was wrong, that her need for physical affection was not unnatural. Other times, she had understood his concern. What else but depravity would set her entire *body* to vibrating from the excitement of those kisses?

Violet mulled a variety of scenarios in which she found a way to lure Arthur into lying with her. Or standing with her. She'd even seen a naughty etching once where both partners were . . .

"I will take over whatever intelligence work needs to be done, Kneland." Grantham's voice intruded on her daydream. "Set yourself between Violet and any flying objects, like you did with Dickerson. How hard can it be?"

Shamed by his offhand manner, Violet admonished him. "Grantham, stop. You are rude."

"There is enough security for Lady Greycliff that I might follow up on new information," Arthur said. "I must have as much information as possible so I can predict any dangers."

"Grey didn't hire you to lead an investigation," Grantham argued. "What's needed is brawn, not brains. He hired you to take a bullet."

"Don't say that," Violet gasped.

"I've taken a few in my day." Arthur took no obvious offense, his face impassive as he began a recitation. "I've taken bullets, fallen off a building, and been set on fire. I've even ingested different poisons and built immunity so I could taste one man's food. That was nasty. Involved mushrooms. Even worse, I had to eat American food for a year. Lucky I didn't lose my sense of taste after that."

The contrast between the violent images and Arthur's nonchalance took Violet aback. What must his life had been like to speak of such things as though they were commonplace? No wonder he held himself removed from everyone else. Those rare smiles of his took on even greater value.

"That is horrible," she said. "I had no idea the government would subject a man to such tortures. I assure you I would never ask such for such a sacrifice."

"You aren't the one who hired me. Grey did," Arthur reminded her. "He expects his money's worth." One finger held back her protestations, and he shot an enigmatic glance at Grantham. "I've learned seven languages, eaten meals prepared by Carême, and lived in twenty different capitals on four continents. My work does, on occasion, call for more than standing between a bullet and its target."

"My word." Violet shook her head in amazement. "What a remarkable life you've led. You must be exhausted after your adventures."

Grantham harrumphed. "I've been shot at as well, if you'll remember." He crossed his arms. "And stabbed. Have *you* been stabbed?"

"Stabbed?" Arthur bent his head in recollection. "Three . . . no, four times."

"Drowned?" Grantham snapped.

Arthur nodded. "Twice I've been on guard aboard a ship attacked by pirates. One time, they managed to get me overboard. I caught the ship at the next port and rescued the man."

"Hanged?" Grantham persisted.

Arthur shook his head while he scrunched his nose. "Can't say anyone tried to hang me."

"Stran—"

Violet smacked Grantham's arm in dismay. "That is enough, Georgie." She shook her head. "Men. Must you turn everything into a contest?"

"Hmm." Grantham tossed his head, sulking at either the interruption of his macabre inquisition or the fact she'd used his childhood nickname. Or both.

"Ingested poison on purpose, eh?" Grantham said. "Doesn't sound clever. Probably rendered you infertile."

Arthur shrugged. "Don't plan on having a family, so it isn't a concern."

Like the snick of a lock, his expression closed. Once again, Violet wondered what, or who, was the reason for Arthur's distance.

Before she could think about it further, Grantham spoke again. "Point is that Kneland is here to do one thing, and one thing only."

Arthur turned to Violet and pinned her with his stare. "However I choose to do it, my job is to keep you alive. Until you finish your work, I will not stray from your side."

"Neither shall I, my dear." Grantham smoothed back a lock of buttery-blond hair and crossed his booted feet. "Fetch out your prettiest gown. I'm looking forward to having the most beautiful woman in London on my arm tomorrow night."

9

I DON'T REMEMBER HER being such a dowd. Mind you, that extra stone she's put on, and her ghastly complexion from hanging about her *club* doesn't help. I worry for her health."

Violet paused in the act of tasting a biscuit from the refreshment table, her skin pebbling in discomfort at the overheard comment coming from behind a large column. The unknown woman's emphasis on the word *club* had made it sound illicit or nasty. Could the woman be speaking about her?

Extra stone?

Such a dowd?

Violet glanced at her ball gown. She'd finished with mourning, but she hadn't bothered to order any new dresses since Daniel had died. Not considering how much fashion had changed, she'd had her old gowns let out. Within moments of arriving at the ball, she'd understood how outmoded and ill-fitting the gown she wore tonight was.

She set down her biscuit. Grantham, with input from Phoebe, had decided the Thornton-Hammersmith ball was well suited to Violet's need to appear at an event and to reassure everyone of the club's respectability while trying to recruit new members. She'd arrived an hour ago and was waiting for Grantham to make his appearance before she'd attempt to socialize. Happily, Violet recognized some familiar friendly faces from before she went into mourning.

There were others, however . . .

Peering around the column, she spied a thin blond woman with a regal nose and stern-looking eyebrows. Mrs. Fanny Armitage.

"Such goings-on," another woman lamented.

When Violet leaned over more, the second lady came into view. Aha. Lady Olivia. She and Fanny had come out a few years before her.

"A social club for ladies?" Lady Olivia continued. "What a ridiculous—why, even dangerous—notion. Those women would be better off tending their homes and children."

"I'm not surprised Lady Greycliff conceived of the idea, seeing as she never accomplished either of those things," Fanny opined. She'd aged since Violet had seen her last. A picket fence of wrinkles bisected her mouth, the result of pursing her lips so tight with unremitting disapproval.

Lady Olivia tittered, her dyed purple plumes hanging over one ear, her bulbous eyes perusing the dance floor, in search of someone else to judge. "She cannot be blamed for the latter, Fanny. Greycliff was three times her age when they wed."

Fanny disagreed. "Greycliff had a son. The fault must have been with her." As an afterthought, she added a sickly sweet lament: "Poor woman."

Violet wasn't surprised at Fanny's indulgence in such gossip. She was prone to picking over the most salacious of rumors under the guise of concern for the person in question.

"It may be for the best she never had children." Lady Olivia's words were sympathetic but laced with a thread of disdain. "Not everyone can create a model home in the way we can. Still, she might have appeared to try."

Whipping back out of sight, Violet leaned against the column for support, setting a hand to her churning stomach, eyes closed tight against the pain.

Violet had found Daniel's steady presence, quiet life, and reserved demeanor attractive. His assertiveness and practicality had captivated her after an upbringing surrounded by dreamers and thinkers. She had wanted so much to be worthy of his regard.

Hours were spent writing invitations to dinner parties, memorizing the names and habits of Daniel's guests, and overseeing the domestic staff instead of pursuing her work. When he'd left her bed, she'd gone through ridiculous lengths to lure him back, until his illness put an end to those dreams.

She'd outgrown that youthful optimism, bringing her energy to bear on creating a place where other women wouldn't suffer as she once did.

Violet had hoped the pain would fade over time.

Some hurt never healed.

"Hello, Lady Greycliff. What a pleasure to see you here."

Violet opened her eyes to behold Miss Althea Dertlinger. A tall, bespectacled young woman with an adventurous taste in turbans. She was a second cousin to Lady Potts and shared her kinswoman's love of science. Fortunately for the rest of their family, Althea confined her interest to nearly invisible animals, in the form of bacteria.

"My cousin and I enjoyed the lecture on care and cultivation of orchids at Athena's Retreat the other night," she said. "In fact, I have asked Mama"—here, Althea wiggled her fingers at an older woman standing near the orchestra—"and she has given permission for me to attend the upcoming Evening of Education."

"This is wonderful news, Miss Dertlinger," Violet replied, swallowing her hurt.

"Miss Dertlinger, you may wish to reconsider. Does your mama know what goes on at that place?"

Violet and Althea turned in unison to confront the sight of Fanny and Lady Olivia, staring down their noses at them with identical sneers.

Lady Olivia issued a thin sigh and fluttered her fan. "A day doesn't go by without the club and Lady Greycliff's name in the popular press, and lately there have been other rumors too salacious to mention. You are young and innocent," she said to Althea. "It might affect your reputation to be written up in such a manner."

"Indeed." Fanny's thin fingers clenched in glee at Althea's bewildered dismay, like a stringy old lioness regarding a nice, plump doe before supper. "Your mama has gone to great trouble and expense to bring you out, my dear. It will be for naught should you cultivate a reputation for eccentric behavior and radical views."

Althea's spectacles slipped while she twisted her reticule strings. "Mama is a high stickler," she mumbled.

Violet suppressed a burning urge to slap the feral expression from Fanny Armitage's face. How many times had Fanny sat across the table and gobbled Violet's discomfort and embarrassment as though ill feelings sustained her?

"Do be reasonable, Lady Greycliff. She's no beauty," said Lady Olivia, waving her fan in Althea's direction. "Throwing in with your club brings her chances down even further."

Before Violet could stop and consider, she shot her hand out to the side, grabbed the arm of a vaguely familiar young man, and pulled him to her side.

"What a delightful coincidence," Violet said to the youth. "How have you been keeping since we last saw each other?"

The sandy-haired young man stared at Violet in shock, but good manners prevailed. "Good evening. Delightful, indeed," he stammered.

God bless the youth of England, carrying on the tradition of politeness in the face of even the most absurd situations.

Violet pulled out her most brilliant smile as she tried to remember the boy's name. "I haven't seen your godmother in ages. How is she?"

"Oh." The man's brows drew together in consternation. "My godmother? She's . . . she's dead."

Fanny, Lady Olivia, and Althea's heads swiveled between Violet and the man, with identical expressions of confusion.

Drat.

"Of course, I was sorry to miss the funeral. And how is your aunt?" Violet willed the man to help her.

"Do you mean my father's sister, Mrs. Penelope Forthbright, or my mother's—"

"Yes, exactly," Violet cheered. "The Forthbrights. We're close, as I'm sure you remember. You are named for Penny's husband, are you not?"

"Ahem . . . You misremember," he stammered. "I'm named for my mother's brother, Robert Fish—"

"Robbie," Violet declared with relief, "you must know Lady Olivia and Mrs. Armitage if you've been in the vicinity of the punch bowl at any ball the past three seasons." She mimed the throwing back of a few drinks. "However, I'd wager you haven't met Miss Althea Dertlinger. Her cousin Lady Potts is excited to bring her out this season."

"Erm," Althea ventured, "this is my second—"

Violet stepped on her toe. "I am charged by her mama to protect her from the ne'er-do-wells who might be fortune hunting tonight. However, seeing as you come from such an excellent family, I will grant your request to partner her in the next dance."

At this point, Robbie's stricken face brightened with interest.

"I say," Robbie exclaimed. "Would your cousin be the same Lady Potts who authored a letter to the editor in the latest edition of the *Journal of Arthropods*?" he asked Althea.

"If you mean the letter decrying the current subclassification system of Opiliones, then yes," Althea replied.

Lady Olivia dropped her fan in surprise, and Violet held in a sigh of relief. The young people headed off toward the dance floor while Fanny transferred her scrutiny back to Violet.

"Accosting strange young men won't help your reputation."

"My reputation is sterling, Mrs. Armitage," Violet countered. "As someone who spends a prodigious amount of time keeping watch over everyone else's behavior, you are well aware of this."

Lady Olivia stepped forward and locked arms with her friend. "You may not have been discovered in a scandal, but this club of yours pushes the boundaries. You admit women like Lady Phoebe—and we all know the type of crowd she runs with. And there are rumors that some members of your staff have unsavory pasts."

Violet didn't give a fig about the scurrilous gossip Lady Olivia chose to spread. Her staff were under her protection, and she'd defend them tooth and nail.

She swallowed a nasty retort and pulled her lips into what she hoped wasn't a grimace. "If you are so interested in what happens at the club," Violet said, "you are welcome to attend our Evening of Enlightenment and . . . And there will be lemonade and a presentation by a well-respected authority from the British Museum. You will find our members to be congenial and amenable. Unlike some."

"And will you be serving langoustines?" Fanny's gaze widened in mock curiosity.

A tremor of red-hot rage shook Violet from toe to head. Streams of unforgettable and unforgivable curses pushed against her clenched lips. As she opened her mouth to deliver them, a low voice prevented her from such folly.

"My lady. Please forgive my tardiness. If you would consider honoring my request for this dance."

He did not wait for an answer. Before Fanny's eyebrows could hit her forehead in surprise, Arthur had swept Violet onto the dance floor and into a waltz.

"I didn't require rescuing," she told him.

A twitch of his lips down and to the side was his eloquent response.

At her scowl, he pulled her closer and took a soft, round turn, spinning them away from the nasty prying leers of Fanny Armitage and her petty friends.

His hand, warm and firm against the small of her back, soothed her. She relaxed into his arms as the crowd swirled around them. He'd accompanied her to the ball, then melted away the instant she set foot in the oversized entrance hall, blending in with the crowd without a word of goodbye.

Why should he have said anything? He was there to guard her, not dance with her.

Or so she'd thought.

"You look quite handsome," she told Arthur. Indeed, the deep burgundy of his cravat made a dramatic contrast with the brilliant white of his shirt collar and the brassy gold of his waistcoat. Unlike most of the men here tonight, he did not need any padding to fill out the broad shoulders of his evening jacket.

The golden threads in his deep brown eyes flickered in the buttery candlelight. He dipped his head and cleared his throat. "You look fine tonight as well," he told her.

Liar.

Across the dance floor, hundreds of tiny sparks from glittering gemstones winked in and out as the couples made their turns. Purple, pink, white, and blue blossoms of watered silk unfurled to the pure crystal notes of a composition by a talented Polish composer, Chopin. Beneath a ballroom chandelier, everything appeared richer—colors deepened, and even the cheapest of jewels could be blinding.

Violet had forgotten how sensual it could be to dance the waltz. Silk glided against her skin, and she relished the freedom of letting a partner push her through space. The press of his palm sent tingles down her spine and the backs of her legs.

As she swayed in Arthur's arms, the aftereffects of her confrontation with Lady Olivia and Fanny muted her pleasure.

"You are trembling," he said, lips close to her ear.

"I suppose I am cold," she lied.

"Aha. I thought you were angered by what the ladies said."

"Angry?" Her forced laugh grated against the backdrop of the orchestra. "You misread my expression."

She fixed her attention on the cheap brass pin holding together his cravat.

A jarring note of reality amid the finery he wore tonight, it reminded Violet that Arthur had no one who took care of him and might have gifted him with something nicer. No doubt, he'd purchased the pin out of expediency, thinking only of its function.

Never in a million years would it be appropriate for her to buy him a cravat pin. Some other woman would take care of this man when the job was finished. A different set of hands would brush the shoulders of his jacket and push back an errant lock of hair.

Tonight, though, Violet was his partner, if only for a minute or two. As the music hit a crescendo, she leaned into his arms and relished her stolen time.

ARTHUR HAD BEEN on a ramble once with his wee sister, Deoiridh, when they'd spied a grouse caught in a snare. Deoiridh had cried out in dismay and pointed to the trapped bird. Too young for words, she'd flapped her arms in distress, mimicking the animal. Wild thing calling to wild thing. Unable to deny her, Arthur had clipped the snare. He and Deoiridh had then watched the bird claim its freedom in silent joy.

The same distress lived in Violet's gaze when she'd stood at the side of the dance floor, crowded by two sharp-featured women. An urge to rip open the ballroom doors for her had propelled him out of the shadows. The crowd wasn't the snare she struggled to free herself from, however. Instead, the words of a dead man kept her from flight.

He'd been punished for clipping the snare; the grouse was to be someone's dinner, after all. The relief on Deoiridh's face had been worth the punishment.

There would be similar consequences for what he did here tonight. No good reason existed for him to sweep Violet onto the dance floor. How to explain the urgency firing in his veins when he saw her struggle to protect herself? They were words, not slaps.

Groping for the answer, he beheld the woman in his arms. Despite, or perhaps because of, her drab dress, she held an undeniable allure amid the garish gowns and sparkling jewels. Her low bun had come partly undone. Ringlets had escaped the confines of her pins to brush the gentle dip of her shoulders. He strained to see his reflection in her irises, which lightened from chocolate brown to the color of tea.

"Ah yes, a lady never gets angry," he said.

"That's right," Violet said.

They spun once more, into a sharp turn, and he splayed his fingers, holding her closer than necessary.

"I suppose they don't get furious, either?" he asked.

Her nose scrunched. "Furious? Never." Two lines between her eyebrows smoothed away. Arthur took note.

"Livid?" he asked.

"Out of the question," she countered.

"Wrathful."

An upside-down curl appeared at the corner of her mouth.

"That sounds almost biblical. I'm afraid certain excesses in the Old Testament are considered unseemly, so the answer is no."

This piqued Arthur's interest. What might be unseemly in the Old Testament? He left his curiosity unsated and returned to the matter at hand.

"Corybantic?"

"Cory . . . ?" The simple tilt of her head caused his chest to constrict. Her smile had a powerful effect on that circulatory system she talked about so often.

Shaking her head in disbelief, Violet answered. "That one I wasn't expecting. Corybantic. Well played."

A ridiculous gush of pride filled him. "Means 'frenzied,'" he explained.

"So it does," she said. They beamed at each other.

The last few notes of the waltz plucked at Arthur's conscience. "Shall I escort you to the refreshment table, my lady?"

"Oh, no, please. Just . . . take me home."

The sadness in her voice had him hustling her out of the ballroom as though they were being followed by armed marauders. Within moments, he had plucked their groom from a huddle of gossiping servants and had Violet ensconced in the carriage, pulling out from the long lines.

She sat across from him, staring out the window as they moved forward in small fits and jerks, the roads crowded with strident London traffic. Ten minutes went by in silence, the longest he'd been in her presence without her speaking. A curious discomfort pulled at his chest at how forlorn she appeared.

Not that her distress was any of his concern. Worrying would divert his attention. Fiddling with the carriage locks, he let another five minutes pass before he could no longer stand it.

Clearing his throat, he stepped over the border between a bodyguard and something more.

10

SHALL I DIRECT the coachman to take you to another venue? Lady Phoebe did mention she would be appearing at a nearby rout this evening."

Distracted from her brooding, Violet shook her head.

"If I tell Phoebe what happened, I fear for Fanny's safety. Not that I like the woman, but sometimes Phoebe does go too far." She sighed. "I shall never speak to Grantham again for leaving me to those biddies—and leaving it to you to rescue me."

When he would speak, she held up a hand. "I know it's your job. You remind me of that daily. I hope Grey's paying you a pretty penny for the trouble I put you through."

Arthur shifted in his seat. "He doesn't . . . I didn't dance with you out of obligation."

"Well." A trickle of color stained her cheeks. "That's nice to hear." She sighed and glanced at her skirts. "I am a crow in a field of poppies. I suppose I must purchase new gowns for these dratted parties."

"You would do this again?" he asked. "Go back and subject yourself to the pecking of those hens? Why?"

"What should I do? Stay home? I am the public face of Athena's Retreat. According to Letty, it inspires respectability and trust for me to go out and speak with the ton about what we do."

Arthur frowned. Why hadn't Grantham come and helped her tonight? What else was the man good for? "You could send the earl in your stead. Or Lady Phoebe."

"Lady Phoebe? I think not."

The red velvet curtains billowed in along with a gust of freezing wind. Violet turned her face to the cold. "For years, I buried myself away, hoping time would dull my rough edges or my brain might wrangle hold of my tongue, or a female chemist would cease to become anathema. None of these things happened. Life is marching on." Her voice wobbled with uncertainty. "If I go out enough, they will become used to me—eccentric Violet Hughes, with her grubby hands and ugly dresses. Someday, I might even win them over."

Arthur had spent a lifetime reading the unspoken cues of men and women around the globe, and he knew Violet told the truth. Despite her age and accomplishments, she lacked the skills of subterfuge and dissembling that her peers possessed, blithely unaware that many women of his acquaintance would have paused here, waiting for him to object to her blunt description.

He did want to object. She didn't have ugly hands; she was beautiful and kind. More important, she was genuine. The only time she tripped and stumbled was when she tried to be anyone other than Violet.

"It wasn't till Fanny mentioned the langoustines . . ." She pulled her shawl tight against her shoulders. "I supposed you've heard the story."

Arthur shook his head.

"Daniel told me they were Lord Insley's favorite dish, and I ordered them prepared tableside in an elaborate display. To keep them fresh until right before they were flambéed I dipped them in an anesthetic solution of my own devising."

She sighed. "I miscalculated the strength of the solution. During the first course, they woke up. As you can imagine, they didn't sit around on the platter waiting to be set afire. They wandered away. The first we noticed was when one made its way up Lady Whitsley's leg."

Dipping her chin, she appeared to brace herself for Arthur's ridicule. He kept his face impassive instead, picturing how she must have reacted, her expression crumpled in dismay as she faced her husband's disapproval.

"It was cruel of her to remind you," he said.

"I am resigned to how they mock me, yet I cannot stand it when women like Fanny pick on others who cannot defend themselves. They make life onerous for a girl like Althea. Scaring her away from Athena's Retreat, the one place in the world that can protect and shelter a girl like her, makes me so . . ."

She sucked her lips inward to keep the word from escaping.

He waited for the eruption, leaning forward as if to catch her words.

"So . . ." Violet balled her hands into fists. "So *angry*." She burst into tears.

Tears.

Arthur stared, frozen in horror.

"I am furious." She shuddered with emotion. "Livid. Incensed."

Scrabbling through his pockets for a handkerchief, Arthur tried to fathom how it had come to this.

My God, he'd made her cry.

"If you are angry, why are you crying?" he asked, aghast at the sobs that racked her body.

"I don't know," she wailed. "I—I broke something. I never cry. Never."

Arthur located the square of cambric and shifted across the carriage to her side, pressing the handkerchief into her limp fingers.

"Is this what it feels like to let go of anger?" she said. "I don't like it at all. Help me put it back, please."

"*Na bith a' gul.*" He patted her hand. "*Na bith a' gul.*"

As the carriage swayed, he pulled her bonnet off and settled one arm around her shoulder. Violet buried her face in his coat, and they rocked back and forth until the tears came to a stop. He'd never been so relieved as when she pulled away and dried her face.

"*Na bith a' gul,*" she repeated. "Did your mama whisper that?"

"It's what I would say to my wee sister when she was upset," Arthur replied.

Reddened eyes peered up at him, and Violet sniffed. "You must be a wonderful older brother. I always wished for an older brother myself."

Odd how grief could cut you open even after years. Had he been a wonderful brother? God, he hoped so.

Violet set his handkerchief down and pulled her gloves off. Taking his hand, she laced her fingers through his.

"Is she the person you lost?" she whispered.

How could she know? Had someone told her?

He opened his mouth to tell her he'd lost nothing. His history was of no importance to anyone.

"Her name was Deoiridh."

A rusty lock broke open, and the terrible sweetness of memory flooded his chest. Deoiridh loved plum tarts, and her plaits were forever unraveling. Her fingers were plump, like bannocks, and she had terrified his eight-year-old self whenever she threw herself into or onto or off immovable objects.

"What happened?" she asked.

"Influenza." One word. One word for devastation from which he'd never recovered. Bright red cheeks one afternoon, which wouldn't go away after teatime. A fever that couldn't be checked. Then racking coughs ending with a terrible stillness.

"Was it a long time ago?"

Lifetimes. Dozens of years and millions of miles ago.

"I was eight, and she was three. My parents died as well." His father gave up the day after Deoiridh passed, turning his face to the wall while great, heaving coughs shuddered through his body. Mam tried her best to hold on, but the fever's grip was unbreakable.

"An enemy you couldn't guard against," Violet said.

Arthur took her chin in his fingers. "Death can slip past any guard." He willed her to understand before they went too far. Before he forgot this most important of lessons, despite the pull of the sweetness and comfort she offered.

Turning her head, she studied his face. "You're guarding me. I've never been so safe and cared for."

He bent his head to hers. "You're not safe." His lips traced the words on her skin. "None of us are. This is an assignment, and you can't matter to me."

THERE WAS NO sweetness to what happened next. No tentative exploration. He shook his head in denial, but his closed lips dragged against hers until they could no longer hold back. Flames came to life at his touch. Desire charged the air between them, crackling in the wake of her thighs brushing against him.

Raw and carnal, his kisses melted her bones. They came together, again and again, teeth bumping, tongues tangled. Tiny sparks raced beneath her skin as his fingers tightened in her hair. She bit and sucked at his mouth as though devouring him. He tasted of spice and fire.

The heat of his body burned through the layers of cotton and canvas that stood between them. Wool brushed beneath her fingertips until she found the slick silk of his cravat. She fumbled at the knot, unwilling to stop kissing long enough to see what she was doing.

The rough thrust of his tongue contrasted with the gentle sweep of his thumb against her cheek. Enormous strength lay in the hands cradling her face. His control excited her almost as much as his passion. His kiss was so deep it was as if she were falling into him, falling like a woman drugged, over and over until she lost sense of time.

He broke the kiss to put his mouth at the side of her neck, and she swallowed a gasp at the throb of pleasure between her thighs when his teeth grazed the skin.

Violet raised her arms to grasp his shoulders, but she came to her senses and put them back at her sides. It wouldn't do to act eager.

He turned, laying her against the cushioned carriage seat, then followed her down, his narrow hips cradled between her thighs, one foot on the floor to brace them as the carriage swayed back and forth. A dark velvet growl came from deep in his chest when she suckled his tongue, and he thrust against her, delivering a glorious pressure where she ached.

Pulling off a glove with his teeth, he ran his thumb beneath the edge of her corset, releasing her breast from its confines.

Violet longed to reach her fingers through his hair, and her hands fluttered up and then back down again. When he paused, she flinched. Had she made a noise?

Putting her fears to rest, he set his mouth to her breast and traced the outline of her nipple with his tongue. The lick of damp heat sent shivers through her. She took a risk, fumbling her gloves off and sinking her fingers into his thick curls.

Was she moving too much beneath him? She should stop.

She *couldn't* stop.

When he freed her from the entire top of her dress and suckled her nipple, an exclamation of delight left her throat. Her cry sounded so desperate and wanton the sound pulled her back from pleasure and slammed her into reality.

"Sorry. I'm sorry," she whispered, letting go of Arthur's hair before he complained.

Her wet skin pebbled in the chill air when he let go. Too late. Tears of shame sprang to her eyes.

"You are like a mad hummingbird with your hands never settling," he said.

"I'm sorry," she whispered again.

"Why are you sorry? What is stopping you from touching me?" He brushed the curve of her cheek, his scrutiny stripping away any chance that she might dissemble.

"I did not want to seem too eager. Or to raise my voice," she said. "I apologize for the indelicacy. I won't do it again."

"Breathe."

Not until he gave the command did Violet realize the speed of her shallow inhalations.

"First, breathe," he said. "What do you want, Violet?"

What did she want? The truth pushed from the inside out, tearing holes in her fear and forcing it to the surface.

"I want to touch and be touched. I want to want and be wanted."

While she spoke, his fingers toyed with her nipple. It took all Violet's willpower not to raise her hips in delight.

"Of course you do. It's what we all want. There is nothing unnatural about such desires." He spoke with the same surety that he used when he told her to stay away from windows and walk to the left of him.

Leaning forward, he blocked her view of anything but his face. "Was it pleasurable, what I did to you, Violet?" His voice drizzled over her like thick, dark honey.

"*Yes*," she said. "No? I didn't mind."

A predatory grin lifted the corners of his mouth. Dropping his head, he set his lips to the place where her neck met her shoulder, opened his mouth wide, and bit down. Heat surged through her body, and the pulse between her thighs throbbed.

He lifted his mouth from her skin and brought his lips to her ear.

"Did you like that?" he whispered.

"Yes."

"Never be afraid to tell me when it's good," he told her.

Hovering over her again, he set his forehead to hers. A stray sliver of moonlight swept the edge of his jaw. "Even more important, never be afraid to tell me what you don't like. Pleasure must be mutual."

Violet had heard some men felt this way. "Do you mean it?

The moment that the last word left her mouth, she wanted to pull it back. She sounded like a child.

Taking no offense, Arthur cupped her chin. "Can you trust me?"

Before they'd exchanged a single word, this man had awoken a piece of Violet she'd long buried. She'd trusted him from the moment he first touched her.

"Yes," she said.

"Let's practice, shall we?"

Once again, he bent to her breasts. This time, he teased her nipple with the flat of his tongue until she squeezed her eyelids shut.

He stopped. "Violet?" he asked.

"Oh, yes. I like it. I like it."

Arthur chuckled against the undercurve of her breast and licked a path around to her throat.

"Ooooooh," she moaned. "Oh, I like that, too."

"I am happy to hear that."

"I want to touch more of you," she told him.

She wanted to see him, to feel the dark thrill of holding him in her hand. The prospect of exploring him with her tongue and tasting the salt of his skin dampened her drawers. She reached for the fastenings of his split-fall trousers.

With uncharacteristic clumsiness, Arthur tried to push up her petticoats at the same time. He cursed when they fell back down again, a waterfall of frustration. The sight of this cunning predator being flummoxed by yards of lace and muslin made Violet giggle. He looked up at the sound, abashed, with a wide, unhurried smile.

A stranger sat before her, hand halfway up her skirts, lips swollen from her kisses. An Arthur who wasn't waiting for death to come at her. An Arthur who might laugh at a joke or stroll, loose-limbed, in the park without worrying who might follow.

He was *beautiful*.

Reaching over to kiss the laughter away, his hand paused in midair. The carriage shuddered into a turn.

"Damn," he whispered.

They came to an abrupt halt. Violet turned her head in surprise. "Are we home already?"

"I wasn't paying attention. I can't believe . . ." With hurried, graceless movements, he pulled up her bodice, twitched her skirts back around her legs, and moved to the seat opposite her.

"We can tell the coachman I forgot my wrap," she pleaded, desire throbbing still between her legs. "We don't have to stop."

An instant of regret was all she glimpsed before Arthur disappeared and her bodyguard returned. An impassive, unaffected man now handed her the gloves she'd thrown to the carriage floor.

"What if I . . . ?" Her words faltered at the grim set of his mouth.

"I have been derelict in my duties. Please accept my deepest apologies," Arthur said in a calm, unhurried tone as the carriage lurched when the footman dismounted. "In the meantime, we shall forget this happened."

Violet pursed her lips, saying nothing as the door opened and a young man pulled out the steps. Arthur handed her down and walked away, leaving her alone beneath a waning moon.

Forget this happened?

How?

She made her way upstairs to her bedchamber and stood before her looking glass. Trembling, she set her fingertips to trace the swollen outline of her lips. A lock of hair had escaped her prison of pins and fluttered with her rapid breaths.

Violet couldn't remember the last time anyone had kissed her like she was treasured, like she was extraordinary. What had happened in that carriage was chemistry.

Violet had no idea how to manage seduction, but she *did* know her elements.

If Arthur thought to school her on when the chemical reaction between them was over, he should think again.

11

❦

U P AT DAWN, Violet went to work with a vengeance. Three hours later, she'd created black sludge that smelled like beet salad and ate through her wooden table.

"This won't do," she lectured herself.

She needed a distraction from reliving what had happened in the carriage with Arthur. From imagining what *hadn't* happened. Frustration had left her restless and aching.

For once, Violet's work could not pull her out of her head. Her thoughts circled back to the moment she'd burst into tears, when her walls had broken. Arthur's expression was the same as it had been the night of the first explosion. He'd been prepared to save her again if she split open too wide to pull herself back together. Not a hint of disgust or pity.

This moved her more than the delicious kisses, more than Arthur's heated touch. Dizzy with an inexplicable lightness, she abandoned her work, roaming the house, until she found Alice tidying the dressing room.

A *dowd*, Fanny had called Violet last night.

Reviewing her wardrobe, Violet had to agree. Nothing in this closet resembled anything half so pretty as the dresses on display at the ball.

She'd sent Alice out for a stack of ladies' journals, and the two of them now sat in Violet's antechamber, examining the latest fashions before a small fire. Strewn with books, loose paper, mismatched furniture, and a half-constructed pendulum draped with a pink and orange lap quilt, the room had lost all traces of genteel repose once Daniel had passed away.

"Why do the women in the advertisements for corsets have bodies that don't actually need a corset?" Violet asked.

" 'Cause it's men what does the drawings, my lady," Alice replied.

In her hands, Violet held a picture of a green and gold gown with daringly low shoulders, a pretty swath of embroidered vines twining around the hem. She set it aside, then picked it back up again.

A woman confident in her power to seduce would wear that dress. Such a gown was an unspoken invitation. She traced the outline of the skirt with her finger and sighed.

"Did you enjoy the ball last night, my lady?" Alice asked.

"Hmm."

Fanny Armitage would find the green dress scandalous since most of the extra weight Violet had put on resided in her chest.

She had a deep-seated desire to upset Fanny Armitage.

"Mr. Kneland did not seem to," Alice continued.

Violet's head popped up. "What?"

"He snapped at Winthram something awful when you got back. He isn't friendly, not like Mr. Thomas."

Violet arched an eyebrow, waiting for Alice to continue. The little maid stared at the fashion plates in front of her. "Told him I was from near Dingwall. Asked him did he have kin near there, and he frowned at me," the little maid lamented. "Wasn't prying. It would be nice to speak with another Scot."

"Maybe he is homesick as well, Alice. For some, it hurts more to speak of home than to not speak of it."

As Alice mulled over that concept, Violet considered her own words. What might it have cost Arthur to share the story of his family with her last night? Could it have been their emotional intimacy that had disconcerted him more than the physical?

"Maybe," Alice said. "Maybe he isn't even from the north."

"What do you mean?" Violet asked. "He's from a small farm in the Highlands. Lord Greycliff said so."

"No such thing anymore. All that's left there are the great estates and sheep. Rest are crofts—it's why we had to leave."

So Arthur had lost more than a family. He'd lost an entire way of life.

"Well, hello, darling." Phoebe strode into the room and stared at the shawls draped over a chair, then let her gaze drift toward Alice. "Taking tea with your maid. How . . . democratic of you."

The poor girl jumped to her feet and scurried to tidy the offending garments. With a regal nod of approval, Phoebe plonked herself in the chair, giving the stack of ladies' journals a disinterested perusal.

"Thank you, Alice," said Violet. "We will continue this conversation after Lady Phoebe has said whatever she came here to scold me about."

Alice curtsied and made a quick exit.

"How did you know I came here to scold you?" Phoebe asked.

"You have that look. Like I've set fire to your boots or matched a striped bonnet with a paisley shawl."

"Paisley and stripes are a crime against humanity. You are a murderer of fashion, and I will never stop wanting justice for it," Phoebe complained. "Do you have anything to drink?"

"Why do you pretend?" Violet asked.

Phoebe froze for a moment, then tossed a journal to the floor and tilted her chin sideways, showing the line of her neck from the most flattering angle.

"What you said to Alice . . . ," Violet began.

Twitching away from Violet's remonstrations, Phoebe adjusted her skirts. "You cannot expect the daughter of a marquess to slurp tea with an uneducated—"

"You were the one who introduced Alice to the works of Giovanni Plana in the first place." Violet threw aside her lap blanket and went to the fire, prodding the smoldering coals in frustration.

She turned and examined her friend. The beautifully trimmed gown of bruised rose silk hung loose at Phoebe's waist, and her mahogany hair did not have its usual shine.

"Why play the pompous aristocrat when we both know you don't believe that nonsense?"

A shaft of sunlight fought its way through the gloom, and Phoebe reached out a hand as if to catch the beam.

"Odd, isn't it?" The drawl slipped from her voice as she turned her palm this way and that in the slanted square of illumination. "However much I try to slip free of my father's influence, it is his prejudices I parrot."

The muscles in her face constricted, creating a smile so taut it exposed the skull beneath her porcelain skin. "Prodding at someone weaker when one feels low is a Hunt family failing, I'm afraid. To my credit, I don't limit my antipathy to the lower classes. Grantham came in for his fair share."

So much energy wasted erecting a facade of ambivalence. The truth was that Phoebe Hunt felt too much, cared too deeply, to walk comfortably in her skin.

Sunlight brushed past Violet, washing the walls with timid strokes.

"You rescued Maisy White from her husband," she said. "You stood by me when everyone mocked the idea of Athena's Retreat. Why not let the rest of the world see your heart?"

"Shine a light into the dark corners?"

For a fleeting moment, their gazes met, and another woman stared out through Phoebe's eyes: uncertain, lost, and in need of her friend. Violet froze, but a trace of sympathy must have revealed itself. As if sensing their attention, the sun withdrew, and Phoebe closed her fist hard on the sudden shadows. Throwing back her shoulders and baring her teeth against the very idea of vulnerability, Phoebe forced a brittle laugh. "Darling, the heart is nothing but a muscle with an outsized reputation."

Letty popped her head around the door. "I'm sorry to intrude, my lady. I hoped . . ." She faltered when she saw Phoebe. "Oh. Excuse me, Lady Phoebe. I did not see your card downstairs."

Silently, Violet cursed the interruption with a naughty word she shouldn't know.

For her part, Phoebe squeezed her misery behind a mask of cool amusement and tossed her head, determined to act as though her encounter with Violet had never happened. She gestured to another armchair, hidden beneath a pile of books and papers.

"No, it's good you've come, Letty. We're here for the same reason, I suspect."

Letty turned and regarded Violet with such sweet seriousness Violet's stomach pitched.

"Nothing's exploded, has it?" she asked. Milly and Willy had seemed suspiciously cheerful yesterday.

"Fanny Armitage's head last night," Phoebe answered. "It nearly separated from her scrawny little body with excitement at gossiping about you."

Letty nodded in reluctant agreement. "I heard the story from Lady

Olivia's cousin. She was at my father's emporium, gossiping with her aunt. It wasn't terrible, not anything they haven't said before . . ."

"It was bad enough," Phoebe said.

Drat.

"Grantham is to blame for that mess," Violet said, brushing coal dust from her hands. "He picked out the Thornton-Hammersmith ball and then never showed up. If he'd been there, Fanny would've never noticed me. What use is that blond gorgeousness of his if he won't distract those nasty hens from pecking defenseless young ladies to death?"

Letty's brows drew together in confusion, and a sense of unease climbed Violet's spine. She crossed her arms, tucking her hands against her chest, chilled despite the fire.

"Lady Olivia reported your behavior as beyond eccentric," Letty said.

"The ladies of my family have always had reputations as originals," Violet reminded them.

"Yes, that is the problem." Phoebe straightened in her chair. "You already have a history of social failure. Until now, you've managed to walk the line between unorthodox and outrageous. Your title and the support of members such as myself help keep you upright."

The sight of Letty nodding piqued Violet's temper. Weeks of rows between the two of them, and they picked today to link arms and lecture her. She'd been debauched (in the best way possible) in a moving carriage, and her world now stood upside down. Who had time to listen to a speech on etiquette?

"All I did was introduce Althea to a young man whose name I'd forgotten."

Phoebe's brow quirked. "This has nothing to do with Althea."

"What else could it have been?" Violet asked.

Letty and Phoebe exchanged incredulous glances. Foreboding

fluttered in Violet's stomach, and she sat back in her chair. At her feet lay the ladies' journal splayed open to the picture of the green gown.

"I saw you with him," Phoebe answered, her voice soft with rare sympathy.

For one terrible moment, Violet thought Phoebe was speaking of what had happened in the carriage—the unbearable intimacy of her tears and Arthur's touch.

"How could you have seen anything?" she whispered.

"I was there. You waltzed right by me," Phoebe retorted. "I'm not surprised you didn't notice, considering the looks that passed between you."

"It was just a dance." The lie was unmistakable.

Phoebe leaned forward. "I poured champagne down the front of Sir Peter Forthingull's pants when he called Miss Lucy Petershaw a cow, and no one blinked an eye, because they were watching you dance."

Letty nodded her approval at Forthingull's fate, but the furrows between her pale brows remained. "According to Lady Olivia, Mr. Kneland hauled you away like a brute, without saying a word. She says you pressed yourself so close the cellist tipped over his chair in shock at the display."

"How lurid," Violet exclaimed, pulling the blanket back onto her lap, fussing until it lay perfectly smooth. "I had no idea Lady Olivia had the brains to invent such a story."

"That was Fanny's description, you can be sure," said Phoebe. "As soon as the ladies began talking, I told everyone Kneland was the man who took a bullet for Dickerson. That may not have helped. Dickerson is a boor, with questionable ideas about hygiene."

Curse Fanny Armitage. She'd stained the kindness of Arthur's rescue.

"Regardless, you cannot act like the rebellious daughter of a marquess 'giving one' to a groomsman," Phoebe scolded. "The end result will be worse than an irate papa running after the man with a bull-whip."

"Mr. Kneland is not a servant, and that is a bizarre analogy," Violet said. "It was one dance in public, not my first kiss behind the barn."

Letty couldn't help herself. "Did your papa really take a bullwhip to your groom?" she asked Phoebe.

Phoebe snorted. "Of course not. He wouldn't waste the energy on a mere groom. He had his valet do it for him. Papa saved the real punishments for . . . Never mind. You are correct, Violet. Kneland is not a servant." She dropped her air of bemusement. "He's not a gentleman, either."

"The reason everyone remarked on it is because you don't go out to parties or balls, my lady," Letty said. "They don't know what you look like when you are happy."

Violet turned her hands over in her lap. She'd managed to smear coal dust not only on the palms, but over the back of her glove as well. The situation required her close examination until she gathered her composure.

"Happy or in heat, it doesn't matter," Phoebe said. "If you're going to tumble with the help, do it after the event." She stalked across the room and peered out the window. "I have to get back to my work this afternoon. I've long overdue correspondence to finish with Herr Kolbe before I get to the next step in my research. Now, let's make this clear. You are in trouble, Violet."

"No one has said anything directly . . . ," Letty began.

"They will," Phoebe interjected. "You've caught Fanny Armitage's interest. She's the worst of the lot and has never liked you since you married Daniel. She'd been angling after him for ages."

"They would have been much better matched. I never lived up to his expectations."

Phoebe turned, a militant light in her eyes. "That is because he was cruel. He couldn't stand that you had a better mind and tried to make you small in other ways."

Was this true? Did Daniel cause Violet's insecurities, or were her faults there all along, and he merely pointed them out?

"Blaming Daniel is easy because he isn't here any longer," said Violet. "If I had stood my ground in the beginning and insisted my work come first, things would have been different."

"How could you? You wanted him to love you," Letty whispered, as though it were shameful.

There it was, said aloud for all to hear. Violet's greatest regret. She had wanted Daniel to love her, and no matter what she sacrificed, how she stuffed away anything he found objectionable—he never did.

If her husband couldn't find a way to love her, why would anyone else?

"All this introspection is fascinating," drawled Phoebe in a manner designed to let them know it was the opposite. "It doesn't change the facts. The rumor mill is turning. This is the opposite of what we wanted. You must remain as far away from Mr. Kneland as possible."

"Lady Phoebe is correct," said Letty, as surprised as any of them that she and Phoebe agreed. "Rumors of any impropriety on your part spells disaster for us all."

ARTHUR DONNED A mask of indifference and nodded at appropriate intervals, hands folded in his lap, body still.

No one would guess that all he could think of was kissing.

Kissing and . . .

"Have I not made myself clear? Shall I repeat my objections for the thousandth time, Mr. Kneland? Are you even listening?" Letty's voice flattened into an unintelligible drone as two sides of an argument raged in his head.

One part of him insisted he should never have touched Violet in the carriage last night. Grey had hired Arthur to protect his stepmother, not seduce her. Even worse, Arthur cared about her feelings. He'd spoken to her of Deoiridh, let himself comfort and be comforted.

How long would it take to push those memories back down?

A darker, more forceful part wanted to follow Violet to her room to finish what they started. It hadn't been enough, that one taste of her. If only they'd had more time.

Unaccustomed to his basest urges having any part of his decisions, Arthur suspected the fault lay with Violet. She might be an evil genius who'd invented a concoction to make men insane. Why else would his hard-won experience and common sense go flying out the window at the sight of her?

Hell, even at the scent of her.

If anyone had told him three weeks ago that the combination of slate, lilies, and ethanol would arouse him, he'd have laughed in their faces.

Well, not laughed. He wasn't one for laughing. Since he met Violet, however, he'd been visited more than once by the urge to chuckle. Grin, even.

"In conclusion, as the Athena's Retreat club secretary and in compliance with the bylaws of our club, specifically rule number 13, subsection 6, paragraph 18b, you cannot station a man at the connecting door between the front and the back of the club to check members' names and likenesses against your list."

Letty was pelting Arthur with arguments from behind a desk in the Athena's Retreat office, the polished rosewood gleaming in a slice of sunlight. An echo of the softness of Violet's skin tickled his fingers as he argued with himself.

"You need to stay away from Lady Greycliff."

Jerking his head in surprise, Arthur cursed himself for his inattention. "I beg your pardon, Miss Fenley. What was that about subsection 6?"

"I finished speaking on that subject five minutes ago," Letty snapped. "You were paying as little attention to our rules as you have the rules of society and the state of Lady Greycliff's reputation."

Could she know what had happened in the carriage? How?

Arthur swallowed his apprehension. "I aim to oversee security so Lady Greycliff can work on the formulas. If this conflicts with her reputation, so be it. The safety of the public takes precedence."

"The safety of the public compelled you to dance with Lady Greycliff at the Thornton-Hammersmith ball?"

Arthur tapped his finger—once, twice—on the arm of his chair, regarding Letty without blinking.

The tiny mathematician was made of sterner stuff than most women, for she returned his stare with a fiercer one. "And after you pasted yourself to her like a stamp to an envelope . . ."

What? He'd done nothing of the sort, for goodness' sake. Pasted himself?

". . . you proceeded to drag her outside, like a marauder flinging his spoils over his shoulder and disappearing into the night."

"That is a description straight from Minerva Press," Arthur said. "I didn't *fling* anyone. I offered to dance with Lady Greycliff so I could protect her."

"From the bomb-wielding radicals on the dance floor?" she asked, her sarcasm as pointed as her chin.

He resisted the urge to cross his arms. "No. From the insult-wielding ladies."

Sighing in acknowledgment, Letty rubbed at a spot on the desk with her finger. "It is not your place to intervene, Mr. Kneland. Those women are bored and vicious to an unreasonable degree. Fanny Armitage lives for another woman's downfall, spreading spite across the ton as though it were butter." Her finger pressed so hard against the wood the material began to pill.

"Do you know her well?" he asked.

Letty's movements stilled, and she thrust her hands into her lap. "Only by reputation. I am not of sufficient social standing to mix with such elevated personages as Mrs. Armitage and her friends."

"Lady Greycliff has family who will rally around her," Arthur said. "Greycliff won't stand for any slander."

"And if it is not slander? If your past comes to light, Mr. Kneland?"

The crack of the broken arm of his chair punctured the sudden silence. With great care, Arthur unwrapped his fingers from the wood.

"Who did you hear it from?" he asked.

She jerked her chin up, her voice thinning in defiance. "Does it matter? The story is out there. I am not the only one who has been told. It is a matter of time before Lady Greycliff hears it."

The longer the silence stretched, the more Letty fidgeted. Either she hadn't meant to speak of the old scandal, or she felt guilty about how she'd revealed it.

"My past has nothing to do with my ability to protect Lady Greycliff," Arthur said. This was the truth.

Letty frowned as though disappointed with him. "That is a matter of perspective. She will still have to go out in society after the Omnis have been thwarted and you have moved along. You know how those people are, Mr. Kneland. London society, the aristocracy—all of them. They won't let people like us be happy."

While not "of sufficient social standing" to be welcome in high society, Letty Fenley must have somehow suffered at their hands. Who had thwarted her happiness? Was she now seeking revenge?

"Lady Greycliff might be able to salvage her reputation," she said, "but she will not be able to save this club if it is mired in scandal. This club is her life."

"It is not much of a life if she cannot be herself."

"Mr. Kneland," she said, a thread of pity in her tone. "Lady Grey-cliff survived years of ridicule and cruelty to create Athena's Retreat. A place that guarantees security and respect. She has a good life here among us. Please, do not be the one to take it away from her." Compassion cushioned her words. "Grantham can take care of that lot. Once he marries her, Lady Greycliff will be protected. There is no good can come of people like us mixing with the aristocracy. It's as I said: They are bored and cruel and cannot be secure of their elevated status unless they're standing atop of the rest of us."

She walked to the door.

"I'm sure you meant well," she said over her shoulder, then left the room.

Meant well? He hadn't meant to do anything. Last night was the result of pure instinct. Discipline honed over the years had deserted him in the face of Violet's distress.

Arthur wrestled with the question of whether he would do it differently if given a chance.

When the answer presented itself, he leaned his head back and studied the ceiling as if there might be an alternative written in the sagging plaster. As it stood, a chasm yawned on either side of him, and before him lay a narrow path.

If he fell, he'd pull down more than just himself.

12

CHRIST JAYSUS!"
Insofar as explosions went, the one that had Grantham racing into Violet's workroom and shouting profanities was too small to account for such a reaction. Folks nowadays were too easily ruffled.

"What the devil was that?" he cried as he waved away an *infinitesimal* amount of smoke.

"Oh, that noise? Part of a simple experiment posing no danger to anyone. Tea?" Violet smothered a cough as thick flakes of ash came drifting down from the ceiling.

"Tea? Vi, we were supposed to be at Dunby's dinner party twenty minutes ago," Grantham grumbled. "If you'd take a moment away from your blasted . . . Damn, I'm not supposed to say 'blast' anymore." He stopped. "Or 'damn.' Blast!"

When they were children, he'd been a gangly boy with long, skinny legs, enormous feet and hands splayed everywhere. He'd filled out over the years, grown into a beautiful man. As he apologized for his language, Violet acknowledged how hard he'd worked to acquire polish upon receiving an unexpected title.

It hadn't come easy.

"Do you remember Cook said she would wash your mouth out with soap when you taught me to curse?" she asked.

Grantham sauntered over to her worktable and surveyed the mess. "Was that the first time we ran away together?"

Growing up the oldest of what seemed to her an excessive number of sisters, Violet had searched out a more restful companion. Grantham, the stepson of a well-liked tenant, was the closest in age of the neighborhood children. He suited her perfectly, as it never occurred to him to cry if he fell and scraped a knee, and he was tall enough to boost her up where she shouldn't have been. Together, they had been the scourge of cooks, nurses, and various servants, who washed their hands of trying to tame them and focused instead on keeping them alive. Grantham was the brother she always wanted, with the added benefit of being sent home whenever he smelled bad.

"The second time," Violet said. "We made it as far as Asher's Grove in the wolds and got lost. I cried, and you told me not to worry, that you would hunt for us—except you twisted your ankle, and a bug got stuck in my nose."

Grantham chuckled. "That was a grand adventure, wasn't it? Remember how we both contracted influenza and weren't allowed outside for weeks afterward?"

Violet did not remember that part as being so grand. "Remember the time we stole Squire Pelletier's prize orchid, because it looked like the magic flower in the book of stories your mother read to you? That was great fun as well. Except when they came searching for it and we ate the flowers to turn us invisible, but they didn't, and we were sick on the upholstery in Mama's parlor."

Wrinkling his nose, he tossed her pen back and crossed the room to throw open a window. With a suspicious air, he rattled the gate that Arthur had fixed to the outside.

"What am I supposed to say to Dunby?" he complained.

"You abandoned me at the last ball," Violet reminded him. "I stuffed myself into a ridiculous gown and nearly drowned in watery ratafia waiting for you to appear. This is your punishment. Say whatever you like, I have work to do."

"I'm sorry I wasn't able to get word to you. The prince summoned me, and it took ages to get away—you know how he talks. He's worried about the Omnis as well, especially after what happened with Edward Oxford two years ago."

"You're an earl now, not a soldier." She scratched out a number and started over. The ratios were wrong. "You don't have to be at the prince's beck and call. Didn't you want to spend more time at the estate?"

"I did," Grantham said. "Then I got your letter asking for help with the season, remember?"

Violet measured the amount of liquid left in a canister and did a few calculations. "I panicked, didn't I?"

"*Georgie, it's like sailing through a lavender-scented hurricane of pettiness with one oar and half a sail. Can't you come back and use your curst good looks in the service of science rather than self-indulgence?*" he recited, in a perfect imitation of her.

"You'll note I complimented your looks," she pointed out.

"Yes, and here I am. You, on the other hand, are nose-deep in formulas and setting off explosions left and right." He wandered over to a small flame, where she'd been distilling a solution.

"I am helping Grey—"

"You are putting yourself in danger," Grantham said. "It doesn't have to be you figuring out the antidote. There are plenty of other scientists who can do this work."

"I *like* it, Georgie."

Not true. She *loved* it. Nothing else left her so centered and confident. When Violet was working in her lab, the humming noise in her head quieted and the world showed her its mysteries.

Having grown up watching her create enough potions to poison an army, Grantham stopped arguing. He'd never understood her fascination with chemistry, but he never shamed her for it.

"Vi, I didn't come back to bring you to balls. I meant what I said before. About coming to the point."

Numbers squirmed on the page, and she raced to pin them down. "I'm trying to work, if we could—don't touch that jar."

Moving over to a set of drawers, Grantham busied himself opening them and rummaging through the contents, juggling a handful of pumice stones. "We could do it. We rub along well."

He stopped playing and put the rocks back. "Mama is getting worse. With her memory fading, I'm lost as to how to go on."

Violet gave Grantham her full attention. Was he proposing? No, it couldn't be. "I'm sorry about your mama."

"I need help managing the estate." He ran his hand over the back of his head, mussing his hair. "I have to get this right, even if my mother is too far gone to know it. Then there's Lizzie. She'll need to be brought out. You can help her since Mama cannot."

No. Not this.

The walls of the room closed in, and Violet pulled air into her lungs with effort. "Your sister is a dear, and I want to help your mama. I can do this without marrying you."

She pushed aside her pen and went over to the bank of windows, struggling to open another one.

Grantham lounged against her worktable and studied her notes. "You aren't getting any younger. What about children?"

Her clammy fingers slipped on the window lock. "I was married for five years. No children came then."

She pressed her fingers to the bridge of her nose. "I cannot think about this now. The evening event is next week. My first concern must be the club."

"Is it marriage in general you wish to avoid?" he persisted. "I am not Daniel. I would be nothing like him."

Violet willed away the worst of the memories. Day by day, Daniel had whittled away at her confidence until she became the woman he told her she was and not the woman she longed to be. Loath to endure the sympathy of her friends and family, unwilling to admit to her youthful mistakes, she'd closeted herself in Beacon House, first tending to Daniel as his health failed, then throwing herself into running Athena's Retreat.

"Is it marriage to *me* you don't want?" he asked carefully.

What could she say? If she married Grantham, she would be moving backward.

Oh, he would let her bring her instruments and chemicals, clear out a room next to the nursery he'd like her to fill. At first, there would be a handful of requests. Taking care of his mama as she grew more confused. Bringing out his sister. Organizing a church fete. Seeing to his tenants.

Little by little, dust would gather on her papers. Time with her work would be put off, just this once. Then once more. Years would pass, and who would she be? Someone's wife. Someone's mother. Someone who would gaze longingly up the stairs toward what could have been.

Pulling back the curtains, she tried to summon a blank expression.

"You will make someone a wonderful husband," she told him.

"But not you?" he asked.

"I don't—"

"I'm wondering if there is any other reason you wouldn't want to be married." Grantham studied her. "People have been talking. I breakfasted at my club this morning, and someone mentioned a waltz."

The scolding tone irritated Violet. She spun around. "Would *you* lecture me? One waltz, and everyone acts as though I'm a common baggage."

"The first waltz since you married Daniel. I know what that means, even if you don't." He sighed. "In many ways, you are an innocent. Let me take care of you. I don't want to see you unhappy."

Was this what Violet had to choose from? Either the ruin of her club or another loveless marriage?

"What if I wish to . . . waltz with someone? If it makes me happy?" she asked.

"Are you talking about an affair?" He punctuated his question with a condescending chuckle.

Violet's hands fisted at Grantham's amusement. Why wouldn't he laugh, though? Who would want an affair with her? What had Arthur said in the carriage? She was like a mad hummingbird. A man couldn't want a love affair with a woman who had to be told what to do. Arthur hadn't even looked at her since that night.

What if Arthur's beautiful words were just that—words?

The proposal made sense. No doubt if her family were here, they would echo the warnings of her closest friends. The club would stay safe, Grantham would treat her well, and there would be an end to her lonely nights.

Why couldn't she say yes?

What was holding her back?

WHAT WAS HOLDING him back? For the love of God, all Arthur had to do was knock on the door and ask his question, but on his way to

Violet's workroom, he'd spied Grantham's carriage out front, and now indistinct voices murmured behind the door.

What were they doing? Why might they want the door closed?

Arthur shook the questions from his head. Even if they were doing something—which they weren't—what business was it of his? Letty was correct. His past would come to light sooner or later. He should stay well away from Violet.

He had no claim on her. He was the employee of her stepson. No reason to act like a nodcock. Putting his ear to the door, he pressed against the wood.

If she and Grantham were doing anything, there would be sounds. Wait—was that the rustle of clothing being removed?

He scoffed aloud and took a step back from the door, then turned to make sure no one had observed his *ridiculous* behavior and leaned forward again.

That noise might have been a tiny moan escaping when someone had discovered a particularly sensitive spot.

He pressed his ear even closer. Was that the soft exhalation after a—

Arthur slammed open the door, unannounced. The sight of Grantham at one end of the room (fully clothed) and Violet clear across on the other side (also fully clothed) made up for the shock on their faces.

"Sorry. Forgot to knock," he blurted.

They stared at him as though he'd lost his mind. Which he might have done, truth be told. He'd once saved a man from three knife-wielding Corsicans in the middle of the crowded dining room of Le Grand Véfour without a single patron noticing anything. A few weeks in Violet's company, and he couldn't even walk into a room without making a fool of himself.

He needed a cold bath.

In another country.

"I'm not interrupting anything, am I?" he asked.

"You are, as a matter of fact," Grantham answered, puffing like a popinjay.

Violet scowled at Grantham as she tucked a clump of curls behind her ear. Her topknot was loose, and her creamy skin appeared pale in the wan grey light. He hadn't seen her since the carriage ride, nor had she sought him out. Instead, she'd closeted herself in the workroom.

He missed her.

"You are not interrupting," said Violet. "We were discussing—"

"Marriage," Grantham announced.

Violet took a small step backward and shrunk as if he'd shifted an unwanted burden over to her.

"While it was delightful visiting with you, Grantham, I have to get back to work. You'll both be pleased to hear I have come a long way in the past two days." She straightened suddenly and clapped her hands in excitement. "As a matter of fact, do you remember when I spoke of Avogadro's law?"

"Have you discovered something new?" Arthur asked.

"I told you of the difficulties I've had proving this particular theory. However . . ."

Like a skipping stone across a lake kicking up beads of brilliance in the sunlight, Violet's mind raced ahead of everyone's around her. Within seconds of her explanation, Arthur was at sea.

Fearless, that intellect of hers, jumping forward without the worry of where it might land. The woman who stood before him glowing with happiness was a far cry from the woman he'd rescued at the edge of the dance floor.

Ever since the night in the carriage, Arthur had struggled to put his finger on why Violet Hughes turned him inside out.

Was it this simple? Was it so easy to care for Violet because all she needed was someone to tell her to go ahead and be who she already was?

"Fascinating," Arthur said, once he figured she had finished.

"Indeed," Grantham said, blinking hard. His eyes had glazed over midway through Violet's recitation. "That Avogadro. He's a tricky one."

Recognizing she'd lost them both, Violet settled back behind her worktable. "So, you must understand that I need to get back to work as soon as possible."

"I need to speak with you regarding security," Arthur said. "There was another committee meeting. There is disagreement over whether to limit the attendees to one guest per member."

"Another meeting?" she said in dismay. "Why wasn't I told?"

He frowned. "You've been on assignment. That takes precedence over the club."

Violet objected. "Nothing takes precedence over the club."

"Is that so?" Grantham said with a strange intensity. From the way Violet jumped, one might have thought the earl had shouted the question. "Sounds to me as though you are confused about what comes first. Your club or your commitments. The sooner you decide on what you value the most and how to safeguard it, the better for all of us."

Violet stood with a protective hand clenched over her abdomen, desolation plain on her face. "All I know is that I have work to do. The sooner I finish, the sooner I can be left in peace. If I can't have peace and quiet in my own home, I'm going to the laboratory at the club. Why don't you"—Violet pointed at the earl—"and you"—she pointed at Arthur—"bother each other, while I"—she pointed at her chest—"go away. Good night."

With that, she brushed past Arthur and left the room.

The urge to follow and apologize took him aback. He hadn't done anything wrong. Had he?

"Oh, *well* done," said Grantham. He'd draped his oversized body over Violet's armchair, his dinner jacket littered with tiny pieces of ash.

"What?" Arthur asked. "What did I do?"

"Telling her about the meeting. You've upset her."

"*I've* upset her? She was already upset when I arrived. What did you say to her?"

Grantham blew out a derisive snort. "Nothing that concerns you. Everything was fine before you barged in like a bloody elephant. Speaking of which, why did you barge in here? Door was closed. Whatever question you had could have waited."

"Barge in?" Arthur echoed in disbelief. "I did my job. If you don't care enough to want me protecting her, then—"

"I do care, Kneland," the earl said. "That cur Daniel stomped all over her when he was alive. For years, she buried herself in her club, and now that she's finally venturing out of her laboratory, someone is trying to blow up her work. Not to mention she's on the verge of embarrassing herself again in front of the ton."

Grantham stood and attempted to leverage the minuscule amount of height difference between the two of them by looming. Pointing a finger, he stabbed it into Arthur's chest. "I see the way you gawp after her."

"I have never gawped," Arthur said.

Had he gawped?

"You make your living pushing petty tyrants out of the way of bullets and blades and whatnot. You're hired muscle, not a savior—and certainly not a gentleman."

Arthur's social stature had nothing to do with his unsuitability as anything other than Violet's bodyguard, but he didn't bother to argue.

Grantham took the silence for agreement. "Lady Greycliff is the granddaughter of an earl and the daughter and the widow of a viscount, and the most gracious and generous woman I know. Soon, you will be a jobless no one. You are not good enough for her. Keep your distance. And if you know what's good for you, you'll stay far, far away from her bed."

Arthur could detect no real malice in the observation. The earl was correct. Violet was gracious and generous, and so much more.

And yet . . . he could imagine more for himself.

Not a title—he'd seen men far more exalted than he up close and never come away impressed. No.

He imagined being more to Violet than her bodyguard. Imagined being the man she came home and shared a drink with on a cold winter's night. What would it be like to follow her to bed and wake beside her every morning?

If he had a woman like Violet at his side, he would do everything in his power to make her happy. The sweet flare of pain in his chest burned bright for one bittersweet second before reality doused it.

Even if Violet were to ignore the difference in their stations, she could not forgive the notoriety his past would bring.

"The Omnis managed to get the drop on you once already," said the earl. "How am I to trust they won't surprise you again?"

"Don't worry about the element of surprise," Arthur replied.

Reaching over, he grabbed the earl's obnoxious pointing finger and pivoted on one heel.

Grantham's arse hitting the floorboards made a massive noise. More gratifying was the sheer astonishment on the earl's too-pretty face. It couldn't banish the pain, but it made Arthur chuckle.

"Come back here, you insufferable ba—"

Arthur flung open the door and nodded at the gaping footman, ignoring Grantham's complaints as they followed him down the hall.

Violet would be settling for less if she married Grantham. The man treated her like a younger sister. She deserved a man who found her irresistible. Who got down on one knee and told her that life could not and would not be worthwhile if she wasn't at his side.

Violet deserved to be loved.

13

❧

"*B*OLLOCKS!*"*

There were many benefits to Violet's widowhood. The most obvious being that she no longer had to tolerate her husband and his bullying tirades.

Widowhood also allowed liberties like cursing at the top of her lungs without having to hear a single word of reproach. As she rubbed her sore head, Violet reviewed her other vocabulary options.

Bollocks was fun to say and covered an extensive range of circumstances. Much better than *damn.*

Of course, her favorite word was . . .

"Are you all right?"

Violet smacked her head against the bottom of her coffee table for the second time at the sound of Arthur's voice. She had been certain she was alone. Cautiously, she backed out from under the table on all fours until her head was clear.

Arthur stood in the doorway of her workroom, a candle in one hand and a frown on his face. He leaned a hip against the doorframe,

one leg crossed over the other. He'd left off his coat and loosened his
cravat. She'd never beheld him in shirtsleeves before. What a fascinating body he had. Violet wagered he would look as compelling out
of his clothes as he did in them.

That blow to her head must have knocked the sense out of her.
She should not be thinking about seeing Arthur naked.

"I am fine, thank you," she said. "Why do you ask?" She pulled at
the neck of her dressing gown, struggling to appear unruffled even as
her skin heated.

His thick black brows dipped in confusion. "You shouted, 'Bollocks.' I assumed something was wrong."

"I did not shout . . . that word you said," Violet said with a sniff. "I
shouted, 'Buttons.'"

"Why were you under the table?" Always on alert, Arthur scanned
the room from corner to corner as he set down the candle.

Violet rose from the floor and collapsed onto her sagging sofa. "I
set up an experiment and knocked over a jar of lemon drops—for me,
not the experiment."

Winter held London in its grasp, tapping at the window glass, finding its way in through tiny cracks and fissures, even through the sturdy
walls of Beacon House. Despite the fire laid earlier, the workroom had
a slight chill, and she'd donned an enormous old night rail of thick
knitted wool. Beneath it, a simple, unadorned cotton gown covered
her from her clavicle to her ankles.

"Will you sit?" she asked, patting the cushion next to her. "Come
now. I won't bite."

The memory of Arthur setting his teeth against the soft column
of her neck made her flush. "I mean, I won't bite in a rabid dog way . . .
Not that I would bite you in any other way . . . Unless you wanted me to."

One thick eyebrow lifted in question, and Violet sighed.

"I told Caro Pettigrew we should never use the word 'stupid.' Yet that is how I am around you. Tongue-tied and stupid."

For the past two days, a chorus of voices had been raised against her association with this man. The fate of Athena's Retreat hung over her every minute of the day, and yet she could not believe what she wanted was wrong.

He made his way toward her, and Violet marveled at the way his body moved beneath his clothing, the waistcoat pulling against the breadth of his shoulders.

"I don't care what everyone says," she muttered. "I wish I could..."

"You wish you could do what?"

"More than anything, I wish I had the confidence to seduce you," she confessed.

There it was again—that way he had of switching from protector to predator in an instant. A shift in the way he held himself, thighs tensed and ready to spring, fingers flexed. He cleared his throat as his gaze dropped to her bare toes.

"I wish I could get my hands on whoever took away that confidence," he said.

His words smashed the walls around her to pieces.

"I cannot believe you doubt your allure. It hasn't gone without notice that I am ... affected by your company." He rubbed his jaw. "Not that it's a good idea, seduction. I shouldn't be here."

"I have been given the same warnings." Violet hugged herself at the memory of Letty and Phoebe's critique. "From the moment we returned from the ball, I have been told what not to do."

A fire had smoldered in her chest since her friends' visit the other day. Grantham's words had added fuel to the blaze.

"Do you know how it made me feel, to be told I was irresponsible and letting down the club members because I chose to dance with you?" Her hands clenched into fists.

"Angry?" For a moment, pride filled his eyes. The next second, his brows lowered in worry as he hunted for a handkerchief.

"I'm not going to cry," she promised. "Yes. Angry. And guilty. And sad."

Still holding the handkerchief, he waited for her to finish, cradling them both in that miraculous stillness he carried with him.

"Mostly, I was tired," she said. "Tired of hiding my passions to accommodate others. Tired of pretending to be what I am not. Tired . . ." Violet's voice broke. "I am tired of being alone."

A precipice awaited, and she threw herself over, wrenching herself wide open to him. "I do not want to be alone tonight."

Had she ever not known him? He must have lived on the edge of her dreams. Only years of familiarity could have allowed her to read the stillness in his face. Prickles of anticipation lit her skin even before he lowered himself to the sofa, ready to give in to desire.

"It has been a long time since anyone offered to seduce me," he said. His weight on the couch caused her to tumble toward him. "How will you begin?"

She exhaled, squeezing her thighs around a quiver of pleasure. "Well, you are retiring to a farm, are you not?"

The hard body now pressed against her made it difficult to concentrate, even more so when he wrapped an arm around her shoulders.

That must be why she blurted out the least seductive suggestion one could imagine.

"We could examine the subject of agricultural use of chemical methods to increase yields and disease resistance in various strains of wheat."

He tilted his head as he considered her words. "Or I could kiss you."

A tiny squeak of relief emerged, and she tilted her head upward for the promised kiss, but he set a finger to her lips.

"I want you to ask for anything you want. *Anything.*" He wiggled his eyebrows. "Tell me as well if there is anything you do *not* want," he said, his voice softening as he traced the arc of her bottom lip. "I will be listening."

Violet wanted him to stop talking and start touching, but he hesitated. "Tonight is about *physical* passion. There can be no sentiments involved. We cannot be discovered."

"Of course." She nodded like a fool. "We are going to indulge in our physical urges, nothing more."

She paused, then added, "Maybe in more than one position?"

He laughed. He *laughed*. Low and smooth like the rush of river water over rounded stones, the sound covered her in a lusty awareness, and she plunged ahead without fear.

Dark and soft and tasting of smoky gunpowder tea, Arthur kissed her over and over again, and she met his mouth with an unabashed hunger, her fingers running through his hair as she pulled him flush against her.

He'd pounced on her hungrily, pushing her further into the couch, like a wolf hovering over his prey, and the image sent a wicked thrill through her.

Arthur broke away and raised himself up on his forearms.

"Why are you wearing so many clothes?" he asked.

She chuckled in answer, and his predatory grin made her open her legs beneath him. In response, his heavy cock stirred. The lightness of the moment vanished, and her hands fluttered to the ribbon at her neck.

Arthur stood from the couch, pulling her with him. He kept his gaze locked on hers while he unknotted the frayed ribbon at her throat and slipped the worn wooden buttons through the holes on the front of her hideous robe.

"You have beautiful eyes," he told her.

"Oh." She was fascinated by his clever fingers as he worked to free her. "What a lovely compliment."

When the robe hung open, he slipped it from her shoulders.

"It's a terrible compliment," he said. Spinning her around, he put his mouth close to her ear, his breath tickling it. "I should be telling you that your eyes are like the pools they talk about in fairy stories. The ones that call to men in the darkest part of the forest, pulling you in with the promise of pleasure, where even as you drown you are grateful for such a perfect death. I should have said that, but better."

Gently, he lifted her hair back over one shoulder, fingers brushing the base of her neck as he now attacked the tiny buttons down the back of her gown, huffing in frustration. She turned her head, and his movements stilled.

"No one has ever said anything half so nice about my eyes, Arthur," she whispered.

"Then you have been surrounded by fools. Where do I start?" he asked. "Odes to your lips? Sonnets praising the line of your neck, the sweetness of your mouth?"

"Oh, yes, please," she murmured. "Then it will be my turn. I am particularly enamored by the angle of your jaw and the backs of your hands."

This was meant to be Violet's seduction of Arthur. Instead, he'd turned it around.

Fairy pools.

What would fall next from his lips? Compliments to her skin? Perhaps he'd recite a piece of poetry to her, stroke the hair from her forehead, hold her hand and kiss her palm as he gently—

"What the devil?" she cried out as a freezing draft from the nearby window lashed her naked arse.

He'd torn off her nightgown!

Allowing a fraction of a second for her shock to subside, he spun her around and pulled the tatters of the gown from her arms, picked her up, and set her back on the couch. Violet pulled an afghan blanket from beneath her and covered herself. The room was cold!

"Now I understand why you curse using the word 'buttons,'" he said. "There must have been thousands of them. Much better like this."

No trace of his smile remained. Instead, he stood over her, hands busy removing his cravat, the outline of his thick erection pushing at the confines of his trousers. His gaze swept her body like that of a starving man surveying a meal.

She should be outraged.

Instead, she was thrilled—right down to her bare toes.

"I never liked that nightgown anyway," she said.

"Stop covering yourself," Arthur growled. "I worked hard to be able to see your body."

A sweet lash of pleasure warmed her skin at the command. He pulled the cravat from his neck and ran the strip of cloth over his knuckles. Something about the way he glanced between the cloth and her body aroused her even more, and she licked her dry lips.

His expression bordered on feral. "Another time," he mused, his voice low and dark with need. "Not tonight. Tonight, I have no patience for games."

Had she found the room cold? His words had heated it to one hundred degrees. Good thing, because she discovered the thrill of watching Arthur's face as she peeled back the blanket. His eyes darkened to black, and he dropped the cravat. As the rough yarn snagged on her nipples, he rubbed a hand over his mouth, making a sound she interpreted as *interested*.

"Will you undress as well?" she asked, eager to view the body she'd imagined all this time.

His fingers went to the fastenings at the front of his trousers, then paused.

"Do you remember my disdain for distractions?" he asked. When she nodded, he reached over and pulled the rest of the blanket away from her.

When she opened her mouth to object, he swallowed her words with his soft lips, curled his velvet tongue around her grievances, and stole her complaints. The slick caress of his satin waistcoat against her skin made her restless, and he broke the kiss. Carving a trail of bliss down her neck with the tip of his tongue, he lingered in the gentle dip of her clavicle. Wanting to assuage the need at the juncture of her thighs, Violet shifted below him.

Large, calloused palms gripped her thighs, and he widened her legs. A fleeting embarrassment at her wet core against the fabric of his trousers vanished in the wake of pleasure.

Her hands slipped over his shoulders, hard and heavy as rocks beneath the linen of his shirt. He held the bulk of his weight on his elbows; there was not an ounce of give in the back beneath her roving touch. Growing impatient, she dug her fingers in and pulled him even closer. Tiny sparks set off beneath her lids when he rewarded her by thrusting his hips at the right angle while stroking her nipples with the flat of his tongue. Violet groaned at the sensation.

"I'm sorry," she whispered.

"Not sorry," he whispered against the curve of her ribs. "Never that."

Not content making her crazy with his tongue, the wicked man proceeded to take her hardened nipple in between his teeth and lightly bite down.

She cried out as he alternated between suckling and nipping, while pinching and rolling the other nipple with his fingertips. Her awareness narrowed to his hands and his mouth and the havoc they wrought on her. A prickly swath of heat exploded through her. She shuddered, craving something out of reach.

Her body begged for the warmth of Arthur's skin against hers. She wished more than anything to give him pleasure in return, but he continued to deny her. Instead, he abandoned her nipples for an open-mouthed exploration of the valley between her breasts, then her belly, and finally, toward her aching center.

"Are you . . . ?" She forced the words out in anticipation, wanting to be certain this appealed to him.

"Oh, yes," came his reply.

Arthur's thick curls tickled the bottom of her stomach, and she threaded her fingers through them, relishing the texture of his hair. When his thumbs parted her vulva, she bit her lip to keep from making any more noise. It wouldn't do to divert him from his path.

The instant his tongue tapped at the tiny bud at the red-hot center of her, she let go a cry of approval. Threads of bliss spread out through her body while he traced ever-tightening circles. Every time she made a sound, he rewarded her with more pressure. Even so, her culmination was unattainable. Whenever it approached, he would slow his pace until she could no longer bear the torment.

"Oh, you are cruel," she cried.

A horrible moment ensued when he paused. "My apologies," he said. "Did you want me to stop?"

"No, no, no," she begged. "When I said 'cruel,' I meant 'clever.' Please, please . . ."

Stop? Never. Never in a million years. She wanted to tie him to her couch and never let him leave. Having only read about this activity, the real-life experience far exceeded her most heated imaginings.

"Please, Arthur. Please," she mumbled in an unsteady chant of need.

Taking pity on her, he accepted her command, tending to her intimate flesh until the coil of tension snapped, and a blaze of pure bliss tore through her.

Her shouted praise—of him, of the heavens, of whatever god might be responsible for such a sensation—echoed through the room, and she melted into a puddle of joy.

THREE YEARS AGO, Arthur had stopped a man from being pushed off a building by throwing himself across a gap between two town houses. Hanging by his knees from a gutter to save the bloke was an incredible sensation.

His sense of accomplishment at that stunt was nothing compared to the ocean of satisfaction he was swimming in right now.

"... understand the underlying physiological mechanism to a certain degree," Violet rambled, eyes closed and hands waving as she emphasized her points. "The reality cannot compare. This was ..."

Sublime. Amazingly, he'd given her control, although she was the one lying supine beneath him. Her sighs had commanded his attention. Each moan, each plea was a directive to him for more or less of what she needed.

Arthur raised his head from its comfortable resting place on the soft swell of her stomach. His hand made lazy circles on her plump thigh, relishing the delicate skin beneath his calloused fingertips.

"You've answered many questions tonight," Violet said. "Still, I am curious." She slipped her hand to where his aching cock was trapped behind the fall of his trousers.

Clasping her hand, he stilled her exploration. "Of course you are curious. So am I. There are many sweet and silky places I have not yet discovered. What if I ..." He leaned over to kiss a charming spot below her ear, but stopped when she stiffened.

A quick glance at Violet's face, and Arthur cursed himself for his stupidity. Tiny question marks appeared at the corner of her mouth; her confidence had ebbed. He couldn't tell her that pleasure must be mutual, then push her away.

"Who am I to deny a scientist her discoveries?" he asked, and released her. Her squeak of delight made him laugh out loud and turn them both until she rested atop him. He'd hoped to hold this piece of himself apart from her so it wouldn't hurt so much when he left.

For Violet's sake, he welcomed the pain.

When she opened his trousers and pulled him free, he almost came at the sight of her work-worn hands on the column of flesh. Any other woman of her station would hide the scars and imperfections. On her, they were a badge of honor, a symbol of how hard she toiled and to what end. They were rough and unsteady, and he had never experienced anything so erotic. She crouched over his shins, wrapping those fascinating fingers around the base of his cock, and stroked him.

"Perfect," he assured her. "Just right," he praised. The words spilled from his lips in an effort to light her from the inside.

The entire world disappeared.

All that remained was this bed and this woman and the way she watched him as she leaned over and set the tip of his cock between her damp lips. Then even she disappeared, because his eyes could not be open at the same time his focus centered on her sucking him. Her palms strong and warm around him, she pulled and twisted with measured, torturous strokes. Arthur's entire body came alive, every inch of his skin awake to the smallest friction.

"Agh...uh..."

She was making speech an impossibility. His conscience was prodding him, however, so he managed to form an important question.

"Is this what you want?" he asked. It would kill him if she'd taken on this act out of a sense of obligation.

Her slick hands kept their rhythm as she stared at him, lips swollen, hair in wild disarray.

"I have been longing for the taste of you on my tongue almost from the beginning, Arthur. I want this very much."

Her words slammed into his stomach, and a surge of lust fired through his body. Reaching down, he held her hair taut and angled himself so that when she took him, he would see her expression. Her flush deepened, spreading from her cheeks to her chest.

The sensation was almost more than he could bear as he slid in and out. Lightning gathered at the base of his spine. He lost himself to the feel of flesh on flesh, the sight of her cheeks hollowing, and the sound of the wind hammering against the walls—until the pressure built too high, too fast, and the sky came crashing down.

It could have been seconds or hours—days?—later that Violet made her way back into his arms. He pulled the afghan over both of them, letting a spill of silky curls tumble across his chest. In an act almost painful in its intimacy, he ran his fingers through her unbound hair as she fell asleep.

Gently, so as not to wake her, Arthur pressed the curls to his nose, inhaling lemon drops and cordite—uniquely Violet.

Despite the discomfort of the sagging cushion and an elbow in his groin, it took forever to bring himself to slip from her arms and walk away. Better to leave before they pushed their luck.

This would only get harder the next time.

Because there would be a next time.

This connection between Violet and himself had a power that Arthur—a man who'd practiced twenty years of penitence—could not resist.

14

ARTHUR LEANED AGAINST the windowsill and watched as pale grey clouds bled into an indigo sky. Tiny pellets of snow tumbled into the corners of an alley, swept by brutal wintry winds.

Spring adamantly refused to take up residence in London this year, no doubt put off by the uncanny fogs, clammy tendrils of black and brown that turned the city into a warren of gloom.

By God, it was a beautiful morning.

He turned and took one last look at Violet's workroom door, then ambled down a narrow back staircase, loose-limbed and at peace with the world. There could be hail the size of boulders and swarms of locusts outside, and it wouldn't bother him.

Too early for Cook to be up. The kitchen boy still snored on his cot by the fire. Arthur hung a pot of water over the smoldering coals. A nice cup of strong tea would be just the thing.

Leaning his chair against the wall, he let his mind wander to the workroom upstairs, to where Violet lay tangled in her afghan on the sagging couch. So decadent and sweet were the images filling his head, he almost ignored a slight tickle at the back of his neck. The front legs of his chair hit the floor.

Something was off.

Arthur cocked his head and paid attention to the sounds around him. The boy snoring. The crackle of coals in the fireplace. A horse clopping on the street outside, its cart rumbling along behind it.

Nothing out of the ordinary. Except there was another sound as well, so low as to almost escape notice.

And a scent reminiscent of . . .

Behind him, boiling water began to hiss. Arthur was already dashing through the hallway connecting Beacon House with the club.

"Fire!" he bellowed, knocking on doors as he ran past. He'd set guards in the club. Where were they?

Pattering footsteps heralded a rapid approach.

"What the hell have you been doing?" he yelled. Except it wasn't one of his men. Letty Fenley came racing around a corner, wearing one of the thick brown aprons used in the club's laboratories.

"There is a fire in the storage cupboard," she cried. "That's where Lady Greycliff keeps her flammable supplies."

At the same time, someone else came stomping down the stairs from the third floor. "I put away the canisters, but—" Caroline Pettigrew stopped in surprise. She was dressed like Letty, but her apron was a far sight messier, covered in grease and a slick, acrid-smelling substance.

"What are the two of you doing here at four o'clock in the morning?" Arthur demanded.

Surely someone must miss them. Letty Fenley was an unmarried young lady, daughter of a shopkeeper or no.

At last one of Arthur's men made an appearance, hurtling down the stairs. "Third floor is clear, sir. I checked the rooms when the lady called, 'Fire.'"

More men came running, and Arthur set aside the question of what Letty and Mrs. Pettigrew had been up to. He made his way to the fire, following Letty's directions through the narrow warren of twisting hallways and tiny rooms.

Smoke billowed from under a closed door at the back of the building. Arthur called out orders to his men while trying to convince Letty to leave.

"Get to safety, Miss Fenley. We can manage a small fire," he barked.

Holding buckets sloshing with water, Thomas, Winthram, and two other men came up the stairs and headed toward the closet.

"Wait!" Arthur called to them. "Lady Greycliff said something about this cabinet." Precious seconds ticked past as Arthur tried to remember. "You need to fetch sand instead."

"You remembered. Well done."

Arthur's stomach clenched at the sound of Violet's voice. Masses of curls had escaped from her messy braid. The ragged hem of her robe almost tripped her up as she pushed the locks from her face.

An icy shiver lifted the hairs on his arms as he remembered ripping open the back of her nightgown. What the devil was she wearing beneath her robe now?

The cool, calm part of his brain that was tasked with keeping everyone alive directed the servants to open the windows at either end of the corridor.

The red-hot animal part of his brain was consumed with the image of Violet naked beneath her robe.

Arthur could not stop from reaching out an arm to pull her away from the heat of the fire. She shivered beneath his touch, but her manner remained bright and determined, and her voice was steady over the hubbub.

"Winthram, there is a bucket of sand in the room next door. Show the men to laboratories three, six, seven, and nine," she said. "There are buckets in there as well."

A tarlike stench emanated from the storage cupboard, where an inverted waterfall of blackness rolled out from the bottom and sides of the door. While Letty helped the footmen open the windows, Mrs. Pettigrew edged away from the chaos.

Arthur blocked her escape. "Why were you here so late at night?" he said.

"I am at a critical part of my work. I was in the common area to make a cup of tea when I smelled something burning." She was nervous, her glance darting between Letty and Violet.

"Haven't you perfected the aerosol delivery system? What more was there to do?"

"Caroline," Letty called, "I could use your help over here."

The woman darted clear of Arthur, and he made no protest. Time enough to question her once the fire was out.

Arthur approached the first footman to sound the alarm. "Did you see anyone on this floor?" he asked him.

"No, sir."

Damn. Someone must have seen something.

He turned to Winthram. "Where were you?" he asked.

"I locked the outside doors at two thirty, like always," the doorman said, one hand half raised as if to protect himself from Arthur's frustration. "Then I did my last round—"

Thomas and the other footmen returned with the sand just then. Violet took charge of them, explaining what to expect. Smoke was rising past their knees, flowing along the sides of the corridor, making its way into each of the open rooms.

"Do not try to save the contents of the cupboard at the expense of your safety," she told them. "This may do damage to your lungs."

They opened the door and a mushroom of smoke burst out, curled into a giant wave, then fell to the floor as if it were trying to hide from them. The footmen began dousing each of the shelves with handfuls of sand.

Arthur continued to question Winthram. "What time would you have walked past this corridor?"

"Two forty or thereabouts," the doorman replied.

"Miss Fenley, where was she?"

"I . . . I don't know. Her workroom is on the first floor."

"She came down the stairs from this floor to warn us of the fire," Arthur said. "What was she doing here then?"

They both fell silent, watching Letty and Mrs. Pettigrew handing out water-soaked cloths for the men to put over their mouths.

"Miss Fenley is one of Lady Greycliff's best friends," Winthram whispered.

"Friends are like tin farthings," Arthur observed. "Two-faced and easy to manipulate."

Winthram's shoulders drooped. "Suppose you don't make many friends in your work."

Arthur regarded the man beside him, then returned his scrutiny to Letty. "Friendship requires trust. Trust is easy to shatter and near-impossible to fix once broken."

"Aye, that's true." Winthram adopted a knowing air, but he couldn't fool Arthur. Winthram wanted to believe in the goodness of a man's soul.

Violet bustled around praising the footmen, consoling Letty as to the state of the whitewash, and casting quick glances at Arthur.

"All will be well," she said. "Is that not correct, Mr. Kneland?"

He didn't answer her question. The acrid stench of destruction burned the inside of his nose as he studied the scene.

Thomas took a position at Arthur's side, fingers worrying his unshaven chin. "Whoever it was, they threw rocks at her windows to scare her off."

"Aye. Next came the bomb on the second floor," Arthur replied.

"Then a thief breaks in to steal the lady's papers, and now someone sets out to destroy the materials she needs to finish the work," Thomas concluded.

"What are you thinking?" Arthur asked.

The older man raised his brows and shifted his gaze to Letty. "The explosion and the broken windows. Those are grand gestures—noisy, like."

"A show of intimidation," Arthur said. "Not something a woman would think to do."

"Could be," Thomas said.

"You don't have to pretend your good ideas are my ideas," Arthur chided. "You're better at reading people than me."

"That's because I like them," Thomas pointed out.

Friends are like tin farthings.

Arthur pushed the thought out of his head. "The attempt at theft and the fire. Those are different?"

"Wasn't for show," Thomas said. "Had a purpose."

"To stop Lady Greycliff from completing her work."

Thomas nodded. "Someone knew she wouldn't be intimidated by bricks and bombs. They could have set fire to her workrooms, but they didn't. Someone took care that she wouldn't be hurt."

"Something a friend might do," Arthur said.

"Better an open enemy than a false friend," Thomas said.

Arthur couldn't agree more.

15

ARTHUR READ A smudged copy of the *Morning Chronicle* while he sipped his tea. The kitchen was empty this time of the morning, and he relished the quiet.

In other households, he took his meals apart. Here, Mrs. Sweet had insisted he join the rest of the staff in the cheery kitchen. So much noise—laughter and easy banter, stories told and retold. He knew if life had been different, none of that would feel foreign. His parents had joked together at the table, and he remembered them having company, with a fiddler in the corner and a thick linen cloth to cover the scratched oak table.

Too long ago. No matter how hard Arthur tried, he could not stop listening beneath the noise for the *whoosh* of a blade or the click of a barrel being loaded.

Before the kitchen door opened, he had folded the newspaper and slipped his hand to a hidden pocket where he kept a knife.

Alice was backing into the room, using her hip to hold open the door, since she held a covered tray in both hands. She jumped and uttered a soft cry when she turned to see him sitting there.

"Good morning," he said.

She lifted her chin in a regal manner—no doubt she'd been watching Lady Phoebe—and nodded with composure. "Good morning, sir."

The accompanying sniff of disdain was masterful. Arthur opened his newspaper, covering his amusement with the smudged pages.

Who could blame her? He'd declined her friendly overtures in the last few weeks. He imagined Deoiridh having to work in London, far from home. If his wee sister were in Alice's position, he knew a kind word would go a long way to warm the heart.

"Cold out," he said.

Her eyebrow lifted like a fringed wing. " 'Tis."

Coals popped in the fireplace.

Arthur racked his brains for what to say. He never had difficulty talking to Violet. She was most animated when he asked her about her work. Should he try this with Alice?

"What is on that tray?" he asked.

"Tea for my lady," she said curtly, emptying the tray onto the kitchen counter.

"Did she eat anything?"

Alice glanced at him, then away. "She didn't. There's nothing to tempt her with, either. Could do with a nice batch of black buns, but Mrs. Sweet won't hear of it."

On the counter was an untouched plate of what Mrs. Sweet called digestive biscuits and Thomas called "indigestives."

When one fell off the counter, it bounced three times until it came to rest beneath the kitchen table.

"Well, since we can't eat them, I suppose I could load my pistol with them," Arthur said. "They're less costly than bullets."

Alice turned in surprise. "Was that . . . Was that a joke, sir?"

He considered the question. "Was it funny?"

Alice approached the table, sucking in her bottom lip. "A little."

"Then, yes, it was a joke."

They regarded each other for a moment across the distance. A tiny smile pulled at the corner of Alice's mouth. Arthur's chest filled with pride. He *could* do this, after all.

"Black buns," he said.

"Sir?"

"You . . . you mentioned black buns. Haven't had one in years. I liked the way they smelled coming hot from the oven."

Alice clasped her hands, eyes softening with remembrance. "My mam makes the worst black buns."

"Does she now?" Arthur asked, confused.

Alice laughed. "Every time. No one knows why they taste so odd, when her tatties are heaven and her bread is so fine. One time, my da walked home from Inverness rather than stay one night longer away from her, and he teased her it was because he couldn't live without the taste of her black buns."

She sighed. "What do you miss about home?"

Arthur rubbed his chest while he considered his memories of Deoiridh, but he kept her tucked away for now. It frightened him how easily he'd shared her with Violet. What if he took the memories out too often and they began to fade?

"Well, I don't miss parritch," he said instead.

Alice giggled. "My brother Finlay hates it more than anything. One time . . ."

The maid shared stories of life with five brothers, a ferret, and two terriers while Arthur chuckled and inhaled the comforting smell of tea and onions.

Was the key to making friends the same as the secret to making Violet happy?

Accept people for who they are?

Just be present?

Seemed simple enough—unless you'd spent your life running away.

"ARE YOU SURE we should be doing this?" Letty asked. "What if Mr. Kneland comes in and finds us?"

"Don't be silly," Phoebe retorted. "Who cares what Mr. Kneland thinks? We are justified in using any and all measures to achieve our goals."

"I'm drunk," Violet said.

The three of them were shoulder to shoulder on the couch in Violet's workroom. Upside down.

Violet, Letty, and Phoebe had secreted themselves in the room with a supply of port. ("Father will never notice, and if he does, all the better," Phoebe had declared.) Letty had snuck a box of confections in under her cloak. ("Bilious complaint be damned," she'd whispered at Mrs. Sweet's disapproval.) Like the early days, when they were envisioning a plan for Athena's Retreat, Phoebe had marched around the room, spreading curses aplenty. ("A man can't *really* do that to himself, can he?" Violet asked.)

Violet had missed this camaraderie in the past few months. Letty and Phoebe somehow managed to balance the intensity of their belief in Athena's Retreat with a practical sensibility about how society truly worked. Even more important, laughter with friends was a balm for the soul.

"What if Earl Grantham catches us at it?" Letty continued. "He'll make a terrible fuss."

"Darling, do shut up," Phoebe complained. "You are giving Violet the headache."

"It isn't Letty giving me the headache. I have to sit up."

"How *do* we sit up?" Letty asked. "What if we—ow!"

"Your foot is so large," Phoebe grunted. "Oh . . . oof."

"You are kicking me in the—oh, this dratted corset," Violet cried.

In the end, it took them ten minutes to stand upright. Violet had to have Letty yank her dress in one direction while she twisted her body in the opposite direction to settle her undergarments back into place.

It had been Phoebe's mad idea, as usual. She'd been dressed down by her father again and confined to her house for the past two nights. Although she treated these punishments as a joke, from the occasional bruises glimpsed high on Phoebe's arms, Letty and Violet had their suspicions about how the marquess quelled his daughter's rebellions.

The one time Violet tried to broach the subject, Phoebe gently set her hand over Violet's mouth. "Darling," she'd said. "We leave our nightmares behind in the dark for a reason."

"He found a bundle of my notes regarding Herr Kolbe's work with Herr Schmitt and thought they were billets-doux, so I missed the excitement," Phoebe said now. "I can't believe that Mr. Kneland had the nerve to question where I was last night. Told him I spent my evening lighting metaphorical fires. Less dirty and smelly than literal ones. What were you even doing here so late, Letty?"

"I was simply . . . Oh dear." Letty's port had slopped over the side of her glass. She crossed to a set of cabinets and rummaged through for a rag to clean the mess.

Phoebe turned her attention back to Violet. "The faster you figure out this formula, the faster everything can go back the way it was."

Violet popped a tart in her mouth and moaned with pleasure, then made a face at Phoebe. "It isn't as if I haven't been working on this for the past month. The ratios must be exact. I cannot risk exposing anyone to a mixture that might sicken them even more."

"The problem is not the ratios," Phoebe countered. "The problem is that you've been distracted."

Letty intervened. "We don't blame you for the fire, or the explosion, or any of the current upheaval. Anyone would be distracted by such goings-on."

It hadn't been the fire keeping Violet from her work, but she declined to correct Letty's misconception.

Phoebe frowned. "What you need to do is clear your head of any other thoughts and then concentrate on the formula."

That is how the three of them found themselves with their legs over the back of the couch and their heads touching the floor. Phoebe swore by the practice, but Violet's corsets were unforgiving in any position other than sitting at attention. Even more so after having stuffed herself with tarts and half a bottle of port.

Phoebe managed to appear unflustered and invigorated by the whole experiment. "That was amusing. Did it work, Violet?"

Violet considered the question. "I learned how difficult it is to clear one's mind when confronted with what lives beneath my couch. Does that count?"

Phoebe's amethyst eyes darkened with irritation. "Give the work to me, then. I know enough chemistry of gases to finish the antidote. Then the event can go ahead as planned."

"And put you in danger?" Violet shook her head. "I have Arthur and his gaggle of faux footmen watching my every move. You have no one. I won't do that to you."

"They weren't watching for a fire," Phoebe said with exasperation.

"It doesn't matter. I will finish by the end of this week. I promise." Violet clasped Phoebe's hands in her own. The contrast between her broken nails and the supple cream leather of Phoebe's gloves was lost on neither of the women.

"I believe you." Phoebe smoothed the annoyance from her face. "You can do anything you put your mind to. In fact, the three of us will change the world, each of us in our own way."

"You are prickly," she said to Letty, "but your brain is magnificent." She handed her a glass of port. "You hate the aristocracy, and you have a good reason for it. The Earl Melton treated you poorly."

"Poorly?" Letty said. "You two are the only members of polite society who acknowledge me anymore. He ruined my life."

"No. He is not responsible for your life. You are," Phoebe said. "You are brave and strong and will someday make Melton and his son feel like insignificant toads."

Next, she handed Violet a chipped mug, also filled with a generous dose of port. "And you are kind and generous," she said. "The only woman who could come up with the idea for Athena's Retreat and have the utter lack of self-preservation to see it become a reality."

Phoebe held the bottle aloft and leaped onto a chair. "I am rich and fearless. Too highborn to ignore and too pretty to be taken seriously. We built this club together for women who need our protection. I pledge on all that is holy, namely the gods of sugar and alcohol, that Athena's Retreat will continue its work. No matter what—or who—might stand in our way."

16

~~~~~

RUMOR IS YOU gave Earl Grantham a thrashing the other day. Do you think he had anything to do with the fire?"

In a narrow alleyway in Shoreditch, Arthur and Winthram scrutinized a tiny coffeehouse on the opposite side of the street.

"No," said Arthur. "Grantham's a pain in the arse, but he wouldn't do anything to hurt Lady Greycliff." The earl's affection for Violet was genuine, Arthur would bet anything.

She had that effect on men.

More than once, Arthur had to reach out to the wall and steady himself. Scraping his hand against the rough bricks, he hoped to puncture the disorienting numbness. The aftermath of the fire and the strange emotions plaguing him since he'd left Violet's room this morning had him mistrusting his senses.

He was in deep trouble. Matters of the heart were throwing him off his stride and leading him to doubt like he hadn't since he was a boy.

In the years since he'd left England, there had been women, most of them more sophisticated and experienced than Violet. In all that time, he'd never been so shaken during physical intimacy. He had a limited vocabulary for interactions with other people. What to call his current state? There was a frightening softness at the center of him, as if Violet's untutored caresses and delighted explorations had punctured some vital barrier.

His judgment was damaged. Arthur no longer recognized the inside of his own head. Calling a halt to any thought of continuing his affair with Violet was the smartest thing to do. Time to pick up the threads of the investigation into the Omnis and get out of the club before he did something stupid. Like go back and let her seduce him again.

"He's a big bloke, the earl," Winthram continued. "James said the earl was flat on his back when you left the room, and you hadn't a hair out of place."

"A trick I picked up," Arthur said. "You can toss a man twice your size over your shoulder if you do it right. Not much to it."

A group of young laborers walked by. Arthur shrank into the shadows. For two days straight, he'd run down every clue he could find, and the same name kept popping up.

Adam Winters.

This coffeehouse was a gathering place for suspected Omnis, and Adam Winters was scheduled to speak there. Winthram had insisted on tagging along to point his brother out. They examined the crowd of older, sober-looking men entering.

Winthram scuffed his boot against the crumbling yellow brick of the building next to them. Shilling-sized snowflakes sped past in a crazy spiral and settled in the doorman's hair and eyelashes.

"Might run into trouble you don't want," Winthram said, gaze cast down and away. "I'll stay for a while and help keep watch."

Arthur frowned. "This is a rough crowd. You could get hurt."

Winthram's head shot up, and he scowled. "I can take care of m'self. I've had to fight my way out of a tight spot before."

Arthur held his hands in the air. "I didn't mean hurt from a fight."

Winthram's mouth moved as he chewed on this. Clear as day, the younger man didn't want Arthur's sympathy.

"I've had plenty of time to get used to Adam's words to me. It doesn't matter anymore."

Arthur had been five when Deoiridh was born, a late-life surprise to his parents. He might have resented the interloper in his snug, ordered existence. Instead, he'd lost his heart to the tiny creature the first time she smiled. Arthur's sister had opened his eyes to the beauty of the world. Her giggles broke the oppressive silence of the empty landscape, and he threw himself into the task of guiding and protecting this tiny, fragile being through life. In turn, she greeted him every morning with arms wide-open, trusting him to keep her safe.

When influenza came to their vale, she died as she'd lived, holding her arms out to her older brother, asking him to help her.

If Deoiridh had lived and made the same choice as Winthram, Arthur would have been conflicted—but he never would have abandoned her. Could Adam Winters not accommodate himself to his brother's decision, as strange as it must have seemed at first?

Arthur knew little about love. However, he'd always imagined it grew to encompass other people, not narrowed as time passed.

"It's his loss," Arthur said. "He'll come to regret it."

Disbelief twisted Winthram's pinched features. His shoulder jerked up and to the side to signal his discomfort with the subject. Silence settled between them as the carters shouted to one another and the crowd shuffled by.

"There he is." Winthram pulled Arthur back into the recess of the alleyway. "The meeting must be starting."

Sure enough, Adam Winters was descending from a hackney across the street. He resembled Winthram, with his slight build and neat features, but he was older, heavier in the jowls, and broader in the chest. A few burly men accompanied him, their heads swiveling as they surveyed the pedestrians in either direction.

"Right. I'm going in," Arthur said. "I'll listen to the speeches, then stay on afterward and see what I can learn about what the Omnis have planned and if anyone mentions the club or Beacon House. You stay here."

Winthram's slender frame sank in on itself.

Arthur sighed. "Simple physics, that over-the-shoulder move. Shouldn't take long to demonstrate. Half an hour at most."

Winthram lit up like a candle. Arthur wagged his finger. "One move. I haven't time to muck about. In a matter of days, I'll be on my way."

"ARE WE SERFS, to labor in a lord's fields? Why is it assumed that if we use our bodies to carry out a full day's work, then our minds must remain blank? What do these men fear from educating their labor force? They fear accountability. They fear consequences. They fear *justice*."

Warped walls of pine, stained black with age, vibrated from the stomping of dozens of feet and the scraping of chairs as a group of thirty or so men shuffled around to find space in the tiny back room. The sagging plaster ceiling released the odors of the thousands of pipes smoked in here over the years and, mixed together with the smell of a roomful of unwashed men, made Arthur's nose itch.

Adam Winters stood at the front of the crowd. Winters's deep-set eyes and high cheekbones were the mirror image of Winthram's, but he exuded a dark charisma that his younger brother lacked.

Sweat glistened on his forehead as he continued to speak about universal suffrage in an eloquent takedown of the Reform Act of 1832. The men followed his words with an astonished intensity, as though bemused by their own excitement for his message.

If Winters could bend this group to his will, what effect might he have on his younger brother or even an impressionable young woman? Both Letty and Mrs. Pettigrew claimed to have lost track of time when the fire broke out. Difficult to argue when he'd seen the same thing happen to Violet.

"Mark my words, he's a man to watch," opined a man next to him. Arthur turned in surprise to see Earl Grantham at his elbow.

"What are you doing here?" he asked Grantham in a heated whisper.

"The Crown considers the Omnis to be a threat," the earl answered in a low voice, adopting an authentic working-class accent. "Edward Oxford's assassination attempt on Her Majesty wasn't a one-off. Better question is, what are you doing here?"

Arthur inspected Grantham more closely and grimaced in surprise. Dressed in a plain pair of brown trousers beneath a loose-fitting coat, his glossy hair was hidden by a felted cap, his boots as dusty as the next man's. Other than his height, the earl fit right in with the crowd full of laborers.

Grantham nodded in acknowledgment of the scrutiny. "Wasn't always an earl. There's a group of us who came from like backgrounds and now can do some good with our changed circumstances. I've been to a few of these meetings before with them. No one will question my being here today."

"As a spy or as a supporter?" Arthur asked.

The earl scanned the men closest to them, but they were intent on Winters's words. He leaned over and whispered through clenched teeth. "Leave this to me, Kneland, and get the hell out of here. Violet sent me word about what you did."

The floor dropped out from beneath Arthur, and his palms grew damp. What the devil?

"She said the fire was an accident," Grantham growled. "You and I both know better. It happened on your watch. You failed."

Giddiness washed through Arthur, and he nearly laughed aloud. For a terrifying few seconds, he'd thought Grantham knew what had happened in Violet's room. Relief must have shown in his face, for Grantham's stern mouth twisted into a sneer. "Start packing, Kneland. Your days in Violet's presence are numbered."

Of the fifty-two methods Arthur knew to bring a man to his knees, thirty-one of them were lethal. For a long moment, he considered the ones left to him, especially those aimed at an opponent's nether regions.

Lucky for Grantham's hope for offspring, common sense prevailed.

When the crowd roared in response to Adam Winters's words, Arthur made his way to the exit, leaving an enemy at his back.

17

⁘

ARTHUR SHOOK HIS hand out, then touched the tip of his thumb to the tips of his fingers. No matter he'd worn gloves and scrubbed his hands, the shadow of ink still stained his fingers. It had taken him hours to complete the first of two letters he'd written today, and he'd gone through a shilling's worth of paper in the process.

The missives he'd penned had forced an examination of the choices he'd made since one grave sin had set him on his path twenty years ago. The process left him restless, pacing the halls while his hand settled over a tender ache in his chest.

He'd told himself to walk this particular hallway because a bank of windows at one end made it more vulnerable. This was a lie. He knew very well who was working in this wing today. In fact, if Arthur was lucky, he'd turn the corner and run into . . .

"Aaachooo!" Johnson staggered into the wall opposite an open doorway, propelled by the strength of his sneeze.

Huh. Not who Arthur had expected to see.

"Are you all right, Johns—"

"Meeerchoo!" The poor footman was gasping now, eyes red and

watery. He pointed at the room and shook his head. "Can't . . . breed . . .
Ub sorry."

"I'll take over from here. Go see Mrs. Sweet." Arthur flinched in
sympathy as more sneezes racked the footman's powerful body.

Once Johnson was out of sight, Arthur scanned the empty corridor, then peered up at the heavens and nodded in acknowledgment.

He knocked gently at the open door of a small stillroom. Violet
stood across the room, next to a low ceramic basin set into a counter,
her head bent over a sheaf of paper, her toes tapping in a furious
rhythm. Her experiments must not have been going well. Soot clung
to the tight sleeves of her cambric gown, and she'd discarded the
apron he'd seen her in earlier.

"Come in," she called in a low, sweet voice, never looking up from
her work.

Johnson having left, Violet needed a guard with her. That was the
reason Arthur stepped inside, locking the door behind him. Not the
sliver of creamy skin exposed at her collarbone, where her shawl had
slipped away, nor the impulse to cover that vulnerable part of her.

Bunches of dried flowers and herbs hung alongside three large
cabinets full of glass jars and bottles, and the scent of mint and sage
hovered in the air. The sole light filtered through faded crimson curtains covering a bank of high windows.

"Johnson appears to have a sensitivity to something in here," Violet said. "I know you always want a guard with me, but if you wait . . ."
She scratched out something and then sucked the end of her pen.

Her manner could be interpreted as absentminded or naive, but
Arthur knew that Violet walked in two worlds at once: the world in
which everyone else lived and the world within her mind, where myr-
iad connections were made every second.

While Arthur waited for her to return to him, he examined a series
of spigots and pipes overhanging the basin.

He would miss this place. Each time he turned around, a fascinating discovery sat waiting for him. If he were a different man or if this were a different time . . .

"My work has been progressing much faster than I'd anticipated," Violet said.

Arthur nodded, spinning a knob to let a flow of water rush past. So he would be leaving sooner than he'd expected. What was he to say?

"That is good news."

She set aside her pen and gave him her full attention. "However, I've reached a point in the work where I can't progress. I'm wondering if you could help me."

He stooped to examine her papers. A trail of numbers and symbols lurched across the page, devolving into a mess of scratches and naughty words scribbled in the margins.

"I'm not sure how I can help you, other than mentioning that this part here . . ." He pointed to a word. "This is anatomically impossible."

"I had something less challenging in mind." She swallowed, turning to the basin of water and washing the ink from her hands. Peeking at him, she continued. "It became apparent from our mutual enjoyment the other night that you and I are physically compatible."

Arthur raised a brow at this *massive* understatement. Unless *compatible* had another definition. Explosive, perhaps.

She continued. "Sometimes, when I reach a block in my work, vigorous activity will help."

"Vigorous activity," he repeated.

"Extremely vigorous. In the interest of science, of course."

"Of course."

He should make this easier for her, but he admired the darkening color on her cheeks.

The tiny smile slipped away from the corner of her mouth.

"I remember you saying you did not want a child," she said. "I never conceived a child with Daniel. It doesn't mean, however, that pregnancy is out of the question."

The urge to tease her melted beneath the wave of sadness swirling around her. Instead, he placed a palm on her shoulder, and she tipped her head to rest her cheek on the back of his hand. For a moment, he forgot to breathe.

Violet gestured to a glass bowl filled halfway with a clear, citrus-smelling liquid. "There are many ways to prevent conception. A few of our members—" She paused. "You must keep this a secret," she pleaded. "We could get into serious trouble if anyone found out the ladies are refining methods to control a woman's fertility."

Arthur gave her a nod of encouragement. "I would never say anything."

They stood so close their sleeves brushed. A ghost of pleasure from their night together rose beneath his skin.

Curious, he nudged the bowl with a finger, and the contents swayed back and forth. At the bottom of the bowl lay a sea sponge, whittled to a tiny sphere, inside a finely netted bag, with the ends in a loop made of silken thread.

He thought he knew what it was, but a strange idea occurred to him.

"Do you drink this?" he asked.

"Oh, no. The sponge soaks up the liquid," she explained. "You can use vinegar, but this particular liquid contains a distillation of quinine."

"The malaria cure?" He knew about sheaths, of course, but hadn't much experience with any other type of conception prevention.

"One inserts the sponge in through the woman's vagina until it is flush against the womb. It acts as a barrier. Afterward, you remove the sponge by pulling on the loop."

Arthur frowned. "Will this interfere with your enjoyment if we make love again?"

Make love.

The words had popped out unplanned.

"No," she said. "If anything it may enhance it for both of us if we do not have to worry."

With that, the final leash on his self-control was lifted and questions of right or wrong fell away. He tried, one last time, to hold on to sanity.

"There is nothing prudent about this," Arthur said. "I leave in a matter of days. You cannot risk the scandal if this affair is discovered, Violet."

He was speaking to himself, too.

"We will be careful. We can keep secrets," she said.

He took her in his arms from behind, and her shawl slipped to her ankles. Trapping her in his embrace, he covered the tiny knobs at the top of her spine with his mouth. Unhooking the back of her dress, he traced the outline of her bones with the tip of his tongue. She tasted like a warm summer night in Brest, like salt and starlight and the knowledge that home lay so close and yet so far away.

"Keep secrets? Oh, no," he whispered, lips still pressed to her flesh. "Why keep secret how much I liked the feeling of your mouth on my cock, the way you moved beneath me, and how much I want to be *inside* you."

The *shush* of her dress sliding to the floor produced a counterpoint to the rhythm of their breathing. Violet trembled as he pulled the ties of her petticoats loose. A cascade of ivory cotton puddled at her feet.

"What if someone . . . ?" she said.

"I locked the door. We are safe."

"We are not safe," she disagreed. "The way you touch me. I will come to crave it. The things you say. I will come to believe you, Arthur. That is dangerous."

What could he say to this? He kissed her again in answer to her fears as he pulled the pins from her thick, heavy curls, freeing them from the tiny metal prisons. He'd dreamed about Violet's unbound hair since their first night together. Roamed the hallways in search of its bright, clean scent. Now, masses of it were loose in his hands, and he memorized the texture.

Her wild tresses created a frame for Violet's face, and a younger, hopeful woman peered out at him. Sympathy for the person she'd been as a bride swelled within him. If he went back in time, what could he have said to eighteen-year-old Violet? What would he have told the eighteen-year-old Arthur, come to think of it?

Don't love? Don't invest your heart in something destined to bring you pain?

Their younger selves would never have listened.

Her dark brown eyes, her fairy pools, remained fixed on him as he took his leisure in appreciating her beauty.

"I agree this is dangerous," he said, tracing the line of her jaw to the arc of her neck with his thumb. "The silk of your skin might be fatal."

The straps of her worn chemise slipped from her shoulders to her elbows. The thin material hung on her full breasts for a moment before he pulled it off, and her nipples hardened. Angry red lines streaked across her breasts and ribs, marks from the corset boning.

He bent and soothed the welts with his tongue, growing harder each time she gasped in pleasure.

"The sweetness of your breasts could prove lethal," he teased.

Picking her up, he turned them both around, and Violet wrapped her legs around his hips. He walked them to a low table, set her on the edge, then fetched the glass bowl, placing it to one side of her.

It should have been him with the power in the room. He stood fully dressed and carrying a dagger or two on his person. She wore nothing but a transparent pair of drawers and her stockings, her house slippers having fallen off.

Instead, Violet took command of the encounter. Reclining onto her elbows, she arched her back, grinning with a pride in her appearance he'd never seen in her before. In the crimson light, the edges in the room blurred. Lambent with desire, she shook her hair and spread her legs wider.

Arthur set the tiny sponge to her tender flesh. She yelped in surprise, coming off the table and grabbing his arms. Pulling her into a kiss, he licked the giggles from her lips, holding her tight against him with one hand while the other brushed the sponge lightly over her entrance. As their kisses grew deeper and more heated, he pressed his thumb against the center of her in a gentle rhythm.

In between kisses, she directed him, praising him with enthusiasm as he worked his thumb in circles. The slit in her drawers teased him with glimpses of her, and he pulled away to watch his fingers disappearing inside.

"You are beautiful," he rasped, hands shaking with need. "No, not beautiful. There isn't another word that comes into my tiny male brain at this moment to describe you. It might be grace that sets you apart from any other woman I've encountered," he declared. "Grace and, of course, the most astonishing brain in England."

Head tilting in flirtation, Violet reached for his coat and pulled him between her spread legs. "I'd have never guessed, from the way you hauled me about on the first night we met, how silver-tongued a charmer you could be, Arthur Kneland."

In all his years of watching men and women perform terrible acts of cruelty and ignorance, he'd stopped hoping to find someone like her. Not perfect, but a light in the world nonetheless.

Essential to know such a light existed when one lived close to the darkness.

Reaching up, Violet set her work-stained hands on his cheek, holding his gaze.

"Don't worry," she said. "I understand we are bound by the same limits you set the other night. This cannot be permanent."

Her history of rejection and disappointment lay in the tiny creases above the bridge of her nose and in the wariness with which she received his compliments. She was not a child, and Arthur did not treat her as such by denying her words.

"I can't undo twenty years of vigilance," he said. "We cannot forget who I am. Who I am not."

Leave aside who he wished to be. Leave everything aside for this moment.

"I would never expect sudden declarations. I ask only . . ."

She threaded her fingers through his hair, clenching them, in an echo of how he'd held her the night before. The slight pain gave an edge to his desire, and his balls tightened in anticipation. Wrapping one leg around his waist, she pulled him to her and licked the closed seam of his mouth. When he opened his lips in response, she drew his tongue into her mouth and suckled, then broke the kiss, lips damp and swollen.

"I ask that you let those reasons stay outside that door," she said.

"I wish . . ." Arthur fell silent.

A wish is a weighted object, heavy with history and the burdens of expectations and responsibilities. It would crush them both if he were to speak his aloud.

Instead, he told her, "I promise."

Promises could be made with the softest caress of her breasts and belly. Made in the gentle worship of her round knees and curved thighs. Promises could be made while honoring the sweet center of her with all the skill at his command.

If he could not say the words and would never hear them from her lips, he could plant his promises beneath her skin.

WHETHER HER THROAT was sore from letting loose words of praise or from the pain of holding back an unnamed emotion, Violet could not be certain. Thoroughly spent, she lay spread on the table in front of Arthur, one leg draped over his shoulder.

When he raised his head from between her thighs, a self-congratulatory smile on his face, Violet realized he remained clothed while she was bare except for her garters and stockings. Unhooking her leg, she rose and tugged at the waistband of his trousers. His erection strained against the material, evidence that he was not unaffected by her pleasure.

"That was a passable attempt at turning the human body from a solid to a liquid," she teased him.

"Passable," he scoffed, his relaxed tone at odds with the way his palm covered her hands, as if uncertain whether to stop her or not. "Is that a challenge? If so, you may not have voice to issue another if I accept."

He allowed her to unbutton the fall of his trousers, glancing first at the door, then at the bank of windows.

"Do you sleep, Arthur?" Violet asked.

"Yes, of course, I . . . ah—" His voice broke into a hiss when she held him in her hand. Stroking him from root to end, she clasped the thick length of him with enough pressure to wring a groan from him.

"Your attention is distracted for those few hours of the day, yet nothing terrible happens?" she asked, feigning innocence while her thumb circled the tip of him with deliberate gentleness, teasing a reaction.

Ruddy and engorged, the head of his cock glistened in the low light. Violet considered taking it into her mouth and bringing him to his knees. That wasn't what she wanted, though.

She wanted to see him bare before her. She craved the sensation of his skin beneath her fingertips. His trousers clung to his slim hips, and the long tails of his linen shirt hid his flat stomach from view. How maddening this attempt to keep his distance by hiding behind layers of wool and linen.

Didn't he understand? She didn't need to see his flesh to know he was human.

"There is so little time left," she reminded him. "I won't have you leave behind this one regret."

After the slightest hesitation, he slipped the sponge inside her. Scooping her up, he took a seat in a hard-backed chair, settling her in his lap. The rough weave of his pants abraded the soft skin on the inside of her thighs as she straddled him.

"Just this once," he whispered, dusting her cheekbones with tiny kisses. Holding on to her hips, he shifted, so she hovered above the length of him.

She'd told him they would be honest, and as she let the tip of him inside her, she spoke the truth.

"I will not ask of you more than you can give. You have seen every piece of me." She stopped speaking for a moment to relish the slow stretching of her passage in his wake.

"So sweet," he whispered as he nuzzled the curve of her neck.

"Hmm," she said, too full for words as gravity did the work drawing out the pleasure/pain of him filling her. Invisible threads pulled with a delicious tension, from the tips of her fingers to the top of her scalp. When she did not think any more of him would fit, he pressed her hips down another inch and ground against her. They rocked against each other with tiny thrusts. Friction sent blissful pulses through her body.

To gain purchase, Violet clutched Arthur's waistcoat in her fists. The raised threads of embroidery rubbed against her nipples. She writhed on his lap, wanted to pull the clothes from his body, baring him to her gaze.

"I can see you," she warned. "Through your layers of cloth, your seventy thousand daggers, and the grim facade you wear every day. You are beautiful, Arthur, and I wish you would not hide it."

All movement stopped. Deep within, Arthur pulsed in time with her heartbeat. Violet clenched around the length of him. He filled her utterly: thoughts, body, and heart.

With a tenderness that made her ache, he brushed a tear from her cheek and let his armor fall apart.

One second was all he gave her.

One second to see him bereft of protection. One second, and everything he felt could be read upon his face.

One second was all it took for her to fall in love.

She shuddered against him. With an inarticulate cry, he lifted his hips. Wrapping his arms around her back, he took control of the tempo, pushing Violet past the point of breathlessness to a place outside her experience.

When her climax came, and the world turned upside down around her, Violet could still see Arthur's face in that last unguarded moment.

18

❦

HAPPIER THAN A well-fed tarantula in the desert, Violet crooned sweetly to her formulas when Phoebe burst in on her and slammed a bonnet on her head.

"You are due at the Mensonge studios in half an hour," Phoebe cried. "Do not 'But, but, but.' Fanny Armitage has been comparing your last gown to a chewed-up jellyfish, and I won't stand for it."

"But . . . but . . . ," Violet said, though she knew it would do no good. "I canceled that fitting."

Phoebe hustled her downstairs. "I rescheduled it. You will have a new gown for the event, or I will make you wear mine."

Violet beheld Phoebe's yellow silk skirt covered in waterfalls of lace beneath an ermine cape with matching muff. Each stitch lay perfectly straight; every material was of the highest quality. The very existence of such an ensemble intimidated Violet into submission.

"I told Mama I would be back within the hour," Phoebe said, "so I will have to trust you not to panic. Now, go forth and fashion."

"Tell Mr. Kneland where I'm going," Violet called out to Mrs. Sweet as she left. "I'm taking a guard with me, but you can be certain he'll be cross when he finds out."

In the luxurious fitting rooms of the Mensonge studios, she stood upon a pedestal flanked by purple velvet curtains. Violet had forgotten how unbearable she found the process of being fitted for gowns, especially those designed for slimmer women. It pained her to see her flaws in the dressing room mirror. Daniel's complaints rang in her ears, and she fretted about being away from her work for so long.

Did no one else have places to go and dangerous criminals to thwart?

To her surprise, Madame Mensonge presented Violet with a dress made of watered silk the same color green as new shoots in spring. With a scandalous bodice and a cunning underskirt of bright gold peeping out from beneath the draped overdress, it fit as though it had been made for her.

"This isn't what I ordered," Violet said. Still, she held the dress to her chest.

One reason Lady Potts was fascinated with tarantulas was their ability to shed their skin, leaving the empty replicas behind when it was time to change. Violet felt an itch beneath her skin as though her body were readjusting itself.

At the last moment, Violet lost her courage and sent the dress away. Instead, she chose a copper-colored gown of a more modest cut.

"Ridiculous waste of time," she muttered to herself on the ride home. "Who cares about stupid gowns and stupid gloves and stupid— oh!" The carriage swerved, and she fell to the floor. Outside, angry men shouted, and her coachman screamed at the horses.

They rounded one more turn, then the carriage shuddered to a halt.

On the left-hand side of the road, a group of large, rough-looking men had cornered a thin, frightened youth in front of a small lecture hall. Something in the way the youth held himself drew Violet's notice.

She leaned out the coach window and shook her fist at the men. "Stop, you bullies. Stop it right now!"

Ignoring her coachman's panicked protests, Violet jumped from the carriage. Hurrying across the street, she pushed her way through the circle of angry men to try and reach Winthram's side. With an astonished curse, the guard vaulted off the back of the carriage and followed.

"Run and fetch the watch," she cried to him. "They won't do anything to me, but Winthram is in danger. Please!"

Two burly men stood to either side of Winthram but stepped back at Violet's approach. The doorman's thin face twisted in dismay at the sight of Violet coming to his rescue.

"Oh no, my lady," Winthram cried. "How could Mr. Kneland let you out on your own? You must get back to the carriage right away! This is no place for you."

A small part of Violet acknowledged this was not a sensible choice of actions, but her back was up now.

"My groomsman has gone to fetch the watch," she said in a loud, clear voice, "and there are pistols in my carriage. The coachman is not afraid to use them."

For a moment, the men surrounding Winthram hesitated, until one man scoffed and spit at her feet.

"Think we're scared of the watch? You've no idea what we c'n do to 'em," the man crowed.

A current of malice charged the crowd. Violet's heart jumped to her throat as the loose circle of men tightened around her. Winthram tried to push her behind him at the same time she grasped his arm, hoping to pull him back to the carriage.

Arthur would be furious.

Here, in a most inconvenient place for an epiphany, an elemental fact about Arthur became clear to her. The impassive facade he presented to the world, that curtain of stillness, was not erected to keep people out. His walls were meant to keep his emotions within.

Arthur would be furious, but he'd hide that rage and worry. If something happened to Violet, he would never forgive himself, and never show the slightest hint to anyone how much it grieved him.

Violet gripped Winthram's arm tighter. She wanted, more than anything, to see Arthur again. She would not be the cause of any more pain to him.

Sweet relief rushed through her when a door to the hall behind them slammed open. The threatening crowd froze when a tall man emerged.

"Stand down, stand down!" he shouted. "If you want to be treated with dignity, behave with such."

He wore the clothing of a laborer but without the patina of grime. The rakish set of his felted cap gave Violet the impression that his garments were more a message than protection from the elements. Auburn sideburns glinted in the watery March sunlight, and the man squinted at the sky when he adjusted the plain cambric scarf at his neck.

"Winthram, is he family to you?" Violet whispered to the doorman when she noticed the striking similarities of their features.

"Not according to him," Winthram replied.

Winthram's brother—for, surely, it must be—strolled with apparent unconcern into the circle of men and let his gaze travel over Violet's person in a manner a fraction shy of offensive.

"There are too many men out here," he said. "We don't need the Riot Act read. Get on your way."

With a few muttered protests and a half-hearted show of reluctance, the men backed away, filing into the hall.

This was the man Arthur believed to be behind the threats to her. A ripple of apprehension tinged with fascination pricked the backs of her hands when he fixed his gaze on her. While she wouldn't classify him as handsome, something compelling emanated from his person.

"I regret we have no one here to introduce us," he said. "I am Adam Winters." Winters sketched an insolent bow.

Winters? Violet looked at Winthram in question, but the young man's attention was fixed on his brother's face. He stepped between Violet and his brother, despite the slight trembling in his frame.

"I won't let you hurt Lady Greycliff," the young man declared.

"Look at you." Winters shook his head. "You told me you were leaving everything behind, including the people who loved you, to be true to yourself. Is this how you define 'freedom'? Bowing and scraping to highborn ladies. Is that who you are, Hen? A servant?"

"I *am* being true to myself," Winthram protested. "I do honest work for my wages."

"He does indeed," Violet seconded. "He is invaluable to us and is paid well for his services."

Winters scoffed. "Paid well according to whom? Do you even know what it costs to keep a family in London? Are you familiar with the long hours and backbreaking work involved in domestic service, my lady?"

"Lady Greycliff isn't like other toffs," Winthram said.

"No?" Winters's response bordered on sarcastic. "What has she done to earn her fortune other than marry into it? Does she or anyone in her class make anything? Contribute to the common defense? What does the ruling class do other than perpetuate itself and hinder the growth and well-being of the lower classes? How exactly is she different?"

Despite the showy flourishes of his deep voice, Winters's sincerity rang through. Violet had never considered these questions and had no ready answer.

Winters focused on Winthram. "And your honest work is to serve these people?"

"You make a compelling argument," Violet said. "You are a member of Omnium Democratia, I assume?"

Winters smiled, but his expression held an edge and he stared at Winthram when he answered. "That organization has recently been made illegal, my lady. Though I admit to sharing their ideals, I've never participated in any of the riots the government tries to blame on the Omnis."

"You haven't said anything against them, though," countered Winthram. "You have so much sway, Adam. I've seen you change folks' minds with a speech and a handshake. Now, you travel with a group of bully boys. Your crowds are getting rowdier and angrier. This will end poorly."

Winters dropped his veneer of amused distaste and squared off with his brother. "Come now, Hen. I taught you this myself. Never in history has power shifted in a civilization without radical movement."

"Fear and anger are like fires," Winthram argued. "When they burn out, who's left hurting? You once talked about hope. About solidarity."

"If you want things to change, stand with me, Hen. Come home."

Unabashed longing colored Winters's voice. Winthram must have heard it, too. Shaking his head, he sighed. "If I did, would you call me 'brother'?"

The older man's expression closed, although he could not manage to put the facade of ambivalence on again.

"No. I want my sister back, not . . . whoever you think you are now." Winters's voice hovered between grief and dismissal as he walked toward the hall. "If you change your mind, if you miss your family even the slightest bit, you know where to find me."

Winthram watched his brother turn away and shut the door.

"I'm sorry, Winthram," Violet said. "Someday . . ."

He rolled his shoulders, took off his hat, pushed his hair into a neat coif, then settled the hat back on his head. Mouth thin with resolve, he stared at the closed door.

A shrill whistle sounded as the watch approached. Violet accepted the arm Winthram held out to her, and they returned to her carriage.

Violet turned to him. "Why were you there if you knew what he might say? My goodness, there's a chance you could have been hurt."

"Chances are meant to be taken when it comes to love," the young man said. He spoke without inflection, as if unaware of the power in his words. "We can't always choose who we love, my lady. Even when a person disappoints us, it doesn't kill the part of them we care about. Caring for someone else is half the story."

"The other half is yourself," she said.

"Yes," Winthram said. "Love can't be in one direction. If I go back to them as Henrietta, I'm asking them to love a lie. Can't be loved by my family—by anyone else—unless I love myself."

Tears pricked at the back of Violet's eyes.

Since Daniel's death, she had convinced herself that love might have come had she been a better wife or given him a child. Had love been waiting for her all along? Did happiness have nothing to do with setting up a nursery or throwing a successful dinner party?

She'd cut off her anger, her hopes, her true self, to fit into a box labeled *lady* and *wife*.

Years wasted trying to be good enough for Daniel to love, when she could have been taking a lesson from Winthram.

Everything inside her had been frozen.

Up ahead, the sun waited.

❧❧❧

"YOU COULD HAVE been *killed*."

Arthur's jaw clenched so hard the muscles in his cheeks bunched.

"The watch was there before anything could have happened, and Winthram did a fine job of protecting me. My, you have a lengthy stride." Violet huffed, cheeks red from keeping pace with him as they walked down the hallway.

Arthur relented, and she patted her chest as they slowed. "Consider, please, the average lung capacity of a woman wearing a . . . It's unladylike to say the word out loud, but it starts with a 'c' and ends in '-orset' and has me in its steel grasp."

He sympathized and slowed his tread even more, remembering the raised red welts on her waist yesterday.

"As I was saying, there was no immediate danger. Winthram had complete control of the situation."

They were on their way to the third floor, where the fire had broken out. Arthur wished to test a theory about the exits and entrances there. He was not convinced that Letty Fenley and Mrs. Pettigrew were telling the truth.

"What did you think of him?" Arthur asked.

"Winters?"

It was delightful to watch Violet when she considered a question. Her thoughts ran through a complex system of twists and turns, much like the spigots and pipes in her lab, at such a rate he could almost hear the process.

Was it mad to find a woman's mind as alluring as her body?

"He is compelling—in a dark, magnetic fashion."

Obviously, Violet's brain was working sluggishly today.

"Dark and magnetic, eh?" he grumbled. "Anything else? Smell nice? Well-made?"

"Well-made?" She tapped a finger to her chin, and his jaw clenched even more. He'd have a headache later. "I'm afraid I didn't notice."

Excellent. Her faculties were working again.

"However charismatic he wished to appear, he seemed lonely and nervous. Yes, there was an undercurrent of fear in his manner," she said. "He misses Winthram."

"The Omnis are in trouble," Arthur said. "You are close to nullifying their weapons, and, more worrisome, the government is poised to break up the movements in the north. A scared man does stupid things."

He hardened his voice. "Which is why you should not have left without telling me."

Therein followed a convoluted explanation about copper gowns and yellow silk and intimidating capes. All the while, scenario after scenario where the watch did not come, where she and Winthram did not emerge from the carriage to find him waiting and ready to wring their necks, played out in his head.

Disturbed by the images, he picked up the pace.

"Have you tried walking?" she asked him.

He scowled. "I am walking."

"You are prowling," she said.

"What does that mean?"

"That way you walk as though you are hunting prey, rather than simply strolling along a corridor like the rest of us mortals."

Arthur couldn't think of a reply. *Rest of us mortals?* When they reached the doorway connecting the two parts of the club, a tingling in his neck halted his steps.

Something about the door was different. He bent to examine where it sat flush with the carpet, running a finger along the door's edge.

"Wouldn't it be easier to lock the door and give each of the club members a key?" he asked.

When Violet didn't answer, he glanced up to find her examining him with blatant appreciation. Some of his anger melted away.

"Is anything amiss?" he asked, biting down on a smile.

"No. Nothing missing," Violet said. "All where it should be, in exactly the right proportions."

He pivoted on his heels to face her, bringing his knees close enough to touch her skirts. Taking his time, he brushed against her body on purpose as he stood, admiring the flush that entered her cheeks.

"I asked you about a key," he said.

"Of course. You asked me about . . ." She frowned. "Are you trying to mesmerize me, Arthur?"

"Mesmerize you?"

"Yes. Is it taught in assassin school?" she asked. "How to make a woman confused with a look?"

"You are the one distracting *me*," he countered. "Lady Greycliff, is there a key to this door?"

"Oh, back to business, are we?" she teased. "We tried a lock once. Everyone kept forgetting where they put their keys."

"Everyone?"

Arthur stared at Violet.

She stared back.

"Me. It was me. I kept losing my key." Violet pushed past him and reached for the door handle. "Now, I have already lost precious time— first with the fitting and then with your lectures. Don't forget to duck."

"What the . . . ?"

For two seconds, Arthur's entire misbegotten life flashed before his eyes as a giant metal ball covered in two-inch spikes came hurtling directly toward his face. Within the space of an inhalation, he bent his knees, twisted his torso to the right, and grabbed Violet around the waist. On the exhalation, he continued the descent, pulling them both to the floor a mere half second before the missile completed its near-fatal path.

"I said, 'Duck,'" Violet complained from beneath his prone body. "Not 'Throw me to the ground.'"

Above Arthur's head, the spiked metal ball swung back and forth, suspended from a chain.

He rolled off Violet but kept hold of her arms as he stared at the instrument of death while waiting for his heart to dislodge from his throat.

"*Duck*? That was your warning?"

"I trusted your reflexes," she said.

Peering over at her, Arthur couldn't tell if she was joking. "Why is there a mace swinging over our heads?"

"That is what I wanted to show you. It was Caroline's idea. She thought you would appreciate its simplicity," Violet explained with cheerful calm.

As though they hadn't just *narrowly avoided death*.

"A clever mechanism," she said. "Once you open the door, a hook is released and—"

"For God's sake, how could you think a mace was better than a key?" He was coming undone. The women in the building were turning him inside out. Later, he would take Winthram and Thomas out to drink beer and, if he was lucky, punch things—thus restoring sanity to his world.

"I wasn't the only one who voted against keys," Violet muttered. "The last time we had them, Milly locked us in. Poor Winthram broke a toe kicking in the door. Another time, Miss Orphelia Higgins picked the lock with her tools, but they kept breaking and getting stuck in the lock. Then there was that fire once when someone else hypothesized that if we lit pressured gas on fire to melt the—"

"Stop," Arthur begged her, tilting his head so that their foreheads touched. "This hurts my ears. Flying maces. Pressured-gas fires." He lifted his head. "What happens if the club members forget to duck when they open the door?"

A slight headache awoke at the scenarios the question conjured, and he filled his lungs with Violet's calming scent: an absurd mix of lilacs and copper. "Again, a key would solve . . . Could it be the excess use of your brains somehow interferes with the instinct for survival?"

"I thought you'd be pleased," Violet said, pouting.

Arthur forgot his objections at the sight of those plump lips pressed together. "Five minutes in your presence, and twenty years of training disappears from my brain as though it was never there. You are the one who is mesmerizing me. I am utterly . . ."

He let go of her and shifted onto his back, staring at the metal ball overhead.

Utterly what?

What was the word he couldn't allow himself to say?

VIOLET LAY STILL, despite her increasing discomfort. She'd donned a new corset today and gone in search of Arthur, to see if he'd be amenable to removing it. Unfortunately, Alice had tied the strings too tight. The boning dug into her back.

Now, however, she could have been wrapped in bands of steel and she wouldn't have moved. She rolled onto her side, pressing her chest against Arthur's arm, and set her head in her hand.

"Will you tell me?" she asked.

He didn't pretend to misunderstand her. Of course, he wouldn't. Arthur had never deceived her. He had been brutal with his honesty since the beginning.

"I don't know if I can," he admitted.

Arthur's walls might be too well-built for him to see the emotions hidden on the other side. What of her own defenses? What did she hold close to her own heart?

Joy. Regret. Hope. Confusion. Desire . . .

Taken all together, was this love?

"I don't know if I can," he repeated. "It is so foreign. I think . . . I might be happy?"

The world spun beneath her.

Happy. Violet made him happy.

She lay back and stared at the ceiling, giving him the privacy to wrestle with the epiphany. Maddening, frustrating, embarrassing: These were the states of being she so often invoked in others despite her best intentions.

Not in this man. She moved her little finger a centimeter to the right, touching the back of Arthur's hand.

"Deoiridh, my sister." He stopped, and she let her whole hand slip over his. "The summer before she died, I made a swing for her name day. It wasn't anything to look at. A piece of wood I polished for her seat. Two lengths of hemp. You'd have thought I made it from gold."

He stopped again; between his words rested long afternoons when a little boy would play with a baby sister while the sky gazed down and the wind ruffled their hair.

"Sometimes, she would insist I sit with her on my lap so we could swing together. 'So high,' she would tell me. 'So high.' When I am with you, I have the same sensation as when I watched the ground from the top of that swing."

Violet blanketed Arthur in acceptance as the minutes ticked by, until he flipped over his hand and linked their fingers.

"I would like to have seen it one more time," he said. "That swing. The farm. Home."

"Is it gone?"

"Aye." He ran his thumb over the mound of her palm. "I wanted to stay, but I was too young. A cousin had already immigrated to London, and I went to live with him. While I was gone, the landlord enclosed the land and tore down the house. I couldn't save any of it."

"I have a theory about ghosts," Violet whispered. "They aren't ethereal forms sent from the other side. They live in the heaviest part of the body, invisible weights that pull our feet onto paths they otherwise wouldn't have followed."

"Can you be haunted by a piece of earth?" he asked.

Searching within for the answer, Violet closed her eyes. "You can be haunted by any loss. Someone you loved. A place of safety. The person you might have been."

"That doesn't sound scientific," he said.

She sighed in agreement. "Setting aside the weight doesn't mean we forget them, or never loved them. It means learning to move ahead on our own without guilt."

"Are you free of your weights?"

The question was not asked unkindly. Violet didn't take offense. It took brass for her to tell Arthur to let go of his ghosts when Daniel still grabbed at her ankles.

Arthur could hurt her more than Daniel ever did.

She'd lied when she said there would be no attachments between them. Long before Arthur had been inside her body, this silent, solid man had found a way inside her heart. She wouldn't have had it any other way.

He'd ushered in her spring.

"We'd better stand. Unless there are more surprises to come?"

Even as he finished the sentence, Arthur's sense of ease vanished, and he sat up. Only one person in Violet's acquaintance could make that much noise merely walking. The pounding footsteps coming down the hall toward them belonged to—

"Sweet Jesu," Grantham bellowed. "What are the two of you doing?"

Arthur called out, "Watch your head."

"Watch my . . . What the—" Grantham stopped short just in time. Even so, the mace almost caught him right between the eyes. "What the hell is that? Beg your pardon for my language."

In one fluid move, Arthur rose and offered Violet a hand without looking at her.

"That is what the ladies of the club have devised for their protection," Arthur explained.

"What . . . Why would anyone in their right mind . . . ?" Grantham spluttered as he walked in a circle around the mace, his face red with irritation or incredulity, Violet couldn't tell. "Lock. Key. A club full of geniuses, and the simplest solution is beyond them."

"Fine. We shall revisit the question of a key at the next club meeting," she allowed.

The satisfied smirk on Arthur's face set Grantham's hackles on edge.

"Never mind that," the earl said. "What were the two of you doing messing about on the floor? I told you to keep your distance, Kneland. Do you think this is a game?"

Not a hair on Arthur's head moved. Not a sound escaped him. Deoiridh's brother disappeared, and the man who jumped in front of bullets returned.

"This has never been a game," he said.

Beneath Grantham's bluster, concern deepened the lines on his brow. "You should have listened to those Valkyries of yours when they warned you," he said to Violet. "I've written to Grey. He will be here by Thursday night."

Arthur twitched. In any other man, it might have gone unnoticed. For Arthur, it meant he was readying for attack.

"Georgie, you had no call to do so," Violet protested.

Now the earl rounded on Arthur. "All that talk of eating poison and letting yourself be stabbed to protect your charges. That isn't the whole truth, is it?"

Arthur absorbed Grantham's anger without a word. An unsettling blankness blurred his features, making Violet sick with worry.

"What are you saying, Georgie?" she asked.

"I'm saying he'll do anything to keep a man alive," Grantham sneered. "Unless he's fucking their wife."

19

GRANTHAM'S EXPLOSIVE ACCUSATION yesterday had gone unanswered.

A full armory might have been hanging within reach, yet nothing could have penetrated the bedrock of Arthur's reconstructed walls as he took in Grantham's words.

Arthur had begged their pardon and left, closing the connecting door and setting the mace to swinging again.

"Where d'you think you're going?" Grantham had called after him.

But the damage had been done. No amount of bluster on Grantham's part would pull Arthur back into the world now. Whatever doors had opened when she and Arthur had lain together for those blissful moments were once again locked.

Unable to talk to Arthur, Violet had turned on Grantham, furious that he would throw out such a serious charge.

"What on earth are you talking about?" she'd said.

"There were stories in the gossip rags at the time. It was a full-

blown scandal. He had an affair with the wife of a man he was supposed to protect," he'd hissed. "Three different men confirmed it."

"I never heard a word about this," she'd countered.

"Because it was twenty years ago. You were a child in Lincolnshire
when it happened."

"You were a child as well, Georgie. And so was he—how old would
he have been twenty years ago? Seventeen? Eighteen?"

Even as she defended Arthur, doubts crowded behind her words.
Young enough to be reckless, yes, but old enough to know right from
wrong. Old enough to end up in a married woman's bed.

"What does it matter his age? They packed him off to the continent
afterward, and he hasn't been back to England since. He cannot be
trusted," Grantham insisted. He ran a hand through his hair, exasper-
ated, no doubt, that she wouldn't fall into his plans as she had in their
youth. This time they weren't sneaking off to go fishing or purloining
a handful of plum tarts. "I want what is best for you."

"Then treat me like a grown woman and not a child. You are feeding me rumors. There is more to this than you are saying, and none of
it has any bearing on me."

Ducking beneath the mace, Violet had yanked open the door and
slammed it shut behind her, then cursed *herself* for acting like a child.
Still, she ignored Grantham's bellows and hastened to her workroom,
hoping to lose herself in her formulas.

Instead, visions of what she and Arthur had done together had
superimposed themselves over the loose scrawl of her formulas. Such
a difficult man to read. What did she know of him, truly? Had he been
so enamored of this other woman that integrity and duty ceased to
matter? He spoke so sparingly—was there another story entirely amid
his silences?

Falling into a restless sleep, she'd awoken with a deep sense of foreboding in the pit of her belly. In a fit of sentimentality, she'd taken the afghan from her workroom couch and secreted it in her bed. Now, as a cold rain struck the windowpanes, she held the blanket to her nose. Wool and winter.

"Don't be such a ninny," she told herself. "Of *course* he's made love to other women before me. That doesn't change the words he said to me."

Self-doubt writhed beneath her skin as she rose and went to her dressing room, widening her hips and thickening her torso, so that every dress she donned made her look lumpy and ungainly. Her hair fell in messy clumps, and Alice did not answer the bell to come help her fix it.

"I don't need a lady's maid," Violet argued whenever Phoebe upbraided her on her appearance. "I don't leave the house except to go to the club, and I can't wear anything too fine when I am conducting experiments."

She'd stopped caring about her appearance when she'd stopped thinking of herself as desirable. Her poorly mended chemises and ugly gowns were symptoms of a deeper malaise. She'd heard so many times that her intelligence made her less feminine. This, along with Daniel's distaste for her physical self, had prompted her to see clothes as merely covering a body she found flawed.

However, Arthur had convinced her that he wanted her *because* of her enjoyment of the act, not despite it. She wasn't a sexless drudge. She could find pleasure in her body and her mind.

A powerful message.

What if Violet had simply been one of many women he'd tutored in the affirmation of desire?

It didn't matter. She shook the thought out of her head as unworthy. Unworthy of Arthur, and unworthy of the woman she was on her way to becoming.

Nevertheless, her hair was still a fright. Rather than ring the bell one more time, Violet went to the kitchen. It might be that Alice was engaged in duties somewhere else and another maid could help.

"This must remain a secret," she heard as she approached. "You can't tell a soul." Arthur's deep voice gave an outsized gravity to the command, although he'd delivered it gently.

"I won't, sir. I promise," came a quiet vow in response.

Violet peeked around the door to the kitchen. Arthur and Alice sat in the corner. Cook and Mrs. Sweet would be in the housekeeper's parlor, planning the week's menu about now, so the two of them had the room to themselves. On the long wooden table before them sat a covered basket.

"Go on, try one," Arthur ordered.

Violet knew better than anyone how difficult it was to defy the man, so she was surprised when Alice hesitated.

"What if they don't taste the same?" the girl asked.

"They won't," he said with his usual bluntness. "Everything changes. You. The folks around you. Where you live now, and where you'll be in ten years."

Arthur pulled back the cloth and sniffed. "Your memories won't change, though. When I smell these buns, I remember my mam taking a batch from the oven and turning her back on my sister and me. I snatched two for us to eat later, thinking I was a clever one. She did it apurpose, of course."

Alice laughed.

"See." Arthur nodded. "Don't even have to taste them for the memory to come."

The maid picked up a round, dark bun and brought it to her nose. "One time, Cam—he's the youngest boy—one time he cut a neep to look like a finger. I don't know how he did it, but . . ."

Violet retreated into the corridor and pressed her back against the wall, one hand against her beating heart.

Everything changes.

Her own life was a study in change. She'd gone from child to woman, from wife to widow. She'd tried to build a marriage and watched it fall to pieces around her. She'd founded the club and created a shelter for others like her.

She thought of Lady Elva Perllan, a young woman from Herefordshire, who had recently joined Athena's Retreat. Her interest lay in botany, and one night she'd delivered a lecture on tulip bulbs:

They lie beneath the earth, where no sunlight can reach them, yet they never despair. Even in the silent dark, the bulb waits with an unerring belief in spring. Do not think of them as sleeping. Think of the blossoms as crouched and ready, poised to push their way toward the sun at the smallest encouragement.

Arthur's tiny moment of connection with Alice, despite trying to stay detached from them all, was a sign of how small gestures could punch through the strongest of barriers.

Violet could buy a hundred new gowns, but the same woman would be staring back at her. For all the changes she'd wrought at Athena's Retreat, had Violet been too frightened to take the final step and shed her old skin?

Pushing through to the light wasn't just change; it was growth.

"There are still some left, if you'd like to try one."

Arthur had come out into the hallway. Playacting a man at ease, he struck a familiar pose, leaning against the wall. As ever, he swept the corridor with his gaze, and one hand hovered, ready to draw a knife at the slightest hint that something was wrong.

"Forgive my intruding," she said.

"It is your home, my lady. You can go anywhere you please without considering it an intrusion."

My lady.

Violet's thoughts were so disordered from her earlier self-revelations she didn't bother to hide her hurt. She pulled her shawl close, grasping for something to say. "You will cause an insurrection by Mrs. Sweet if you keep bringing sweets into the house."

"That will not be a problem, as I am leaving today."

A draft snuck beneath Violet's petticoats and grabbed her ankles. She could not remember a spring so cold. Surely, it must be a trick of the light that it seemed darker with every word out of his mouth.

"Today?" she echoed. The word frosted the tip of her tongue.

Arthur glanced into the kitchen, then back at her. "After what Earl Grantham told you yesterday, I am surprised you didn't order my dismissal immediately. I've written my own letter to Grey. An apology."

His shoulder lifted, then dropped. "I'm ready to go," he said, as though his words were of no consequence to him, sending Violet falling down a dark hole.

"MR. KNELAND, SIR," Alice poked her head out the doorway, oblivious of the tension. "There is a delivery wagon outside. It's supposed to go 'round to the club, but the driver says he won't go, and ... Oh dear. Did you catch your hair in Mrs. Pettigrew's spinning whisks again, my lady?"

Violet let Alice tease her, but her smile was tempered with melancholy. She did indeed appear disheveled. Her gown was buttoned wrong, and Alice was not far off in describing the state of Violet's hair. She must not have slept well.

Arthur wanted to coax her back upstairs and run a brush through her lemon-scented tresses. Then he wanted to push her against the wall and do things to her that would leave her hair an even bigger disaster. Too late now. Too late for that and anything else he'd put off.

He knew his words had hurt her. Once again, his lack of experience with intimacy had left him in the dark as he tried to figure out how to make it better. What would Grantham say to her?

Goodbye. You look pretty?

Arthur went to sort out the delivery before he said anything idiotic.

"Oy, what's this I've got to go another street over?" A wagon driver was arguing with Letty Fenley out in the mews, next to the carriage house.

"This won't do at all." Letty Fenley delivered her scold to a driver twice her size without fear. "I specifically told the warehouse not to send them to Beacon House. They were to come directly to Athena's Retreat without delay."

Letty's dress hung loose and wrinkled on her thin frame, and dark lavender smudges beneath her eyes gave them a hollowed appearance. Like a nervous shadow, Caroline Pettigrew hovered behind her. An outsized cape with the hood drawn far over her head obscured her face.

Arthur slipped toward the back of the carriage house so that they wouldn't catch sight of him.

Peering from beneath the cowl, Mrs. Pettigrew leaned over the side of the wagon and read the labels aloud.

"Ethanol, acacia gum, ferrous sulfate," she muttered. "This should be enough to get us through until Thursday night, if we're not discovered."

Arthur's fists clenched in anger. Here he'd been worrying over Alice and fantasizing about Violet's hair, and in the meantime these women were receiving secret shipments right under his nose.

The driver pointed at a trunk buffered from the rest of the boxes by heaps of blankets. "That there is Lady Greycliff's special order. When it's my lady's order, I come to this entrance. I have to pack it different than the rest, on account of it's contemptible."

Mrs. Pettirgrew blinked, and Letty paused in her pacing.

"It's what?" Letty asked.

"Congestible," said the delivery man, staring at them as though they were deaf. "Explodes if you shake it around."

"Combustible?" Mrs. Pettigrew asked.

"'S what I said, innit?"

"Has anyone from the household seen you arrive?" Letty asked.

"Why would that matter?" Arthur said as he stepped out from behind the carriage house.

Mrs. Pettigrew squeaked in surprise, but Letty scowled.

"It matters because I don't want to worry Lady Greycliff's staff with a minor inconvenience," she snapped.

Arthur crossed his arms, letting his disbelief show. "Is that it, or have you something planned with these chemicals for Thursday night? Something combustible?"

"Comestible," corrected the driver.

"Oh dear," murmured Mrs. Pettigrew.

"Unless you are trying to keep Lady Greycliff from completing her formula by diverting her supplies?" Arthur took another step closer, examining Letty's expression for signs of guilt.

"What on earth?"

Even Arthur gave a slight start of surprise at Violet's query. He hadn't heard her come outside. He'd been too busy pretending his anger was due to some scheme rather than his own despair.

There was no victory to be had when Letty paled and Mrs. Pettigrew pulled her hood down even further. The sight of Violet confronting her friends' deception twisted his insides with sympathy. Alice must have taken her in hand, for her cap was now straight and the hair beneath fixed into a tidy bun. She pinned each of them in turn with her stare.

"There's nothing to be done but come clean, Caro," said Letty.

Beneath the hood, Mrs. Pettigrew whimpered but offered no resistance when Violet tipped her head toward the house.

"Follow me."

Arthur followed, in case they tried to slip away as they trooped through to the club's office. Violet took a seat behind the desk, while Mrs. Pettigrew and Letty stood, hands folded and heads bowed in penitence before her.

Arthur settled between them and the door. They appeared to be chastened, but appearances were deceptive.

"It was my fault, my lady," Mrs. Pettigrew burst out.

"Now, Caro," Letty said, "there's no need to be dramatic."

This was the outside of enough. "Admission of attempted murder is indeed reason to be dramatic," Arthur sneered.

"Murder?" Mrs. Pettigrew gasped.

"Have you lost your mind?" Letty cried. "We didn't try to murder anyone—except one another when this all went cockeyed."

"Surely that is too strong a charge, Arthur," Violet remonstrated, leaning over to catch his gaze.

"What do you call throwing bricks, or setting off bombs and lighting fires?" he said. He pointed at Mrs. Pettigrew. "Even if you weren't trying to kill Lady Greycliff, you've betrayed her trust and endangered everyone around you."

"Throwing bricks? No, no. When I said it was my fault, I meant my head," she said, pointing to the hood. "I used up all our supplies trying to get the formulaic proportions right. The night of the fire, I went to borrow some of your acacia gum, my lady, and that's when I saw the smoke. I meant to get you more before you noticed it was gone, I swear."

Violet threw her hands up in frustration. "Formulaic proportions and acacia gum for what?" Her confused gaze shifted between the two women. "What have you been keeping from me?"

Mrs. Pettigrew glanced at Letty, who signaled her permission, then pulled off her hood.

Violet gasped, and Arthur leaned forward. Though overcast, enough daylight lit the room that they could both see the remarkable . . . transformation in Caroline Pettigrew's hair.

"It looks . . ." Arthur circled the woman, peering at her head from all sides, and tried to find a descriptor. At least it wasn't pink.

"Solid," Violet said, finishing the sentence and setting a hand to her cheek in shock. "Caroline, what have you done to your hair?"

Mrs. Pettigrew's hair was dressed in a coiffure more suitable for the ballroom than the daytime. It was parted down the middle, with four or five barley curls hanging on either side of her face. The back was braided and twisted into an elaborate design.

The style was not itself out of the ordinary. What fascinated Arthur was the fact that not a single hair was out of place. Caroline's entire head reflected the light, as if she wore a helmet of polished marble.

God save them if Mrs. Pettigrew tried to invent something for internal use.

"Ahem," Letty said. "If I may?"

Arthur went to stand next to Violet, one hand behind his back. He'd a clever little folding knife secreted there, handmade by the sole female bladesmith he'd encountered. She lived in London, and Arthur had considered introducing her to Athena's Retreat.

After today, he decided against it.

Letty began, "Imagine never having to worry about your hair if the wind blew your bonnet, or your hat, from your head."

"Imagine," Arthur repeated, trying to remember if he'd ever wondered about that. Since he began this assignment, outlandish scenarios had become commonplace.

Letty gestured to Mrs. Pettigrew's head with her palm facing the ceiling, a trace of obsequiousness in her manner. With a wave of her hand, she'd transformed from Athena's competent club secretary to a Piccadilly shopgirl. "If a lady's hair remained as lustrous and shapely at the end of the day as in the morning," she said, "she'd save hours of time when dressing for dinner or a party."

"What does any of this have to do with Lady Greycliff's supplies?" Arthur said, interrupting Letty's recitation. "The two of you are still hiding something, and it isn't Mrs. Pettigrew's head."

Violet said, "You've used the aerosol deliver system to spray—"

"Hair lacquer," admitted Mrs. Pettigrew. Red spots of shame stood out against her wan skin. "We are perfecting a formula for hair lacquer to sell at Fenley's Fantastic Fripperies. I never meant to keep this secret."

"I did," Letty declared. "Blame me."

Violet and Letty shared a glance that, as angry as Arthur was, he envied. They'd history between them.

"I didn't think you would approve, my lady," Mrs. Pettigrew explained.

"Approve of your hair?"

"Approve of making money from it," Letty said. "The bylaws state that our work is for the advancement of knowledge. When I suggested we add the words 'wealth and benefit of the members,' you and Lady Phoebe voted me down."

"We need the mixture perfected by Thursday," said Mrs. Pettigrew.

"The night of the event," Arthur pointed out.

"Thursday's when my father places orders for the beauty selection," Letty explained. "If we are to sell the hair lacquer before the season, the materials must be ordered now."

"Why couldn't you tell me?" Violet asked, hurt written on her face.

The grim set of Letty's mouth softened, and Arthur moved as close to Violet as he could without touching her.

"We couldn't involve you in such a mercantile project, my lady," Mrs. Pettigrew said. "A gentlewoman doesn't sell cosmetics or household cleaners."

Letty continued. "We wanted to split the profits with Fenley's Fantastic Fripperies and put our half of the earnings back into a fund for our members."

"A fund?" Arthur said. "For what?"

"Not all our members have means." There was a hint of apology in Mrs. Pettigrew's voice, but Letty simply crossed her arms. "They must pay for supplies or hire childminders for the hours they come here to work."

"I never thought . . ." Violet bit down on her bottom lip as she considered Letty's words. "I never considered the matter from any point of view other than my own—as a woman with means."

"Who else knows of this project?" Arthur asked. "Any of the club members? Lady Phoebe?"

"Of course not. Imagine what Lady Phoebe would say if it were known the social club was being used for commerce," said Letty. "Why, it would be an even larger scandal than experimenting with science."

Violet shook her head. "You do Phoebe an injustice. She is in favor of women supporting themselves."

Letty scoffed. "She spends more money on a bonnet than entire families spend on coal for a year, and that's after her papa has halved her pin money."

Violet turned to Arthur. "Would it draw too much attention if we allowed our members to sell their inventions?"

Arthur considered the question, pleased she'd asked for his counsel. "I suppose it depends on where they sell them," he said. "Perhaps a discussion between your members is in order? The nature of Athena's Retreat means you will always be balancing the greater good against the desires of individual members."

He hadn't meant for it to be a reminder of his and Violet's own predicament, but the echo of his words hung between them as Violet asked the ladies to hold off on producing more of their wares until they called a meeting of the entire club.

Arthur and Violet were free to make whatever choices they wanted. Today's discovery served as a reminder, however, that the consequences of their choices would affect everyone else around them.

20

❧

"Y OU DON'T TRUST them, do you?" Violet asked.

She didn't believe her friends were responsible for any of the mischief Arthur had accused them of, but she admitted to being disappointed that neither woman had included her in their plans.

Arthur had been contemplating the threadbare rug in front of the desk since Violet ushered Letty and Caroline out into the hall.

He answered her now. "They tell a compelling tale, but, no, I don't trust them. Do you think it is coincidence that Mrs. Pettigrew's aerosol invention resembles the one used by the Omnis in their riots?"

"Often, scientists develop similar work without having contact with one another," Violet replied. "Think of how Leibniz and Newton discovered calculus at the same time but in different countries. Caro Pettigrew is a member of Athena's Retreat. She made a vow never to reveal the secret of the work we do behind the oak door."

"A vow?" Arthur scoffed.

The man who had gifted little Alice with memories of home was nowhere to be found. Instead, the cynical enigma from the night they'd first met had reappeared. From the moment Grantham had accused Arthur of negligence, he had begun to retreat, readying himself for another loss.

Not this time.

"You know how important this club is to the members," she argued. "You've seen them working all hours of the night on their creations. If you cared—"

"I *don't* care," he blurted. "Worrying about aerosol pumps or pink teacups is not my job. This assignment—"

"You do." Violet marched over to him and stood toe-to-toe. "We are not assignments any longer. We are people who care for you, and you care about us as well."

"What do you think happens if I become involved in the lives of the people I am meant to protect?" The syllables fell from his mouth, dense and wooden with despair. He lifted his eyes from the floor but didn't look at her as he spoke. "What if I grow to care about them or, conversely, *not* care about them?"

It didn't take long for understanding to dawn.

Arthur's shoulders inched up in discomfort while his gaze rested on the curtains behind her. "Most of my . . . assignments were horrible men. Men with black souls and no conscience. Some molested their servants and cheated other men out of their fortunes. Some beat their wives."

What must it feel like to live cheek by jowl with such men? Daniel had never been deliberately cruel, but his disappointment had worn her down, seeping into her skin and bones. Might Arthur have kept away from ordinary people for fear of contaminating them with the ugliness of the men he served?

"If I had become involved, I might not have been willing to do anything to keep them safe. Those men would be dead. That would have been on my conscience. Worse. Their deaths would have had dire consequences for the country—and in some cases, the entire continent. I protected them, and by extension, I am complicit in some of their deeds."

Violet raised her hand to offer comfort, but he shook his head.

"A bodyguard cannot feel anything for the people he is protecting. He cannot hate them, and he cannot . . . What Grantham said was true. A man died because my focus was not on him. My focus was on his wife."

She stiffened at the slap of his words, and the space between them filled with ice. Still, hadn't she wanted him to explain what Grantham had meant?

"On my first assignment, I committed the ultimate betrayal of my duties," Arthur confessed. "The first time I went into the field, the man I was supposed to protect was murdered."

She said nothing as she turned Arthur's words around this way and that.

His chin dipped to his chest, and his voice dropped to a whisper. "I knew better. I had been trained to avoid any entanglements. I did it anyway. I never made that mistake again. Until you."

For every word spoken aloud, a thousand more shouted out to her across the silence that followed.

"Was it love?" she asked.

"What?" He stared at her as though she'd spoken another language. Perhaps she had.

"The woman with whom you . . ." Violet didn't know what to call her. "Did you love her?"

"Love," he repeated. The word sounded awkward in his mouth, as though his tongue could not find the shape of it. "Yes. No. I was . . . fascinated by her."

A tiny coil of jealousy unwound itself in the pit of Violet's stomach. Fascinating, eh? "Was she poised and beautiful?" she asked.

His brow raised in query. "I suppose? I had little experience with

females, other than my wee sister and mam. I missed them every day."
He sighed. "Her name was Maria Bellingham. She wasn't just beautiful; she took notice of me. That's all it took for me to lose my mind a little. A woman's kindness."

While he searched for words, Violet studied his profile for traces of the boy he'd been. Once, he'd been inexperienced and unsure of himself. Difficult to imagine Arthur as anything other than invincible. The mantle of command he wore and the aura of leashed power surrounding him often obscured any trace of uncertainty.

Tilting his head upward, he studied the shadows on the ceiling. "I'm hard-pressed to describe Maria as anything other than devastatingly compelling to a young man who should have known better yet wanted to be needed. To be essential."

Ghosts hovered between them. Uncertain as to how she might dispel them, Violet remained silent and gave them their due.

"We were seven assigned to the Bellinghams. He sold guns to the Greeks—not a nice man but not a brute, either. Out of all those men, she took an interest in me. We recognized the loneliness in each other. Sympathy rather than love, but no less powerful."

Violet shifted her weight from one foot to the other, torn between wanting to console Arthur and wanting to stay clear, so that his words might flow undisturbed.

He studied the shelves full of books and files as though they contained vital secrets.

"I didn't love her, did I?" he said finally, sounding surprised. "How could I? I never said more than a handful of words to her. I fancied myself Lancelot. She was Guinevere. At the time, I hoped she saw something special in me. I imagined myself giving comfort, giving succor."

Humility flashed across his face. "On the afternoon I was to meet her for our first assignation, I asked another man to take my shift. I'd a bad feeling all day, but I ignored it—thought it was guilt. I was impatient. Instead of waiting for him to relieve me in the parlor, I left as soon as I heard him in the corridor outside. He was almost to the door when we heard glass breaking. By the time we got there, it was too late. *I* was too late. Bellingham was dead, and the man who'd replaced me took a bullet in the leg, trying to stop the assassin."

Facing her at last, Arthur tilted his palms outward in supplication. "Distracted. Dead."

"And since then, you have made certain never to repeat your mistake?" Violet asked, careful to keep any judgment from her voice. "Never allowing affection for the people you protect or anyone around them?"

"When my sister died, the memory stayed with me, so sharp and clear. I hoped by saving others, I could blunt the pain. The first time I had the chance, I failed." He set his fingertips to his lips, as if shocked by the flow of words.

"You did not invite the assassin in, Arthur. There were six other men assigned to the house. You didn't even have an affair with her."

When he shook his head, shadows filled the hollows beneath his cheeks. He stared at the floor as though Bellingham's body lay in front of him even now. "I was . . ."

"Yes. You were distracted." Violet's voice cut through the darkness, surprising them both. "A young man, with all the feelings and flaws inherent at that age. You made a mistake."

"When I lost my family, there was such a hole . . ." Arthur pushed the words out as though they burned his mouth. "I tried to fill it with Maria, but she was the wrong shape. Then everything went to hell. Bellingham is dead, and in all these years it stayed empty."

"Our lives are not the product of the mistakes we've made and the wrongs we committed." Here, in this place she had created to escape her own failures, Violet spoke to her younger self as well as Arthur.

"Our lives are what comes afterward. The journeys we take in search of forgiveness. The lessons we learn along the way."

"Forgiveness?" he whispered. "There is no one left to forgive me. They're all gone."

"There is yourself, Arthur. If it were anyone else, might you allow them absolution?"

FORGIVENESS?

What a large and unwieldy concept. The syllables wrapped themselves like soft wool around old wounds.

Arthur pushed on with his confession, wanting to purge the last of it. "Maria blamed herself and divulged everything to the prime minister's assistant when he questioned her. I managed to keep my employment, but the assistant was indiscreet. There were stories. I don't know if they printed my name, but enough people knew that I had to leave for the continent."

"It was a long time ago," Violet said.

"Not long enough. Earl Grantham heard. Miss Fenley knew even before Grantham."

"Oh. She never said."

Arthur frowned. "If we caused a minor scandal with one dance, imagine what folks will say once they know what happened with Maria and me."

"But you never consummated the affair," Violet argued.

There were stacks of papers piled high atop every surface in the office. A newly purchased brass-and-teakwood hygrometer sat on the ledge behind her desk, and Arthur studied its polished base.

"I never denied it. I let the story take on the veneer of truth, and nothing will change it now. People think I murdered Bellingham. You cannot have a murderer walking the halls of Athena's Retreat. It will

undo everything you've set out to achieve with your Evening of Eleva-
tion. Soon I'll be a pariah in London. That's why I am retiring to the
anonymity of the country."

"Yes, that's right. You are going home."

"Home," he repeated.

The finality of that word blanketed them.

"Where will you go?" she asked.

"A place where I wouldn't be responsible for anyone's life." Where
he would sleep through the night without worry or fear. No longer living in someone else's house and following someone else's direction.

Her skirts brushed the back of his legs as he placed his fists on the
polished sheen of the rosewood desk. A perfume of the chemicals
she'd been experimenting with mixed with scented soap wafted from
her, the smell of comfort and compassion.

He pictured, once again, the never-ending expanse of sky above
his parents' farm, all the colors between black and blue dipping to kiss
the gentle hills and exposed rocks of the silent landscape. When finally he found a home, there would be no place for men of politics or
passions or greed.

Home meant a life of peace and simplicity. *Home* meant an absence
of pain and blessed solitude. Arthur ached for such a place. Still, in his
heart of hearts, had he wanted more? A tiny girl with wild curls. A boy
who loved jam tarts. Ribbons of laughter floating outside in the summer gloaming.

Had hope lived deep within him this whole time, pushing toward
the sky despite his best intentions? A foot away from him stood hope
personified. Light made flesh.

How terrifying when dreams walk the earth. Perfect in their imperfections: messy and flawed and more beautiful for it. When you let
a person in, they mattered, and when you lost them, worlds ended.

"You must be so tired." Violet leaned against him, wrapping him

in rain and flowers. "Twenty years, and never a place to call your own."
When he turned, she reached beneath his jacket to pull him into her
soft warmth.

"I am," he said. "Twenty years without a full night's sleep, and each
day spent in the service of strangers." So tired of endless nights alone,
his only solace now was to dream of an empty house and an empty life.

"Don't leave, Arthur." Violet lay her head against his chest. "Not
yet."

"It can't last," he warned her.

He ached for tenderness, but when they came together all he allowed himself to sate was his hunger. Tasting tea and oranges, he
sucked her lower lip, falling into the cushion of her body, spinning her
around and leaning them both against the desk. These inelegant, fran-
tic kisses only fed his need.

"Can I touch you here?" he panted, fingers searching for the tapes
of her drawers, coveting her skin, as smooth as the polished wood beneath them, as hot as the flames flickering in the candelabra.

"Anywhere. Everywhere," she whispered. Her wicked tongue
traced a path from his chin to his cheek while he slipped the drawers
over her hips.

Thus freed, he pulled her bodice with one hand while the other
searched beneath her skirts for the sweet syrup at her center.

"I want to feel you," she said, pulling at the buttons of his trousers,
yanking his shirttails free, and reaching beneath his linen smalls to
stroke him from root to tip.

"Let me inside," he begged her. "I won't come in you." He ate at her
mouth while he slid his fingers through the soft hair protecting her
cleft, then pressed lightly on the delicate pearl beneath his thumb.
When she moaned, he slid one finger into the slick heat, holding her
firm as she bucked against him.

Breaking the kiss, Violet gasped her consent and pulled Arthur even closer, hooking her leg around his waist. Despite the yards of material around her, Arthur managed to fit himself to her, though he nearly came at the need in her face alone.

Tight, so tight. It took forever to push the whole length of him inside her. They locked stares as he nudged himself, inch by inch, into her sweet embrace.

"Tell me how it feels, Violet," he begged. "Give me your words."

Caught in the traps of her petticoats, there was barely room for Violet to widen her thighs and accommodate him. He kept one hand between them, circling her clit, while he bore down on her in tiny thrusts. She drummed her heels against the back of his thighs, whispering words of encouragement.

Sweet, tight, harder, and *yes. Thick, hot, wicked,* and *more.*

She gave him what he asked for, pouring exclamations and exhortations over and around him. They filled his ears and drowned out any questions of guilt or innocence. There were no more thoughts of what might come next once they left this space. Nothing but sizzling pleasure and a tension too much to bear.

"Let go," she crooned, lifting her hips to meet his strokes.

The rest of the world fell away at her urging. Arthur's entire existence narrowed to the sound of flesh against flesh, the taste of salt on her skin, and the sight of Violet's lips moving as she granted him absolution.

21

THE CORRIDORS OF Beacon House sounded empty in the dregs of the dark March morning. The pewter sky smothered the building, and tiny fists of hard snow hammered at the windows. An anemic fire in the grate failed to ward off the gloom, but Violet had a fondness for this parlor. The walls were a simple whitewash, the furniture coverings were a soothing mixture of pastel shades and whimsical embroidery, and the ancient silk drapes pulled back from the windows by brass curtain hooks were a pleasing emerald green.

A bowl of hothouse gardenias sat on the end table next to Violet's chair.

Grantham had brought them, along with an apology. "Not just for my language," he said, "though I apologize for that, too. Shouldn't have shouted the word for what Kneland did."

"What he didn't do, rather," Violet said while picking at a tassel on her armchair. She told Grantham the story, but he remained unimpressed.

"I can't go around town explaining he *almost* cuckolded Belling-

ham. The man is still dead on Kneland's watch." Grantham peered
over at the bookshelf. "Did you see that? Looked like a spider, but
huge, a—"

"Dust ball," she blurted. "Appears larger because of the shadows. I
shall scold Alice tonight for certain. Come sit by the fire."

Grantham wouldn't care about Lady Potts's feelings for one second. If he caught sight of a tarantula, it would be stuck to the bottom
of his shoe within seconds.

"Hmm." He crossed to a small drinks table and poured himself a
brandy. Sniffing it, he set it down, squinted into the decanter, then
picked it back up again. "The story is out there. Ran into Victor Armitage."

"Hiding from Fanny, no doubt," Violet said with a sniff.

"He is not to be underestimated. Very highly placed in government, and not pleased with the idea of a club for ladies. He asked me
what I knew about Kneland," Grantham told her. "Fanny must have
said something. If Fanny Armitage knows something nasty about
someone, you can be certain all of London will know by the end of the
week."

Violet examined her hands and picked stray threads from her
skirts, shifting in her seat. Her bottom was a tad bit sore from what had
happened with Arthur on the desk yesterday. It was worth every ache
and twinge, the sensation of being filled with the whole of him. The
sole regret she had was that once again he'd remained clothed, holding on to the last bit of distance between them even as he'd bared
everything else to her in his confession.

She had meant to speak with him about that, but when she'd
returned to her workroom, another way to formulate the antidote occurred to her and she forgot about . . . well, everything, until her work
resolved itself.

She'd finished the formula.

There had been no one to tell at two in the morning, and rather than crow about her success right now, she carried the knowledge in a space beneath her heart, where difficult truths usually sat. Lodged in her chest like a burr was a complex tangle of fierce pride, relief for the safety of others, and the bleak reality that Arthur had no reason to stay.

"Armitage asked about Dickerson, too. Kneland didn't take the Queen's honors when he saved the man, and Armitage wondered was there some reason, some hidden shame. I hope Kneland has the sense not to make another appearance in public with you." Grantham pushed aside the decanter and searched on the lower shelf for something else to drink while he spoke. "Vi, this won't just be a disaster for you. The rumors will attach themselves to the club as well."

"I told you he's done nothing wrong," she insisted, irritated with how petty folks could be to spend time disparaging others instead of lifting up kindness.

Grantham quit his search, rubbing his eyes as though the conversation pained him. "Listen here, Vi. I've seen you bring home any number of wounded birds over the years. And snakes. And bugs."

"That boar one time," she added.

"Wounded boars, ladies who science—it's a far cry from protecting a man knee-deep in scandal," he said. "You're too softhearted. Let me fix this for you."

"I don't want to be fixed. I'm not broken." Beating wings of frustration propelled her from the chair. Why did everyone persist in seeing her as deficient? "I don't want to be taken care of. I want to be *loved*."

Grantham's mouth opened and closed. He seemed disappointed in her.

"How'm I supposed to . . . ? I brought you flowers. Do you mean poetry and such?"

Violet's heart broke a little for her friend. "That isn't even close, Georgie. I want real love. The kind that lifts you up and splits you open. The kind that changes everything."

She might as well have asked for the moon from Grantham's expression.

"Don't you want that, too?" she asked.

"No," he said, hands out in front of him as though warding off the notion. "I don't want someone to fall in love with me. How could I live up to that?"

Violet crossed to where Grantham stood and set the stopper back in the bottle. "I married Daniel hoping to feel secure and found myself trapped instead. I can't go back."

"I don't care about your work," Grantham said. He took her hand, then tutted over a scorch mark on her glove. "I can protect you *and* the club."

"I don't want to be safe," she cried, pulling her hand from his grasp.

"Then you will lose everything," Grantham argued.

"I'll have myself back," she countered. "The Violet I could have been—before Daniel, before losing my confidence."

Grantham scratched his head. For all he played the sweet-tempered oaf, he'd a fine mind and a well-honed ability to read others.

"You *have* been different lately," he said finally. "Can't quite put my finger on what it is."

"Happy," she whispered. "He makes me happy."

ARTHUR STOOD IN the hall outside of Violet's parlor.

I want real love.

He couldn't help but overhear. Violet's words had carried out into the hall and he'd run headfirst into the declaration.

I want real love.

Thomas found him there, pacing with indecision over whether to interrupt or run in the opposite direction. "Got a note from Ham Millerton," Thomas said, "Grey's man up north."

Arthur stared at the door. "And?" he asked when Thomas's pause grew overlong.

"Miss Fenley got herself in a bit of trouble a few years back. Her father spent a fortune trying to get her launched in society. Seems she put the cart before the horse with the son of Earl Melton. The boy told her he'd marry her until his father caught wind of it and sent her packing."

"Huh."

Violet assumed Letty to be innocent in the fire and attempted theft. Arthur hadn't disabused her of the notion, but he'd asked Thomas to do some investigating.

Someone close to her could not be trusted, and he wanted to find that person before they hurt her even more.

"Didn't say it outright, but the earl made clear Miss Fenley wasn't welcome in his circles anymore."

"Explains her antagonism toward anyone with a title," Arthur said, "but how is it connected to the trouble here?"

Thomas considered the question, shaking his head. "Melton owns a few mills that went on strike, but that is the only connection I could find to explain a link between her and the Omnis."

"Pretty thin link," Arthur acknowledged. "Doesn't strike me as a compelling motive, but we should inform Grey anyway."

"No worries about that."

Arthur tilted his head in question.

"Melton is Lord Greycliff's cousin," Thomas explained. "Grey already knows about Miss Fenley's adventures."

This shed new light on the tension between the two of them. Had

Melton's son and Grey been rivals for Letty's affections? Arthur suspected something more complex than simple jealousy, but Grey had
seen no reason to mention it.

"Anyone else you want me to investigate?" Thomas asked.

"You still have a man following Adam Winters?"

"Aye. He talks to whoever will listen about bringing down the government, but none of his crew have come anywhere near her ladyship
since she ran into carriage trouble last week."

Behind them, voices were raised. The door to the parlor flew open,
and Violet stormed down the hallway in the opposite direction without seeing them.

Arthur debated whether to follow her, but decided instead to confront the man who caused her upset in the first place. He let Thomas
go with a quick nod, then checked that his knives were in place.

"I ought to thrash you." Grantham had uttered the threat matter-
of-factly when Arthur entered the room. "Have a drink first."

Arthur shook his head. "I'm working."

"Right. And there's the rub, eh?" The earl set the bottle down and
cocked his head. "You plan on staying, do you?"

Did he?

Arthur could defy society and stay, taking Violet to bed each night
and waking her in the morning with scorching kisses and words of
devotion. In between, her days would be empty, as her friends, her
acquaintances, and the club members would all distance themselves
from her.

"No. I'm damaged goods, and she's . . ." Arthur tried to find the
words to describe Violet, but that vocabulary was beyond him.

"Better than you," Grantham said.

"Better than you, too."

Grantham didn't argue.

"I want you to do something for me," Arthur said.

The earl snorted but nodded for Arthur to continue.

By God, he wanted to wipe that smug grin from Grantham's face. Instead, he ripped out his heart and held it out for the other man to see.

"Don't let her marry anyone unless they would take a bullet for her."

Grantham's head jerked back for a moment, but he recovered quickly and quirked an eyebrow. "Right. Take a bullet. Anything else?"

Arthur growled. "This isn't a joke, Grantham. You do this, or I will come back and shoot *you*."

The earl held up his hands in surrender, and Arthur continued. "Take a bullet, but there's more. Make sure he can't eat if she's hungry. Don't let anyone touch her unless they can listen to her explain Avogadro's law all the way through without falling asleep. He can't be afraid of spiders, and . . ."

In for a penny, in for a pound, he supposed.

"He has to love her with all that he is and all that he will ever be."

Grantham pursed his lips, then blew out a long, slow exhalation. "Is that it?"

"I heard what she said," Arthur confessed. "She wants to be loved."

"You heard what she said, eh? Are you sure everything is working up here?" Grantham knocked on Arthur's head as though it were a block of wood.

With incredible strength of will, Arthur did not pull a knife on the big oaf.

Heedless of how close to death he was skirting, the earl continued to speak. "She said she wants to be loved *by you*, you blockhead."

"No, she said she wanted to be split open and lifted up," Arthur argued. "She didn't say by whom."

"Split open and lifted up by a fool who won't eat if she's hungry and wants to get gored by a bullet. Jesu wept, the two of you make love sound like one of the Four Horsemen," Grantham marveled.

"I . . ." Arthur ran his fingers through his hair. "It doesn't matter. This club is more important to her than ever. It's the core of who she is. It is her *home*, and I won't let her lose it."

He'd been hollowed out when he lost his family and the farm, scraped clean of sentiment by his misfortunes. How could he visit that upon Violet?

"I'm leaving as soon as Grey arrives," he said.

"You'll do no such thing," the earl said, poking his finger into Arthur's chest.

"Don't do that," Arthur warned him. The shock of Violet's words had worn off. A rising tide of frustration and panic had replaced it and would need some release.

"Do what? Do this?" The earl poked him again. "You will not leave her. It will break"—the earl poked Arthur even harder—"her"—this time, he used the flat of his hand to shove Arthur back a step—"heart."

The first punch Arthur landed was ill-timed. Grantham leaned forward as Arthur's fist flew, and the blow glanced off his ribs instead of square in the middle of his stomach.

"You asked her to marry you, you giant gudgeon," Arthur said in disbelief.

Quick on his feet despite his size, the earl grabbed Arthur's arm and wrenched it behind his back. Arthur had forgotten Grantham was once a soldier.

"Yes," the earl spat from between gritted teeth. "But she wants to marry *you*."

Arthur shot his right foot back between Grantham's legs and yanked him off his feet. They landed in a heap behind the settee and rolled around, each trying to pin the other to the ground.

"No, you are an earl. You can protect her. *You* should marry her," Arthur insisted.

Grantham pulled Arthur's head back and grabbed his cravat. "No, *you* do it."

They hit an end table and sent a tower of books flying.

"What in the name of the Merveilleuses are you *doing*?" cried Lady Phoebe.

They froze, Arthur with his fingers mere inches from Grantham's eyes, and Grantham with one hand around Arthur's throat, holding a fireplace poker above his head.

"Are you two fighting?" Violet pushed past Lady Phoebe and set her hands on her hips. Both women wore matching expressions of disgust.

Arthur and Grantham traded sheepish glances. An overwhelming urge to laugh tore through Arthur, and an answering grin split Grantham's face. When the earl's shoulders shook, Arthur bit down hard on his bottom lip and smothered a snort.

"Fighting? No, my lady," he said with as straight a face as he could manage. Grantham shook even more.

Lady Phoebe's mouth flattened in disbelief. "What are you doing, then?"

"I lost something," Grantham sputtered, covering his laughter with a cough.

"Your bloody mind," Arthur whispered.

"Why are you *both* on the floor?" Clearly, Violet didn't believe a word of their story. Arthur got to his feet and held out a hand to Grantham, but he twisted Grantham's wrist as he did so.

"It fell under the settee," the earl wheezed, stepping on Arthur's foot. "Kneland was helping me search for it."

Grantham wrenched his arm free of Arthur's bruising grip and brushed a smudge of dust from his lapel, then proceeded to do the same to Arthur, whacking at his chest with undue enthusiasm.

"If the two of you are finished with your search, I have an announcement to make," said Lady Phoebe. With a flourish, she executed a deep curtsy in Violet's direction. "The unsung heroine of noxious gases everywhere has triumphed."

Arthur's joy at *finally* pummeling Grantham bled away at the news. She'd finished her formula.

Grantham swooped Violet into his embrace, but Arthur remained frozen in place.

"I surprised her in her workroom and wiggled the news from her. She wasn't even going to tell anyone until after the event tonight. Such humility, although admirable, shan't rob me of a midmorning glass of champagne," Lady Phoebe declared.

Violet ducked her head, but she couldn't hide her pleasure in the accomplishment. Why should she? Of all the chemists in the country, the government had come to her, and she'd delivered.

"All these years of listening to you yammer on about Avocado's law, and it turns out you weren't spouting nonsense, after all," Grantham teased, his handsome face awash with genuine admiration. "Good work, Vi."

Arthur swallowed a bitter pill of grief and self-loathing, ashamed that his first thought was of his own loss, rather than of her great achievement.

"I shall tell Cook and Mrs. Sweet to prepare something celebratory," he said. Holding Violet's gaze, Arthur bowed and spoke with as much honesty as he could bear. "Well done, my lady. Well done."

Despite the roses of pride blooming on her cheeks, Violet's thin smile told him that she, too, recognized what her success meant for them.

As she made for the doorway, she paused and glanced over her shoulder.

"Did you find what you'd lost, Grantham?" she asked dryly.

"No, but you know what they say . . ." Grantham laid his hand on Arthur's shoulder. Arthur stared at the big man, but he didn't move away. "You have to lose something first to realize it's what you've been looking for the whole time."

22

❧

Freezing rain beat at the few buds brave enough to emerge from the branches. Summoning a hansom, Arthur carried out his errands without stopping, mindful of the time slipping away from him.

It didn't matter what Grantham had said; the assignment was finished. Everything would return to the way it was before Arthur first met Violet.

Nothing would be the same.

By the time he'd finished his errands, the upper floors of Beacon House were deserted. Staff were gathered in the club for last-minute preparations. An army of silver raindrops marched double time down the roof, throwing themselves against the battlements of its walls and windows. To the rhythm of the tiny pellets against the glass, Arthur climbed the stairs, an unwieldy package beneath his arm.

Shifting his parcel, he stopped to check that a casement window lock was secure. How often had he walked the back hallways of houses over the world on afternoons such as this? All those years of self-imposed distance to save lives. A terrible irony that on the one assignment he could not keep his distance, the stakes were the highest he'd ever encountered.

He never should have allowed that first kiss.

He would remember that kiss till his dying days.

Arthur's thoughts continued in circles as he made his rounds until he paused at the doorway to Violet's bedchamber.

Violet's bedchamber.

Those two words still had the power to set Arthur back on his heels.

When no one responded to his knock, he entered the antechamber and walked through to Violet's bedroom. Here, the walls were painted a vibrant pink; grey skies and the lone light of a candle had mellowed them to a dusty rose. Mounds of pillows and thick, quilted counterpanes of deep plum and burgundy topped the bed.

Scandal was one whisper away. Despite his best intentions, he would never be the man Violet needed. She deserved someone who had words at the ready when tears appeared. A man without scandal attached to his name. A father to her children.

Children.

A tiny flame of hope he'd thought died long ago burned deep within him. Best put it out before he fell prey to Grantham's words, before he forgot the world outside these doors.

Setting the package on her bed, Arthur leaned over and set a finger to the dent in her pillow. He imagined himself resting here, Violet lying at his side. Were he a different man, his first thoughts on wakening would be of pleasure: admiration for the plump curve of her arm, the arc of her dark lashes against her skin, the sweet half gasp she made when she came. Were she a different woman, it might be his touch guiding her from untroubled slumber to early morning bliss. Instead, she had a dream, and he was going to find a home.

"A man!"

To the left of Violet's bed, a square of light fell on the floor from the opening to her dressing room. The call had come from within.

"This is . . . help . . . so ridiculous . . . ," Violet's muffled voice came again. Arthur decided her words comprised a request for help.

Far be it from him to disappoint a lady.

"What woman would formulate such a stupid, torturous . . . Hello? Alice, is that you, dear? If you can give me one good reason for my bosom to be pushed up to my chin other than for the amusement of men, I will double your wages. All my breasts are good for, aside from the suckling of children, is balancing the heft of my bottom."

"The problem is your vantage point," he remarked as he entered the room.

"Arthur?"

She must have been conducting an explosive experiment in her dressing room. The chamber, papered with a pattern of pink and gold chrysanthemums, was carpeted with a blanket of garments in varying shades. Rows of shelves stood empty except for a solitary pair of boots and a crumpled straw bonnet. A glass bowl filled with orange pomanders and dried lavender stood precariously close to the edge of a dresser, next to a small table lamp and a basket of handkerchiefs.

Arthur could see no sign of Violet, however. For a panicked second, he considered whether she was buried alive beneath the mess. Instead, her head popped out from the side of a tall screen, camouflaged by even more discarded dresses hanging over the top.

Shutting the door, he leaned against a counter and again surveyed the disaster.

"What on earth . . . ?" he said.

"Don't ask," Violet warned. "I've made a mess, and I will clean it up. In the meantime, I am not a contortionist. I am stuck in this dratted corset."

Only a tiny lamp and a small round window lit the room, yet her skin glowed like a pearl. The powdery scent of cloves hovered in the still air. Beneath her distress rung a note of amusement, hinting at an ability to find humor in any situation, including those of her own making.

Part of Arthur wanted her to remain frozen in time after he left. To never know any heartache or loss again, to never find melting pleasure or heated passion with any other man. Not until he met Violet had the selfish, possessive part of his character become so prevalent. He wanted her to stay right where she was without him.

The better part of him, the man he hoped she might remember, sent a silent prayer heavenward that Violet Hughes would never stop being herself. He imagined an octogenarian Violet, mumbling about the uselessness of undergarments and the tyranny of fashion while she tossed her dresses left and right. He hoped she continued to drive her household to distraction, never stopped delighting in educating the people around her, and always kept her sense of humor.

"Alice disappeared once she drew a bath. I've tried to undo the ribbons on my own, and I cannot loosen the knots. Can you fetch me that robe, and I will cover myself while you help me?" She came out from behind the screen. "As I said before, I cannot imagine why . . . Oh. You heard my reasons why, didn't you? That nonsense about bosoms."

Staring at the floor, Arthur hid his delight at how her words went stumbling into one another each time he called forth her blushes. There had never been anyone like Violet in his life before, and there would never, ever be another woman who moved him as profoundly. It took all his willpower not to leave and pretend time had stopped.

"Are you laughing at me, Arthur?"

"I am smiling," he said, dropping his hand from his mouth. Why trap his delight and admiration within him? If anything, it did her good to watch him set it free. "Reflecting on my good fortune at being the one to rescue you. I can appear heroic at least once before I go."

"Are those the heights to which you aspire?" she asked. "Catapulting yourself across a table to stop a bullet is nothing, I suppose. Catching my fall from the top of a bookshelf, chasing off a thief, putting out fires left and right. Are these not heroic?"

Arthur hated the word *hero*. Heroes were feckless men at the head of the pack, heedless of the damage left behind. Cowards were those who had seen the end of a battle and knew that was one place they never wanted to be again.

A coward would walk away right now. Minimize the casualties. Put a quick end to the suffering.

A hero was a fool. A hero would run straight over the edge to feel the fall one more time.

"DID YOU SAY you needed my help?" Arthur asked.

"Yes, please. Pass me that wrap?"

"Your wrap? I can't seem to find it," he purred.

Thrills of excitement ran beneath Violet's skin. She'd donned a new corset this morning, and the chemise beneath was a pleasing shade of ivory.

She supposed she didn't need a wrap. He had seen her naked many times before. Violet bit her lip and stepped over a pile of petticoats.

Arthur's expression revealed more appreciation than any of his inventive compliments could.

"You must come closer, my lady," he said, his teasing tone at odds with the hunger in his eyes. "It may take time for me to complete this task in such low light."

When Violet hesitated, he stiffened. After a quick sweep of the room, his gaze returned to her. "Unless you want me to call Alice?"

"Oh, no."

A standing mirror showed her a glimpse of her rounded hips, and her breasts flowing over the top of the corset. Bowing her head, she presented him with the tangled mess she'd created.

Twice, she opened her mouth to speak, and twice she swallowed the words, afraid she might ask for more than he could give.

What could she say? The truth?

He'd broken her apart when he'd first entered her life, cracking open the shell she'd spent years constructing around herself.

Now, when he left, he would break her again.

It would be a necessary breaking, though, and the pieces would fit back together in a different way. Violet was a scientist, first and foremost. An object remained forever at rest unless acted upon by an outside force. If Arthur hadn't come into her life, she would have remained the same lonely, insecure woman she'd been at the end of her marriage.

"Am I pulling too tight?" he said.

Violet regarded Arthur over her shoulder. "No, of course not. I was thinking of something else. Everything is fine."

Those eyes of his missed nothing. But how inconsiderate that he wouldn't let her lies stand.

In the city of London, hundreds of thousands of people woke, fought, loved, and prayed in a cacophony of sound and color. The premature end of a lady's affair with her bodyguard was an inconsequential event in the grand scheme of the history being made outside her walls.

Why then, did every exhalation, every blink, every small brush of their fingertip against the other's skin feel so momentous? How could the vast world shrink to an afterthought when she was in the company of this man?

The corset came apart in his hands. He tossed it to the side, exposing her with a flick of his wrist.

"I wish I could see you," she told him. "In all the times we've been together, you've kept yourself hidden from me. If you are leaving and this is to be our last time, I need to be . . ."

"On equal footing?" he asked.

"On equally shaking ground."

Arthur hesitated, and Violet held her breath. Leaving off the corset made this easier. The moment stretched and, as so many other things between them, took on outsized importance now that time was running out.

This would be the last of the barriers between them to fall.

Intent upon his expression, she nearly missed the act of him untying his cravat. The strip of linen slipped to the floor next to a dressing gown. His coat came off with little effort, his clothing having been tailored for ease of movement. He was not an indolent gentleman with a valet to dress him. If nothing else, the speed with which his simple garments fell away was a reminder of their places in the world outside.

Not here, however.

Not now.

She said nothing as he unbuttoned the fall of his trousers and reached behind his head to pull off his shirt. Biting her bottom lip, she drank in the sight of him, bare-chested, pants hanging low on his narrow hips. The head of his erection pushed against his linen smalls, and dampness bloomed between her thighs in answer.

The outline of his secret anatomy was visible beneath his skin. A deltoid expressed in the slope at his shoulder, the delineation of his obliques appearing as rectangles with rounded edges. Open him up, and she could give a scientific name to each part of him. The bones of his arms and hips, the major and minor muscles, the organs that kept him moving and breathing.

All that knowledge meant nothing when she beheld the sum of him: the dark curls covering his chest between two copper-colored nipples, the way his thighs bunched then lengthened as he bent to remove his stockings, a smattering of pebble-sized white scars dotting his side, and a larger scar rising red and angry above his left elbow.

"Can I . . . ?" Violet made to touch his chest but waited for permission.

With a sweet hesitance, he nodded. True to form, he reached out and took her hand, placing it on his sternum and holding it there for a moment. Determined stay in control and remain on guard.

"Let go," she coaxed him.

With a wry shake of his head, he dropped his hand, and the walls came down.

Violet explored his body with the wonder and anticipation she had for a new theory or a challenging experiment. She reveled in the noise he made when she set her open mouth against the skin beneath his clavicle and sucked. A rational part of her mind noted that Arthur was as pleased when she set her teeth to his nipple as she was when he nibbled hers. The rest of her brain dissolved into a pleasant fog. All that mattered was sensation, the search for a way to sink *into* him.

"Why have you hidden yourself this whole time?" she demanded, running her hands up and down his arms, marveling in the texture of the hair on his legs and the way his jaw clenched as she caressed his cock.

"Easier to take on an assassin when your dangling bits are tucked away," he explained.

Trailing her fingertips over his scars, Violet walked around to view Arthur's body from all angles. The history of his life could be charted on the map of his skin.

The scrutiny rattled him. Twisting her around, her back to his stomach, he maneuvered them in front of the mirror. Her first impulse was to cover her heavy breasts. Instead, he grasped hold of her wrist and held her arm up, while his other hand rested on her belly.

"Here I am," he said to her reflection. "Here we are."

Outside, the wind hammered at the brittle glass windowpanes in a bid for their attention. A table lamp flickered an impudent reply.

Neither of them paid any attention to the back-and-forth between the elements. Once again, Violet marveled at the intensity of Arthur's gaze. Focused, as though he could discern the future if he didn't blink. His hand moved downward with maddening deliberation, leaving fire in his wake, and he pulled up her chemise.

"Don't," he whispered when she let her head fall back against him and averted her gaze. "I want you here with me. If I cannot see and hear your pleasure, I can't find my own."

It took courage for her to watch him touch her, to silence the critical voice in her head that whispered insecurities about her belly and her hips.

Even more difficult to accept his genuine satisfaction with what he saw and touched.

"You are so soft and warm," he told her. "And here, in the sweetest part of you . . ." He slipped his fingers into the slit in her drawers and touched her between her thighs. "You are slick and smooth, like satin."

His erection pressed at the small of her back as he worked his palm against her mound. She held on to him to keep from falling forward.

Pulling away, she turned in his arms, closing the distance created by their reflections. Now, face-to-face, she saw the tenderness in his smile when he guided her to the ground and settled them both onto a mound of gold and blue satin. His weight was on his elbows, and his hips pinned her beneath him.

"When I decided to clean out my wardrobe, I didn't imagine it would serve this function," she said.

Their goodbye stood outside the doorway and muffled any laughter. Still, a wicked gleam lit Arthur's eyes. Within seconds he'd divested her of her drawers, keeping only her chemise.

Pulling the material tight against her breasts, he sucked her nipples through the translucent material. The warmth of his mouth and the friction of the cloth against her flesh combined to heighten her sensitivity.

Craving the heat of his skin, she searched his secrets with her hands. She memorized how his stomach muscles jumped when she brushed her fingertips against them, cupped his heavy sac with eager fingers, and stroked the broad expanse of his shoulders.

A golden haze lit the room, muting the brilliant colors to either side of Violet. Free from the constraints of his clothing, Arthur appeared larger, more elemental. A wash of blue-black shadows painted his jaw, and a few grey hairs glinted in his thick curls. He was radiating power, even though he'd made himself vulnerable at her command.

"Before we go any further," he said, "do you have another sea sponge?"

"I am not in the fertile part of my cycle. We should be safe if you withdraw," she replied. "But nothing is certain, Arthur. If we do not want any risk, we can finish now. You are the one man—"

He took the rest of her words in his own mouth and kissed her without finesse. Kissed away what they could never say aloud. Kissed her so that he impressed himself upon her, and no other kiss would ever taste the same.

Within him lay the sun; the burning star covered her body and sent its heat deep within her. The lick of flames—against her lips, her breasts, the very center of her—woke the woman buried deep within.

Never using a single word, he told a story of springtime.

With a soothing languor, his hands and mouth readied her. She heard the unspoken relish in his touch, saw the way his jaw clenched with anticipation, tasted the beads of sweat at his temple. Violet let go of the last of her inhibitions and trusted him as she'd never trusted another.

"I have never been so firmly within my skin as when you touch me," she said. "For the first time, the weight of my body does not drag me down. It holds me steady beneath you. Not until I met you had I truly felt beautiful."

She'd lost years of happiness buried beneath the blanket of Daniel's words. Being with Arthur had burned away the suffocating weight.

Hovering above her, Arthur set his lips upon her forehead as though pulling the scent of her skin into his lungs.

"You have an extraordinary gift, Violet Hughes." He brushed her eyelashes with his lips in a butterfly of a kiss. "Whether you take someone's world and upend it like a globe or shift their position so they can see farther, you have the power to remake everything and everyone around you better. Especially me."

He whispered the last few words, and Violet hoped, more than anything, that what they did today would sustain him in the years to come. She prayed it would bring Arthur the comfort and peace he deserved wherever he found his home.

They were two pieces of a puzzle coming together when he fit himself to her and she hooked one leg around his hip, her heel pressing into the base of his spine.

"Please," she told him. An invitation and an appeal.

"Yes," he said. An answer and a surrender.

So sweet were the first careful but deliberate strokes. She opened to him, tight but wet with anticipation. Gentle at first, they lost their sense of time in the smooth, slow glide of him finding his way. In their silken cocoon, the only sounds were the slick slide of flesh and Violet's low gasps in time with Arthur's thrusts.

Climax beckoned when he increased the pace, pulling more clothing beneath her and tilting her hips upward. When he raised himself above her, mouth drawn, a wild look in his eyes, she dug her fingers into his hips, urging him on. Unable to hold back, she cried out when he thrust deep within her, reaching to her womb. He dropped his gaze and watched himself parting her flesh, and he groaned in satisfaction.

Every part of her body trembled with need as she met his thrusts with her own. Outside, the wind shook the city upside down. The room spun away, untethered to any world other than that of their own creation. Faster and faster, they came together and parted again, relentlessly seeking friction, trying to find a way into each other's skin.

Blossoms opened, and colors exploded behind Violet's eyelids. In the instant before she flew away, she called out Arthur's name. Underneath her noisy cries of release, she might have heard him say, "Always."

SOON AFTER, ARTHUR left her.

In body, he remained at her side, but in the aftermath of their lovemaking his warm manner disappeared in that way he had of receding into silence, still aware yet removed. Did he pace the boundaries of his future farm? Was he seeing himself eating solitary meals and reading a book by the fireside as the nights wept down from the Highlands and blanketed his fields?

"When . . . when I am gone," he said in a careful monotone, "do not let Greycliff burden you with another such assignment unless he remains here to protect you."

The demand pinched, and Violet arched away from him. "You are not my protector any longer," she said. "After tonight, you will find yourself limited to directing the security procedure for your cows and goats. Or perhaps your advert will yield success, and you will find domestic bliss and a wife to protect."

Taking one of her curls between his forefinger and thumb, he pulled it straight, then let it spring back a time or two before he answered.

"I was never going to do that—place an advert for a wife. I can't imagine I would make a good husband."

Violet sat and examined his face. "Are you truly going to spend the rest of your life alone? What will you do without company? What if you get sick?"

She pictured the man Arthur might become if he continued this way. Silent for days on end, fearful of caring for anyone or anything. Unforgiven. Unforgiving.

If she had more courage, she would ask him the question that had been haunting her for days:

Why are you choosing a lifetime of isolation rather than staying here with me?

Instead, she asked, "Who will bake you tarts and wait up for you if you are out late?"

A clear drop of liquid ran down her cheek and fell to the floor. How odd. The ceiling of the dressing room must be leaking. She would investigate the source of the leaks if her vision weren't blurred.

"Oh, my dear. Do not cry." Arthur spoke gently, as though his words could cushion her.

But Violet had fallen already. Fallen hard. And it broke her open so wide that everything spilled out.

Violet pulled a wrinkled petticoat over herself, lurched to her feet, then stumbled.

With his customary grace, Arthur sprang to his feet and caught her, keeping her from knocking over the bowl of dried flowers.

"If you'll excuse me," she said, "I must . . ." She cleared her throat and tried again. "Alice will return soon to help me dress for tonight's event."

"Of course," he replied. "Tonight will be a success, I am certain. I wish—"

What good would it do to hear his wishes? They'd made their choices. Unless the world outside had changed, they were bound by them.

Putting off the inevitable farewell, Violet fled into the bathing room. She closed the door and curled into a tiny ball on the floor. For a while she stared at the ceiling and found pictures in the plaster cracks. The faint odor of attar of roses filled her nose.

Why didn't it hurt more?

Instead of pain, her overwhelming feeling was . . . nothing. With a detached interest, she pressed her fingertips into the cold tiles beneath her, watching her skin turn from pink to white. Nothing.

Freezing rain iced the windowpanes loud enough to draw her attention. Not loud enough to cover the sound of Arthur leaving the dressing room.

At last, Violet pulled herself to sitting with excruciating slowness, then to her feet. Hadn't she told Arthur, told everyone, that the club took precedence over everything?

Everything must now include her broken heart, she supposed.

She filled a basin with water and washed off the scent of him, scrubbing away her tears, until the remaining evidence of their desire was the ache within her chest. Outside the bathing room lay heaps of gowns and undergarments on the dressing room floor. Strange to think it would take mere minutes to clear away the witness to what she and Arthur had shared. How long would the effect of his words last inside her head and inside her heart? Could she continue to believe in herself after he left?

Shivering, Violet went into the bedroom to fetch her warmest robe. There, on her faded counterpane, muslin of the palest blue covered a lumpy package, tied with a length of red ribbon, the faint scent of dried orange peels rising from the cloth.

She reached out gingerly, as though the package might leap up and bite her. For a moment, her hand rested in the air, above the knotted ribbon.

With trembling fingers, Violet opened the package.

The dress from Madame Mensonge's lay before her. The one she hadn't allowed herself to buy.

Unshed tears muted the colors of gold and green as she ran her hands over the cool silk. An emotion that could be either joy or pain clenched at her heart. She lifted the gown to shake out the wrinkles and spied another bundle beneath it. Setting aside the gown, Violet tugged at another ribbon, blue this time.

Fairy wings. The words popped into her head upon spying the transparent material. It might have been fashioned of something lighter than gossamer. Lace, the lightest of pinks, trimmed a blush-colored chemise with tiny rosebuds embroidered at the neckline.

Violet pulled the chemise over her head and walked to the mirror, hair down and still wet, trickles of water pasting the chemise to the swell of her breasts. Without the armor of corset, petticoats, dress, and shawl, she barely recognized herself.

Who stood here before the looking glass?

A widow.

A chemist.

A lover.

A friend.

Violet inhabited more roles than she had dresses. Which would she choose?

Or would she give them all up?

23

AT SIX TWENTY on Thursday evening, forty minutes before the doors of Athena's Retreat were to be thrown open to the public, Milly Thornton claimed she'd lost her gloves and made for the back door.

"I must have left them in the carriage. Or at home. Or in Herefordshire," she called over her shoulder as she hurried to the exit.

"You are going nowhere," declared Lady Potts, blocking her way. Over multiple stiff petticoats, the older woman's aubergine skirts flared in a cascade of loose gathers, taking up more space than two other women standing side by side.

Milly didn't stand a chance.

"We stand together, or we fall together. Now, buck up and help me put out the folding chairs."

"All well and good for you," said Willy. "You've a title. We have only each other if tonight goes poorly. There are so many people coming, what if someone finds out about our work?"

Lady Potts lowered her chin slowly—her coiffure would not survive sudden moves—and regarded Milly and Willy with surprise.

"Don't be foolish. You have us. Athena's Retreat is your home, and we are your family."

They stood in the small lecture hall, preparing for the talk by the renowned Sir Thaddeus Limpenpot, as uncontroversial and uninteresting a lecturer as they could find. Huge sprays of lilies and roses from Violet's family stood artfully displayed throughout the room, alongside cards and notes of encouragement. The scent in the room was evocative of spring storms.

While her friends spoke, Violet fussed with a pretty arrangement of violets from Grey. In the accompanying letter, he expressed his sincere regrets that a delay in travel meant he would miss the event itself, but he said that he hoped to return to Beacon House the next morning.

Violet was feeling melancholy, but she attributed it to Grey's absence rather than Arthur's impending departure.

"Do you promise not to blow anything up?" said Phoebe to Milly. "If you stay away from your lab and content yourself with small talk, all will be well."

"What if I slip and begin a discussion of acid catalysis?" Milly asked.

"Let us make a rule," Violet suggested, squelching her blue devils and returning her attention to her friends. "We promise not to discuss any topic we wouldn't broach at the Queen's drawing room."

"Oh, that's an excellent idea," said Milly. "I don't see as how we'll get in trouble discussing the weather."

"Unless one is a student of the work of Joseph Priestley with an interest in the phenomenon of lightning . . ." Willy trailed off when the other ladies glowered at her. "Never mind that. Sticking to rain."

At six forty, Violet had finished speaking with the musicians and had the footmen light the candles. She was discussing the timing of refreshments with Mrs. Sweet when Letty grabbed her arm and dragged her into an alcove.

"Reginald Pettigrew is here, and he isn't well pleased." Letty wrung her hands, and a terrible falling sensation filled Violet's belly.

The specter of Maisy White's terrified face while her husband dragged her away loomed between them.

"Fetch Winthram at once," Violet told her.

Letty hurried off while Violet made her way back toward the connecting door, pulling her grey shawl taut and wrapping the comforting material in her fists while she considered whether to end the evening before it even began.

"Brilliant. Just brilliant, don't you think, Mr. Kneland?" came a man's voice. "It's simply brilliant, my dear."

The oak door stood open, and Caroline Pettigrew, dressed in a pretty gown of robin's-egg blue, walked through on the man's arm. Bringing up the rear, Arthur closed the door and, when he was certain of Violet's attention, mimed fitting a key to a lock.

She nodded. Point taken.

"Lady Greycliff, may I present my husband, Mr. Reginald Pettigrew," Caroline said, her face bright with happiness.

Reginald Pettigrew, a whip-thin man with high, angular cheekbones, stood almost the same height as Arthur but took up half the space. Clad in a brown cutaway coat and buff-colored trousers, he sported a buttercup yellow stock at his throat, which matched the trim of Caroline's gown. His hair sparkled, and the smell of acacia gum hung in the air.

Violet professed herself pleased to meet him, while trying not to gape at his head.

"I'm ashamed to admit it, Lady Greycliff, but I began to suspect that Caroline had grown tired of my company," Reginald said after the introductions were over. "I work long hours as a clerk, and I'm afraid I neglected her."

"Not at all, Reginald," Caroline protested.

He shook his head. "It's true. I grew more and more suspicious of her 'charity work' until finally I followed her here tonight. I had no idea, Lady Greycliff, that my Caro is a *genius*."

Caroline bit her lower lip and blushed while Reginald beamed with pride.

"I met Mr. Pettigrew wandering the halls looking for his wife," Arthur said. "We had a conversation about the necessity of keeping the work here a secret."

Reginald cleared his throat, and some of his color faded at the mention of the conversation, but he nodded in agreement. "Yes, enlightening little chat. Mr. Kneland explained how the club works. I agree wholeheartedly with his philosophy about my duty as a husband."

"What duty is that, Mr. Pettigrew?" Violet asked.

"My duty to protect the members of Athena's Retreat," he answered. Reginald glanced at his wife's hand resting on his arm and covered it with his own. "Husbands don't just protect their wife's bodies; we protect their hearts."

"Their hearts?" Violet asked softly. Although she was speaking to Reginald, her gaze was fixed on Arthur's face. He gave nothing away from his expression, as usual, but Violet searched anyway.

"Indeed," Reginald replied. "Caro's heart is here. I am her protector— and, by extension, yours and all the lady scientists'. And would you look at my hair?"

Reginald whipped his head back and forth, in a vigorous demonstration of the efficacy of Caroline's invention.

Even Arthur, the most stoic man Violet had ever encountered, had to hide a laugh.

They promenaded back to the public rooms as the orchestra played the first bars of a cracovienne.

Arthur waited until the Pettigrews were distracted, then whispered in Violet's ear. "Is there a new fashion for large grey shawls, my lady? I thought this a more formal event."

Violet peeked at him from beneath her lashes. "The doors haven't opened yet. I am not ready to display my finery."

"Lady Greycliff," Letty called to her from across the room.

Before Arthur could pull away, Violet faced him. The pain from their parting mere hours before was still fresh, but something had shifted inside her when she'd donned her new dress. She wasn't ready to say a final goodbye.

"The orchestra has been told to play a waltz for the last dance," she told him.

Arthur graced her with a rare smile.

"Well then, consider yourself claimed."

AT PRECISELY SEVEN o'clock, the doors of Athena's Retreat were thrown open, the lemonade was poured, and Lady Greycliff stood in the entrance of London's first ladies' social club to welcome her guests.

Newly lit beeswax candles stood at attention in candelabras placed at the side of the dance floor. Two huge tables, covered with fine white linens, were set in the center of the club's common area. Refreshments stood in tidy piles to greet the guests after the evening's lecture and before the dancing.

Miss Althea Dertlinger hurried over to greet Violet, her mother trailing behind at a more sedate pace.

"What an exciting evening," the girl exclaimed. "I don't remember everything being so fine when we were here last. I suppose candlelight makes it more romantic, doesn't it?"

"Indeed," Violet said. "Are you looking forward to the lecture tonight?"

Althea frowned. "Mama says it is the most exciting part of the evening. However, and this is in the strictest confidence, my lady . . ."

Violet nodded her consent and leaned her head toward the young woman. "You may tell me anything, my dear."

"Well, Mr. Smithfield says—"

"Who?"

Althea blinked. "Mr. Smithfield?"

Violet lifted her shoulders in question.

"Mr. Robert Smithfield? You are good friends with his aunt?"

Right. The boy from the ball. "Oh, yes. Sorry. Dearest Robbie."

Althea frowned, but recovered her story. "Mr. Smithfield says that Sir Limpenpot has a somewhat . . . archaic view of natural history."

"Is that so?" Violet asked. She'd never heard Sir Limpenpot lecture, but he sat on the board of the Royal Society. Perhaps more ominous, though, he was the only scientist to reply to their invitation to speak. "Well, let's hear what he has to say."

Lady Potts clapped her hands and announced the commencement of the lecture. Althea was snagged by her nervous mama, who settled them in the front row of the small lecture room. So many guests were in attendance that Phoebe, Grantham, and Violet had to remain standing at the back.

"Imagination? Fairy tales? No, oh, no. *Dragons*, my dear ladies, were real, and they lived right here in England."

Sir Thaddeus Limpenpot stood at the front, nodding at the shocked gasps following his announcement. He strode out from behind the lectern and positioned himself in a pool of light thrown from the sconces dotting the room, ensuring the flattering illumination of his profile. Behind him stood a rendering of the skeletal remains of a fantastical creature.

"Talking asses, my dear ladies," Phoebe whispered. "They are real, and they live right here in England."

"If there are no such things as dragons, what is that?" Grantham asked, pointing to the picture behind Limpenpot.

The skeleton's skull resembled a lizard's head, and the spine curved in a sinuous manner. If one was a writer of fiction, it could easily be described as a mythical beast. Sir Limpenpot, however, billed himself as a geologist and an expert on fossil science.

"That is an animal long extinct, not a dragon," Phoebe said. "Men like Limpenpot spread stories about these fossils in hopes of notoriety, the old fraud."

"Are you going to challenge him to a duel?" Grantham teased.

Phoebe frowned. "You jest, but he's making a mockery of years of scientific work. Why can't women challenge men when they've done something unforgivable?"

Grantham's shoulders tightened, and he broke off his observation of Limpenpot's prancing. "You are supposed to ask another gentleman to intercede if you need help. Instead, you make a spectacle of yourself."

"A spectacle because no one will heed me," Phoebe hissed.

A few heads turned their way.

"If people listened to me," she said. "I wouldn't have to go to such outrageous lengths to draw attention to injustices."

The anguish in Phoebe's voice broke an invisible tether within Violet. Glancing over at Althea Dertlinger, whose face was pinched in misery as Limpenpot carried on with a disingenuous pile of steaming claptrap, Violet knew something had to be done.

Althea and Phoebe weren't the only women objecting to Limpenpot's nonsense. Doris Whitstone, mouth thinned in irritation, was making to rise from her seat. An amateur fossil hunter, she was quite strong from climbing the cliffs and moving rocks and earth. Violet had no doubt who would prevail should a conflict turn physical.

Enough.

Blowing out a breath of courage, Violet walked toward the stage.

If she was willing to let Arthur leave her to protect Athena's Retreat, then the Retreat should be a place worthy of such sacrifice.

She paused at Doris's shoulder and whispered in her ear, then made her way to the front as Doris hurried from the room.

Amid the bright lights, Violet's courage almost deserted her, until she caught sight of Letty Fenley giving her a nod of approval. Willy and Milly grinned madly in their seats, Phoebe and Grantham left off their squabbling to lean forward, and out of the corner of her eye, Violet spotted a tall, solid figure standing, as always, in the shadows.

She could do this.

They could do this.

Sir Limpenpot did not see Violet at first as he continued expounding his theories to the audience. "Indeed, ladies," he said, "some believe the dragons died out in the great flood, expelled by Noah from the ark."

"Except no self-respecting scientist would posit such a ridiculous notion," Violet said. Employing the most luminous smile in her collection, she came to stand next to a startled Sir Limpenpot. "Our distinguished lecturer has done an outstanding job of presenting an outmoded school of thought. He had you fooled, didn't he?"

A confused murmur rippled through the crowd. Althea turned her head this way and that, then gazed back at Violet with relief.

"I did?" Limpenpot's eyebrows quivered in confusion.

"You were magnificent," Violet assured him. "Isn't he magnificent? It takes a talented mind to play *advocatus diaboli* as well as you did."

God bless Lady Potts, who caught on quickly and began a hearty round of applause. In response, Sir Limpenpot's chest puffed to twice its normal size, and he beamed at the audience.

Violet nodded like a cuckoo and continued. "Why, no one would believe a scientist in this day and age would peddle the same sensationalism as the British Museum did when it labeled this fossil a flying dragon all the way back in 1828."

Doris Whitstone had returned, a sheaf of papers beneath her arm, and Violet waved at her to join them.

"Of course not," said Limpenpot weakly. Perplexed, he twisted around to regard the illustration behind them. "But, if it isn't a dragon, what—"

"A pterosaur." Doris spread her notes on the lectern and nodded at the illustration. "This particular find was discovered by the great fossil hunter Mary Anning in 1828, and I believe it to be the first of its kind found outside of Germany. There remains still a great deal of controversy surrounding this order." Doris lifted her head and stared at Sir Limpenpot. "Is that not so, Sir Limpenpot?"

Limpenpot, having by now twigged to the situation, nodded. "Indeed, Miss . . ." He leaned over, adopting a serious mien as Violet whispered in his ear.

"Indeed, Miss Whitstone," he continued. Flinging his arm to encompass Doris and the illustration, he turned to present his stentorian profile to the audience. "The fair lady will carry on with the conclusion of our joint presentation. Afterward, I will happily address any questions you might have on our subject of expertise."

Doris squinted with disbelief but showed restraint by clapping politely. After a second round of applause, Limpenpot took a seat, and Doris returned to her notes, delivering a thorough, if less sensational lecture on the order Pterosauria, and a bit about dinosaurs more generally.

Miraculously, Sir Limpenpot seemed to enjoy his new role as devil's advocate and participated with good grace in the round of questioning afterward, deferring the bulk of questions to Doris.

In fact, to Violet's astonishment and great relief, the entire Evening of Edification and Entertainment was an unqualified, unmitigated *success*.

After the lecture, guests descended upon the refreshment tables and exclaimed with delight. The dried-then-reconstituted lemonade was heralded as both delicious and time-saving. Mrs. Sweet's seaweed canapés disappeared the moment they emerged from the kitchen.

The story of Mrs. Pettigrew and the pink china had slipped out. Rather than making her a laughingstock, she was the center of a crowd of ladies eager to learn about this marvelous invention that could both hold their hair in place *and* paint a teacup.

Wincing, Violet shifted her weight off her left toe which had been stomped upon during a boisterous country reel. That reel had been the first of many dances she'd enjoyed tonight. Her newfound popularity with the gentlemen must be due to Madame Mensonge's creation, she guessed. The silk caught the candlelight and threw it back ten times over, setting the tiny crystals in her hairpins sparkling.

Madame's neckline was as arresting as her materials. More than once during the evening, Violet wished she hadn't abandoned her shawl. Arthur might not have known what he was letting her in for when he gave her the gown.

Grantham didn't bother to disguise his opinion when he brought her a glass of lemonade. "Sweet Jesu. Wentworth was going to fall in, the way he leaned over the top of your dress. Where's Kneland?"

"I don't know." The only time she'd caught a glimpse of him tonight had been in the moment before she'd made that mad gamble in front of everyone. The thrill of her bravery still set her heart to beating.

"He should be here right now," Grantham said.

Violet cocked her head in surprise. "Why's that?"

"Not my job to fight off your admirers," he said cheerfully.

Well, here was a surprise. "Tell me, Grantham, what exactly did you lose in the blue parlor yesterday?" she asked.

"My bearings," he said, depositing the lemonade in her hand before wandering off.

Letty joined Violet sometime later, having spent the evening skulking in corners. Because of Melton, speculation about her character meant that she normally eschewed large events. That she'd worked so hard on the evening anyway was a testament to her devotion to Athena's Retreat.

"Lady Phoebe has stabbed Earl Grantham with a shrimp fork," she announced. "Also, there was smoke coming from Reginald's hair earlier, but Caro fixed it in time."

A twist of silk by the door caught Violet's notice as Phoebe stalked from the room, and Grantham stomped off in the opposite direction. Two matrons stood in the corner holding their pink teacups to the light. Althea and young Robbie swept across the dance floor. Milly fetched a plate piled high with tarts for Willy, who was engaged in animated conversation with Lady Potts. The last dance was next, and then they could breathe easier.

All except for Violet.

The instant Arthur entered the room and leaned against the wall, the air became charged. The black of his evening jacket stood in stark contrast to the powder blue stripes on the wallpaper behind him. Violet marveled that the length of floor between them did not burst into flames at the heat in his gaze.

"Are you all right?" Letty asked. Following Violet's gaze, she sucked her teeth in annoyance. "Why is Mr. Kneland dressed so fine? He can't think he is a guest."

Violet pressed a hand against her stomach. Butterflies had taken up residence there as it dawned on her: He knew what she was wearing beneath her dress.

How wicked. How absolutely, *amazingly* wicked.

Arthur must have read her mind, for a wolflike grin appeared as he leaned forward. A pulse of desire beat between Violet's thighs, and she ran her tongue over her bottom lip.

"He shouldn't be staring at you like . . ." Letty's head whipped back and forth between them. "You shouldn't be looking at him like . . ."

"Will you excuse me, Letty?" Violet said, her gaze never leaving Arthur's. "There is a question of security I must discuss."

"You can't, Lady Greycliff," whispered Letty. "Everyone is watching you tonight. What will they say?"

"Why would they say anything?"

Letty stepped back at Violet's tone but wouldn't be cowed. "Mr. Kneland is not a gentleman. He isn't even a parvenu, like me. He is something else altogether." She paused. "You know what people have been saying: That he let a man die so that he could have an affair with the man's wife. It's repellent."

"It is a lie." Violet's voice rang loud and clear. Two women a few feet away from them stopped speaking and turned their heads.

Letty's cheeks flushed, and she coughed to cover Violet's words, but it was too late.

"He was part of a mission that failed," Violet said, "and he's carried the weight of that failure every day since then. He may not be a gentleman, but he is a good man. A kind man. A decent man, and if you truly are my friend you will never speak ill of him again."

Across the room, Arthur tipped his head at her, then wandered through the crowd, deftly avoiding the couples trying their best to manage in such a tight space.

"What will Lord Greycliff say?" Letty whispered, peering around the room. "Your reputation is important if he wishes to court a lady from a good family."

"Grey would tell me that I deserve happiness," Violet declared. "Even if it is for a short time."

Hours.

Only hours were left to them now.

Letty's brows twisted. "Happiness is fleeting. The pain and hu-

miliation of damage to your reputation—that stays with you forever."
Her petite features scrunched with worry; Letty's unease was genuine. She'd run up against the rules of society and come away scarred.

Violet sympathized—hadn't she spent years in a futile attempt to
impress the same people?

Walking the same path as Letty would mean never taking another
risk. It would be safe, but safety wouldn't ease Violet's doubts or erase
her failures. No matter what path she took, she would be carrying her
imperfections with her.

Better to choose a path of joy as a flawed person than to live a life
devoid of love in the search for perfection.

"He won't stay past tomorrow. There are things he must do," said
Violet. "I will not abandon you or the club, but for tonight . . ."

Looking even more miserable, Letty protested. "My objection isn't
on behalf of the members. I want you to be careful of your heart."

Be careful of your heart.

As Violet skirted the elbows and knees of the ton in her pursuit,
the fragile, hopeful little organ beat double time.

It might get battered.

It might even break.

The only way it would stay unharmed was if Violet never used it
at all.

24

❧

AS HE EXAMINED the pink cups and saucers lining the refreshments table, the unique scent of wet slate and lilies warned Arthur of Violet's approach. His throat ached when he greeted her.

Though her skirts shimmered in the candlelight and the jewels in her hair and around her neck nearly blinded him, neither were a match for the radiance of Violet's smile.

Madame Mensonge might be an extortionist, but that dress was worth every shilling he could scarce afford.

How odd. He'd been waiting for this moment since setting the parcel on her bed this afternoon. What should he do with his hands? Why had he tied his cravat so tight, and was this a huge mistake?

"I wanted . . . ," she said.

"You should . . . ," he blurted out at the same time.

They stopped and stared at each other. Arthur might have done something irrevocably stupid at that moment—commented on the crowd size or, worse, gone to check with Winthram to see if all was secure—if Violet hadn't pressed one hand against her waist. Left hand to the side, little finger angled out. Waiting for an invisible strike.

Not tonight. Not from him.

"Blush," he said.

She did, and his nervousness disappeared. Every last worry about anything or anyone else fell away.

"Wh-what?" she stammered.

In dangerous situations, Arthur's training took over. He could fight as easily with his left hand as with his right. Blinded or deafened from an explosion, his marksmanship never faltered. Over the years, his killing skills had become second nature.

The connection between himself and Violet was the same: like breathing and sleeping. Blind or deaf, now or a hundred years from now, Arthur would know what to say to make her color that gorgeous shade of crimson, to make her stammer and set her pulse beating at her throat.

There was a name for this feeling. He wouldn't say it. Even to himself.

"The color of your chemise," he said. "I called it pink and was quickly corrected. It's blush."

"How did you know?" she asked, smoothing out the skirts of the gown for his perusal. "Of all the dresses I tried on, how did you know this was the one?"

"It's my job to know," he replied, echoing what he'd said the night they first met.

"Did you purchase undergarments for Lord Dickerson as well?"

Keeping a straight face, he bowed. "Lord Dickerson favors wool over cotton and is less partial to lace trim."

Violet's dimple deepened in approval, and the floor tilted sideways for a moment.

"You look . . . ," he said. "My paltry store of compliments cannot come close to describing how lovely you are tonight in that dress."

Violet's eyelids lowered; a sultry smile curled the corners of her luscious mouth. An unfamiliar sensation of joy skidded along Arthur's veins.

Six musicians had crammed themselves into the well beneath the lecture stage. It could have been an orchestra the way the music swelled around them.

One-two-three.

The count of three is where great leaps of faith begin. A three-count is the time it takes to take a breath, swear a vow, or dance a waltz.

"May I have the pleasure of this . . . ?" He paused when Violet's dimple disappeared and her skin blanched, all light extinguished.

A low hum reverberated in one corner of the room, and a few heads turned Arthur's way. Following the direction of Violet's stare, he spied Fanny Armitage by the dance floor, malice gleaming in her beady eyes. Lady Potts stood next to her, wringing her hands, while Althea Dertlinger had a hand to her mouth in shock. Letty Fenley was heading toward them from the opposite direction.

Caught among them all, Violet tilted her head to meet Arthur's gaze. A rapid succession of choices examined and discarded grew thick between them.

Violet's theory of ghosts made sense. He'd lived with the loss of his home for thirty years, and the pain had steered him into a life devoid of connections. Athena's Retreat was Violet's home. What would happen to her if she lost it? Dredging up a polite expression, he forced his facial muscles to rearrange themselves. Tonight was a celebration of everything she'd worked so hard for, and he would ruin it if he stayed.

"My invitation was selfish," he said. "You have other claims on your time. I will take my leave. Good night, Lady Greycliff."

The murmurs had grown louder, and Arthur had half turned to leave the dance floor when Violet did the unthinkable and took his hand.

One.

The low note of a cello tracing the arc of a turn in the honey-scented air.

Two.

The only places he touched her—the small of her back and the palm of her hand—as they began the dance.

Three.

One step forward, one step to the side, one step together, and then the dance reversed.

A pattern repeated over and over until the end. What had Violet told him about the laws of physics holding their world together? For every action, there is an equal and opposite reaction. One stepped forward, and the universe dictated that a step backward must follow.

In the end, you stepped together.

For a handful of golden moments, Arthur relished the sensation of dancing with a woman in his arms who knew the whole of him. He'd stopped trying to hide from her. Whatever she saw was the truth, and the truth was . . .

Invisible needles pricked the back of his neck.

There, to the left, Grantham appeared in a doorway, squinted at him, and frowned.

Not yet.

Stubbornly, Arthur guided Violet through the spinning tops of brightly colored gowns and sparkling cravat pins. Two men stood with their backs to the guests, one with auburn hair glinting in the candlelight.

The prickle turned to jangling nerves, and his nostrils flared.

Time was up.

"I have to go," he whispered in Violet's ear.

"Now? I thought . . ."

Thomas was nowhere to be found, and the sounds and smells of the party had faded to nothing. The two men he'd spotted had disappeared as well. Arthur held himself in check, aware that he and Violet were still the object of speculation.

"Do not go anywhere with anyone alone," he warned Violet. "Remain here until I return for you."

As he left, the breeze from Fanny Armitage's skirts ruffled his pant legs, but he did not glance back over his shoulder. If Arthur was sure of anything in this world, it was that Violet could handle Fanny from now on.

Especially in that dress.

VIOLET WATCHED ARTHUR as he parted the crowd like a cutter, slicing through waves of pale, limpid aristocrats. It made no sense that the Omnis would try anything tonight. There were too many people, and she'd finished her formulas. They were locked away in a cabinet in her workroom.

She'd almost forgotten her surroundings in the sensual excitement of the waltz, but the sight of Fanny Armitage brought her awake like a bucket of cold water. Violet's lips and fingertips went numb, and she pressed her hand to her stomach. There was no escaping the laws of physics. Newton taught that every action in the universe had an equal and opposite reaction.

London's social scene was as perilous today as it had been 150 years ago.

"I can't fathom why there is so much to-do over your club," Fanny told Violet. "All I can see is some tatty rooms and garish plates. Although I suppose anyone can maintain appearances for one night."

Ignoring Fanny's grating voice, Violet calmed her thoughts. How deeply ingrained in her the instinct to hesitate when it came to her desires.

"That gown resembles a Mensonge creation," Fanny went on. "The woman charges shocking prices when you consider how little material is used in the bodice."

Fanny's earbobs dangled like rattles as she shook her head in disgust, and her small, sharp teeth flashed in the light. "Who was that gentleman you were speaking with by the refreshments? He looked familiar," she said. "Or should I say, infamous?"

"You are not stupid," Violet said.

Fanny's sneer disappeared, and her lips formed an oval of surprise. "I beg your pardon?"

"You are not stupid," Violet repeated. "You are not poor. You married well, and you have three healthy children. You are invited most places and, as far as I know, you've never been bullied or slandered."

Fanny didn't know whether to preen or object. Her lips opened and closed, the thin skin beneath her chin shaking with confusion. "What is your point, Lady Greycliff?"

"My point is that you have everything you could want, yet you spend your time tearing apart others who do not. You exude malice rather than joy. Instead of extending a hand to help, you use it to slap women down."

The hectic flush of nastiness drained away from Fanny's cheeks, leaving her gaunt and unsure.

"You are an unhappy woman." Violet shook her head as Fanny started to protest. "I should know. So was I."

There were still loads of people in the room, but Violet and Fanny stood miles apart from them, with one foot in the past as they reviewed the choices that had brought them to this place.

"I don't know what has stolen your joy," Violet said. "It could be a lifetime of comparing yourself to others. It could be you had someone in your life who spoke to you the way my late husband spoke to me."

Fanny shrank in on herself. "You . . . you are drunk. Where did you find the nerve to say such things?"

Arthur. Arthur helped Violet to find her voice.

"Go home, Fanny. You are not welcome back at Athena's Retreat, but I do not wish you ill."

Despite Fanny's snort of disbelief, this was the truth. Violet did not hate Fanny Armitage.

"I wish you change. I wish you empathy. I wish you happiness," Violet said. "There isn't enough of that in the world. Maybe if you find some, you can spread it around."

Leaving the past behind, Violet joined the rest of the club members in bidding their guests farewell. Whatever expression she wore must have served to warn her friends not to broach the subject of Arthur and the aborted waltz.

All except for Lady Phoebe.

"Fanny Armitage has forgotten how to breathe. She's gasping like a dead fish," Phoebe said. "Her coloring is much the same, if you think about it."

"Hush, Lady Phoebe," Letty scolded.

"Keep your voice down, dear," Violet added. "It's bad enough I created a spectacle on the dance floor. Have you seen Grantham? I wanted to ask him if he knew when Grey planned to arrive."

"I have," said Phoebe. "There was a message delivered to him just now."

"This is taking forever," said Letty.

The two women spoke to each other while Violet replayed the conversation with Fanny in her head. Could she sacrifice her position at Athena's Retreat?

Everything was about to change; of that, she was certain. Was she ready for a life so altered?

The answer eluded her until her friend leaned over and whispered into Violet's ear.

While everyone around them was carrying on as though nothing had happened, everything Violet had ever believed was falling apart.

25

ARTHUR ELBOWED PAST a gaggle of servants outside the large assembly room, searching for the two men.

"Blast," he muttered to himself. Foreboding cramped in his gut as he questioned the staff. Although none remembered seeing two men leave by this exit, one had seen Grantham poking his head into the room earlier.

Johnson left off his flirting with an upstairs maid and added to the account. "He grabbed Winthram and told him to come along with him back to the house. Winthram wanted to stay here, said he had to keep watch over my lady, but the earl told 'im that's your job."

Arthur rubbed the back of his neck and took off toward the entrance to Beacon House's kitchen. The connecting door between the two buildings stood open, and dismay flooded him. Thomas was slumped in a chair before the fireplace, and Cook was wringing her hands. An acrid stench like burnt onions hung in the air.

Mrs. Sweet was kneeling before Thomas, wiping his face with a wet cloth and murmuring soothing words.

"What and when?" Arthur asked without preamble.

Thomas looked up with red, swollen eyes, his breath labored. "Two men. They had a canister like what the Omnis used. The spray . . ." Thomas coughed into a rag, which came away speckled with blood.

Mrs. Sweet came to her feet. "Enough. Don't make him say anything else. He must rest his lungs."

"Listen to me," Thomas rasped. "They were on their way upstairs—"

"They barreled through here," Mrs. Sweet said, "and were headed for the servants' stairs when Earl Grantham and Winthram arrived. Thomas got the spray full in his face, but they all inhaled some of it. The men ran out the back with the earl on their heels."

"I tried," said Thomas.

"You are not to blame yourself." Arthur set a hand on his shoulder when Thomas made to protest. "They will pay for this, Thomas. I swear it."

His fury on behalf of Thomas was tempered by the knowledge that Violet stood safely among the crowd of guests in the other building. Adam Winters and his conspirator must be on the hunt for the formula.

"They left not five minutes since," said Mrs. Sweet.

Arthur went out the back door and picked his way through the tiny kitchen garden. At the end of the path stood the mews, where a paved drive led out onto the main street. The light from the house did not reach here, and the carriage house was unlit. He slowed his steps, listening intently.

A whisper of air behind him was the sole warning, but it was enough for Arthur's instinct to take over. He twisted to the right as a meaty fist flew past his cheekbone. Throwing a punch of his own, he heard a satisfying grunt of pain erupt as his fist connected with a soft, vital part of another man's anatomy. As Arthur's sight adjusted to the darkness, he could make out the outline of the hulking figure, a man larger even than Earl Grantham.

The big man must have inhaled his own poison. His punches were sluggish, and he swayed on his feet. Thinking to himself he ought to teach Winthram this move, Arthur swept his foot out in an arc and kicked at the back of the man's knees, toppling the giant to the ground.

"Where's Winters?" he demanded of the man, crouching and grabbing him by the hair. Arthur had done his job too well, however, and the man's eyes rolled up into his head, his body sagging like a dead weight.

"Right here."

Arthur dropped the giant's head and peered over his shoulder.

Arthur hardly recognized Winters at first glance. He was dressed in fine evening clothes, with his auburn hair pomaded. His cravat was askew, and he was shaking as he wheezed. The arm holding a canister was steady enough, however.

"It's over, Winters. Put down the canister," Arthur ordered. "The formula has already been finished. Your weapon is useless."

"It's over when I say it's over," Winters said. A note of peevishness lay beneath his words. "I don't care about the damned formula anymore. Don't care about your lady, either. Move aside, and I won't have to use this."

"Why risk coming here at all?"

"That heartless woman ruined everything, and I will get revenge."

"What did she do?" Arthur rose from his crouch, hand on his knife handle beneath his jacket, ready to throw.

"What did she *do*? She misrepresented herself to me." Winters set a hand to his chest, and it settled right over the spot where betrayal hurt the most. "She came to hear a speech of mine and approached me afterward. Said my message *moved* her. I described to her how women have been treated as chattel for centuries, not unlike the common man, and she claimed I understood her as no man had before."

"You explained the subjugation of women to her, did you?" Arthur asked.

Winters nodded, oblivious to the irony. "When I confided to her that we planned to bring the fight to the streets, she supplied us with the gas canisters." His brows drew together then, the corners of his mouth drooping. "I didn't mean to kill anyone. I should have listened when she told me to dilute the solution."

Arthur cocked his head, and Winters scowled at the silent admonishment. "You have no idea how much that woman can talk. I can't be bothered to listen to everything she says when I have the fate of England's workers in my hands. Besides, Lady Greycliff was working on an antidote."

"Which you tried to stop her from completing." Arthur had lost patience with Winters's self-absorption and took a small step forward.

Winters shook his head. "No. At first, yes, but then I had the brilliant idea . . ." He paused at Arthur's huff of disbelief. "*We* had the brilliant idea that I would steal the antidote, then turn around and present it to the Queen, thus delivering our country from fear of the rioters."

Arthur took another step. "What about the Omnis? Have you abandoned your support for republicanism and universal suffrage?"

"All that will come in good time. More important, I need funds." Winters shrugged. "You can't eat good ideas. Legitimacy brings with it the security of a steady wage."

A touch of the confidence Winters had displayed in Shoreditch now returned, and he gestured with his free hand, letting his voice rise and fall. "If you rush to change, you risk losing everything. My followers understand that nothing valuable can be lost by taking time."

He shook a clenched fist in the direction of Beacon House. "Of course, this is a concept beyond the comprehension of that female. She stole my canisters, intending to travel the world from Albania to Afghanistan—wherever there is war—and sell the gas canisters to one side, then sell the antidote to the other side. Perfidy, thy name is woman!"

Arthur blinked. "I don't think that's the exact quote."

Winters didn't care. "Let me pass, I say. I will see her face one last time and curse her soundly. She has no honor. But I will confess, at one time she had my heart." He gazed past Arthur's shoulder at the lighted windows of Beacon House. "Love brings us all down in the end, doesn't it?"

His moment of reflection finished, Winters raised the canister. Aiming the nozzle at Arthur's face, his eyes widened with sudden surprise. He let out a groan, then crumpled to the ground. Behind him stood Winthram, holding a brick and looking as though he might cast up his accounts.

"Will he be all right?" the doorman whispered.

Arthur stepped over Winters and held Winthram's gaze. "He will be fine. You've done the right thing. I'm proud of you."

He clapped Winthram on the shoulder, letting his hand rest there for a moment. Despite his anger at Winters, a tiny flicker of happiness lit in his belly at Winthram's courage.

"I've got to go find Letty Fenley and bring this to an end," Arthur said. "Do you know where Grantham went?" He'd known Letty's story about the hair lacquer was too far-fetched to be true.

"Oh no." Winthram's face fell. "The earl is searching the club—didn't you know? Miss Fenley was the one who came to fetch me. She says Lady Greycliff and Lady Phoebe left not twenty minutes ago, and she can't find them anywhere."

Ice-cold fear robbed him of his breath, and Arthur slapped his palm over his chest. "Why would they do that?"

He knew the answer before he'd finished asking the question.

"I tried to tell you," said a weak voice. Winthram and Arthur turned to stare. Winters sat up, rubbing the back of his head. "She doesn't have a heart within her, but she does have a gun."

THE DISTRESS AT having a gun shoved into her ribs was nothing compared to the shock of Phoebe Hunt being the one to hold it.

Whispering into Violet's ear, Phoebe had cautioned her to follow directions and not to scream. "Matters are become quite serious, darling."

There'd been no trace of humor in Phoebe's voice, and Violet did as she was told. She exited the club in front of Phoebe at a calm but brisk pace. In the commotion of the departing crowd around them, no one noticed them walking away without their coats.

"Your Mr. Kneland will be watching the connecting door to Beacon House, so we enter via the servants' entrance," Phoebe explained. "If you try to warn anyone, trust me when I say that a bullet will ruin the line of your gown. I'm willing to shoot anyone who comes to your rescue. You don't want to be responsible for that, do you?"

Violet said nothing until they were in the house and climbing the back staircase.

"Phoebe Eleanor Margarethe Hunt," she hissed. "What is the meaning of this?"

Phoebe sighed in exasperation as though speaking to a young child. "I am threatening to shoot you unless you give me your work."

"I know that, but . . ." Violet pushed open the door to her workroom. She'd hoped someone might be waiting there, but the room stood empty.

Phoebe stuck the gun deeper into Violet's ribs. "No one here to save you." She gestured to Violet with a brushing motion. "Fetch me the formula, darling."

"You didn't answer my question." Violet pushed the gun aside, twisting around to glower at Phoebe. "I understand why Adam Winters would want to keep me from neutralizing his weapon—"

"*His* weapon?" Phoebe cried, genuine anger in her voice. "Violet, not you, too? I cannot believe you would credit that pompous ruffian with my work."

Phoebe's words sank in, and Violet's hurt and exasperation solidified into bone-chilling horror.

"*You* created poisonous gas canisters? My God, Phoebe. A man is dead because of them. Why?"

"Why?" Determination hardened Phoebe's jaw. "Because I will no longer sit and wait for the world to change. *I* will change the world."

"Change the world?" Violet echoed, stunned by Phoebe's rationale. "You said the three of *us* would change the world with Athena's Retreat. Instead, you worked with the Omnis? You don't give a fig for the rights of workers."

"I care about the rights of women," Phoebe retorted. The low, squared bodice of her gown, an elegant creation of saffron silk, revealed her delicate clavicle protruding under her chalk-white skin. The pulse at her throat was beating extraordinarily fast. "The corrupt old men in this country will never let us out from under their bootheels. Groups like the Omnis are tools we can use to climb out from beneath their weight."

Violet clasped her hands in supplication, desperate for Phoebe to return to her senses. "You don't need to poison people to advocate for political reform. You're from one of the most powerful families in England. Your voice alone—"

"*My* voice?" Phoebe's rage was awesome to behold. Anger blazed hot enough to burn her skin away and reveal the muscles and bone beneath. "I have been shouting at the top of my lungs my whole life." She gasped the last few words, straining to make herself understood. "My station makes me less powerful, not more. I could stand in the middle of a ballroom and recite my entire paper on carboxylation from start to finish, and the next day all anyone would remember is the color of my gown."

Part of Violet sympathized, even though she understood Phoebe was traveling a road past righteous toward no redemption, until her gaze landed on the clump of solid menace in Phoebe's hand.

"Have you no thought for anyone else?" Violet asked. "Everything you've done to slow my work could have had fatal consequences. Your canisters *killed* a man. Setting off bombs, causing fires . . . who *are* you?"

"I am the villain," Phoebe announced, tossing her head and posing as though for a portrait of a warrior queen. "In every story and every play, it is always a man who takes that role. I am snatching it away from them. I am the mad scientist, you are the damsel in distress, and this time, the hero is nowhere to be seen."

She snapped her words like the tail end of a whip. "I'm the one who told Fanny about his scandal, you know. I'd hoped he'd be halfway to Scotland by now, in a valiant effort to save your reputation."

"You are selfish, is what you are." Violet shook her finger in outrage. "You betrayed my friendship and the trust of every other woman in the club. How can you speak of wanting a woman's voice to be heard when you broke faith with the one community that has always listened to you?"

"I've no time for this." Phoebe brought the nozzle of the gun back into line with Violet's heart and jerked her chin toward the oak cabinet where the formula was locked up. "Open up the drawer and give me the formula."

"I've forgotten where I keep the key," Violet said, feeling rather sly.

Phoebe shook her head slowly. "Everyone knows you keep it in the jar of lemon drops."

Drat.

Violet stomped over to a row of shelves and climbed up on a stool. Standing on her toes, she pushed aside jars of powders and vials of liquids.

"There must have been ways to make your point other than violence." Violet rooted about until she located the jar. A handful of lemon drops rolled around at the bottom, alongside a rusted little key.

"It's the only way to get their respect." Phoebe's voice had softened. "Weren't you tempted to do violence in those years married to Daniel when he pressed you into smaller and smaller spaces?"

She lowered the gun as she made her case. "First, he turned you from a brilliant young woman into a mere hostess. Then just a wife. Then even smaller. A place setter. A tea pourer. How did that make you feel?"

"I hated it," Violet confessed, holding the jar tightly to her chest. "I hated him, and sometimes I hated myself."

Phoebe's intensity faded even more, and she nodded in agreement. "Since the beginning of time, they've had power over us because of their physical strength. Whenever we objected, they beat us into silence."

"Oh, Phoebe." Violet's heart broke for her friend and whatever injuries she'd taken at the hands of her father, both on the outside and the inside of her body.

Phoebe shook her head, refusing to acknowledge Violet's sympathy. "Science has given us the opportunity for parity. Do you know the canisters were not meant to be lethal? Adam ignored me when I told him to dilute the mixture in order to decrease the chances of fatalities. He wanted to raise the stakes, damn the consequences. Well, the

stakes are now ours to raise. We can develop weapons to protect ourselves and keep dangerous men at bay."

If Daniel had lived, if Athena's Retreat hadn't come about, would
Violet have joined Phoebe's mad undertaking? Rage as clean and pure
as Phoebe's was indeed compelling. Hadn't the same invisible barrier
trapped Violet from the world when she'd tried to make a point and
the men around her would stare right through her?

"To use our discoveries for harm is . . ." Violet tested the theory
aloud.

"Balancing the scales," Phoebe insisted.

Compelling, but ultimately destructive. What did it accomplish to
harm someone else because you had been harmed, other than beginning a cycle of pain without end? What would happen to the friendship and the community they'd created if their goal was to frighten
and intimidate? Eventually, the anger would poison them all.

"There has to be another way, Phoebe. You don't fight tyranny by
engineering an even greater threat."

Phoebe stared at the lump of grey metal in her hand. "Violence is
the only language they hear."

"No." Violet flung her arm out as if to encompass Phoebe and the
women on the other side of the walls. "You and me, Letty, the members, all the girls out there who will one day follow in our footsteps, we
don't have to accept that language. We can use science to create an
entirely new vocabulary. Violence is easy. Changing how people think
is difficult. We can do it if we work together."

Believing Phoebe must be moved by these sentiments, Violet went
to embrace her friend. Tragedy struck when she hopped off the stool
and promptly stepped on the skirts of her gown. Both women gasped
in horror at the sound of ripping silk.

"My dress," Violet cried in dismay.

"The first decent gown you've had in years." Phoebe bemoaned the wanton destruction of fashion. "A Mensonge creation, at that."

When Violet took another step, she tripped on the torn hem and fell to the ground in a clumsy heap, the jar flying from her hands. Broken glass and lemon drops lay everywhere. Violet let loose a hearty curse.

Phoebe gasped. "I had no idea you even knew that word," she said. "Impressive."

Violet preened, but her mishap had recalled Phoebe to the task at hand. Despite Violet's hopes, Phoebe was too far gone to let their moment of camaraderie deter her.

"No more delays, Violet," she said calmly. "The key is next to your knee. Pick it up and open the cabinet."

"I've twisted my ankle," Violet complained. She sat up and grabbed at her foot. "You are not going to shoot me anyway. Are you?"

Phoebe readjusted her grip on the ivory handle of the gun and pulled back the hammer. A small click meant the cylinder had locked into place. The sound caused Violet's heart to plummet. A folding trigger dropped, and Phoebe set her thumb to the side of it.

"You're right. I won't. I will, however, point my gun at the door. Whoever walks in risks a bullet to the heart. Do you want that?"

Violet shook her head. "Neither do you. Put the gun away."

A blanket of regret settled over Phoebe. "I cannot stop now, Violet. My father terrorizes every person in his life without any repercussions—the opposite, in fact. If there's one lesson he's taught me, it is that fear is power, and I want power. I won't be at anyone else's mercy ever again."

Certain she could talk her friend into reconsidering, Violet racked her brains to find an argument strong enough to win the battle between love and fear.

ARTHUR TOOK OFF running, not bothering with the servants' staircase, pounding up the main hallways without care, terror grabbing at his ankles. He'd *known* this would happen. He'd violated his cardinal rule and allowed something beautiful and warm into his barren world.

He'd killed Violet. He'd killed her with his stupid, selfish need for something precious to call his own, if only for a few hours. Lady Phoebe had been in front of him the whole time, and what had he been doing? Eating black buns. Chasing tarantulas. *Waltzing.*

The door to Violet's workroom was closed, but Arthur burst through as though it were made of paper. Phoebe stood a few feet away from Violet, aiming a revolving pistol straight at him.

"Go away, Mr. Kneland, if you do not want Lady Greycliff hurt."

Rage roared through him.

Arthur had never hit a woman in his life. Even when Mirabelle Delacroix had knocked him over the head with a plank while attempting to assassinate a Spanish *duque*, he'd subdued her without coming to blows. However, the sight of Violet, face as white as paper while sitting huddled on the floor, tested his resolve.

Arthur put his hands out, willing his heart to slow and his mind to sharpen. "Adam Winters has been apprehended," he said. "He confessed to his part in your scheme."

"Confessed?" Phoebe snorted. "More like bragged, then speechified, then complained."

As she spoke, Arthur noted her awkward grip and checked the distance between them and Violet.

"He also treated me to a lecture on the perfidy of certain females," Arthur added.

Phoebe pursed her lips to the side. "He loves that word."

"He claims to love you, as well," Arthur said.

"Love?" Phoebe waved the gun as though it were her pointer finger, and Arthur's stomach lurched. "He has less understanding of that word than he does the word 'perfidy.' Sex is not love. Control is not love. Possession is not love." She let loose a frustrated groan. "Why is anyone surprised that I wish to put men in their place?"

"It wasn't just men you hurt," Violet pointed out.

"You set off a bomb," Arthur said, raising his voice and drawing attention back to himself. "And that man who died had a family."

Phoebe gripped the gun so tightly the seam of her glove split at the side. "Yes, I designed the bomb that went off in the second-floor rooms last month. It was meant to create the greatest amount of noise and smoke with the least amount of damage," she said. "Do you know what Adam did?"

Arthur shook his head, glancing quickly between the gun and Violet.

"He asked his men to check my work," Phoebe said. "They took my bomb and rewired it—because what would a lady know? I *told* Adam not to tamper with the canisters, that adding too much of the reactant would render the mixture lethal. I might as well have been speaking another language. Or no language."

Her arm remained steady, and Arthur knew a round could get off before he could grab the weapon.

"You can hold yourself to blame for everything after that," she said. "If you hadn't become one of Violet's lost causes, she would have finished the formula weeks ago."

Fear threatened to suffocate him when Phoebe gestured toward Violet with the gun.

"She is forever trying to change men's nature. It won't work. Patience." Phoebe spat the word out as if the taste disgusted her.

"Kindness. To powerful men, those are another way of saying 'weakness.'"

"You have it wrong," he said. Though facing a gun and possibly worse, he opened his heart. "Violet is one of the strongest people I have met, and her patience and kindness are the source of that strength. Even more impressive is her compassion. Her knowledge, her friendship, her home: She shares it with a generosity that amazes me. Humbles me. Makes me want to be a better man."

Arthur paused. Not because Phoebe's outstretched arm now shook, but because he wanted, he needed, to say this before he left Violet forever—one way or another.

"You treated these gifts poorly and should be ashamed of yourself," he told Phoebe. "Such gifts are rare. They are precious, and when they come into your life, they change you, for the better, forever. The closest a man might come to heaven would be if he were loved by Violet Hughes."

Phoebe's beautiful eyes misted with unshed tears. Given time, she might have apologized or confessed to a change of heart. Declarations of love tend to have that effect on people.

She never got the chance.

Arthur took advantage of the moment and rushed toward her. She wouldn't have gotten off a shot if he hadn't stepped on something round and hard. His feet flew out from under him, and he toppled Phoebe to the ground. A blinding flash lit the room, everything spun, and the rank smell of gunpowder burned his nose.

Damn it. Not again.

Beneath the rushing of blood in his ears was the sound of Violet screaming.

He wished she would stop. He wanted to tell her how much he would miss her.

For in a matter of seconds, he would say goodbye.

26

IDIDN'T MEAN TO shoot anyone."

Exhausted by the night's events, Violet bit back a curse and glared at Phoebe. "You do not carry a weapon designed to kill without tacit acceptance that it will achieve its objective. You loaded it. Your intentions after the fact are irrelevant."

That Violet could see Arthur's chest rise and fall as he slept was the sole reason Phoebe stood here in Mrs. Sweet's office and not in jail or worse.

Leaning against the far wall, Grey crossed his arms. He was watching Phoebe's every move—when he wasn't peeking at the skeleton hanging in the corner.

He'd arrived home to find Grantham wheezing and crawling up the front stairs to Beacon House, then he'd burst into the workroom as Violet and Phoebe were stanching Arthur's bleeding. Once Arthur had been transferred to Mrs. Sweet's care, Grey had bundled Phoebe out of the room, keeping her confined until Violet arrived.

Grey spoke in a low, flat voice. "Arthur may have officially left the service of the government, but he was shot protecting government secrets by a woman who might be considered an accomplice to murder."

Phoebe pulled at the waist of her gown, now wrinkled beyond repair and spattered with the rust red stains of Arthur's blood. "My father would never allow a member of his family to sully his name by standing trial for so heinous a charge."

Grey flicked a speck of dust from his coat sleeve. "I wonder how he will resolve that problem when I deliver you to him."

Phoebe flinched, her fingers clenching the thin fabric of her skirts.

"No," Violet said.

"I cannot permit her to simply walk free." Grey studied Phoebe as one might examine the specimens floating in Mrs. Sweet's jars, with a mixture of curiosity and revulsion.

At first, Phoebe met his gaze, but she dropped her eyes after a moment.

"Why?" Violet whispered.

Phoebe frowned. "I told you. The Omnis were a tool—"

"No," said Violet. "Why couldn't you tell me? Why couldn't you speak to us about your father?"

"What could you do?" All of Phoebe's fire had been smothered with Arthur's blood and Violet's tears, but the anger remained, a sullen, stubborn pulse beating beneath her words. "My father owns me until I am sold to a husband. Every step I take out of doors in the shoes he purchased is dictated by the length of his leash. Will you upend the legal constrictions on women? Can the ladies of Athena's Retreat change the marriage laws? Property laws? Could you have convinced Parliament to reverse the Reform Act and grant women suffrage?"

Violet rubbed her forehead, moved by Phoebe's pain but frustrated by her friend's twisted reasoning.

"We don't have to choose between acting like a mob of angry men or doing nothing," Violet said. "Why can't we find a third way? Look what happened at the lecture. We didn't let Limpenpot continue his drivel, but we didn't blow him up, either."

Phoebe crossed her arms and pushed her toe against the coal scuttle. "You wanted to blow him up, though," she muttered.

"Sir Thaddeus Limpenpot?" Grey asked. When Violet nodded, he snorted. "I'd want to blow him up, too."

Violet resisted stamping her foot. "My point is, we found another way to counter his harm without doing any damage of our own."

Addressing Phoebe, she continued. "The world can be a terrible place, and I suspect your father is guilty of perpetuating those terrors. You let your rage blind you. Your constant battle against this world has left behind innocent victims. Winters may have changed your formula, but it was your idea and a man is dead."

Two tiny lines appeared on Phoebe's brow, the only outward sign of fear Violet had seen on her face all night. "I know that, Violet," she said. "I've retraced my actions from the first time I met Adam at one of those stupid lectures I attended with Grantham, all the way to when he and the Omnis took over production of the canisters. It's clear where I let my pride and anger override any better judgment I may have had, but if I let go of the anger, who am I? Who is left but that frightened girl I used to be before I found a way to fight back?"

"You are still Phoebe Hunt," Violet reassured her. "Still a scientist, still a champion for the protection of women." She smiled. "Still a firmament in the fashion heavens."

"Still a friend?" Phoebe asked.

Grey opened his mouth, then shut it, wise enough to let Violet make her own decision.

She stared at the jars full of specimens lining Mrs. Sweet's walls and considered dreams deferred, the ache of impatience with the world's unwillingness to change, and the slow boil of frustration so many women accepted as their lot in life.

"You must find a way to atone," Violet finally said. "Think of Letty, who already suffered a terrible betrayal by someone she loved. Learning about your lies will compound her pain. What of the club members who trusted you with their work, only to find you've used it to harm people?"

Phoebe's gaze skittered to the side, and she nodded. "All of them. I owe all of them an explanation and an apology. And the man who died . . . I owe his family reparations. Somehow . . ."

Meeting Grey's cool gaze, Phoebe pulled her shoulders back and let go of her skirts. "If you can keep me safe from my father, I will find a means of restitution. I won't change my goals, but I will change how I attain them."

It was lucky for Phoebe that Grey had the final decision over her fate. He would understand better than most how a father's disappointment or neglect could shape a child's actions. Daniel had despaired of his son's condition, embarrassed and frightened by his sudden seizures. An upbringing in isolation while suffering through punishing "cures" gave Grey a unique empathy toward the outcasts and the forsaken.

"I know of a group who might be able to use a female agent," he allowed. "You'll no longer be Lady Phoebe, and you won't see home for a long time."

"I don't suppose I'd want to come back until I've changed a few things," she said. Worry still lingered in her amethyst eyes, but Phoebe's face appeared younger, lighter somehow, and Violet could not resist smiling.

"Will you forgive me, Violet?" Phoebe asked.

Violet tapped a finger to her mouth in consideration. "I might, after a while."

"If anything happens to Mr. Kneland," Phoebe said, "would you be able to forgive me then?"

All these years, Violet had excused Phoebe's carelessness for others as a clumsy attempt to keep a cruel world at bay. There were limits to absolution, however.

Violet answered with complete honesty. "I will always love you. But if Arthur does not recover, I will see you stand trial without a shred of remorse."

"I HATE BEING shot," Arthur said.

Mrs. Sweet glanced up at his complaint, then returned her attention to his wound. Pulling on a length of catgut, she finished the last of her stitches.

"Maybe stop jumping in front of bullets," she suggested.

"I didn't jump," he muttered. "I slipped."

Distraction from the pinch of the needle had come when Thomas, Alice, Winthram, and even Grey filed through Mrs. Sweet's treatment room and offered opinions, sympathy, encouragement, and critiques in the same order as the visits.

Although Arthur made light of his injury, Alice was especially upset. Risking Mrs. Sweet's wrath, she brought him three stale black buns she'd been saving for herself. Arthur ate one under her watch, pronouncing it almost as delicious as his mam's.

He enjoyed it more than the bag of boiled lemon drops Thomas had placed on the bedside table with a devilish wink.

"Seems you have made a few friends," Mrs. Sweet observed.

Friends. Imagine that.

Mrs. Sweet packed the wound with honey and rosemary, admonishing him not to disturb the dressing.

He must have fallen asleep then, because he'd closed his eyes on Mrs. Sweet and opened them back up to see Grantham looming over his cot.

"Shot again, eh? Don't you look where you're going?" Grantham groused.

As the anesthetic properties of fear and shock wore off, Arthur didn't know which was the greater pain, Grantham or the gunshot wound.

"Chrissakes, I didn't fall," Arthur said. "I slipped."

Grantham cleared his throat in disbelief. "Suppose you thought to woo Violet by literally falling at her feet?"

Every nerve in Arthur's body screamed a protest, but he forced himself to sit. "I have no plans to woo Lady Greycliff."

"No?" The big man scratched his head. "Must I thrash you again? Poor form to pummel a man with a hole in his chest." Grantham leaned over and squinted. "Huh. Not so impressive up close."

"You realize I still have my knife," Arthur said.

Grey popped his head in at that moment to give them news: Violet had a strained ankle. She'd refused Mrs. Sweet's treatment last night, insisting on sitting by Arthur's bedside as he slept, until Alice had tricked her into eating a bowl of Mrs. Sweet's soup. They'd dosed it with large quantities of laudanum and carried her upstairs.

"All that seaweed masks the taste," Grey explained. "Mrs. Sweet is binding her ankle right now. I'm off to question Winters. Are you coming?"

Arthur swung his feet to the floor. When Grantham put out a hand to stop him, Grey intervened.

"He's made of stone, that one. Doesn't feel a thing."

Made of stone, indeed.

Grumbling something about stubborn Scotsmen, Grantham helped Arthur to stand.

"Post came today," said Grey. He pulled an envelope from his waistcoat pocket and handed it to Arthur. "This one is addressed to you."

Grantham whistled when he caught sight of the franking. "What's the Queen have to say to a leaky little Scot?"

"Possibly the same thing she'll say to a toothless earl," Arthur replied, flexing the fist on his good side.

"I've the train ticket you asked for as well," Grey said. "Staying or going?"

"I don't know," Arthur answered. "I'm not the one who has a decision to make."

27

⁂

Arthur closed the lid of his worn traveling chest and lay on his bed.

Once he had a home, he would furnish it with an eye toward permanency. Enormous wooden beds that would have to be taken apart to get out of the room once he died. Oak dressers and toile curtains, and whatever else other folks filled their homes with, would sit in piles in each of his rooms.

Or so he told himself on this first morning the sun had deigned to reappear in London since he'd come to Beacon House. He'd told himself any number of silly stories since waking, lying like a corpse in his narrow cot, staring at the ceiling. His wound throbbed beneath his dressing, but Mrs. Sweet had checked it an hour ago and declared him sound in body, if somewhat damaged in the head.

The tea she'd given him for the pain soon took effect, and he slept for a while. He woke to a tingling at the back of his neck.

"Sheep!" chirruped a voice from the corner of the room.

"Feck!" Arthur shot into the air, then fell off the cot. Scrambling like a lunatic, he pulled open the bedside drawer and grabbed for a pistol with one hand while unsheathing his knife with the other, pulling at his stitches in the process.

"According to Flavia Smythe-Harrows, they are intelligent animals. Their reputation for stupidity is the result of herding behavior. Flavia's father owns a large sheep farm, and she took an interest in their habits, although her first love will always be *Tetrao urogallus urogallus*."

Arthur released his grip on the pistol and groaned. Opposite him in a chair by the cold hearth sat Violet.

Her brilliant green camail trimmed with gold braiding covered a silk dress the color of roses, like a spring garden blooming in his room. A heady combination of wet slate and jasmine filled his nose. He had to ask.

"What is '*Tetrao urogallus urogallus*'?"

"That would be the western capercaillie. The wood grouse. Pronounced sexual dimorphism." Violet's cheerful explanation sounded like the chiming of bells to his ears. She blinked. "Did I alarm you?"

"Not really," he lied. "Why are you telling me about sheep and wood grouse?"

"Grey told me this morning that he'd purchased you a ticket to Scotland. I assume you plan to leave and search for your farm in the Highlands. My research tells me that sheep farming is the largest agricultural occupation in that region. You do remember my interest in the latest agricultural innovations?"

He laughed, and she smiled back with delight.

A tiny finger of sunlight pushed through his curtains and stroked her cheek. Outside, a blue sky covered the city, and songbirds nearly drowned out the rattle of wagon wheels and the cries of coffee sellers.

"I wanted to apologize. You would never have been hurt if not for my clumsiness," she said. The sincerity of her words twisted the anguish in her gut.

"Apologize? I was the one who failed you. Phoebe was in front of me the entire time. I should never have left Adam Winters loose once I learned of the connection between him and the club. He put that bomb there to punish you."

The truth had come out when they'd questioned Winters. He'd confessed to breaking the window but insisted the goal was to create noise and attention, not to harm anyone. When asked about the bomb, Winters had been defiant.

"Henrietta would never have stayed away this long if it weren't for that club. I figured if the club shut down, Hen would have to come home. I know what's best for her. Once I had the formula in my hands, I could have made enough money so that she wouldn't have had to go back to work."

However, he'd disputed Phoebe's story of having his men rewire the bomb because she was a woman.

"'Twas because she was impatient," Winters had said. "You couldn't trust her to do the work properly. Like those gas canisters of hers. She stole the work those other ladies were doing and mixed it together, then claimed it as her own."

"I failed you," Arthur said now.

"You took a *bullet* in the chest for me."

He crossed the room and knelt before her, gripping her hands. "This was my fault. Right from the beginning, there were too many coincidences. I spent weeks investigating Winthram, Letty, even the Pettigrews—the wrong people—the whole time. All because I doubted my judgment," he said. "I let myself get distracted. I always will around you."

Violet slipped from the chair and, with his help, settled on the floor facing him. They knelt together, a hair's breadth apart. He breathed in her scent as though it were air and he'd been locked away in a box.

"It doesn't matter anymore," she whispered, "because I am no longer in danger."

He turned his head, hiding from her imploring gaze. "But you may be again. I am not the man for you."

VIOLET HAD WAITED all day for this moment. Well, not this moment exactly. When she'd pictured their reunion, it hadn't consisted of her clothed and Arthur refusing to even glance her way.

She'd imagined him throwing himself at her feet and declaring his love for her.

Except he hadn't. She'd donned a new dress, which had arrived this morning, but the corset pinched. This and the throbbing in her ankle was making her irritable.

"Arthur," she said. "While I am sympathetic to your sensitive nature, I am afraid my patience with your delicate nerves is nearing its end."

Three lines appeared between his eyebrows as he puzzled over her statement.

"Delicate nerves?" he asked.

"Yes. It is all well and good to harbor a feeling of responsibility for me," she began.

"I do not have *nerves*," he said.

"You are a mere mortal, with the limitations that come with that state. Whether your focus is on me or not, you cannot control the rest of the world. We might be walking arm and arm and lightning strikes me dead. Will that be your fault?"

"No," he said cautiously.

"A carriage might flatten me when I cross the street to greet you. A house could fall on my head while we are sleeping together in bed."

They blinked at the same time when she said those last words, and the tips of her ears buzzed.

Sleeping together in bed.

First things first, however.

"The study of science is a study of the rational." Violet tempered her admonishment with a quick smile. "We do not deal in myths, dreams, or dark forebodings. We deal with the senses; we learn without prejudice, and we test our hypotheses."

"I find it incredibly erotic when you say the word 'hypotheses,'" Arthur remarked.

The corner of his mouth turned up a fraction of an inch, and Violet's heart soared in response.

"Consider the evidence to the contrary of your theory," she continued. "It hasn't been death, but life you've given to me."

He lifted her gently into his lap.

"Oh, be careful. I don't want to hurt you," she cried.

"Put your head here." Arthur positioned her so that she rested on the opposite side of the lump where his bandage lay beneath his coat, then set about removing her gloves.

The heat poured off him, and she snuggled close to the warmth. A shimmering wave of joy started from the tips of her toes and prickled beneath her skin all the way to her scalp.

"By the time Daniel died, I was a tiny version of myself," she said. "I'd shrunk beneath the weight of his disappointment and forgotten how to grow back. Those years I spent building Athena's Retreat never satisfied me. I thought I wasn't trying hard enough, doing enough to support the members."

Fortunately, Arthur found the patience to unbutton her gloves and not tear them off. Alice had spent hours picking them out and would not have been well pleased to see anything happen to them. Her hands freed from their confines, Arthur reacquainted himself with them, running his lips over the backs of her fingers and rubbing her palms against the delightful roughness of his unshaven cheeks.

"I didn't need to create a secret club to make me happy," she said. "I needed to make myself happy. You reminded me of how to live again. To be kind to oneself as well as others. To grab hold of and hang on to joy when it comes." Violet's voice hitched, and she continued in a whisper. "To let go of grief and regrets when they become overwhelming."

Arthur placed his hand at the side of her face, tracing her lips with his thumb.

"I've lost everything I ever loved," he said. "My family. My home. If I lost you? That is a grief I could never let go of."

"As great a grief as if we lived without each other due to fear?" said Violet. "These few weeks have taught me to fight fear in all its forms. I won't be diminished again. I have you to thank for this. You woke me up." She stared into those formidable eyes that once told her nothing and now gave her the courage to lay herself bare in their gaze.

"I love you, Arthur Kneland. You've made me come alive again, and I don't want to live without you. Someone else can be the face of the club. It doesn't have to be me. I am learning how to be brave outside of those walls. My work will continue no matter what. I am not ashamed of you."

She paused. A ticket sat on his bedside table. "But you are in search of a home . . ." Her words trailed off at the way his hand flew to his heart at the word *home*. Better to have lost him to a place than to fear, she supposed.

"I want you to have the same gifts you've given me," she said. "If you cannot be happy unless you have a farm, then—"

Uncanny how fast he moved without making a sound. Before she could blink, his mouth was pressed to hers. The kiss was everything she'd craved since they parted: equal parts dark intensity and gentle tenderness. He tasted of tea and longing, and smelled like the first breath of spring.

Perfect.

Too soon, he broke the kiss. "Home is not a place. It is *certainly* not a sheep farm," he said. "Home is the smell of graphite and lavender. The sound of glass bottles rattling when you forget to take them off the flame."

"One time," Violet said. "Twice. No more than that."

He ate her lie with another kiss, then continued.

"Home is the taste of your lips and the way your eyebrows turn into tiny triangles when you talk about the behavior of ideal gases. You have taught me much about the world, but your most important lesson was about the heart. Home is where I love. Not where I live. I love you, Violet. *You* are home."

His words pushed her happiness to another level. They were a balm upon a wound which still pained her all these years later. This man loved her—the real Violet, messy and awkward and everything in between.

"I suppose this whole time I've been searching for home, too," she said.

"Home is us, together," he whispered against her mouth. "I cannot promise I will find the words to comfort you when you need comforting or to encourage you when you need encouragement," he confessed. "It has been too many years since last I tried. I can promise that I will do my best to show you how I care for you."

Arthur put a hand to his chest, as though whatever rested within there was making itself known. "I am afraid I won't be any good at it."

"You will do fine," she said.

"I have something to tell you," he said. "A while back, when I didn't know how long it would take for you to finish the formula, I . . ."

Violet shifted in discomfort and accidentally knocked her shoulder against his wound.

"Christ," he gasped.

"Oh dear, I am so—"

"If you could just . . . ," he said.

The two of them climbed to their feet, bumping, wincing, and stumbling together.

Violet sat on the bed and patted the mattress. "Come sit here," she said. "I won't bite."

When he frowned in disappointment, Violet laughed. "Or perhaps I *will*."

She winced again and set her foot out in front of her. Arthur sat so his wounded side faced away from her.

"I will never forgive what she did to you," he said.

Violet patted his arm in a soothing manner. "She was selfish and thoughtless."

He froze, then examined Violet's face. "You let her go, didn't you?" Indignation brought color to his cheeks.

Violet took a moment to admire him. "Did you know, Grantham arranged for Winters to resettle in Australia in return for not revealing Phoebe's role in the Omnis. Winters is interested in farming sheep, strangely enough."

Arthur would not be distracted. "Lady Phoebe cannot go unpunished for what she did, Violet. She betrayed you, and she bears some responsibility for a man's death."

"Yes, I know." The pain of that betrayal would take a long time to fade. "Phoebe was so consumed with anger that she lost sight of the ends. Progress made with violence lasts only as long as you are the one holding the weapon. Now, she must learn to live after having set the weapon aside."

"Are you . . . It sounds as though you might forgive her," he said. "How can that be?"

"Do you still not believe in forgiveness, Arthur? You exiled yourself for twenty years because you could not absolve yourself. Will you deny Phoebe her chance for atonement?"

Arthur left Violet's side and walked to the window, pulling back the curtain and staring broodily out at the street.

"She hurt you," he muttered.

"She hurt *you*," Violet said. "Only the fact that you are upright and in excellent looks has saved her from my wrath."

"Hmm, 'excellent looks,' eh?" he said.

"I won't argue that she's caused damage and destruction, but she's suffered damages of her own." Violet shook her head, ridding herself of her secondhand sorrow. "Phoebe is brilliant and fierce. She will find her own way—a new way—in the world. I truly believe she will eventually balance the scales. Besides, Grey has hit upon the perfect retribution."

Arthur crossed his arms in disbelief. "What might that be?"

"She's being sent to America," Violet confided with relish. "The western territories."

"America?" Arthur scowled, scratching his chin. "I suppose that is almost as bad as being transported," he allowed.

"The western territories, you say? It's as democratic a place as you can imagine. Difficult circumstances out there. Hardly any big cities. Full of missionaries and fur trappers." A wicked grin split his face. "She'll *hate* it."

"This means the danger is over now," she reminded him.

His amusement dimmed, and his arms dropped to his sides, hands clenched in loose fists.

"I wrote a letter," he said, staring at the windowpanes. Spears of sunlight fell on either side of him in straight lines, hitting the bare wood floors and melting into puddles of gold.

After a pause, he continued. "To Maria Bellingham."

Violet felt sick to her stomach. It must have been the corset squeezing her lungs.

"When I received the reply, I wrote another letter," he continued. "This time to the Queen."

"The Queen?" Understanding dawned. "Oh, Arthur."

"It is not easy to confess a youthful mistake to a monarch, especially when it had such dire consequences," he said. "I told Her Majesty why I'd declined her offer of honors after the incident with Dickerson. She gave me a second chance to accept her commendations and the honors it entailed. I said yes."

This most guarded of men had reached back into his past and asked for help. There would never again be any doubt in Violet's mind that this man was made to love her.

Arthur turned his back on the world outside and faced her. "I wanted to clear my name. Not just to protect Athena's Retreat, but for myself as well. I would not wish to see any child of mine be marked by scandal."

Violet crossed the room and took his hands in hers. "I do not need the approval of the Queen to marry you, nor a sash full of medals covering your broad chest. Plain Arthur Kneland, son of Highland farmers, is more than good enough for me."

Arthur frowned, but humor lit his gaze. "Are you so certain I was going to propose to you?"

"Not at all." She laughed at his surprise and squeezed his hands. "In fact, I'd convinced myself you would not propose, out of some ill-conceived notion regarding the difference in our stations."

"There are those who will say—"

"I care not a whit for what anyone else might say when it comes to my heart. I will not listen to naysayers or gossips," she declared, setting her palm to his cheek. "Marry me, Arthur Kneland. Wake up with me every morning and fall asleep next to me every night."

Arthur stroked her arm from elbow to wrist, then pressed his palm against the back of her hand and rested his forehead against hers.

"I will wake with you, Violet Hughes," he vowed, "and your eyes will be my morning sun. Your joy will be the air I breathe, your name the last words on my lips each night until the end of my days. I will marry you and count myself the luckiest among men."

Arthur demonstrated his acceptance of her proposal with a kiss both fierce and achingly tender. Then another, and another after that.

With reluctance, Violet broke away. "I'm afraid my need for oxygen must call a halt to this." She peered up at him from beneath her lashes. "Unless you can help me?"

The clever man sprang into action—as much as he could, given the state of his wound. They relied on Violet's superior knowledge of anatomy to find the most comfortable position in which he could help ease her distress.

"Arthur," she said, reaching around and touching the back of his hand to halt the hasty unlacing of her dratted corset. "There is a good possibility that I cannot conceive. Will you . . . ?"

He pulled her into his arms and whispered a vow into her ear. "You and I will create a family. Whether with a child of our own or taking care of the women who come through the doors of Athena's Retreat. Whenever we are together, we make a home. That is what I have been searching for my entire life."

As the last of winter's grip fell away in a blaze of April sun, the trees unfurled their tiny buds, and flowers raised their faces to the sky. All around them, and deep within them, spring had arrived.

Author's Note

WHY A SECRET society? While there were well-respected female scientists in the early nineteenth century, they were few and far between. Only a handful were given recognition by their male peers, including Elizabeth Fulhame, Sophie Germain, and Mary Somerville, who are the inspiration for some of the characters in *A Lady's Formula for Love*. Despite their hard work and important discoveries, society pushed back against their forays into the male-dominated world of science. Female scientists, many of whom were self taught, were often ridiculed, their work was used without credit, and they were labeled as "unnatural." Those of you familiar with scientific history know that some of the club members' discoveries, such as the aerosol delivery system, predate the actual discoveries by a few years. Who knows what other real-life advances were never realized because Athena's Retreat lies firmly in the realm of fiction? And don't get me started on the lack of childcare . . .

All mistakes in this book are my own, and most likely the product of wishful thinking.

Acknowledgments

This book exists because of the unwavering and generous support of my husband. He's one of the good guys. Thanks as well to my children, who light my life and bring me such joy, and to Mom and Doug for all their help. Thank you to my lovely and very patient agent, Ann Leslie Tuttle. Many thanks to my delightful editor, Sarah Blumenstock, for taking a chance on me and the ladies of Athena's Retreat. Thanks as well to Anita Mumm for being the voice I hear in my head when I wonder if I'm being kind to a character. Thank you to Jessica Mangicaro and the hardworking Berkley marketing/PR team. I am so lucky to be blessed with an amazing group of women who lift me up and carry me through the good times and the bad. Thank you to the Park Ave Moms and the Highland Hotties for all the encouragement, wisdom, and laughter. Thank you to my RWA contest buddies, Felicia Grossman and Jeanine Englert, for their support, and a special shout-out to Minerva Spencer for all her advice and reassurance over the past three years. And to all the moms who just put the kids to bed and finished the dishes and are fighting off sleep in order to do what they love most—I see you. It will happen.

Don't miss Letty and Greycliff's story,
coming spring 2022 from Berkley Jove!

London, 1843

"A WOMAN'S PLACE IS in the home!"

Miss Letitia Fenley stopped in her tracks at that declaration. What a choker! Everyone knew a woman's place was in charge, if you wanted something done right.

Another winter had come to London and stubbornly refused to be gone. These bleak weeks of April more resembled late February, an in-between time when a sullen sun did little more than peek out from behind the clouds now and then, waiting for the world to be pretty enough to bother with once more.

Letty Fenley and her brother, Sam, traversed the streets of Clerkenwell. Strung out in a grim leer, buildings stained dark yellow and brown from decades of soot and humidity squeezed together like crooked teeth, the second and third stories leaning over to rub against the ones next door. The cobbles beneath their feet were greasy and half submerged beneath a mix of mud, manure, and straw.

The two of them were headed for the grander environs of Bloomsbury, where, amid its walled gardens and wooden walkways, they'd be more likely to find a hack. Halting their progress was a crowd of angry men blocking the road, holding rudely painted signs and shouting ridiculous slogans in front of a shop where the shingle hanging over the door read *Messrs. Jewell & Hoyt, Candlemakers*. The store was an otherwise unremarkable brick building, and its owner had turned his sign to closed and pulled the curtains tight against the ire of folks marching on the walk outside.

Letty stood on her toes at the edge of the crowd to better view the happenings. Another "pea souper" of a fog had sprung up, and invisible motes of coal smut coated the back of her throat from breathing in the noxious air. She pulled the high collar of her mantle around her mouth and nose.

"Why are you stopping?" grumbled her brother, eyes fixed on the road as he tried to keep his boots clear of the worst of the ruts, his head no doubt filled with work. "Bad enough I have to take time away from the store to escort you to your club. Worse is when time is wasted by your . . ."

Glancing up, Sam took in at the scene before them for the first time. "What nonsense is this?" He squinted through the fog at the commotion. "Who're these never-sweats blocking the street at midday when there is business to be conducted?"

With no time to read anything other than accounting ledgers, Sam had missed the latest news regarding the rise of the Guardians of Domesticity. Groveling at the feet of the aristocracy and blaming women for the ills of society, the Guardians of Domesticity hid behind a facade of respectability with lectures and charity work that claimed to celebrate the traditional British family and women's role as keeper of the hearth. Their true colors came into view when they found a business contributing to the "downfall of civilization" by employing young women in their shops and factories.

"Ladies should be taking care of men's needs instead of taking men's wages," shouted one man, flushed with an angry joy. He'd found a captive audience for his complaints, shaking a meaty fist in the face of a slender young woman trying to sidle past him and make her way into the shop.

A shop's assistant, no doubt, hired for pennies per week, working dawn to dusk for a pittance of what a male assistant might make. Although the girl's poke bonnet hid her face, the set of her shoulders and bowed head signaled distress.

Letty clenched her fingers. Despite the dank mist freezing her toes, angry heat rose in her chest. "How dare those oafs frighten that poor girl. Why, I am going to—"

Sam paid no attention to her threats, pulling Letty by the sleeve away from the crowd. Unlike the shopgirl's threadbare cloak, Letty's deep blue mantle was made of the finest wool, the discreet trim done in costly velvet.

"You are going to do nothing but make your way to your ladies' club," he growled. "Da says I'm to get you there without incident, and that's what I intend to do." Scratching his head, Sam read a large banner near them. "What is this nonsense supposed to accomplish? *Take care of men*, indeed."

His golden hair appeared dirty brown in the low light, but nothing could hide the sudden glint of humor in his piercing blue eyes. "Good luck getting you or those secret scientists you keep company with to have anything to do with men. Unless it's to blow them up."

Letty admonished her brother while keeping an eye on the clerk. "We haven't blown anyone up. Well, one time, but it was an accident. Besides, the purpose of the club is to study all aspects of science, not just the ones that make noise."

Letty was accustomed to defending Athena's Retreat. Ostensibly a social club for ladies to gather for lectures on the natural sciences, behind closed doors it served as a haven for women to conduct experiments, do research, and simply take the time away from the pressures of their duties to reflect on theories and ideas. The Fenley family's wealth allowed Letty the freedom to study her passion—mathematics—but that didn't mean her family understood why she and the other club members were driven to sacrifice their time and, in some cases, their opportunity to marry well or climb higher in society.

"Can't imagine what those scoundrels think shouting at ladies will accomplish," Sam continued, still clutching her sleeve. "If I shouted at you or our sisters, what do you think would happen?"

"We'd tell you to shut up, and put toads in your bed," Letty said distractedly.

"You'd tell me to shut up, and put toads in my bed." Sam agreed with good-natured humor. He craned his neck to see over the thickening crowd.

"If I had a banner and waved it in your faces, would you listen to me?" he asked wistfully. "Big sign saying, *Stop reading in front of the customers* or *Stop trying on the bonnets you're supposed to sell* or *Stop putting face cream in the icebox.*"

"Not likely," Letty told him. "If you want us to work for free at the emporium, you need to give us incentives."

Fenley's Fantastic Fripperies, the largest emporium in London, parted the city's ladies from their coin by offering a dazzling array of articles ranging from the utilitarian to the useless.

"It's a family business," he said. "Familial duty is your incentive. Not to mention free face cream, which does not belong in the icebox despite your incomprehensible blather about solids and temperature and matter of facts."

"Not matter of facts." Letty corrected him. "States of matter. You see, when the temperature increases, certain substances . . ."

"Twice now I've put it on my toast." Sam pulled a face and shuddered. "Tastes like a scolding from Aunt Bess. Ugh."

Letty laughed, but when Sam checked his pocket watch, all traces

of a smile vanished from his face. "I cannot be away from the emporium any longer. Let's slip away from this mess and . . ."

"Bring back the better days of Britain!"

Letty shrugged loose from Sam's grip, the rest of his words muffled by the roaring of blood in her veins.

"Guardians of Stupidity is what you are." Letty raised her voice,
glaring at the men around her. "Fools and bullies who think they
know better than women. Back to the kitchen? As though running a
household doesn't require as many skills as running a business."

Slipping through the crowd, Letty approached the building as a
thin wail rose from the doorway. A beady-eyed man with a pinched
mouth and spidery fingers had grabbed the shopgirl by the wrist, halting her escape.

"Don't bother trying to go back to work. We're shutting this place
down until they stop employing women in their factories and hire the
men back," the man said.

A tinkling of broken glass punctuated his threat as someone
launched their sign at the ground-floor window of the shop. The at-
mosphere turned in an instant from hectoring to predatory. With a
foreshadowing of violence, the group of individuals jelled into a single
organism—a dragon ready to pounce on whatever threatened. This
monster's hoard consisted of power, rather than gold.

"Oh, no, you don't," Letty said through gritted teeth, clenching the
straps of her heavy reticule in one hand.

"Letty!" Sam called after her. "Letty Fenley, you come back here
this instant. I know you don't listen to me, but for goodness' sake, will
you listen to me?"

Fear set her stomach to churning, but Letty allowed nothing to
show on her face. Instead, she stuck her chin out and pulled her shoulders back. Never again would she suffer a man intimidating her into
submission, and she'd be damned if she watched this happen to any

other woman. As Flavia Smythe-Harrows always said, sexual dimorphism does not excuse bad behavior.

Pity Letty didn't have *that* printed on a banner.

Without the benefit of a rival sign of intimidating size, she used what was available in the moment. Swinging her reticule around twice to achieve maximal momentum, Letty brought it down hard on the wrist of Beady Eyes.

"You let go of that girl right now, you weasel-faced, onion-breathed..." Letty's stream of insults drowned in the crowd's protest at the sight of their fellow man being assaulted by what someone deemed a "half-a-pint-sized shrew."

"Half a pint indeed," Letty shouted back. "I'm less than an inch shorter than the median height for a woman of my weight based on— Oy, stop waving that sign in my face."

Before Letty could take another swing at Beady Eyes, the sound of horses whinnying and shouts from somewhere at the edge of the crowd broke the tension; a decrescendo from taunting voices to garbled protests heralded the arrival of Authority. Jumping up for a better look, Letty spied two well-dressed men on horseback.

"On your way," a clipped aristocratic voice shouted to the crowd. "Disperse at once."

The crowd buckled, its mood shifting from dangerous to frustrated. Letty protected the girl as best she could from the sudden shoving around them. Most of her attention, however, fixed on the familiarity of those crisp, clean syllables echoing in the air.

She would know that voice anywhere. Their rescue rode toward them in the form of Lord William Hughes, the Viscount Greycliff. A traitorous wave of relief that he would put an end to the danger was quickly followed by a cold dose of shame.

Six years ago, she'd believed him the epitome of nobility and elegance, until that voice delivered a verdict upon her head. The words he had said and the pain they had caused were etched into her memory forever.

"I don't care if you're Prince Albert himself. Move your arse, man!" A deeper bass, the voice of Greycliff's companion, now carried over the crowd. "Put down the signs, or I'll put them down for you."

"Are they here to rescue us?" the girl asked.

Visions of Greycliff riding up on a snow-white steed flashed before Letty's eyes. A handful of years before, such an image would have set her heart to racing and put roses on her cheeks. She would have caught her ruffled skirts in one hand, ready to be swept away by a hero, lit from behind by a shaft of golden sunlight.

Not anymore. The dirty grey-brown reality of working-class London remained solid and smelly before her eyes. These days, romantic scenes remained between the pages of a well-thumbed book.

"Never wait for someone else to rescue you," Letty advised. "Especially a man. They'll ride away on those fine horses afterward, and where will you be? Still here, cleaning the mess, having to work for an owner who couldn't even be bothered to come out here after you. Rescue yourself, my dear."

"Shall we run for it?"

"We could, but I've a better idea." Letty turned to Beady Eyes and held up her reticule. The man flinched, but she had other plans.

"Want to get rid of two troublesome women?" she asked him. Pouring out a palm full of coins, Letty made an offer. "Here's your chance."

"LATE NIGHT OF drinking far too much, bracing ride on a cold spring morning through miles of mud and rain, and now we've the chance to knock heads together. Life is grand, isn't it, Grey?"

Greycliff shrugged, unmoved by the same zeal for chaos that led his friend, the Earl Grantham, to whoop with glee and launch himself off his horse and into the angry crowd like a cormorant diving into the waves.

Grey was not accustomed to being moved by any emotion, let alone one approaching the strength and intensity of *zeal*. He allowed himself only the slightest twinge of annoyance at this interruption in his journey to visit his former stepmother.

Placing a calming hand against his horse's neck, Grey repeated his threat to the crowd. "Break this up now, or I will have the Riot Act read."

Most of the demonstrators heeded his warning, though not without a show of reluctance. Still shouting their slogans, the men turned their attention away from the shop front and broke into smaller groups. Hoping for a brawl, Grantham chivvied them along.

As he scanned the thinning crowd, Grey caught sight of a man using his sign to force a clear path through the crowd for two feminine figures behind him. The women were too far away for him to pick out their individual features, but a tingling of recognition pricked the back of his hands.

It couldn't be . . . but of course it could. Here in the center of chaos, why wouldn't he find a woman who excelled in stirring up trouble?

Before his mild irritation could grow into something approaching fear for her safety, Grey took a deep breath through his nose and blew the worry away. Setting his shoulders back, he took another breath and reached for equilibrium.

A handsome, square-jawed young man dressed in an elegant greatcoat stood at the center of the crowd. A head shorter than Grantham and slighter of build, the man nonetheless exuded an aura of determination.

"Letitia Fenley, where are you?" the man shouted with ill-concealed irritation.

His suspicions confirmed, the tingling ran up Grey's arms and down his spine. Rationally, he knew she would be safe. This must be Miss Fenley's brother. If the resemblance hadn't proved it, the man's annoyance would—a common reaction after a few minutes in Miss Fenley's presence.

The most logical course of action would be to continue his journey. Why should he care that a woman of questionable character had found herself in yet another predicament? Her brother would protect her. The man was right now . . . walking in the opposite direction than his sister had gone.

Mindful of the men still milling about, Grey urged his horse forward toward a narrow alley running alongside the candle maker's shop, where an abandoned sign leaned against the smutty bricks. Peering through the dimness, he spied her standing in consultation with another young woman. Their escort seemed to have disappeared. Although they'd escaped the worst of the crowd, they weren't clear of danger yet. Yards away, a few die-hard protestors in front of the building held Grantham off, waving their handmade banners and wooden signs.

Make babies, not wages, read one. *Protect the sanctity of the home,* read another.

Reflecting on the petite woman in the alleyway before him, Grey tried to think of any instance when she would do as he wanted simply because he was a man and told her to.

None.

No instance whatsoever.

In fact, Letty Fenley would do the opposite of anything he asked.

On a stoop next door to the candle makers, waiting for the crowd to quiet before he could go back to work, a bemused little street sweeper watched the proceedings. Grey tossed the boy a coin to mind his horse and made his way down the alley toward Letty Fenley.

It must have been the effects of the long ride to London that made his heart beat a tiny bit faster. Not the sight of this miniature termagant.

"... let these idiots tell you otherwise. Women are as smart as men, if not more so," Letty was explaining to her companion.

She'd the same high cheekbones as her brother only more pronounced, appearing almost gaunt in the low light. Beneath a sharp nose, her pale pink lips pursed in annoyance. The uncanny blue of her eyes, clear as the summer sky, shone with a passion visible even in the shadows.

"Not smart to hide in a dead end." Grey raised his voice, tipping his hat when the women started in surprise at the sight of him. The girl executed a passable curtsy, but all Letty Fenley offered by way of greeting was a brusque nod and a scowl.

"Smart enough to get us away from that crowd of beef-headed fools," Letty retorted.

Grey held her gaze as all that had passed before them thickened the air and put a flush to her cheeks. Mutual admiration had been cut short when Letty did the unforgivable, threatening those who Grey held dear. Thereafter followed six years of a frosty truce that broke down after more than five minutes in each other's presence.

Shrinking from the silent confrontation in front of her, the shopgirl glanced between them, then at a door in the side of the building. "Pardon my saying, my lady ..."

Letty broke her stare and gave the shopgirl her attention. "I'm the furthest from a noblewoman you'll find. Plain *Miss* will do."

"Indeed. Don't want you lumped in with the oppressive aristocracy," Grey remarked with an exaggerated drawl.

Her eyes changed from turquoise to cobalt when challenged. Fascinating.

"Exactly, my lord. We have no need for your interference. You can go berate the masses out there without further concern." The smoky curl of her Clerkenwell dialect softened the vowels, smudging the edges of her words.

It sounded almost seductive.

"Ummm, I'm going to . . . er." The girl stepped away.

"Perhaps they would grant me a more mannered welcome," he shot back. "Generally, when one is the object of someone's concern, they . . ."

She interrupted his admonishment with her usual defiance. One time, he'd seen her tell a lord where to shove his quizzing glass when he used it to mock another woman. Grey had liked her back then.

Before she'd revealed her flaws.

"Lecture me on good manners, will you?" she asked. Turning away from the young woman, Letty faced him full-on, hands clenched and resting on her hips.

"I suppose you cannot help but school your social inferiors. This time, however, you are wasting your breath. Too bad." She walked toward him, stomping through the shadows as though kicking the dark away. "Oxygen is what you need, high up there in the social strata."

"I'm not high up, Miss Fenley," he said, then paused to gauge the effect of his next words. "I only appear so to a person of your miniature stature."

His *brilliant* riposte went over her head.

Literally.

"Well, at least my head is proportional to my body, unlike some noblemen, whose ego renders their head nearly as large as their . . ."

"Where did she go?" Grey asked.

"Where did who go? Oh." Letty paused in her tirade and glanced behind her. The alley stood empty.

A rapping came from a window above them. There, the girl, joined by two others, waved and smiled her thanks.

Letty and Grey turned and waved back, smiling, then faced one another and dropped both hands and smiles.

"Well, now that is settled, I must be on my way," Letty said airily. "I'd like to say it was pleasure to see you again, my lord, but lying is bad manners."

Brushing his arm, she sidled past him in the narrow alley. Sometime during her flight from the crowd, Letty's bonnet had come off. Walking past him, she bent her head to examine the tangle of ribbons, exposing the fragile line of her neck above the collar of her mantle, a vulnerable column of smooth flesh and delicate bone.

Odd how someone so fierce could at the same time seem . . . breakable.

"Just going to march back out there into the madness?" he asked as she passed by him.

"I am going to join my brother," she answered, not bothering to lift her head. Grey peered at the heavens and complimented himself on his saintly patience.

"Miss Fenley, if you will allow me to see you to safety?"

She waved him off. "Don't bother. I have this under—"

A knot of men spilled past the corner of the building, a few of them stumbling into the alleyway. Grey, reacting without hesitation, pulled Letty away from their flailing arms and into a recess between the side of the building and its facade, blocking her from the man's sight as one fellow's punch went wild and hit Grey between his shoulders.

Grey didn't flinch. He kept his back to the tumult, leaning one arm against the wall, setting himself between her and danger.

"I suppose now you'll tell me how right you were," Letty complained. A few wisps of wheat-blond hair at her temples had escaped a tidy roll of braids.

This close, he could catch a faint scent of orange blossom and something tantalizingly familiar. Leaning in, he closed his eyes and inhaled, lungs filling with the sweet scent of vanilla.

How unexpected.

Letty Fenley smelled like cake.

"Are you smelling my hair?" she asked.

He opened his eyes, disconcerted. "No. I'm not . . . smelling your hair? What are you . . . ? You're simply so short that—"

"So short?" Letty stiffened and tipped her head up at the same time Grey leaned down to make his point. "I am less than an inch shorter than—"

"Are you standing on your toes to make yourself appear taller?" he accused.

"If I stood on my toes, like this, I would . . ."

Letty rose on her toes, and they both froze.

For an endless moment, everyone and everything else ceased to exist as their mouths came so close they drew each other's breath.

Expressions slid like quicksilver across her face before he could read them. Was she repulsed? Angry? Curious?

What might happen if he closed the distance between them another inch . . .

A rock hit the wall above his head and jerked him out of the moment of madness. For it must have been madness, and not anything else.

"Letitia, where are you? Come here now, or I will remove the heels from your boots," a man shouted. "Then, when customers ask, I will tell them, yes, you *are* well-spoken for a ten-year-old."

"That is my brother. Let me go." Letty pushed at Grey's chest. Taking two steps back, he held his hands above his shoulders as though she'd threatened him at gunpoint, saying nothing as she bolted out of the passageway and into the street. Not even when he heard her mutter under her breath.

"I hate you," she'd whispered.

Before he could decide whether that had been issued as a complaint or a challenge, she'd disappeared.

ELIZABETH EVERETT lives in upstate New York with her family. She likes going for long walks or (very) short runs to nearby sites that figure prominently in the history of civil rights and women's suffrage. *A Lady's Formula for Love* is her first novel, inspired by her admiration for rule breakers and her belief in the power of love to change the world.

Ready to find
your next great read?

Let us help.

Visit prh.com/nextread